Wen...

(Book One of the ...

by K.A. Silva

MW00629868

for Share —

Hope this makes you laugh.

From one monster fan to another!

love, Kris

Copyright K.A. Silva, 2020
Graythorn Publishing
Cover illustration by Sally Jackson, 2020

for my Big Frog, who believes in me

1

Wednesday night at the BookStop was as dead as the cast in a Romero flick, and far less energetic. The steady snow all evening had discouraged even the Lawrence University student crowd who might otherwise have come in to argue over the cash value of last semester's textbooks. Morty glanced at the clock; it was five minutes until closing. He stepped from behind the long trade counter to look for stragglers, when Cracker Joe came howling toward him.

Morty jerked back as the homeless man barreled past, eyes wild, screaming "Winter is coming! Winter is coming!" Joe fled out the front door, leaving a chill behind him. Apparently, no one had told Joe he lived in Wisconsin; the snow had begun three months ago.

The irregular visits of the unkempt homeless man, who invariably fell asleep drooling on one of the store's reading chairs, had become BookStop folklore. Morty and his best friend and co-worker, Kim, had invented an elaborate serial-killer backstory for Joe; adding to the legend of Cracker Joe entertained them during the slow stretches between customers. Other supervisors usually threw Joe out as soon as they saw him. Morty pitied him and generally left him alone unless a customer complained about the smell.

From behind the front counter Kim chortled, giving Morty an elaborate bow. "Better lock up before the white walkers hit us, Mordecai of the Watch!"

Morty Wending glared at his best friend. "You know nothing, Kim Xiong," he muttered, earning a laugh from Kim. "And you're entirely too fond of using my given name." Kim grinned, showing off his perfect teeth.

They'd been best friends for the last five years, shortly after Kim had joined the staff, so Morty endured his teasing about the Wendings' scriptural system of naming their offspring. At least Morty's brother Jed didn't have people constantly mis-hearing his nickname. Morty no longer bothered to smile at people making *Back to the Future* jokes at him. His name was Morty, not Marty. He wasn't fond of people asking where Rick was, either.

"Cracker Joe, man. One of these days he's going to have a complete psychotic break, and when he does, you're not hiding behind me," Kim said.

"He exists to keep us ever watchful, my son. You should heed his wisdom for he sees things we do not."

Kim snickered. "Pretty sure tonight's prophecy is a couple months late."

Morty snorted a laugh. "Great minds." He swung himself over the closed end of the counter, heading for the front door. He doubted there was more than a hundred bucks in the till; snow business was slow business, especially after dark. Weary, he swept the store with sharp eyes for any lingering customers. Sure enough, a straggler in a red hoodie was standing by the classic horror DVD display. Morty had set that one up himself, and while he appreciated its perusal by a fellow fan, it was closing time and this lingering customer should have skulked out the door already.

He walked up behind the patron and summoned his best hi-aren't-I-a-pleasant-fellow voice. "Excuse me, we're closing. Did you have anything you wished to purchase tonight, or can I put something on hold for you?"

Red Hoodie turned, and her grin both relieved and annoyed Morty. "You didn't know it was me!" she teased as she flipped the hood off her salon-tipped blond hair.

"I didn't know you were coming in tonight," Morty said. He managed a smile for her. He was tired and had hoped to catch up on his reading tonight.

Darcy turned in a circle, showing off her newest fashion find. "Like it? Dad will probably complain about it being too socialist." She pointed out the small, stylized gear-and-sickle logo on the front of the hoodie. Morty vaguely recalled it from one of the neo-punk bands Darcy liked. Their taste in music did have some overlap to it, and she didn't object to the metal, house and psy-trance he preferred.

"It's cool," he agreed. "Hey, it's nice of you to drop by, but I'm gonna be stuck here for at least another hour." He gestured at the registers as they walked toward the front.

"Oh, that's okay. JimJams doesn't close until three. It's a private club, so they can stay open late as they want." Darcy ran a finger down the length of his nose, which always made him feel self-conscious. It was also kind of endearing. "I can wait. Just try to hurry."

"Darce, didn't we just go clubbing a week ago?"

She laughed. "Babe, that was last month!" She sighed, though she smiled at him. "Okay. You don't have to dance. You can just sit and watch me, if you want." She wiggled her hips suggestively at him. Morty had to admit to himself he did like watching her slender, toned body move. Especially when she made it clear she was enjoying his eyes upon her as she did so. "It's just that Jessie and Kara invited us. Come on. One night out. I'll trade you for," she paused, considering, then broke into a wide grin. "How about one night of absolutely quiet snuggle-reading?"

'Snuggle-reading' was her term for cuddling together on the couch and reading their respective books, which, he admitted, he liked very much. Especially since those quiet reading sessions often led to quiet kissing. And touching. And then not-so-quiet, equally enjoyable things.

He hugged Darce, finding her infectious smile coaxed a more genuine one out of him. "Okay. Sorry, though, you can't wait in here. Leila busted me last week. No non-employees in the store after close."

She pouted, then kissed him. "Fine. I'll be in the car. Keeping warm." She turned to leave, waving at the young man sorting DVDs at the counter. "Hi Kim!"

Morty followed her, his spirits lifted by her cheerfulness. The view of her pert rear end didn't hurt, either. He locked the door, turning off the neon OPEN sign. A swirl of chilled air lingered at the front of the store, and save for Darcy's car, the street outside was empty.

Three months ago, when Darcy Mueller had first entered Morty's life, he would've been substantially more eager to spend an evening with her. She was ten years his junior, currently a music major, former high-school gymnast, and arousingly eager in all the right ways. In short, not the kind of girl who typically looked twice at soft-bellied nerds with receding hairlines. He still wasn't sure what he meant to her. He'd been stunned when she asked him out. He was more stunned she continued to date him after the incident at the movie theatre when he had spilled his soda on her leather miniskirt. Those first two months, he'd been happy not to think about the future. But lately she'd been saying "I love you" fairly often. He'd thought, at first, she meant it in more of a "hey, you're fun, and I enjoy sleeping with you" kind of way, as she didn't seem to put any special emphasis behind the words. Now he wasn't entirely sure what she meant and hadn't screwed up enough courage to ask her about it. He'd considered this a great deal. He wasn't sure he wanted to examine his own motive or meaning each time he replied the same to her. Darce was a college senior, with a very bright, creative future ahead. Morty had spent the last decade, pretty much since graduating from Larry U, working at BookStop, with no real ambitions.

"She planning your six-month anniversary yet?" Kim asked, grinning ear to ear. Though technically as a supervisor Morty was higher than Kim in the store hierarchy, Morty had never had reason to pull rank on him.

"Yes, which is ridiculous since it's still three months off." Morty shut down most of the lights and punched in the code to empty the last till. "I really don't understand the need to celebrate anything less than a year together."

"Dude, I'm celebrating it. Isn't this the longest a girl has wanted to remain in your company?"

"Bite me," Morty returned, though without rancor. "Says the guy who goes through women like popcorn."

Kim shrugged. "Keeping my options open. Speaking of significant dates, is she throwing you a birthday party this weekend?"

"'Party' is subjective. I somehow agreed to spend this weekend up north at a fancy resort instead of throwing the usual gaming party. I had to promise to cover Tina's time off in April in return for taking the whole weekend off."

"Pssht. You must have a year of vacation days built up by now." Morty's record of being called in last-minute to work when others were out sick was almost as legendary as the number of times he accepted. He usually didn't mind; it was money in the bank, after all. "So, where's she taking you?"

"An old lodge. Darcy's dad is part owner of a wealthy club up north by the big lake."

"'The big lake'? You mean in Door County?"

"No, up by Canada. Great Bigass Frozen Lake."

"Superior."

"Given the kind of money these people have, I'm sure it won't be inferior."

Kim laughed. "Reaching that high for a joke setup? You've lost your skills."

"Yeah, yeah." They walked together past the aisles of shelves toward the office. "Anyway, she's planned a romantic birthday weekend of snowmobiling or ski lessons or something at this swanky resort. With her parents."

"Oho! Go you, big birthday party with the Swanky Family," Kim chuckled. He shook his head in mock ruefulness. "Why don't I score all the rich honeys like you?" Kim could boast exponentially more dates than Morty, if he were the boasting type. His Korean good looks and easygoing attitude attracted everyone around him. From what Morty could tell, Kim had always been the popular guy, even king of the prom in high school. Morty had spent his own prom night at home playing *Resident Evil*.

"It's my aura of not-giving-a-shit. Chicks dig apathy."

Morty carried the till through the darkened store to the back offices. For the thousandth time, he asked himself why he'd accepted his current supervisory position. While the pay and benefits were good, as far as retail went, it also meant more exposure to the public. If he was on duty as shift manager, he was the one called to deal with any suburban Karen who needed to speak to the manager immediately.

Morty had never been a fan of humanity in general, particularly idiots who couldn't find their way around bookstores. His own reading tastes ranged from Hunter Thompson to China Mieville, Dorothy Parker to Octavia Butler, with a little Don Marquis and Chuck Tingle thrown in. His comics collection went from the old Nineteen-forties EC *House of Mystery* to modern Marvel's *Deadpool*. Though working here meant he'd never get rich, it paid the bills, he had a little savings, and he was never short of entertainment. BookStop relied on used books, a rarity in this day of bestseller stores which focused on what was popular rather than what was good. The size of the store itself, in the cavernous City Center building downtown, and of its staff, attested to its success. Fifteen thousand square feet of holy used book glory. Granted, being the only indie bookstore in a hundred miles did tend to draw in more serious bibliophiles.

Seeing a paperback copy of Bradbury's *The Halloween Tree* on the book sorting table in passing, Morty paused, lost in thought. Two months ago, during the Halloween season, flush with the headiness of new and unexpected romance, he'd given Darcy a rarity: one of the signed, limited editions of this book, published before Bradbury died. She'd cooed over it; however, to the best of his knowledge, she hadn't cracked the cover.

She'd teased him, at first, about his neat boxes of comics in archival bags, the only things in his apartment which were organized. The concept of a collectible she did comprehend, though it took her a minute to grasp that those original *Teenage Mutant Ninja Turtles* comics qualified. "So, you're saying this one issue is as rare as my dad's Miró painting? Someone would pay a hundred dollars for this?"

"Well, not nearly as expensive as your dad's art collection, but yes." Morty had dug out the latest issue of *Comics Values Monthly* to demonstrate his shrewd investment strategy; Darcy nodded along and tried to follow his ramblings about the vagaries and fads of comic collecting, though her eyes began to glaze after about fifteen minutes.

On the other hand, she enjoyed reading *Bone* alongside him in bed, giggling at the stupid, stupid rat creatures. And they'd introduced each other to books they'd never read and discovered surprising new things they liked. Although her tastes didn't dovetail with his own, Darcy was an avid reader. And although she hadn't played videogames before she'd started dating him, she proved remarkably good at puzzles. Lately they'd been playing tag-team on *Oxenfree,* a supernatural mystery, and although she squeaked in fear whenever a dark, ominous shape popped up in a mirror, she was better than Morty at thinking ahead and figuring out the clues. Morty couldn't understand why she affected such a carefree, almost ditzy attitude around her college friends. Especially when the first five minutes of serious conversation he'd had with her convinced him her mind was sharp as hell. Then again, he'd never really understood people in general, much less the popular crowd. Shaking himself out of his introspection, he went to the office to finish closing chores.

After he stashed the tills in the safe, he looked around the small back office to ensure he hadn't missed anything. He'd forgotten the alarm code more than twice and had left the tills out once. He was well aware Leila, the owner, only appointed him book supervisor because he knew more about cult literature than anyone else here. Oh well, if he missed anything, he could always fix it first thing tomorrow.

Shitgoblins. Darcy wanted to go clubbing.

He checked the shift schedule by the door. Closing, not opening tomorrow; that wasn't so bad. Plus, after dancing and drinking, Darcy usually insisted they go back to his place. Morty contemplated her luscious lips and other tangible assets, and accepted the cost of a noisy club. Darcy would enjoy herself, at any rate, and she always ensured he enjoyed the remainder of the night. There were worse fates, he chided himself, than being Mordecai Wending, B.A. in English, career bookseller, unrepentant geek, and boyfriend to a playful, sexy, incomprehensible debutante. He grabbed his coat and satchel and left with Kim, watching after him a minute to make sure he didn't slip on the inevitable icy patch on the corner.

When Morty approached Darcy's little red Fiat, she swung open the passenger door. Warmth and Flogging Molly burst out to envelop him as he eased into the tiny seat, and Darcy gave him a smile utterly free of pretension. Morty relaxed, giving himself over to his girlfriend's whims. Darcy revved the engine, threw it in gear, and slid a hand up his thigh as she expertly swerved into the slippery street.

Hell yes. There were worse situations he could be in right now. He smiled at her. Much worse.

2

The Bad River Resort was more crowded than Morty would have guessed. Rich idiots paid a small fortune to be holed up next to a fireplace in near-blizzard conditions in mid-January. Then again, it was a really nice fireplace. He sat near it, sipping a potent whiskey toddy as he gazed into the massive river-rock hearth.

Everything about this place was on a grand scale. He'd researched the history of the lodge before the trip and discovered that during Prohibition, Chicago gangsters favored it as a relaxing vacation site far from the gritty city. And it was near enough to Lake Superior that if a boat happened to lose its way and accidentally drop its cargo of fine liquor here, who were they to argue?

The Chequamegon National Forest surrounded the lodge grounds on all sides, and a stretch of three or four miles of currently frozen Bad River edged the sprawling property on the south and east. Tall pines as far as the eye could see, and Morty knew there were scenic waterfalls somewhere in the area as well. Right now, snow and ice blanketed everything. Evergreen boughs, smelling fresh and green, adorned the banister of the grand staircase and the high log walls of the main lodge. He couldn't decide whether he approved of the turn-of-the-century hunting lodge décor. It wasn't over-the-top tacky like some of the local casinos, but with all the huge tree timbers and mounted elk and moose heads, he kept expecting Teddy Roosevelt to pop up at any second.

He noticed a well-dressed, mature couple across the lobby, and heard them inquiring of the concierge whether any of the tours were running this afternoon. The concierge wore a smartly tailored suit which probably cost more than Morty made in a month. The helpful employee assured the couple most of the tours were running, and that they might hire a Chippewa guide to make the experience more authentic. Morty snorted quietly. *Ma and Pa Rockefeller go slumming with the natives. Too bad my Uncle Vern hadn't known about this racket; he would've made a fortune taking snobs out to his ice-fishing shack by the hour.*

Morty wished his parents had allowed him to spend more time on the Menominee reservation with his maternal Great-Uncle Vern. The old man had been a little around the bend by the time Morty and his brother Jed were old enough to go fishing with him on the numerous Northwoods lakes within the ceded territory. They'd spent the occasional weekend on the reservation growing up, and Uncle Vern had taught them how to track, fish with a spear, how to smoke fish on a rack. All capped with a smattering of old, often frightening, folklore.

The last time Morty and Jed saw Uncle Vern was the night he'd frightened the boys by shooting into the darkness outside their fishing shack, yelling in a mix of English and Menominee about bad spirits. When their mother picked them up the next day, there'd been talk of jail, drunkenness, and a growing instability in the old man's ramblings about the Wisconsin wilderness. Morty suspected his mother was secretly glad for a reason never to visit the rez again. She had always seemed vaguely embarrassed about her country cousins who still lived there, and Morty's father didn't seem to value anything that wasn't football or beer-related. The reservation relatives had been a convenient place to drop the kids off for a couple of weeks in the summer to get them out of the house. Until the drunken raving incident, anyway.

Morty perked when Darcy plopped down next to him and threw her arm over his shoulders. "Dad says dinner's at six-thirty; we have almost three hours 'til then. Wanna explore?"

Her enthusiasm could be mildly exasperating when Morty just wanted to relax, though he had to admit it was genuine. Darcy had none of the stiffness or snobbery of the wealthy students who thronged Lawrence University by the score, both when he was a student ten years back and now. He offered her a sip of the toddy. "What's there to explore? Do they charge by the snowflake here?"

She giggled and took a sip. "There's a snowmobile trail; it runs along a bluff by the river. It's really pretty," she suggested.

Morty was dubious. A glance out the window showed a few skeletal trees where an hour ago there'd been only a sheet of impenetrable whiteness. "I haven't been on a snowmobile in ages. Not sure I remember how to start one. Plus..." He held up the toddy. She took it away from him, grinning.

"Goob. It's easier than a car." Darcy stood, tugging his hand until he rose as well. "And tomorrow, we're going to see the artifacts Dad's archaeology team dug up. Tons of Ancient Native American art. We'll get to see it before it all goes to the museum." She beamed, and Morty chuckled. He brushed his fingers through her soft hair.

"I didn't realize you were into archaeology," he admitted, intrigued.

"Well, yeah. Tribal art is really cool. In tune with the earth. Made for reasons other than trying to impress critics." She gestured at a birch-bark canoe hanging from the lodgepole ceiling. "I love this stuff. So does Dad, actually. He collects it."

"Your father is an AmShale oil exec," Morty reminded her. "He communes with the earth solely for purposes of finding out how much crude he can extract from it."

"They're an energy company. They do solar and wind-power too, you know." Darcy smoothed her hair back, pulling on a knitted ski hat. "Besides, I never said I agreed with everything his company does."

"Aren't you the little rebel," Morty teased, and drew her closer to kiss her. "What kind of artifacts?"

She shrugged. "Don't know. Hopefully, something more interesting than pottery shards and arrowheads. Come on, let's hit the trail before the weather turns again or it gets too dark."

He found he recalled enough to start the skidoo, and for half an hour, Morty tried his best to smoothly steer between looming fir trees without lurching them sideways. The trail proved nicely scenic, winding through pine forest where icy trees sparkled in the cold afternoon, overlooking the Bad River at several high points along a sharp bluff. Though Darcy's arms around his waist were warm and welcome, he was grateful to see the roof of the resort again, his cheeks stinging and the tip of his nose frozen. His reward for serving as snowmobile pilot was a steaming shower which turned into something even more heated.

As they lay sprawled together on the bed, breathless, Morty tugged the faux-fur coverlet over them both and gathered Darcy back into his embrace. She snuggled against his chest, soft hands brushing his flushed skin. "Mmm. You're all cuddly. I like that," she said.

He chuckled, pleasantly sated. "So you keep telling me." He ran one hand down the curve of her back. Darcy's body was lean and nicely toned. She ran in the morning, several times a week, a hobby he'd never tried and didn't intend to start. He sighed to himself. They didn't have any common background, other than attending Larry U at separate points. It was obvious her friends only tolerated his presence because Darcy wanted him along. He hadn't fit in with the popular crowd when younger, and he still didn't.

"What are you thinking?"

He hesitated. "Just wondering again why me. You must have plenty of friends closer to your socioeconomic strata."

She laughed. "Oh, come on, don't bring up the whole 'rich girl' thing again." She tickled his belly, making him squirm. "I like you because you're not like them. Most of the boys are big, muscley jocks with expensive cars and business-school plans."

"Oh, of course. Why would you want that?"

She smacked his chest. "You're too smart for the bookstore. Why don't you think about doing something better?"

Morty shrugged. "I'm comfortable there."

"Paul Foster says you should always challenge your comfort zones."

Morty grimaced. "We're cuddling naked, and you have to bring up a self-help guru? It may shock you to hear this, but I don't give a badger-humping damn what Paul Foster says."

Darcy laughed, pushing him over onto his back and throwing her left leg across his thighs. He shifted agreeably for her to straddle him, enjoying the view of her breasts. "Okay, fine. Really, Mordecai, we both know you could be making a lot more doing something more important than digging through boxes of old paperbacks."

He let pass her use of his proper name. Again. But she did make it sort of appealing. "You'd be surprised what you can find in those dusty old boxes. Did I show you the first-edition—"

Darcy rolled her eyes. "Please, I'm serious. I really think you're wasting your skills. You're smart, you can write, you're funny..."

"Is that you talking, or your father?" She stuck out her tongue at him. "Mm. I have a suggestion where you might put that to better use," he offered. She smacked his chest again, and he grinned.

"Get your mind off sex for a minute."

"You're sitting on me," he pointed out. "It's a little hard to think about anything else. Speaking of hardness." She slid off him, much to his dismay. "Hey!"

"Listen for just a sec, okay?" She locked gazes with him, and he sighed, waiting. After a moment she continued, "I've been talking to Dad about your job."

"Assturkeys," he groaned.

"Shush, you. You're wasting your potential. Dad wants to talk to you at dinner tonight."

Morty reached for the edge of the bed and pulled himself out of the sea of sheets and blankets. "And we were having such a nice moment."

Darcy glared at him, sliding the faux-mink blanket over one shoulder as she sat up. At least, Morty hoped it was faux. "Why do you always do that?"

"Do what? Object to other people trying to plan my life for me?" It came out a bit more caustic than he'd intended. He didn't apologize. He trudged into the bathroom. Cleaning himself off, he raised his voice loud enough for Darcy to hear him. "I appreciate you're trying to better my situation, but I'm not interested. I enjoy the bookstore. It's full of geeky things and staffed by geeky people. I'm a geek. I'm happy there. I'm just not made to sit in a cubicle, chained to a desk by a designer tie." He sighed. "I appreciate this whole romantic birthday weekend thing; I really do. This place is cool, once one looks past the overwhelming aura of conspicuous consumption. But please, please, please don't turn this into a campaign to improve my social standing. Okay?"

He returned to the bed to sit down, and took her hands in his, kissing her fingertips. Her expression was disappointment congealed. Morty sighed. "You knew I was a loser when you asked me out. If I'm not really what you want..."

"You're not a loser. See, that's exactly the kind of negative thinking that's keeping you from realizing your full po—" He touched a finger to her

lips to stop the flow of self-help narrative. Darcy shook her head and caressed his fingers with her delicate ones. The gesture reminded him of her
skill with the violin, and he thought of what she'd told him about her parents' plans for her.

"Darce, you said your dad hounded you to get a marketing degree when
you told him you wanted to go into music instead. I feel just as boxed in
when stuff like this comes up."

"I know." She gazed sadly at him, and Morty's heart melted. He never
could resist that look from anyone, least of all someone whom he knew
genuinely cared. He slipped under the covers and lay with both arms
wrapped around her. Darcy snuggled close, her face on his shoulder and her
warmth wonderful against his skin. "It's just I found out something, and I
was trying to build you up to it, so it wouldn't be a surprise."

His mind raced through the implications. "Please don't tell me your
dad is going to offer me a job."

She pulled back to see his eyes, her own deep brown ones imploring.
"Just hear him out. Tell him you'll think about it, at least. It's not the worst
thing in the world, right?"

Morty groaned. Darcy rubbed her petite nose, and just for an instant
he wondered if she was going to enchant him into working at AmShale.
"Morty, please don't take this wrong, but Mom and Dad are kind of concerned about appearances." He'd seen their house. More like obsessed with
appearances. "Dad just wants a chance to get to know you better, since he
really doesn't know anything about you."

"Yeah, guess we must just keep missing each other at the yacht club out-
ings."

Darcy raised an eyebrow at him, her lips pursed. Giving in, at least for
the time being, he sighed deeply, rolling his eyes for good measure. Darcy giggled, and hugged him tight. He nuzzled her hair; she always smelled
lovely, sweet but sensual. "I'm not the kind of guy who can be anything important, Darce. I have a very specific skill set, limited to reading, writing,
and going straight to the Special Hell."

She wrinkled her nose, smiling. "Star Trek, right?"

Morty sighed. He wished it didn't matter to him she was as far outside
his geekdom as Miranda was from the Core Planets. But, he conceded,

she'd been willing so far to watch and read and play all the things he enjoyed. Hell, she'd once engaged in a friendly, intelligent argument with him about who would win if the Scooby Gang faced off against Buffy and friends, and subsequently made him re-think his opinion on the issue. She rubbed her breasts against him in a very distracting manner, pulling him back to the present.

"Know what I like about you? You're male, but cuddly-soft. Not all hard-as-rock," she said, caressing his bottom.

"That's me," he agreed. "A huggable schlep." He strongly suspected she was only with him as an act of rebellion against her parents. What the hell. He was up for a little rebellion.

"I love you," she said, kissing him.

"I know." Before she could react, he slid down the bed, parted her thighs with his hands, and attacked her with his tongue. Though he was only recently learning to master this specific art, Darcy's delighted squeal made him feel he was improving ten-fold. He forgot all about their differences for several wonderful minutes.

Dinner that evening proved exactly as stilted and uncomfortable as Morty had feared. He engaged in polite, quiet conversation with Darcy and Mr. and Mrs. Mueller. Darcy seemed more subdued around her parents, more fastidious in her table manners than Morty had seen when it was just the two of them. She didn't laugh much, and her smiles at appropriate points were small, brief things, very different from the wide grins she usually gave him. He decided he didn't much enjoy who she was around her folks. Her father commanded the head of the table even though it was only the four of them for dinner. Would her dad not approve if she stretched out in her chair and burped? Morty grinned. Definitely not.

Darcy nudged his foot under the table, and gave him an earnest, pleading look. He blanked his expression, but rubbed his foot up her leg. She rolled her eyes at him.

"So, Mordecai. Darcy tells me you've been in a managerial position at your store for some time?"

Morty stifled a flash of annoyance and turned to Mr. Mueller. "Not exactly. I'm the head of the book department."

Mueller nodded. "A man should be well-read, no matter what job he works." Morty smiled in response and tried to focus on his salmon. Clearly the pitch was underway. "How do you like it?"

"Dealing books? It's great." Morty paused to sip the pinot Grigio he'd ordered at Darcy's mother's suggestion; it did indeed go well with the fish, and he didn't want to seem ungrateful for their hospitality. "This is wonderful, by the way. Thank you again."

Mueller smiled, and his wife beamed. She had limited her conversation tonight to the extreme cold this winter and the scarcity of good, fresh chard in Appleton. Although this was the second time he'd met Darcy's parents, very little conversation had been exchanged during their brief introduction at the family Christmas party. He'd half-hoped to talk a little more with Mrs. Mueller, as she seemed more approachable than her husband; however all this evening she demurred to him. Mueller asked, "How many employees do you oversee?"

"Five. It's not the biggest bookstore by any means, but I like to think it's the best on College Avenue." It was, in fact, the only bookstore in downtown Appleton, which Mueller probably knew. Morty could just smell the proposal coming down the pike. Plenty of people might leap at the chance to take a position with a prominent company such as AmShale; he wasn't one of them. He'd worn the only sedate tie he owned, a ridiculously expensive maroon one, to dinner tonight. It was that kind of a place. And, he figured, his screen-printed Dalek tie wasn't quite chic enough for Darcy's parents. Not that he hadn't been tempted to wear it anyway.

Mueller kept smiling, cutting a precise piece from his thick ribeye. "Darcy didn't tell us you'd graduated in the top ten percent of your class at Lawrence, on full academic scholarship."

Yeah, Mueller looking up Morty's grades wasn't obtrusive at all. Morty replied, "That was a while back. It's not worth bragging about."

Mueller regarded him steadily, making Morty feel like a moth on a pin. "You could've gone on to your M.A. and Ph.D. You'd be teaching by now."

Morty shrugged. "I didn't want to teach."

Darcy jumped in to defend him. "Morty's writing a novel." He wished she hadn't. In truth, he'd futzed around with the manuscript for years, and still hadn't finished it.

"Oh?" Mrs. Mueller sounded vaguely interested. "What's it about?"

"The decay and corruption inherent in a world where corporations control all elections," Morty said. To add the cherry to that sundae, he explained, "It's a zombie story, where every elected official is a zombie controlled by the corporate sorcerers, and the public never realizes because they're all addicted to sugary snack foods and reality TV."

"I see," Mrs. Mueller said uncertainly. She asked Darcy, "Have you read any of it, dear?"

"A couple of chapters. I couldn't get past the gory parts." Darcy flashed an apologetic smile at Morty. "Zombies are popular, though. It could be a bestseller."

"Yeah, maybe," Morty said. The conversation lagged for several moments. Trying to be pleasant, he asked, "Darcy said we'd be viewing some Native American artifacts tomorrow? Sounds intriguing."

"Yes." Mueller paused as if mentally shifting gears, and Morty wondered if this man ever spoke a word which hadn't been thrice-filtered through his superego. "AmShale has been funding the excavation of a burial mound we uncovered a few miles from here. We've been working with Chippewa archaeologists to preserve the artifacts."

"I didn't know the mound-builders lived this far north. I've seen the ceremonial effigies at High Cliff," Morty said.

"It's quite impressive," Mueller replied. "I've only seen photos so far, but the extent of the find suggests this may have been intended to honor a god, or perhaps a well-respected shaman or tribal leader. They've uncovered one actual burial, with a wealth of pre-Columbian artifacts surrounding it."

"I'm not sure an Indian graveyard is really a proper dinner conversation topic," Mrs. Mueller murmured, though she cast a humoring smile at her husband.

"I think it's an amazing find," Darcy said. "And I'm glad all of it will be going back to the local tribe, where it belongs. We ought to respect native cultures. After all, if it weren't for them, our ancestors would have starved at Plymouth."

Morty repressed the urge to point out the centuries of treaty abuse and warfare which better typified relations between the two cultures. Instead, he asked, "How did AmShale get involved in this?"

Mueller gave a small shrug. "Our geologists were testing new prospects in the area. When they accidentally dug into the mound—it was buried under layers of earth, in a forested area, not obvious at all from the surface—they, of course, notified the proper authorities they'd inadvertently found an archaeological site. All the artifacts unearthed to date are being catalogued and will be transported to the new Mitigwa Cultural Center, which AmShale is funding. We'll be able to view them *in situ* tomorrow before that happens." He smiled at his daughter's wide grin. "It's a rare privilege, I'm told. We've had several universities fighting over access; the tribal council is handling all the details. We're just funding the dig."

"In exchange for drilling rights?" Morty guessed.

Mueller shrugged again. "We won't make a move until the team is certain the mound has been thoroughly excavated."

Morty finished his wine and reached for the bottle. A waiter he hadn't noticed stepped up and refilled his glass. Morty murmured thanks, and looked around the table, annoyed no one else was bringing up the obvious. "Aren't we right on the watershed here? There are dozens of little lakes and creeks in every direction. Chequamegon National Forest surrounds this resort. You're not proposing drilling there, are you?"

Mueller smiled briefly, his lips tight. "We've secured all the proper permits and access to conduct hydraulic fracturing operations on state land just outside the Mashkiki Reservation. And obtained a three-year lease from the state, commencing as soon as the archaeological study is completed." He lifted his own glass, ignoring the man who quickly refilled the dark red for him. "All perfectly legal, Mordecai."

Morty's brows went up. "Fracking? Up here in the pristine wilderness?" He shook his head. Next to him, Darcy fidgeted. "Haven't you had any objections from the locals?"

Mueller's tone remained perfectly calm. "As I said, we've been granted a lease by the State Department of Forestry. The site should produce dozens of local jobs, and this region could certainly use the employment."

Morty smiled sardonically at Darcy. "Back to nature, huh?"

"Come along and see our operations sometime," Mueller remarked, returning to his steak. "I don't think you'll find evidence of the horror stories you read in the liberal press. You'll see we're quite responsible."

"I'm sure you're eminently responsible," Morty replied.

"Do they still do horse-drawn sled rides here, even though it's after Christmas?" Darcy asked quickly.

"I don't know, dear," Mrs. Mueller said. "What a lovely idea. We should ask Henri." She and Darcy beamed at one another. Morty held his tongue, though he could think of a dozen more arguments against drilling for natural gas in this supposedly protected wilderness. A busboy began silently clearing their plates. Mueller sat back, twisting his napkin between his fingers as if wiping his hands clean of any unpleasantness at the civilized dinner table.

"That was excellent," he remarked. "Who wants dessert? I understand someone is celebrating a birthday."

Darcy took Morty's hand under the table and squeezed it. He glanced at her, and saw the plea in her eyes: *Don't make a fuss, we're here to have fun.* He managed a smile, though he wasn't at all happy. "Sure. Bring on the celebrations."

3

"Oh wow, this is gorgeous," Darcy exclaimed, peering at an elaborate necklace of shell and bone beads interspersed with jet and copper nuggets. She pushed her hair out of her face, bending over to view the necklace from a closer angle. The young man hovering next to her looked as though he wanted to snatch it away, although Darcy was careful not to touch anything. Morty recognized the anxiety of a grad student afraid his precious project would be ripped out from under him, and gave him an understanding nod. A suspicious glare was all he received in return. So much for being friendly.

They were better off keeping their hands in their pockets, anyway. Although a shanty-like shelter of wooden poles and corrugated metal made the site more or less workable, it was cold as a polar bear's butt. Morty wasn't impressed by the few kerosene heaters spaced around. AmShale's funding didn't extend to comfort levels on-site, apparently. Morty guessed they were working on a very narrow timetable. *'Wait 'til the site has been excavated fully,' my ass.*

His breath formed white clouds, and he wished he'd thought to bring his gloves. Being a native of Wisconsin didn't mean he had to enjoy freezing his balls off in what was supposed to be an indoor work area.

Piles of dirt against the makeshift walls were all that remained of the exterior of the mound. Everywhere, a good twenty feet in all directions, excavation pits were marked with red flags and string grids showing extensive cataloguing well underway. A couple of young women, possibly students, worked quietly using toothbrushes to uncover more of a large earthenware bowl. Morty saw one of them pause to blow on her hands before returning to the meticulous labor.

"Isn't this amazing?" Darcy asked, her eyes alight. The dig site compared well to Tut's tomb, from what Morty could see. He'd expected a few arrowheads, maybe some pots and fragile reed baskets. The wealth and variety of the artifacts here surely indicated they were standing in the final resting place of a great chief, a warrior of renown who'd ruled before white men ever set foot on this continent. He was no anthropologist, but a passing fas-

cination with ancient history in general meant he at least understood this
was one hell of a find.

He studied the carvings on a huge wooden shield nestled in one of the
crates. "It's definitely something. I don't really think I have adequate words
to describe it," he replied. "Of course, 'bizarre' and 'extremely disturbing'
do spring to mind." Trees and animals depicted on the shield all bowed toward a figure in the center, possibly some kind of horned fertility god; he
was sure those were antlers. Then again, the entity had long, wicked claws
and teeth, and last he'd checked, deer weren't predators. Its emaciated ribs
and visible bones reminded him of South American death deities. Pointed
spikes hung from the tree branches and the antlers, and traces of white clay
colored the area around the central figure. "Any idea what this symbolizes?"
he asked the grad student.

"Everything here indicates this was a ceremonial burial, possibly to ap-
pease *Kabibona'kan,* the Winter-maker," a voice said from behind him.
Morty turned. A solidly built man stood there in thick flannels and duck
boots, with a graying ponytail and the long, straight nose and high, broad
cheekbones of the local tribes. He gestured at the ceremonial shield. "He
was the one who brought the cold winds and the snow. He was cruel; he
enjoyed keeping the people huddled inside their lodges all season. He may
have been the early basis for stories of Old Man Winter."

Mueller strolled up. "This is Dr. Lightfoot, chief archaeologist for the
dig." Mueller introduced them, "My daughter, Darcy, and her friend Mr.
Wending."

As Dr. Lightfoot didn't seem inclined to shake hands, Morty simply
gave him a respectful nod. "This is quite a find, I'm guessing?" he ventured.

Lightfoot agreed with a subtle incline of his head. "No one has ever
seen a burial this extensive in the region before. We'll be studying the objects here for decades to come."

"I'm really glad all of it is going back to your people," Darcy said.

"We Ojibwe know very little about the people who made these artifacts," Lightfoot corrected gently. "It will be an honor to study them, and
to rebury the elder where he will not be disturbed." He didn't so much as
glance at the white man standing next to him. Morty suddenly wondered

if everyone on the tribal council was thrilled about AmShale drilling near their ancestral land, regardless of how many jobs it created.

"Oh," Darcy said softly, blushing. "The Ojibwe didn't make this?"

"No, my ancestors migrated here well after this was made. We believe the mound predates our ancestors' arrival to this area by as much as a thousand years," Lightfoot said. "However, the clues left here will help us learn more. For example, the workmanship on this war club is more sophisticated than others of the same period." He nodded toward a massive club, green with age, where it lay half-wrapped in a tarp atop a crate. "Perhaps they had mastered refining copper ore, or perhaps it was traded from other Great Lakes tribes." Morty crouched to examine the ornate weapon.

Even a Klingon would've been impressed with the heft of the club. It appeared to be cast from pure copper and was far too massive for anyone short of Thor to lift. Morty took a closer look at the oxidized metal; there were dark, dried splatters along one side. "Is that blood?"

"My theory is the entire burial was a sacrificial offering," the grad student said, sounding pleased with himself.

"A sacrifice," Darcy repeated, touching one hand to Morty's shoulder. She stared uneasily at the club.

Lightfoot gestured to a collection of covered clay pots and baskets of wood and birchbark. "Could be. There are remains of food in all those. Grains, rice, seeds, bones from rabbits, fish, and deer."

Morty looked at the area marked off from the rest of the dig by plastic tarpaulin walls. Presumably the lone occupant of the mound lay there. "Like a pharaoh. Everything he'd need for the afterlife."

Lightfoot raised one angular brow. "Or enough for a whole family to get through a harsh winter. They put an enormous amount of work into all this."

Darcy picked her way toward the main attraction, stepping daintily around open holes and crates nestling pottery in wads of cotton and straw. "Could he have been a great chief?"

The grad student hustled ahead of her to the cordoned-off area. "Careful!"

Darcy made a plaintive face at her father. "Dr. Lightfoot, is it possible we could take a peek?" Mueller asked. "We'll refrain from touching anything."

Lightfoot assented with a nod to the irritated grad student. A frown scrunched up the young man's sallow face, but he peeled back the top sheet and turned on a large work lamp beside the grave. Darcy leaned forward, then recoiled as if slapped. "Ugh!" Darcy's disgusted reaction meant it had to be amazing. Morty quickly moved to join her. "Sweetie, be careful!"

"Darce, relax," he scoffed. He heard her startled intake of breath as his sneaker slid on a frozen slab of rock. Desperately he thrust his arms out as the slip turned into a full forward slide, his feet unable to find a stopping point. *No oh shit don't break anything don't break anything don't—*

His knees slammed the ground, skidding over the cold mud. Morty threw both hands forward, knowing it was going to shred his palms; better that than destroying a millennia-old artifact. His right hand bore the brunt of his fall; he grunted as the ice cut into his skin. The lip of the pit crumbled suddenly under his left hand, and something slashed his palm. He yelped, and fire bloomed in his hand.

Hands went under his armpits and hefted him up immediately. Morty blinked back tears, grimacing at the myriad hurts competing for his attention. He bit back curses, trying to salvage his dignity, though he knew it was a lost cause. "You all right?" Mueller asked. Morty sucked in a breath, trying to take stock of himself. Lightfoot was on his other side. Together they walked Morty back a few steps and sat him down on a trunk. Darcy approached fearfully, her eyes flicking from his knees to his face.

"Babe, are you all right?" He felt warmth dripping from his hands. Blood trickled steadily from a nasty hole in his left palm, and the right was scraped raw.

"Not really, thanks." He calmed his breathing, angry at himself. A dirt floor full of holes, so of course, he almost fell into the most avoidable one. "Please tell me I didn't just obliterate a priceless archaeological discovery."

"I think both of you will live," said Lightfoot, a tinge of amusement in his gravelly voice.

Morty shot him a wry look; the poker face he saw in response upped his appreciation of the archaeologist a notch or two. Mueller appeared far more unhappy, and the grad student's face said *This is why we don't let you cattle around our priceless discoveries, moron,* as he hurried to the other side of the room for the first aid kit.

The other archaeologists had stopped work, asking whether the visitor was all right. Morty wrapped his hands in his shirt to staunch the flow of blood. His jeans had held up, though the lines of brown seeping through informed him he had more scrapes and bruises on his shins. Wet, red gashes marked his forearms, the blood soaking the fabric as he gingerly pushed up his sleeves. Darcy paled, turning away. Morty peered into the grave to see what had cut him.

The skull gaping sightlessly back wasn't what he expected. Instead of mummified remains or a ceremonial mask, the mud-darkened skull of a huge elk lay atop a long humanoid figure. Mangy, half-decayed furs covered the stark ribcage. More unnerving than the hybrid corpse, however, was the wet gleam of red on a pointed antler-tip. He leaned forward, squinting. "Holy shit."

The grad student returned with bandages and antiseptic. Morty gingerly pressed gauze to his wounds. Darcy crouched next to him, trying to wrap the gauze roll around his hand without viewing the blood and not making a professional job of it. He forced his attention away from the pain. "What do you make of that?" he asked, indicating the body.

Lightfoot knelt by the hole, tugged a handkerchief from a pocket, and carefully wiped Morty's blood from the antler. "Well, we know they sharpened the antlers and teeth," he remarked. Instead of the dull, grinding teeth common to ungulates, pointed incisors stuck out of the bone of the upper jaw. Lightfoot regarded the strange composite skeleton with the detached curiosity of a dedicated academic. "For whatever reason, this man was beheaded and buried with the skull of an elk, all the bones ceremonially altered. We haven't found his head here anywhere." Everyone was silent, staring at the blind, accusing eye sockets of the skull. Darcy gave it a repulsed glance, then gently dabbed the gashes on Morty's arms with peroxide. He gritted his teeth.

"They buried him as an effigy of the god depicted on the shield," Grad Student announced. Morty and Mueller both looked at him. Defensive, the kid shrugged. "It's a theory."

Lightfoot didn't offer any comment. He stood, brushed dirt from his pants, and gently set about re-covering the body, securing the tarp walls and laying another over the grave. He switched off the lamp and came to Morty, examining his injuries more closely. "Anything broken?" he asked quietly.

Morty shook his head. "Just my self-respect. Couple months in a cast and it'll be fine." He thought he saw a flicker of a smile on the older man's lips. "Good thing all that jagged, frozen ground was there to catch me."

Lightfoot nodded. "Good thing. Or else you'd have bigger worries. Such as the cleaning bill to get all the blood out of those priceless furs."

Morty managed a weak laugh. Yeah, the old guy was all right. "I don't guess I could put it on AmShale's tab."

He saw a cloud pass over the archaeologist's face. "I am glad your injuries are minor. Perhaps you ought to check in with the resort nurse, however. Who knows what terrible bacteria might be preserved in this cold soil." Morty wasn't sure it was meant as a joke.

"Good idea," Mueller agreed. He offered his hand to Morty. "I'm sure an Old-Fashioned or two won't come amiss after that, either."

"Just whiskey, if it's all the same."

Mueller smiled. "I think we can find something suitable." Morty declined any help up, though fresh fire up his shins made him clench his jaw. Limping slowly, well clear of the open pits, he looked again at the shield as he approached the exit. The creatures depicted weren't bowing toward the entity in the center; they were lying dead at its feet. The long claws of the antlered, emaciated being in the center of the design echoed the sharp icicles depicted covering the trees, and the vicious spike of bone which had just drawn his warm blood. Chilled, Morty realized it wasn't a fertility god. More likely a god of death, of desperation, of cruelty.

He turned away. He didn't want to know anything else about the people who had created this cache of plenty and craftsmanship to honor something like that.

4

Marie Bois du Nord was bored. Hungry and bored; mostly bored.

She'd been prowling the Northwoods for a few days now, but hadn't encountered anyone along the snowmobile trails or campsites abandoned for the long winter. The irregular neon flash of the Leinenkugel beer sign beckoned to her from the trees. The small bar, barely a shotgun shack, was one of many peppered along the miles-long snowmobile route. The inside would reek of unwashed men right out of deer camp, but there would be food. And perhaps an amusement.

She stood in knee-deep snow and listened to the country music floating out from the squat building. Four snowmobiles and one hardy Jeep were lined up, more or less, out front. She thought she might have visited this place before, last winter perhaps, or the winter before. Then again, all these backwoods clubs looked identical to her. Same awful beer, same dull clientele.

A harsh gust blew her dark hair across her eyes, finding every tiny opening in the heavy, hooded coat and slapping snow at her cheeks. Marie sighed. She did not usually mind the cold, but tonight was pushing her endurance. She braced her shoulders into the wind and trudged toward the bar.

The mingled stenches of wet scarves and cooking oil hit her inside the door. She stamped the snow from her boots, unzipping her coat. When she shook her long hair free of the hood, several men looked towards her, appraising. She took an empty seat at the narrow bar. "Whiskey. Neat."

A white man in too-nice hunting clothes leered at her from his barstool. Clearly not a local; his gear could have arrived from a catalog the day before, without dirt or wear. "Well hey there. Wish I'd known something as sweet as you would walk in here before I spent my last cash dollar."

Marie sipped from the glass the bartender set before her, then tossed the rest back in a practiced gulp. She gave catalog man a thin smile. "It is not necessary for you to buy me a drink. I always pay my own way." She laid a twenty on the bartop, then paused, and raised an eyebrow at the bartender uncertainly. "You accept Canadian money?"

He shrugged. "Money is money. Don't expect exact change, though."

Marie tapped her glass. "Another, please."

The man with no more dollars guffawed. "I knew you had to be French Canuck soon as I saw you, honey. Hey, you ever go as far south as Chicago?" He tried to sidle closer, lost his balance, and spilled his drink down the front of her coat and shirt.

Marie leaned back, disgusted. *"Noondezhi,"* she muttered. *Idiot.*

The man pawed at her with a paper napkin. "Aw, shit, I'm sorry. Here, let me—" He stumbled, shoved aside by a younger man with darker skin and sleek black hair. "Hey! Watch it, asshole."

The young man drew up his shoulders, broad hands on narrow hips, displaying powerful biceps sheathed in a warm flannel shirt. "You 'accidentally' spill beer all over her so you can 'help clean her off,' and you call me the asshole?" he asked. The man from Chicago turned toward the angry voice and slowly tilted his head up to meet the much taller man's stern glare.

"Wasn't doing n'thing," the white man slurred, backing away, clearly not so drunk he didn't know when he was outgunned. No one seemed eager to jump to his defense. "Just making conversation, Christ, gimme a break."

The young man kept glaring until the drunk wandered away from the bar. Marie dabbed at her coat, then removed it. The thermal shirt underneath clung to her breasts where beer had dribbled. She felt the appreciative flicker of dark eyes up and down her body. She ignored it, knocking back the second glass of whiskey.

"Shinnob?" the young man asked, easing onto the vacated seat next to her.

Marie turned her gaze to him, and smiled. "Odawa."

He grinned. In Ojibwe, he replied, "Then we are cousins." His use of *niinimoshenh* for cousins didn't slip past her; it could also be used to mean *sweetheart.*

She smiled slowly. "Perhaps." She continued in his language. "Thank you for the help."

He laughed, and raised his arm, signaling for a beer. "You're welcome, though I'm glad I didn't have to hit him."

She favored him with her most playful smile. "In another minute I would have taught him how a real hunter dresses a kill." This brought another laugh from the young man, and from a couple of others nearby, clearly locals. Marie knew a reservation was somewhere in this part of the woods. Several men in the bar nodded appreciatively at her wit as what she had said traveled around the room. She relaxed, feeling more at home.

"I think you would have," the young brave agreed. He offered his hand, switching back to English. "Jimmy Walking-in-the-Snow Jennings."

"Marie Middle-of-the-Lake." She squinted at the dingy menu sign behind the bar. "Is there anything here worth eating?"

Jimmy shrugged. "The venison burger isn't bad."

Marie nodded, and ordered one in her French-accented English. Jimmy kept smiling at her. "So, how did a beautiful lady end up here on the ass end of the rez?"

"I was out for a ride. My Polaris broke down about a mile from here. I followed the trail until I saw lights."

"You walked in that?" Marie shrugged. Jimmy appeared impressed. "Good thing you dressed right for the weather."

"I have lived in this area my whole life," she replied. "Takes more than a little snow to stop me from having fun." Again, she turned a sly smile to him, and again, saw it having its intended effect.

Jimmy switched back to Ojibwe. "What kind of fun are you looking for?"

She shrugged. "Depends on my mood. At the moment, my mood is hungry." She accepted the burger and fries that appeared on the bar, and bit into the meat. The cook had compensated for the dryness of the venison by frying it in butter. Marie allowed a rivulet of it to escape the corner of her lips before she wiped it away. Jimmy kept staring at her, though he ducked his head and drank his beer as if pretending he was not.

He talked to her about the local hunting while she ate, pausing every time she sucked the grease off her fingertips. She acted oblivious to his stare. In truth, the fries were delicious.

Jimmy watched her empty a fourth shot glass. "I've never seen a woman hold her liquor so well before," he commented.

She chuckled. "My mother's family were old-school. That is how you say it, yes?" He nodded. Marie played with the empty glass, spinning it gently. "I had uncles who were actual lumberjacks. I spent a summer in the camp, and they taught me how the real *voyageurs* took their drinks."

"Hey. Listen. I don't want to sound like that Chicago asshole, but can I give you a ride home? Or back to your skidoo? I'm pretty good with engines," Jimmy offered.

Marie studied him, considering it. Her gaze shifted to the men about his age, playing pool at a table a few feet away. They had clearly been eavesdropping, and were silent, waiting to see if their friend would get lucky. "Would your friends mind?"

Jimmy didn't look back. "In this case, it is definitely ladies before bros. They have their own rides."

She gazed out the tiny front windows, though the single lamp outside did nothing to penetrate the swirling drifts or the moonless night. "If you think you can get it started again, that would be nice. If not," Her eyes roved from his angular face to his belt buckle. "I could use someplace warm to bed down."

Outside, they leaned into each other against the wind. Marie cinched her hood tighter, eyes narrowed in the blast of snow. Jimmy guided her to one of the Arctic Cats, larger and newer than the others. She leaned close to make herself heard. "It's a lovely machine."

"Yes it is," he shouted back, starting it up. Marie clasped herself to him, hugging tightly. "And it goes fast as hell, so hold on!"

They roared along the trail, the headlight barely cutting through the relentless snow. Between the whiskey that had warmed Marie's insides, and the heat of the handsome brave, she was almost lulled into complacency. She nearly missed the spot. "Stop," she yelled, pounding his shoulder. "Stop!"

The snowmobile skidded; Jimmy stopped it before it skewed too far. He peered into the howling whiteness. "Where? Are you sure?"

"Yes, I am sure. It was by that big rock." Marie jumped off, searching the area around a large jutting crag of granite beside the trail. When Jimmy reached her, she turned to him in desperation. "How can it not be here? I know this is the right spot!"

He shook his head, surveying the bend in the trail. "Can't have been buried, even in all this. Are you sure?" he yelled, waving an arm at the rock. "You know, a lot of places look the same in snow this bad."

"I am quite sure this is the right spot," Marie shouted back. When Jimmy turned to peer around again, she grabbed his skull in one enormous paw and slung him into the outcropping. The incessant wind muffled the crunch of bone. Jimmy slumped. His blood froze almost as soon as it touched the snow. Marie crouched over the body, dragging a claw through his pretty, pretty hair. "Of course it is the right spot," she purred. "The lake is just over this bluff, about fifty feet down. It's perfect."

When she finished eating the delightfully helpful Jimmy, she hefted his still-sputtering snowmobile above her head, and with a grunt flung it over and down. She heard the thud and crack of the ice below, and trusted the weight of the bike would draw it to the bottom. No one would find it now; perhaps not until spring, if then.

No one would think to look over the enormous rock bluff to the ice far below. It was, indeed, a perfect hunting spot.

5

The hot water pouring down his body felt marvelous, although the dripping off his chin was really beginning to annoy him. Morty blinked, unable to focus. Spikes jabbed his temples, and he groaned. It took him a few seconds to register the tiles pressing against his ass and shoulder blades and tired feet. About the time it filtered into his brain he was sitting in the shower, nausea surged up his throat and violently out. His blurry eyes saw bits of red swirling down the drain. He panicked, one hand going to his mouth, then yanked his fingers away with a loud curse. He peered at the cut on his palm. His idiotic stunt at the dig site came back to him.

Right. Fresh wounds in hot water. He sagged against the tiles, seeing more rivulets of crimson washing from his legs. He started to lean over to examine the cuts on his shins better. Another wave of dizziness convinced him leaning back was perhaps the smarter position. Blood loss and fifteen-year-old whiskey. Good to see his judgment was as sharp as ever. He wasn't sure whether it had been two glasses of better booze than he could normally afford, or three, or five. Mueller seemed to want to use the opportunity to persuade him he was a decent enough guy, and Morty had been mortified enough by his near-disastrous accident to accept. There had been food of some sort involved as well. Morty couldn't remember what. Obviously, it was now decorating the shower drain. Disgusted, he nudged a half-digested lump with his toe until it broke up and washed down the shiny metal designer grate.

"Morty?"

Darcy. He blinked at the frosted window of the bathroom. He didn't remember climbing into the shower. He was naked, dizzy, and still very drunk by the feel of it. It wasn't the first time he'd tried to use a bracing shower to counteract the effects of too much to drink, though generally he went for cold water. Then again, unfamiliar resort bathroom and way more booze in one sitting than he'd indulged in since college. He grimaced as a fresh ache made its presence known. And a tetanus booster from that officiously thorough nurse. Lovely.

"Morty, are you okay?" Darcy came in, wrapped in her plush bathrobe, her hair mussed. He would've found it sexy if he wasn't hurling what felt like his own intestines through his lips.

"More or less," he muttered, making no move to push away from the shower wall.

She paused, looking him over. "Your scratches are bleeding again?"

"They're a bit more than scratches, Darce."

"What happened to your bandages? Do you want me to call the front desk for more?" She glanced at the gauze roll on the counter; it looked inadequate for the various cuts and scrapes to Morty.

He shut his eyes, trying to think past the throbbing in his skull. "What time is it?"

"Almost five in the morning."

"Forget it," he muttered. He leaned forward gingerly, just far enough to rinse his mouth in the heated downpour. With effort, he found the faucet and turned off the water. He slowly pulled himself to his feet, and then across the ledge of the open-stall shower to a thick rug. Something soft brushed his hand; he glanced up to see Darcy offering him one of the wonderfully plush towels. "Oh, thank you," he sighed, hugging it to his chest. "We really have to steal these."

Darcy sighed. "Or I could just buy you some. Here." She produced another towel and began patting his arms dry. Morty flinched, sucking in a sharp breath. "I'm sorry, sweetie! Here, come on, come sit down."

"That is a delightful option." He sank onto the bathroom's ornate teak stool and didn't fuss as Darcy wrapped one of the towels over his shoulders. She began rubbing his head with it, and he winced again. "Ow."

"Well, what doesn't hurt?"

He paused. A smile crept across his face. Darcy smacked his shoulder with one end of the towel. "Really?"

He chuckled, although it sent uncomfortable vibrations through his head. "You asked."

Darcy shook her head. She continued to pat him dry gently. "We're getting their towels all bloody."

"I'm sure that's why they chose this color," he said, peering at the dark grey-and-black tribal pattern on the thick terry. "Of course, that means they don't bleach them. Yuck. Just imagine."

"Oh, my God. Does everything have to be about sex with you?" Darcy asked, giving up. She stood back, trying not to laugh.

"What? I'm a geek. Everything not comics and Firefly is sex. Except Rule Thirty-four Firefly comic book sex." Tiredly, he finished drying his extremities, doing his best to ignore the dull heat wherever the fabric brushed raw skin. With great effort, he rewrapped gauze around his left hand, and Darcy helped him knot the end. "Christ, my head hurts."

"Didn't I tell you to take some aspirin or something before you lay down?"

Morty shook his head, very, very carefully. "Probably. I don't remember."

Darcy left the room, her thick velvet robe a swirl of garnet, returning moments later with pills that she touched to his lips. He took them without question, drinking the entire glass of cool mineral water she gave him. He sat motionless, feeling low in every sense of the word.

"Darce?" he asked quietly. She leaned against the sink-counter, concern in her dark eyes. "Why did you ask me to come with you for this?"

"What kind of question is that? You're my boyfriend and it's your birthday."

He nodded and heaved himself off the chair. No point in bringing up his doubts again when she was determined to be so good to him. Darcy took his arm and guided him back to bed. He let the towels fall to the carpet and rolled gingerly under the blankets again. Darcy shed her robe, slipping in next to him, snuggling near him but thankfully not touching his wounds. "You're too good for me, you know," he murmured into her hair.

She sighed. "My poor baby. Get some sleep. We're supposed to all have brunch before we go home."

Morty groaned. He wrapped his arms carefully around her slender, soft body, giving up any more speculation as to why a girl who could have any man she wanted was trying so hard to make him fit into her world. "Ugly duckling," he muttered, more to himself than for her; she heard him.

"Are you calling me that? That was a swan, though, right?"

He chuckled. "You are a swan. I'm just ugly."

"You're unconventional." She ran a delicate fingertip down his long nose. "Good thing geek chic is in."

"Thanks."

She turned over to spoon with him, and he gradually felt the hammering in his brain quieting. Heaviness overtook his entire body, and with a deep sigh, he released all worries and sank into warm, comforting darkness.

Formal brunch the next morning with both parents, as it turned out, was canceled. Mr. Mueller had received an important business call earlier, an incident at the dig site of some kind which required his immediate attention. Hung over worse than he could recall being in years, Morty was grateful he didn't have to attempt polite conversation with Darcy's father. The bright chattering between Darcy and her mother over coffee and quiche proved a dubious blessing in its place.

Mrs. Mueller offered expressions of sympathy several times for his wounds. Morty had rebandaged the worst one on his left hand, spread antibiotic cream over the scrapes on his forearms, shins, and right hand, and dressed himself with far more care than usual while Darcy tossed their clothes in their bags. He couldn't get out of here fast enough. It would be a long drive back to Appleton.

He'd have to try to get some sleep with a pounding skull and sore guts for a couple of hours before opening the store tomorrow. It was all he could do to offer strained smiles at appropriate junctions in the brunch conversation. He didn't speak much, since his throat felt as though he'd swallowed not only the full set of Ginsu knives but the Act-Now-Bonus-Set-Free! as well. He couldn't recall when he'd last felt this horrendous. It was probably good Mr. Mueller hadn't personally witnessed Morty's bloodshot-eyed, queasy-bellied, very un-Oscar-worthy performance at the table. Darcy's father probably expected a real man to guzzle firewater all night and still eat a stack of flapjacks in the morning like a lumberjack. *Ha—I bet he'd be the guy who can't handle a little toke without going all paranoid.*

With the torturous midday meal concluded, Morty slumped into the passenger seat, finally on his way home. He tried to ignore Darcy revving the engine. When she spoke, her words surprised him. "I think you really impressed them, sweetie."

"What?" he asked, incredulous.

She smiled brightly at him. She was way too chipper for this hour of the hangover. The sky was too bright, the sun too sunny. Couldn't someone do something about all this goddamn brightness. "Mom and Dad. I think you made a great impression. I'm glad we finally could all spend a little time together."

Morty grimaced. "Right. I'm sorry it took me this long to prove to your father what a commie beatnik I am."

Darcy shook her head, turning onto the highway. The stands of white birches in snow, hedging in the light gray sky overhead, did not improve matters visually. A large squirrel stood up at the edge of the hotel's drive, staring at the car as it passed, unafraid. Even the wildlife here displayed a sense of entitlement. Morty shut his eyes as the car picked up speed. The sense of motion heightened tenfold.

"Stop being so down on yourself. He likes you. You may not agree on politics, but I think—"

"Darce, I doubt your father and I agree on anything."

"My dad doesn't order really nice whiskey for someone he doesn't respect."

"Oh, come on. That was pity. I made a complete ass of myself at a project AmShale is using as a pretty PR piece to pretend they care about anything other than making a gazillion dollars each quarter." Morty pressed the heels of his palms into his eye sockets, then hissed in pain. "Fuck me."

Darcy was quiet for a minute. Then she asked, "Why are you so cynical about everything?"

"I'm not cynical about everything. About corporate motives, yes."

"Did it occur to you just maybe my dad really respects Native American culture?"

"No, sorry. Did it occur to you maybe the local tribe had to be really desperate to agree to fracking anywhere near their land?"

"Did it occur to you that you're being completely negative about my parents?"

"I'm sorry, I completely forgot you scraped up your entire body because you slid on an icy chunk of clay and nearly destroyed a priceless creepy artifact. Oh wait, my bad, that was me." Headache erupted into anger.

"Your dad was probably getting me drunk so I wouldn't think about suing AmShale for failing to observe proper safety procedures at their dig site! Did you consider that?"

Darcy looked away, silent. Morty wanted to curl into a ball in a dark, dark room. A mile passed in silence. When he peered through half-closed lids at her again, he noticed the tear-tracks glistening on her cheek. *Ah, shit.* "Darcy." She wouldn't look at him. "Darce, I'm sorry. I'm in pain and I feel like the loser your dad undoubtedly thinks I am, and I'm being an asshole. I'm sorry."

She didn't respond. He tried again, gentling his voice, which was always a bit too scratchy even under the best circumstances. "Darcy, I'm sure your parents are perfectly nice people. They're just not people I'll ever understand. They represent an entire manner of living I find reprehensible, or at the least incomprehensible."

She turned her head to him. Briefly, but it was something, anyway. "You don't understand me, then?"

His throat closed. He hesitated too long, and she glared resolutely at the road. Morty sought a better explanation. "I—you are the best thing that's happened to me in years. And I still don't understand why you're with me. You could be off on some young lawyer's yacht or skiing in the Alps, or something."

"That's what everyone does," she protested. Morty blinked at her. "Everyone I go to school with, all my friends, half of them went into business, or law, or medicine, and the other half are marrying guys who do those things. Not one of them ever sits around playing Call of Thule or whatever, or talks over movies and makes me laugh, or shows me how to get past the Fire Temple dragon thing. Not one of them is—is comfortable enough with themselves that they don't feel they have to impress everyone around them every single day. Not like you." Morty had never heard this kind of fierce determination in her voice.

She took a deep breath, tears sparkling at the corners of her eyes. "I mean, you don't have any money but it doesn't bother you, and you don't care if your shirts come from thrift stores instead of tailors, and you don't care what anyone else thinks of you. And that's what I want."

He tried to wrap his aching brain around her words. "You—"

"I want to be like you," Darcy said firmly. "I want to not care what everyone else thinks. I want to not have to be perfect all the time."

Humbled, Morty reached for her hand. She shot him an anxious glance, then grabbed his hand in hers and squeezed it tight. It hurt like blazes. At that moment, though, he felt he deserved a little suffering.

Good one, Wending. The Insensitive Dumbass is strong in you. He fished a tissue from the packet of them in the glove compartment, and gently brushed it over her cheek. She met his eyes and must have liked what she saw there; she smiled, released his hand, and took the tissue to wipe her face. "You know," he said, "the mascara tracks look good on you." She laughed weakly. "No, no, I'm serious. I see potential here. You'd make a great zombie. There's a Zombie Run in May along the Fox River; want to come with me?"

She glanced over dubiously. "You're going to run?"

"Hell no! I was going to be one of the shambling horrors of decrepitude. All I need to do is shred an old shirt. Got the attitude already." His jaw slackened, and his eyes glazed as he reached a claw-like hand toward her midsection. "Boooooooobsss."

She swatted his hand away. "You're really screwed up, you know that?" she asked, laughing.

Morty shrugged, and reclined his seat, relaxing. He fished a joint out of his shirt pocket and lit it. "You prefer me this way. What's that say about you?"

She noticed what he was doing. "Morty, tell me you didn't have that on you at breakfast."

"Of course not. That would've been completely irresponsible, disrespectful, and only there in case of an emergency such as my utter inability to deal with your father and a massive hangover at the same time." He held in the first drag, slowly relaxing into the comfy cushions of the car seat. "Hey, how do I turn on the massager thing again?"

"You are absolutely shameless." She reached for the joint. Morty reacted faster, holding it out of her reach behind him.

"No, you're driving." He blew out another swirling puff, closing his eyes. The worst was over. He'd survived. Hopefully he wouldn't ever have to deal with this kind of interpersonal stress again. *At least not until she tries to drag me to a family dinner again.* "One of us has to be responsible here. Keep your eyes on the road." He cracked the window down. Another long, sweet inhalation of organic herbal bliss erased the last of his worries and calmed his motion sickness. He shook his head gently. "Young people these days. I fear for the next generation, I really do. Let me know when we come across a Thrifty-Mart. I could really use some Corn Crunchies."

6

Four towns over and two days later, news of the Bigfoot attack reached Garwood Quell. He downed more bottled water and Cheezy Num-o's and tuned the police-band radio as he drove, thankful he'd gone into the truck stop for snacks. If the screaming creature report in Wakefield hadn't been so worthless, he'd still be tromping through the U.P. with a tape recorder right now. If he hadn't given up and come into town right then, he'd never've heard the radio report. Everything happens for a reason.

Garwood Quell had a blog, and four self-published books. His last one, '*SASQUATCH AND THE PARALLEL DIMENSIONS*,' had reached #7 on the Cryptozoology lists. He drove a Nineteen seventy-nine Ford truck which he maintained himself. The beast of a vehicle had high underclearance, useful for driving muddy logging trails with ease. He refused to wear orange in hunting season, confident in his ability to not look like a deer. He was on disability due to the run-in with one of *them* at the cursed old Boy Scout campsite in the Upper Peninsula, sixteen years ago, which had changed his life and his entire worldview.

Garwood Quell hunted monsters.

None of that police-procedural child-molester "monster" crap; no, Quell had come disturbingly close to becoming sasquatch jerky back in the autumn of 2001. While the rest of the world was reeling from the fall of the Towers, Quell lay in a hospital bed in Traverse City, staring numbly at the bandages on his stub of a left leg. Once he'd learned how to walk with the prosthetic, he'd grimly gone right back out into the woods. He'd been there ever since.

The old truck crunched right over an icy patch on the highway without a slip. One of these days, by God, he'd catch one of the hairy bastards. Catch him, gut him, and have the danged beast stuffed and mounted!

From what he could piece together out of the scanner chatter and the curt responses to his questions at the tribal police station—if a desk in a mid-seventies rundown building could properly be called a police station—the attack came at night. The victim, just an ordinary Joe who worked for AmShale, was in the hospital at Ashland. Quell's hope for useful intel went up a notch when he heard the victim was still alive. However, before he drove another forty miles to try and interview the poor fella, he wanted to see where the 'squatch had come out of the forest.

Locating the attack site proved difficult; the tribal sheriff persevered in the sort of stony silence Indians loved to throw in the face of white men. Quell swore to them he was here to help; heck, he'd been to sweat lodges before, considered himself a friend to the native peoples, even offered the sheriff an autographed copy of his latest book, *'SQUATCHES AND 666: THE HIDDEN REVELATION.'* No use. Nada.

At least he knew something he didn't before, which was that oil giant AmShale was drilling in the area. Quell drove every snowed-in dirt road, camping track, and the road to the ritzy resort near the Bad River until he saw what he sought: a small sign with a single word, AMSHALE, and an arrow. He smacked his hands together in the cold cab of the truck; the heater was on the fritz again. "Now we're talking! Okay, fellas. Huh. A 'squatch roars outta the woods to rip apart a guy working for an oil company. How'd it know what they're doing? Did it smell petroleum?" A terrible thought hit him. "Holy smokes, are the danged Indians teaching the hairy bastards how to read?"

Now that was just crazy talk, for cripes' sake. Still, there hadn't been a report from this area in years. There had to be more than coincidence at work here.

There wasn't anyone at the gate. There wasn't really even a gate yet, just a chain strung across an old logging road; it was no obstacle for a dedicated hunter. Quell gave his scarf an extra twist around his head to trap warm breath against his face, tugged his gloves on tighter, and placed his feet carefully into the frozen slush. Not far past the chain, dormant excavators and a plow loomed from the gusting snow. It didn't appear as though AmShale had begun drilling yet; no sounds of heavy machinery, no towering scaffolds. He saw lights ahead, some sort of shanty building, and prudently moved away from it. Pine trees crowded the cleared area; a wall of cut logs, thick with needly boughs and covered in several inches of snow, drew his attention.

A 'squatch coming this close to a place where trees had been recently felled was unusual. Quell didn't like this one bit, no siree. Pretty quiet, though. Logging trucks wouldn't drag this mess away 'til the next clear day, and if they weren't set up to drill yet, the only other machinery sound would just be the plows keeping the road open. Unless the low hum of a gas-fueled generator counted. He saw cables running from it under the corrugated steel door to the shanty.

He studied the clearing. Whatever was going on in that shack, it didn't make enough noise to frighten the beasts away. He walked through increasingly deeper snow, flashlight out, casting this way and that for any evidence. Deer and rabbit tracks crisscrossed the edge of the open area, heading deeper into the swaying trees. Creaking boughs heavy with ice and the moan of the incessant wind played tricks with Quell's ears. Several times he paused and looked carefully all around; nothing. Maybe his intel was wrong. Maybe the guy had only worked here but been rumbled somewhere else.

He was about to trek back to the truck when his light picked up a glint of red. He walked cautiously to the snowplow, a tall industrial model painted school bus yellow. Frozen spatters of crimson marked its side just under the cab door. Quell sucked in a breath when he saw the deep parallel scrapes down its side. Claw marks. Holy Mother of God, the monster chased the victim right to the plow. He examined the ground just below it, pushing aside a couple inches of fresh powdery snow, heedless of the cold that seeped through the tops of his gloves. Spots of pink confirmed his theory. This was where the attack happened. Right here. Quell raised his eyes to the empty cab of the snowplow again, envisioning the horror: a man chased by the monster, leaping desperately for the safety of the plow, claws swiping at him, blood splashing out and freezing instantly. He shook his head. "Bet gettin' into that plow there was the only thing that saved you, friend. Which way did it come from?"

There was no way to find any tracks, not in this. The wet, heavy flakes continued to fall, and Quell's footprints were nearly erased already. He stepped back, taking out his cell phone and wiping the camera lens on his shirttail before snapping a few shots of the crime scene. He studied the angle of the claw marks on the plow's side, aligned himself with them, and did an about-face. All he could see was an endless palisade of pines. He walked toward the tree line anyway, hoping not everything had been obliterated by the winter storm.

Peering into the ranks of trees, he saw rocks and roots at eye level a couple of feet beyond the edge of the clearing. He advanced, one hand outstretched, and discovered an embankment above the site. It was high enough to serve as a danged good lookout point, low enough for an easy jumping-off, and Lord knew, those beasts could jump. He recalled only too well the frightening agility and speed of the creatures.

He bruised both knees before he surmounted the embankment. Clinging to a sturdy tree trunk, Quell looked down. Through a natural break in the forest, he could see the yellow lump of the snowplow even through the blowing gusts of white. Sasquatch had probably stood right here, watching the hapless AmShale guy maybe leaving work after dark, heading for his truck, and then it had bounded down the bank, right at him, roaring, claws outstretched!

Quell shuddered. He forced himself to stop dwelling on the past, no matter how recent, and focus on his surroundings. His wits properly sharpened, he shone his light at the snow where low-sweeping branches brushed the crust smooth. He'd found scat once under an enormous fir. The fool ranger had said it was from a bear; Quell knew the difference. No black bear in the Northwoods took a crap that big.

No tracks, no scat except deer droppings. Nothing. And it was colder than his ex-wife's hands out here. Disappointed, Quell trudged along the edge of the embankment, searching for an easier way down. In a tangle of dead blackberry brush just a few feet away, something fluttered. Something white and black and red. As he drew closer he spotted a print near it, but that turned out to be the track of a big buck elk just within the shelter of a Douglas fir. One of these days, he'd get a good footprint. One nobody could say was a fake. He reached the blackberry thorns. A piece of fabric had snagged in them; when he pulled on it, more came free from the snow below the bush.

Quell held up the ripped, frozen t-shirt, blinking at the brightness of his flashlight bouncing off the white cotton. He read what was left of the logo. "B vampire? What the heck does that mean?" Some teenage rock band, maybe, who knew what kids were into these days.

Whatever; it certainly wasn't the evidence he needed. He had half a mind to carry it down to the AmShale camp and find a trash bin. That wasn't a good idea, though. It would put him too close to the lights of the shack, and possible discovery. Quell had learned years ago investigating 'squatch sightings wasn't considered justifiable grounds for trespassing by most folks. No one could deny those were claw marks, though. And that was blood on the snowcat, no doubt about it. He took a few more shots of the surroundings, for later study.

When he returned to his truck, the temperature had dropped further. Thankfully, the seventy-nine classic started right up. He saw no other vehicles on the roads until he hit the highway. He found a country station on the radio and began to think on why a 'squatch would've attacked someone so close to human activity. With any luck, the victim would be able to describe the assault in detail. And of course, Quell would take photos of the man's wounds. They'd be nasty cuts, with all the blood spatter. He wondered if they'd treated the victim for rabies.

He took a swig of his water. Ahead, a highway patrol car and flares signaled some poor bastard who'd slid off the road. Quell slowed down, frowning at the storm. Now there was a thought: could 'squatches even get rabies?

7

Morty tried to tug the blanket tighter around himself; it seemed to be caught on the edge of the bed. He pulled harder, and suddenly vertigo rushed through him. An instant later he slammed onto the boards of the porch. *Oww. What the hell? Why am I outside?*

He lay still, trying to make sense of what had to be completely incorrect sensory data jumbled in his brain. Blinking and rubbing his eyes, he realized his fingers were numb; little sparks of nerve awakenings shot through his limbs as he moved.

His apartment, a few rooms on the second story of a gently crumbling Victorian house, had little to offer besides the original wood trim along the walls and a halfway decent view of City Park from his bedroom window. The rooms were small, the hot water erratic, and modern insulation largely nonexistent in the original lathe-and-plaster walls. But one thing it did have was a screened-in sleeping porch which overlooked the back yard. During the summer, Morty enjoyed relaxing out here. January was another matter.

Shivering, he wrapped his cold-frosted blanket around his tattered robe and, with considerable difficulty, levered himself off the snow-dusted floorboards. He staggered toward the door, trying to remember last night's activities. Darcy had treated them both to takeout Chinese. A bottle of *sake* might or might not have been involved. He was fairly sure she had gone home since she had an early class in the morning, leaving him ensconced in his favorite armchair playing Zelda. Bewildered, he looked around the porch, seeking anything that might make sense of this. The sudden and incontestable sensation of being watched put his hackles up. *Dammit, don't tell me I accidentally flashed Mrs. Hietpas again.*

Morty wrapped the robe tighter around his waist, turning to see if his nosy next-door neighbor was at her bedroom window already in the grey dawn. Beady black eyes startled him, and he instinctively shuffled back a few steps; a squirrel sat on its hind legs atop a plant stand not two feet away. Morty stared at it. "You're bold," he muttered. He'd lived here three years, and though he'd never bothered to repair the holes all over the porch screen, he'd never seen a creature actually venture inside. And it was far too deep in the winter for rodents to be out of their burrows. Aside from a neighbor's dog occasionally barking, he hadn't seen or heard any animals in a couple of months.

"Dude, I don't have any nuts for you." The squirrel didn't so much as twitch. Morty had never realized just how big these things were. It was so motionless he hadn't seen it at first, despite its size and surprising proximity to the deck chair where he'd been inexplicably sleeping. Its emotionless eyes continued staring right at him, and for a moment he doubted it was alive.

Abruptly, the squirrel turned and leapt from the plant stand to the porch rail, flicked through a tear in the screen, and was gone. Morty shook off the feeling it had been waiting for him to freeze to death so he could be harvested like a slightly furry pine cone. Mrs. Hietpas glared at him from her window directly across the driveway between the houses. Morty shot her a thin smile and a nod. She scowled at him so deeply her bottom lip met her tiny chin, as she yanked her curtains shut.

"Yeah, like you wouldn't enjoy watching me eaten by carnivorous rodents," Morty muttered. "Hypocritical busybody." The doorknob turned stiffly on his third try, and he stumbled from the frozen tundra of porchlandia into his apartment.

Shaking his head, shivering all over as his nerves prickled, he beelined to the stove in the kitchenette and turned on the burner under the kettle. Damned Arctic wind. Though the partitioned old house had multiple cold spots, drafts with the slightest breeze outside, and the necessity for space heaters in every room, it beat setting foot outdoors from November through May. Every summer, the charm of his suite of rooms in the once-magnificent manse in the historic part of town made him forget how damned cold the place was once the mercury dropped. Grateful for the warmth of the stove, Morty dropped his blanket to the floor and huddled in his robe in the galley kitchen. As he reached for a teacup, he heard the crinkling of the frost coating the arm of his robe. What the actual cow-humping hell.

His videogame was still on the TV screen. An empty tea mug and the Styrofoam-coffined remains of his Mongolian beef sat on the coffee table. By all rights, he should've either fallen into bed and slept soundly, or crashed right there in the chair. He touched a hand to his forehead, too chilled to determine whether he had a fever. He stripped off the robe. The frost limning the collar and shoulders crackled. He wasn't sure whether the wind outside had blown out the pilot light for the water heater again. But right now, a hot shower sounded wonderful. He poured boiling water into a mug with a couple bags of chai, then hurried to the bathroom and ducked under the erratic shower faucet. Even ten minutes of standing under scalding water failed to completely warm him. When the hot water ran out, he clambered, shivering, from the tub and pulled on thermals as well as sweats. He must be coming down with something.

Two cups of tea and a plateful of sugary frosted toaster pastries later, he felt somewhat more prepared for existence. By the time Kim called to offer him a ride to work, Morty was planted in his chair, fighting his way through the Earth Temple. "Hey, man. Would you mind bringing over aspirin or something? Pretty sure I have a fever."

Kim sounded more concerned about it than Morty felt. "Dude, not cool. What's your temp?"

"No idea. I don't have a thermometer. I'm getting chills. Probably just that bug going around."

"You coming to work tonight?"

"Yeah, sure. I mean, it's not dire or anything. I just feel a little out of it." Morty eyed the antique cigar box on the coffee table; its contents would undoubtedly soothe this lingering unease, but he'd promised the store manager never to show up to work stoned. He sighed. "Also, I'm wrapped up like Imhotep. Do you have any antibiotic cream or anything? Maybe I'm fighting an infection." He regarded the toilet tissue he'd swaddled around his cut palms. The soft cotton shirt irritated the scrapes on his arms each time he shifted position a little. "Actually, bandages would be boss. Lots of them."

Kim laughed nervously. "What did you do?"

"Some Bruce Campbell-worthy self-inflicted stupidity," Morty said. "Tell you all about it when you get here." He heard Kim's uncertainty in the silence. He dodged the wildly swinging tail of the sand-centipede, grunting when he jerked the controller and his right forearm rubbed against the corduroy upholstery through his shirt. "Damn it!"

"What's going on, Morty?"

Disgusted, Morty paused the game and tossed aside the controller. "Nothing, man. Just bring a ton of first aid stuff, okay? I promise, I'm fine. It's just been a long, weird weekend." He managed a chuckle. "I'll almost be glad to see Cracker Joe tonight."

Kim snorted. "Yeah, nice to know in a world of uncertainties, we can always count on Cracker Joe to make more work for the cleaners."

"He's a secret agent for the ChemDry rep. His drooling ensures no one will object to them drenching all our furniture in psychotropic, experimental mind-control formulas."

Kim laughed. "Right. Sure you're all good?"

"Yeah, I'm fine. Just fighting off some bug, and wishing I was more Van Damme than Von Dumbass."

"Yeah, you're not quite short enough to be Van Damme. Or ripped enough. Or talented enough."

"Bite me," Morty replied cheerfully.

"You owe me for gas and a box of Band-Aids."

"Cool," Morty said, and hung up. He carefully pulled up his sleeve, wincing at the touch of the fabric. His cuts and scrapes had barely scabbed over. Blue blotches which would surely turn all sorts of wonderful shades of painful marked his elbows, and he'd seen worse ones on his knees. The tissues had unraveled from his left palm. He unwound them completely, intending to rewrap them. Seeing the cuts brought up a mental image of the bizarre corpse in the dig site. His momentary good mood evaporated. Life in winter along Lake Superior, far before electricity or thermal insulation, must have been harsher than a run-in with a Republican sheriff at an outdoor concert.

Speaking of Republicans... The cutting voice of a Faux News presenter boomed through the thin wall separating Morty's apartment from Olaf Sturgensen's next door. "Think the Democrats care about the troubles of ordinary small business owners? Of course not! They're still playing their silly game of tax-and-spend."

"Ugh, screw this," Morty growled. He considered banging on the wall, but knew nothing short of going to coupon night at Madge & Buster's All-You-Can-Eat Supper Club would persuade the old geezer to turn down his damned TV. Ever since the retiree's arrival at the house a few months ago, prejudice and misinformation had blared at top volume through the connecting wall from morning 'til evening. Morty had knocked politely on Olaf's door once to ask him to turn down his TV. He'd then endured a ten-minute lecture on personal liberties and the insufferable entitledness of the younger generation. Attempting to debate the old man had only engendered a string of curses in Norwegian. Morty flipped through the playlists on his iPod, selecting the one labeled *Faux News,* and cranked the speaker volume. Nine Inch Nails roared out, the bass thumping the bookshelf.

Morty picked the game controller back up and resumed his boss battle. The cuts and bruises didn't hurt any less; however, his mood was greatly improved.

8

Every winter for the last several years, Marie spoiled herself in a manner her family would find horribly offensive. This was, of course, part of its appeal. Even her closest brother, Wiisini Namegos, the smallest and most ridiculed of the *mishibizhu,* the water panthers, snarled in confusion when Marie confessed she enjoyed spending time at a pleasure-lodge of the *gitchi-mookomaanag,* the white man hunter knife-spirits, without eating any of its patrons or staff. Her family could never comprehend her; part of the nuisance of being a half-breed. She knew other bastard children existed; the world was crowded with humans now, white *waabishkiiwewaad* and brown *Anishinaabeg* with many more cultures and shades of skin. So many, they would never notice a few who weren't truly of their tribes.

As a half-Anishinaabe, half *mishibizhu,* Marie knew she was lucky. The horned, scaled, and furred bodies of the *mishibizhu* were beautiful to behold, but far too fearsome and unsafe to walk in the human world. Others born of claw and fang did not always have a human face to hide behind when they pleased. Or worse, they might only exist in human form, unable to change and forever cursed as abominations by the tribes who slithered or swam.

Marie spent summers among her family, who swam in every lake, river, and ocean of the continent. Regardless of her fetishes, they would always welcome her into the depths when the air turned warm and the sun too bright to bear. Marie was *mishibizhu,* and family was family.

That didn't mean she had to endure their prejudice every hour of every day. Not on a glorious, raging-blizzard day, when slippery back roads produced tasty morsels by the carload and, most especially, not when Marie had a longing to have her nails done at the salon in the Bad River Resort.

She paused inside the grand foyer to stamp the snow from her dainty boots. Honestly, they were very tiny, and her toes had begun to ache, but they had appeared so adorable on the feet of the stranded teenager. Marie had almost let that one go. She'd thought to offer to trade the girl's life for her boots, until the annoying little tramp had panicked and hit Marie with an ice-scraper.

The hotel had a few patrons relaxing in the lounge. A fire crackled in the enormous stone hearth. The mounted heads of moose and elk, along with the giant trophy sturgeon on the soaring log walls, welcomed her back. Marie fluffed lingering ice crystals from her fur coat as she walked to the front desk. The clerk who popped into view to aid her was one she didn't recognize, and he was clearly surprised to see her.

"Good afternoon. Welcome to the Bad River Resort. How may I..." He trailed off when Marie leaned over the desk, exposing a bit of cleavage in the low-cut dress. It was completely inappropriate for the weather but oh-so-useful for disorienting the weak. Marie smiled.

"Bon jour, mon doux apéritif. I am Marie Bois du Nord. You have a suite for me." She waited while the flushed young clerk tried to regain his professionalism and find her reservation in his computer at the same time. A glance at her fingernails dismayed her; a speck of blood remained on her left pinkie. She put her hand inside her coat, smile never faltering.

"I'm very sorry, Miss du Nord. We seem to have lost your reservation." The clerk looked up at her warily. He seemed to be expecting a tantrum in response, so Marie indulged him.

"Today? Today you cannot find my rooms? Did my assistant not speak to you two months ago, and confirm this very date? This very date when I have done so much to arrive? When I have nearly ruined my new boots walking in the snow because my chauffeur could not drive my Jaguar in this tremendous storm?" Her diatribe grew louder and louder, rolling right over the small protests of the clerk. "When I am forced to bump along from the airport in the most horrendous truck thing, and then it is stuck in the driveway because you cannot shovel the snow here fast enough and I must get out and walk to the hotel? Today you pick to tell me you have misplaced my reservation?" At last, Henri, the concierge, appeared.

"Miss Bois du Nord! How lovely to see you." Henri came swiftly to the desk, turning a glare so fierce upon the hapless clerk that Marie had to stifle a grin. He immediately patted the hand she proffered and slipped into flawless French. "I had wondered whether you were going to favor us this year; it is late in the season."

Marie responded in kind, enjoying the embarrassment of the clerk, who clearly didn't speak the language. "Henri. Thank heavens, for a moment I was worried you had moved on to some better establishment over the border. This idiot has lost my reservation."

"I am sure it is merely a technological mishap. Happily, we are able to give you the Witter Suite." In English, "Jeffrey, the keys to the Witter Suite." The desk clerk fumbled with them, and Henri snatched them from his hands. They were old-fashioned iron keys, as befit the most historic part of the hotel. That was one of the things Marie cherished most about this place, the Victorian pomposity of parts of it, where lumber barons and cattle kings up from Chicago would come to play at being "rustic." Cabins had been added later, usually claimed by families with children. Though these were a bit more private, the cabins did not interest Marie. Only the historic, lavish suites would do.

She walked with Henri up the main stairs toward the largest suites in the main building, sparing only a glance back to see the clerk hurriedly gesturing at a bellhop to take up her suitcases. Only one of her cases had anything much in it, just a snack for later; the others were weighed down with rocks to give the impression of the burden of wealth. She slipped her arm in Henri's and leaned in close; the dear man always knew the best gossip.

"So, has Madame Johnson been up yet this season?" she asked, keeping her tone silky and her language the precise Quebecois, the French-Canadian dialect fussier than French itself.

"Oh, no, regrettably."

"How very peculiar. I would have thought she would desire another spa treatment after the holiday parties. All those sweet treats are so devastating to one's figure." She gave Henri the tiniest, wickedest smile, and he stifled a chuckle.

"Well. Her most bosom friend, Mrs. Antwerp, did attend the New Year's party, and I may have overheard Madame Johnson possibly indulged a bit too much, and is instead spending the season in sunny Arizona." He paused for effect. "At a clinic. Let us hope the sun does wonders for her figure. And for her, ahem, tendency to celebrate the finer bottled spirits."

Marie giggled, and Henri allowed himself a small chuckle as well. She waited as he unlocked the suite. "Heavens, I believe the room is a bit stale. I can send the maids around with fresh linens." The bellhop set down her luggage just inside the door with relief. Marie handed him some money without glancing at it or him and ignored his departure.

"No bother," she said, smiling at the familiar antique loveseat and tasteful rugs in the sitting room. This was the most exquisite suite in the old hunting lodge, originally decorated for the first owner's mother. The furnishings were French, the walls papered in the Beaux Arts style popular in the late Victorian era. It was excessively ornate and eclectic; grand windows, rich pastel colors, soft lace everywhere. Marie adored every bit of it. "You know I enjoy the chill of a little fresh air. I will air it a bit while I'm relaxing."

"Oh, perhaps that's not such a fine idea," Henri said, frowning. "There was a—well, they say it was a bear attack."

"A bear?" She laughed. "Here?"

He appeared uncomfortable. "Not far from here. A bit north, by the reservation. Someone was rather, well. It was not pleasant, from what I heard. I would feel better, Miss Bois du Nord, if you would leave the windows locked."

Marie glanced out; snow fell gently past the lace curtains. The woods here gave the illusion all of the north country was pristine forest. From three hundred years of living on this land, Marie knew the forest instead gave way to marsh just a few miles north, where the Bad River snaked toward Lake Superior.

"An unlikely place for a bear to hunt, especially now," she said. "What did you hear, Henri?"

He shook his head. She came closer, purring. "Dear Henri. You must not withhold anything exciting from me. Tell me."

He met her eyes for only a second. "I heard this only third-hand, you know, not from anyone who witnessed the incident. Mrs. Farmingham overheard Mr. Farmingham and another gentleman discussing this. It seems Mr. Mueller's company has an interest near here, and things have been quite stirred up with the local natives."

"Tell me about the bear," she insisted, her voice low and musical. She did her best to sound merely curious about anything out of the ordinary; within her head alarms were ringing. Bears did not come to this part of the woods. Not to her woods. She made a point of marking the larger trees with her claws, rubbing her scent into them, to deter anything which might give her competition.

"It does seem rather surprising. I had thought bears no longer roamed this area, probably not since the grand hunting lodge days. But what else could it have been?" Henri asked. Marie stared at him. Henri swallowed hard. "Really, Miss Bois du Nord, the tale was gruesome."

"It attacked someone?"

"It nearly killed a man," Henri said, again casting an anxious glance toward the window. Marie felt a ripple of irritation; no bear would dare come within a mile of her. "I hear it almost ripped off his leg. Pardon me; really, the whole thing is simply too bizarre for any civilized company."

"How very strange. Bears do not usually attack men."

He shrugged. "All the same, they didn't catch it. A game warden was out hunting it yesterday, I heard. And yet, Mr. Mueller said work at the oil site would resume this week. Don't you think the bear may be out searching for prey still?"

"I am sure it is long gone. The ground will be frozen for months yet. Certainly, it will go back to its den."

Henri shuddered lightly. "I hope the authorities kill it."

And rob me of my entertainment? Marie smiled. "Let us hope so."

Henri shook his head and handed her the suite keys. "I think perhaps Mr. Mueller is moving a bit rashly. Uncovering that Indian mound has caused all sorts of hostilities, and you know whenever the tribes protest, there is sure to be backlash from the loggers and now, from the oil people."

"Oil people and an Indian mound?" She shook her head. "This is beginning to sound like one of those tedious films about sacred land and the clash of peoples which they pass off as art in the movie houses." She gestured disdainfully as she spoke. However, she was troubled she'd heard nothing of this. Loggers were bad enough on her river; now she might also have to be wary of imbeciles drilling for oil. Although it might present better hunting opportunities.

The concierge smiled. "Exactly so. Well. Is there anything else I may provide for you, Miss Bois du Nord?"

Marie considered it. She slowly removed her coat, turning so the afternoon light fell upon her bosom, casting a deep shadow between her firm breasts. "I am very weary from my traveling. Perhaps you would aid me in removing this dress and draw me a hot bath?"

He met her gaze then, and she held his eyes for several beats. She could smell his quickening interest, as always. Gently he shut the door to the sitting room and came forward to assist her with her dress. "Of course. Anything you require." She closed her eyes when he plunged his face into her cleavage. He unbuttoned the front of her dress slowly. Once her breasts were free, Henri took one nipple into his mouth. As he suckled, she began to purr. This was precisely why she enjoyed this place. They always offered such lavish personal service.

9

It wasn't the first time Quell had needed to present his scuffed, laminated "press pass" to be allowed entry to a hospital wing; he hoped it might be one of the last times. If he could only, finally track down a 'squatch and shoot the murderous critter, he might just retire from active hunting. Or go on another book tour. A better one this time, with actual bookstores and such. Quell knocked on the door of the hospital room, hoping the victim would be able to tell him something useful, especially so soon after the attack.

The AmShale worker, a manual laborer named Randy Lamer, eyed him warily as Quell pulled a stiff chair up to the bedside. "So, I hear from the nurses that you're getting fitted for a prosthetic foot today, yeah?"

Randy shrugged. "I guess."

Quell glanced at the man's legs, covered by a blanket. "Rough times, son. Very rough. I am very glad you're going to walk again after how badly you were mauled by that bear."

"Yeah." Randy frowned at him. "Who'd you say you're with? I already talked to the sheriff, and the game warden, and the TV stations."

"Well, a bear attack is pretty big news." Quell smiled, and noticed how the victim looked away, a sullen scowl darkening his face. Quell leaned in, and added in a lower, knowing voice, "Except it was no bear, was it?"

Randy jerked back, eyes searching Quell's. "Game warden said it was a bear," he mumbled. "I lost a lot of blood. Passed out. If there hadn't been some of those Indian grave robbers working on site so late, nobody woulda heard me mash the horn and I'd'a bled out."

Poor guy. They probably had him all twisted around, insisting he didn't see what he saw. Quell sighed and started pulling up his right jeans leg. "If you'll humor me just a minute, son, I got a little story I'd like you to hear. About sixteen years ago, I was a logger. A truck loader." Randy nodded, familiar with most forms of labor in the Northwoods. Quell continued as he took off his boot, "It was a cloudy fall day, still just about the most beautiful conditions you could hope for. We were working in a stand up near this old Boy Scout camp, in the Upper Peninsula. The property had been neglected

54

for a couple years, and the company I was with had bought rights to cut it. I'd just sent the last truck down the road there, and I was clearing up for the day." He met the other fellow's gaze for a second, satisfied he had his complete attention.

"Well, I stepped into the trees for a moment, you know, just for a call of nature, when all of a sudden everythin' went quiet. There were no birds, no squirrels chit-chatting at me, nothing."

Randy gave him a nod, listening. Quell rested a hand on his sock-covered foot. "It was eerie as all blazes. I'd worked the log trucks for over twenty-five years at that point and been out hunting turkey plenty of times as well, but I never heard such awesome silence before in the woods. It was like all a' nature was holding its breath. And just as I zipped up and turned around, *bam!*" He smacked his foot, and Randy started. "Outta nowhere came the most roaring, hairy, frightening thing I ever saw, and here's something you and I have in common; what attacked me was no bear." He peeled off his sock to reveal the hard, plastic shape of a foot. At Randy's wide-eyed expression, Quell nodded slowly. "That's right," he whispered, "It took my leg clean off. Luckily for me, I had my revolver on me, and I put a shot just past its ugly head and scared it off."

He blew out a breath and put his sock and boot back on. "Oh, you don't know how many nights I've laid awake wishing I'd been a better shot. At least, the noise carried down to the truck, and when the fellas couldn't reach me by radio to ask what I was shootin' at, they came back and found me. One guy put his belt on my leg as a tourniquet to keep me from dying right then and there, and they drove me to the nearest hospital. I imagine you understand this full well."

Randy swallowed, then cast a fearful look at the door. Quell had prudently shut it behind him, though there was no telling when a nurse might poke in to poke the patient still more. Dadburn doctors and nurses, always sticking needles in you, or making you pee in a cup for the sixty-fourth time. "So tell me," Quell asked, "what did this 'bear' look like?"

Randy glanced from Quell to the door and back and made up his mind with a firm scowl. "Wasn't a bear. I don't care what the warden says, I know what I saw, and it was no bear."

Quell nodded, taking out his notepad and clicking open a pen. "Can you describe it? How tall was it?"

"I don't know. Taller than me. Skinny, and it ran towards me like a big deer, on all fours; I thought for a second that's what it was, then it leaped up and—" Randy closed his eyes, shuddering. Quell waited, mind racing. He'd never heard of a Bigfoot running on all fours, but it made sense. Gorillas did that, and after all, the 'squatch was most closely related to the great apes. Randy wrestled his voice under control. "It clawed me across the chest." He moved his hand over his body to demonstrate.

"May I see?"

Randy hesitated, then tugged up his hospital gown and peeled the bandages back, wincing. The slashes across the well-muscled chest were widely spaced, much like the marks on the snowplow door. Quell brought out his camera phone with a questioning look, and Randy nodded. Quell snapped a couple of shots, then gestured for the victim to resettle himself. "Then what?"

"I fell back against the snowcat. Didn't have anything I could defend myself with. Couldn't even throw a punch at it, 'cause its horns were really sharp and I knew it would just gore me if—"

Quell held up a hand. "Horns? This thing had horns?"

Randy nodded. "I tried telling everyone that. The warden said only a bear would be big enough to do this to me." He tapped his chest gently and gazed in misery at his legs. "It reared up and screeched. And the smell hit me. God, what a smell. Like something dead three days in the bushes. I bent over, you know, about to throw up, just a sheer gut reaction, and it swung at me and hit the snowcat instead." He shook his head. "If I hadn't ducked right then..."

Quell frowned. Smelled like something dead? That wasn't right. The 'squatch that had attacked him had reeked of pine woods and fresh manure. Filthy animals, all that fur, they didn't even clean their own excrement out of it. Maybe this one had been eating carrion? "You sure it had horns?"

"Huge damned horns. Sharp as my wife's ma's tongue."

"Huh," Quell said. He made himself continue the interview instead of pausing overlong to mull over the details. The nurses wouldn't be happy with him when they found their patient all worked up. Best to press on as quickly as he could. "So then what?"

Randy shrugged, staring off into the distance. "I yanked open the door to the cab and jumped in; it ran at me again. I tried kicking it away, but it bit down on my foot and just pulled." His voice caught, terror coming back to him in a rush. Quell placed a steadying hand on his arm, and Randy turned his frightened eyes on the hunter. "I just yanked the door shut and leaned on the horn. Felt like my foot was on fire. Like," he paused, thinking. "You ever gotten frostbite?"

"Once, yeah," Quell said, nodding.

"Felt like that. So cold it burned. And I saw blood everywhere. And I don't really remember much afterwards. First time I woke up enough to talk to anybody, I was here. They told me the bear ripped off my foot. Bit it off. Bit right through the bone." He stared at the incomplete lump under the blanket where his left foot should be. "They said they haven't found it. Warden thinks the bear ate it."

Quell sat back, blinking. Randy fell silent. After a moment he looked at Quell with haunted eyes. "You believe me, don't you? It wasn't a bear. Nothing at all like a damned bear."

Quell nodded slowly. "I believe you, son."

Randy's expression shifted. "You aren't going to print this, are you? Don't use my name. Doc said in a year I might be able to go back to construction work, but word gets around I'm saying crazy stuff..."

Quell shook his head. "No, I won't use your name. You've been through enough horror without adding injury to it. Are you one hundred per cent sure about the horns? And the smell?"

"Yeah." Randy looked away, grimacing. "Not a smell I'll ever forget."

As if on cue, a nurse knocked on the door, and poked in her head with a smile. "Mr. Lamer? Time to change the dressings." She continued to smile at Quell as she entered. "Excuse us, Mr. Cronkite."

Quell gave her a thin smile in return, and patted Randy's shoulder as he rose to go. Randy grasped his arm. "What are you going to do?" he muttered. His eyes were at once pleading and worried. Quell's face hardened.

"I'm gonna kill the damned thing, son. You have my word."

10

Morty was happy when Kim arrived for their Tuesday game night at his apartment. Kim always brought him decent beer, although Kim's own tastes verged on the cheap and horrible, in Morty's opinion. Tonight, it was a couple of six-packs, a locally-brewed oatmeal stout for Morty and Leinenkugle for himself. He presented Morty with a belated birthday gift of the entire box set of *Ash vs Evil Dead,* which Morty was delighted to receive. He'd need to find time to watch the last season when Darcy wasn't around, as she couldn't stand gore, no matter how comical. The hot wings Morty had ordered showed up with perfect timing, just a minute after Kim's arrival.

Darcy had joined them for a few game nights, sometimes competing with them in MarioKart or yelling in excitement at an all-out Borderlands grudge fight. More often, she would sit behind him on the sofa while Morty parked his ass on the rug between her legs, and she would play with his hair. Kim had teased Darcy once when she was fondling Morty's sleek bangs, "Enjoy that while he's still got it. That comb-over is the hairstyle of a geezer. Wait, how old are you both again?"

"Blow me," Morty muttered, embarrassed. Darcy lifted his chin with a smile, leaned over and gave him a generous view down her blouse while she kissed him.

"He's not that much older than you," she scolded Kim, who was grinning like an idiot, "and I'm smart enough to find his brain very sexy."

"Yeah, Kim," Morty said, "Co-eds dig high foreheads. It's a sure sign of a very sexy brain."

"You're both deeply disturbed people, and clearly made for each other," Kim laughed. He hurled a throw pillow at them. "Either play the game or get a room."

Morty had seen the genuine smile on his best friend's face, and the next slow afternoon, when they'd been talking quietly at the bookstore's trade counter, Morty asked, "Seriously though, you think my hair makes me look old?"

"Stop worrying about it. You do you. Besides, your girl thinks you're cute."

Morty frowned, doing his best to appear deeply wounded. "What, you don't?"

"You are such a narcissist."

"No, the current reality-TV failure in the White House is a narcissist. I'm just persuaded of my own desirability."

Kim smiled. "I'm happy for you, man. Seriously. It's good to see you enjoying company of the female persuasion. Nice to see a nerd finally coming into his own. I put it down to all the great tips I've given you through the years."

"Oh, yeah, right. Just because I don't whore around like you doesn't mean I'm not attractive."

Kim crossed his arms, scowling. "Are you calling me a slut?"

Morty put his hands out, placating. "Of course not. I'm only saying, hiding under the glow of your effervescent promiscuity all these years has indeed taught me how not to display my manly assets."

Kim laughed. "Dude. What the hell did you even just say." He jostled Morty, who shoved him back, grinning. "The glow of my effervescent promiscuity!"

"A beacon of moral decrepitude, guiding me toward salvation," Morty agreed. Kim grabbed a Nerf sword and beat Morty over the head with it, both laughing, until a customer interrupted them.

Tonight, though, Darcy wasn't able to join them. She had concert practice late into the evening and an eight a.m. calculus class in the morning. She was practicing more than usual; she was going to Chicago the coming weekend with some of her strings classmates to participate in a concert hosted by the Chicago Symphony Orchestra. That by itself was amazing, really.

The amount of class hours she was taking this semester concerned Morty a little. So far Darce seemed to be able to handle the workload and she kept saying, "The faster I can graduate, the faster I can move out of my parents' house." She would look at him when she said it, but Morty had no idea what the correct response should be. "High time you were set free from that hive of corporate villainy," he told her, and she'd smiled, but he had the impression that hadn't been quite what she wanted to hear.

He knew her agreement with her parents was that they'd foot the bill for university, as long as she took business classes in addition to her music courses. The double major had added a year to her schooling. Their agreement included remaining under their pretentiously expensive roof in one of the old mansions along the Fox River. Had his own folks offered such a deal, Morty would probably never have graduated, switching majors every year. He didn't voice this thought to Darcy.

He was, truth be told, relieved she wasn't joining them tonight. Although the chills had passed, he wasn't feeling one hundred percent himself. After tipping the delivery driver for the wings, he slumped on the couch, watching Kim unpack the steaming containers. His friend looked askance at him. "You're not hungry?"

Morty shrugged. "I don't know. Stomach's not awesome."

"Good thing you ordered food with absolutely no potential to wreck your intestines, then," Kim said, gesturing at the box of Extra Spicy wings.

The smell of them hit Morty's nose then, and he reached for them. "Now I'm starving." He yanked the box away from Kim when he tried to take one. "Get your own."

"Damn, starve a cold, feed a fever?"

"Definitely," Morty grunted, tossing aside the bones of the first sample and ripping the skin off another. He chewed, frowning, while Kim cued up a team mission for tonight's co-op game in Borderlands 3. "Did they get the order wrong?"

Kim took one and sucked the wingtip. "Hoooo boy, hot hot." He fanned his mouth with his hand. "Nope."

Morty set down the Extra Spicy and tried one of the garlic parmesan wings. "Man, they really overcooked these."

Kim shook his head. "They taste fine to me. I think your taste buds are messed up from the flu."

"I guess." Despite the wings tasting burnt to him, Morty was suddenly ravenous, eating piece after piece as they settled into the game.

Kim stood up some time later to take a piss. Morty finished off his own third beer and reached for the box of Hot BBQ wings, surprised to find it empty. He checked the next nearest container, chewing on the last Buffalo-style wing when Kim returned to the room. "Holy gluttons, Batman! Did you leave any for me?" Kim exclaimed.

Morty paused. "You had half."

Kim turned another container upside-down to demonstrate its emptiness. "Dude. You've eaten like two-thirds of these. Your guts are so going to kill you tonight."

"Sorry," Morty muttered, baffled. "Guess I wasn't really paying attention. Hey, there's pizza rolls in the freezer, if you're still hungry."

Kim waved him off, settling back into his chair. "Nah, I'm good. I worry about you, though. You see Darcy tomorrow?"

"Maybe. We talked about meeting up in the afternoon after her classes."

"Good. You might be recovered by then. Hope she doesn't like playing with your ass because you won't have one left after all those hot wings come out your other end."

"You're so crude," Morty retorted. "You're just jealous because you can't even find your skinny ass."

Kim chortled. "Good thing you have extra you can loan me."

"As if! You wouldn't know how to wear this magnificent flesh." Morty felt his stomach growl. "I think I'll make those pizza rolls."

"Dieting for your figure; good call," Kim taunted as Morty rose from the sofa. He took two steps toward the kitchen and grabbed the nearest chair for support, suddenly dizzy and hot. "You okay?"

Morty nodded, waiting until the wooziness subsided. "Yeah. Guess whatever bug nailed me doesn't like good beer." He forced his feet into motion. "One more run at the tower when I come back. And don't wuss out and hide behind the barricade this time."

"That was you, chickenshit, but whatever." Kim watched him slowly walk toward the bedroom, heading for the attached bathroom. "Hey, maybe you should call it a night."

"Are you calling me old again? I'm only four years older than you. How quickly the vapid youth forget to respect their elders."

"Fine. Get back in here and I'll show you who should be respecting who." When Morty stopped, turning with one forefinger raised, Kim groaned. "Whom. Jesus, I hate hanging out with English majors."

"You gain wisdom, grasshoppah."

Morty's energy dropped quickly afterward, however, and after another half-hour of game time, he set down his controller and rubbed his eyes. "Yeah. I admit I'm not feeling too awesome, no matter how magnificent my shooting skills are."

Kim nodded, and turned off the console and TV. "You do kinda seem beat down. Of course, that's usually how you look when you try to keep up with me."

"Come over here and say that again, you coward." Morty stretched, a deep weariness sinking into his brain and bones. From the adjoining wall, they heard a muffled commercial for gold. Or possibly adult diapers. Hard to tell; Morty knew the ad choices on that network were limited and targeted to the elderly and paranoid. "It just never stops."

Kim rolled his eyes. "Your neighbor needs a hearing aid. And some sanity."

Morty nodded in agreement. "I think I'm going to crawl into bed. When do I work?"

"I think you open tomorrow. I have mid-shift."

"Fuck me," Morty grumbled. Kim shook his head, heading for the apartment door.

"Only if you ask nicely and wear the gimp suit."

Morty threw an empty hot wing box at the closing door. He stood slowly, wavering a bit, viewing the containers and bottles strewn over his coffee table. Screw it. He just wanted sleep. He staggered into the bathroom and spent the bare minimum of time to take care of his bladder and half-heartedly brush his teeth. He turned off the bathroom light and shuffled toward his bed. He nearly tripped over the duffel bag he'd dropped on the floor.

Remembering his favorite tee shirt was probably still in the duffel, he rummaged through it. He pulled a pair of Darcy's lace-edged panties out of a tangle of his jeans, and grinned. However, hunting through and then dumping out the entire bag proved his "Bill the Vampire" shirt wasn't in it. Damn, it probably went home in Darcy's suitcase. He knew he'd had it on under the flannel shirt which had been ripped in his fall at the dig site. He wanted to wear it to work tomorrow but he'd been too hungover Sunday morning to notice what had been packed where. Nothing like a lost weekend with one's best corporate buddies. No more hard booze for a while. It had tasted hideous coming up. Granted, that could have been the Proletariat Tartare or whatever Mueller had ordered for him to go with all those drinks.

He sighed, giving up, and pulled an old T-Rats baseball jersey from the cramped closet, piling it atop his jeans at the foot of the bed to wear tomorrow. He should remember to ask Darcy to search for the shirt. Damn thing cost twenty bucks on sale. Plus, he'd scored the horror author's autograph across the back in Sharpie. He really should frame the shirt. He liked wearing it, though, especially on stressful days; he felt it gave him an extra degree of wiseassery.

He peeled off the bandages on his left hand, wincing at the tug on sensitive flesh, and examined the cuts. The nurse at the resort had decided they didn't need stitches. Morty thought now maybe he should've asked for some anyway. His fingertips still bore dark slices. Fingers bled more anyway. All those capillaries. He flexed his hand and was sure he could feel every single blood vessel. He thought of the possessed demon hand sequence from *Evil Dead II*. He shivered, then frowned. *Right. Soon as it starts squeaking and smashing plates over my head, I'll call the exorcist.*

Trudging back to the bathroom, he cleaned and rebandaged the cuts with a minimum of silent cursing. The skinned meat of his forearms was healing fairly well, and although the bruises were now a lovely shade of purple over his knees and shins, they felt less tender than they had a day ago. Morty stared morosely at his exhausted reflection over the sink. Too bad the zombie run wasn't for another four months. He could win best makeup. Unfortunately, this line of thought led back to the bizarre burial in the ancient mound.

The images of the elk skull atop meatless ribs, and the disturbingly long limbs of the deer-like skeleton, stayed with him as he turned out the lights and slid beneath the blankets. The bedroom felt a lot colder after he'd stripped down; the wind outside was evilly finding every chink in the walls tonight. He shivered for a minute, wishing his body heat would warm the bed more quickly. A sudden stabbing fire in his temples eclipsed his concern about the cold, making him gasp out a curse. He curled up, cradling his head in his hands for several minutes, barely able to think, until the sensation faded. If this was an infection, he'd sue the shit out of AmShale. He drew a shuddering breath. *Sleep. I need sleep.*

His sheets were moderately clean, the comforter atop them warm, and the foam mattress familiar with the shape of his body. He settled himself more snugly in bed, its frame tucked under an eave of the roofline. Cold air whistled in from the dormer window to his left. Morty buried his face in his pillow, glad his workday tomorrow would be spent in the stockroom processing books, though it meant rising before the butt-crack of dawn and walking through six blocks of snow. His head ached. He needed a real vacation. One not involving rich people, oil companies, or snow. The noise from Old Man Sturgensen's TV continued next door. Annoyed, Morty turned on a small space-heater. Its steady, rattling fan lulled him to sleep.

He was used to having odd dreams, especially while under the influence, but rarely were they nightmares. Tonight, though, he found himself in a city buried in snow, but nothing was white or clean. Endless, dirty drifts of frozen, crusty sludgebanks were piled along street curbs, filling vacant lots, covering parked cars. A growing feeling of rage drove his feet through the city. No matter how far he ran, which direction he turned, he found no clean expanse of whiteness nor silent grove of fir branches. The soullessness of the streets, the grey buildings and skies where no star could penetrate the haze of amber lights from below, all filled him with anger.

He ran, and ran, hearing only the muffled crunch of his feet in the snow, hungry, repulsed by the dirt which crowded him on all sides. He could hear something behind him, in front of him, pounding footsteps echoing from the buildings so no matter which way he turned, he felt threatened. He screamed into the frozen street, challenging the unseen monster. The pounding sounded right behind him, and something wrapped around him, smothering his cries.

Morty woke with a start, his comforter enveloping him so tightly he felt strangled. He sluggishly untangled himself. Cool air washed over his bare skin, bringing him close enough to consciousness to perceive the knocking sound wasn't an eldritch, awful thing pounding closer and closer to him.

Dragging himself off the bed and out of the nightmare, he rubbed his face out of habit. The jolt shooting through his wounded hand evoked a heartfelt full ten seconds of cursing.

More knocking. It couldn't possibly be time to get up yet. He fumbled for his phone, managing only to knock it off the nightstand. "Goddammit, fine, hold on!" he yelled. His throat felt scraped raw. When he stood, his gut surged, and he clutched the edge of the bed. The nausea passed swiftly. While his head was down, Morty noticed he was naked. Must've kicked the shorts off. The space heater had warmed the room overmuch, adding to the swimming sensation in his skull when he carefully straightened again. He grabbed his robe, shrugging into it as he staggered into the living room. His legs trembled. He felt sick and weak. Had to be the flu. Just great. He swung his front door wide, ready to chew out whatever asshole had decided to wake him up before his alarm went off at just after dawn.

The gray light bleeding through the leaded window in the hallway was still bright enough to make him waver, blinking, unable to see anything for a moment. Then he heard Darcy's shocked voice: "Oh my God, Morty, what happened?"

"Huh?" Dizzy, he clung to the doorframe with one hand, holding his robe closed with the other. He tried to focus on her face.

Fear filled her eyes. "Did you hurt yourself? Should I call an ambulance?"

"What are you—" Morty noticed his hand was bleeding again. Quite a lot. His fingers left a dark impression on the white paint of the doorframe when he pulled them away, confused. More blood seeped into his robe where he clutched the lapels. Something was dribbling down his neck, and his belly itched.

"Morty, babe," Darcy whispered, "You're bloody all over."

His stomach rumbled. Bile surged. Morty managed to turn just in time not to spew red, pulpy glops all over his girlfriend. He heard her choked cry of fear and disgust. Morty fell on his knees, staring at his bloody palms. "I think I need a Band-aid," he mumbled. The doormat rushed up at him; he had a split second to feel dismay that he was about to faceplant into his own vomit.

The floor cold-cocked him.

11

An hour after being needle-poked, disinfectant-wiped, forced to endure the indignity of a bedpan, and asked more questions than he would've tolerated on a more cheerful day, Morty lay between crisp white hospital sheets. The beeps of the pulse monitor kept him from drifting off to blissful sleep. He vaguely remembered Darcy driving him here. He'd muttered weak protests, but she was clearly worried, so he'd crawled into her car and done his best not to puke on the seat on the way over to St. Elizabeth's. Even with his eyes shut and the incessant beeping, he could hear Darcy pacing from side to side around his bed. "Darce, please, chill out. I'm fine," he whispered, looking up and trying to smile at her.

She paused, eying him worriedly. "Let's just wait and see what the tests say, okay?"

Morty sighed. "If it's not an infection from the dig site, it's probably whatever flu bug has been going around. Mike was out sick all last week. I probably caught it."

"I know. I'm sure that's all it is." Morty peered at her, not wanting to fully open his eyes; the room was ugly-bright. Darcy shot him a smile and resumed her pacing.

In the hall, quick footsteps approached and faded; voices murmured. He wondered which ones were speaking of him. He hated hospitals. This is where people went to die, separated neatly from society so they wouldn't have to be seen by anyone else. Sterile, proper, but always suffused faintly with the smell of death. Unwelcome memories surfaced of the last time he was in such a place, sitting on a hard plastic chair by his mother's bedside. Listening for hours to her ragged breaths and the beeping of monitors, until her lungs had given out. Ironically, it made him want a cigarette. He hadn't touched one since then. His brother still smoked cigars. Jed hadn't seen Mom at the very end. Hadn't sat there and listened to her struggling for every wisp of air. Shoving the memories away, he tried for levity.

"Fair warning," he mumbled, "if that prehistoric creepy deer god gave me some infection no one's seen for three thousand years, I'm totally suing

AmShale for failing to inoculate everyone against Pleistocene Winter Elk Syndrome."

Darcy stopped pacing and reached for his hand, the one not tagged by an I.V. Bandages encased both palms. She caressed the back of his hand, pretty much the only part of him not scarred. He'd been vaguely aware of new scratches on his arms, and small wounds on his collarbone and his belly when the nurses' aides had cleaned him off. Hopefully those were from falling onto his less than pristine welcome mat, where certainly all sorts of gravel bits or sharp twigs might have hitched a ride in on anyone's shoes. "Let's see what the tests say. I'm sure they'll be back with the results soon. It's probably just the flu. Just in case it's not, I'm glad we're here." She frowned, though she didn't stop stroking his hand. "You know you shouldn't have been drinking, if you were already feeling sick."

Morty felt a soft rush of tenderness for her. "Yeah. I know. It's totally Kim's fault. He brought the beer, and who am I to—"

She gave his hand a squeeze. "Nope. You're not pinning this on Kim."

He gave her a pout. "Not even a little?"

"No." She smiled, though, and Morty managed a smile back at her.

A knock at the door announced a doctor bearing a clipboard. Morty noticed his Avengers tie and immediately felt reassured. "How we feeling?" the doctor asked.

Morty shrugged. "When do I get mutant superpowers?"

The doctor chuckled. "A cortisone shot might promote super-healing, but that's all I've got."

"Bummer."

"Do you have the test results?" Darcy asked.

The doctor paged through the papers on the clipboard some more. Morty glanced at his nametag and at first thought it said *Dr. Ock,* then realized it was *Dr. Ost* and was disappointed."Yes, and the good news is you don't have TB, HIV, syphilis, or any indication of kidney stones."

Darcy was far from reassured. "What's wrong with him?"

Dr. Ost lowered the clipboard, shaking his head. "Garden-variety stomach flu, looks like. Though since you don't know what caused those new wounds, I'm glad you're already on antibiotics. We did run a panel for bac-

teria and didn't see anything worrisome. You said this happened at an archaeological dig?" He indicated Morty's bandaged fingers.

"Yes," Darcy said. "The nurse at the resort checked him out and gave
him a tetanus booster."

The doctor nodded. "Your white count is elevated, but nothing particularly nasty came up in any of the blood or urine tests. Though you could
easily dehydrate in this condition, so stick to water for a few days. No caf-
feine or alcohol. We're releasing you. I'll write you a prescription for the
nausea. Go home, bed rest for at least three days, flush out your system."

"Can I get an excuse for work?" Morty asked. He tried to shift himself
upward in bed. Everything hurt and he felt dismayingly weak.

Darcy bit her lip. "It's just a virus?"

Morty squeezed her hand gently. "Sorry, babe. No paranormal sexy
times if I'm not gonna grow fangs." He grinned at her blush; he liked teasing her about the werewolf-and-vampire romances she enjoyed reading.

Dr. Ost flashed a smile. "I'll sign the FMLA paperwork for you and
have it sent wherever you need it. However, what I need from you is for you
to not mix anything with these anti-nausea drugs. Clear?" He gave Morty a
very plain stare, and Morty knew the weed had popped on a test or two. He
nodded, glad the doc wasn't hassling him about his recreational activities.
"All right. In a minute the nurse will be by with your release papers. Do you
want us to go ahead and fill the prescription here?"

"How long will that take?" He just wanted to go home. He didn't think
he could stand being here any longer than necessary.

"I can pick it up for you," Darcy offered. The smile she gave Morty was
full of nurture and warmth. He melted into the pillows. He should stop
worrying about why she cared about him and simply count himself one
lucky son of a bitch. "Is your prescription card in your wallet?"

"I have a card for that?"

Darcy sighed.

She drove him home. He clung to the passenger bar the whole way,
dizzy but at least not feeling on the verge of hurling up his guts again. He
managed to climb the stairs to his apartment mostly by himself, clutching
the sturdy, polished wooden banister.

Darcy insisted on wrapping a couple of throw blankets around him on the sofa before running to the drugstore to get his prescription filled. He was content to drowse there, relieved to be home, listening to the wind building outside. Snow was coming tonight. The wind roared, an angry animal wanting to get inside more than the wall cracks already allowed. Almost soothed by the familiar sounds of his home, he felt something was missing. After a moment of intense focus, he placed it: no obnoxious blare of hateful talking news heads from next door.

A sharp knock on the door startled him. Heaving himself up, Morty opened the door to find a cop standing outside his doormat. Crap. If the old geezer called the cops on a noise complaint, Morty would register one of his own, damn it. The officer gave him a polite nod, a pen hovering over a small notepad. "Your landlord said you went to the hospital there. Everything all right?"

"Yeah. Just a nasty case of stomach flu." They both noticed the glistening vomit just inside the door. "Just got back. I'll get it cleaned up."

The cop looked away quickly, nose wrinkling, his face turning pale. Morty shuffled out into the second-floor hallway of the old house, pulling his door shut to block the smell. "Sorry. What's this about?" He kept a blanket wrapped around himself, leaning against the doorframe.

"Were ya here last night?"

"Yeah."

"All night?"

"Yes," Morty said, and then noticed the door to Sturgensen's apartment was open and people dressed in protective crime-scene gear were going inside. "What happened?"

The cop shook his head. "Ya hear anything from next door?"

"What, last night? Just the old man's TV blaring too loud, again. He leaves it on just about twenty-four-seven." Morty tried to peer into the neighboring apartment. He couldn't see much beyond the crowded bookcases just inside Sturgensen's doorway.

"So you didn't hear or see anything out of the ordinary? What were ya up to, then?"

"I was playing videogames with a buddy until about eleven-thirty. Then he went home and I went to bed." Morty peered at the cop. The younger officer was clearly determined to be professional, though he kept flicking his eyes between the CSI techs and his notepad. Had the old fart yelled for help while having a heart attack, and Morty never heard it? CSI wouldn't be here for death by natural causes. "What happened?"

The officer didn't answer Morty's question and continued with his own. "So yeah, that buddy of yours that was over, what's his name then?"

"Kim. Kim Xiong. We work together at BookStop."

"BookStop. I knew I knew your face from somewheres. Been in there a few times. You folks got a nice kids' books section. I have a three-year-old son." Morty nodded, feeling woozy, clinging to the doorframe. "Say, you need to sit down, there? You don't look so good."

"I'm fine," Morty muttered.

"Kim S-H-O-N-G?"

Morty spelled Kim's surname correctly, and the cop wrote it down. "Was there a robbery or something? What's with all the crime scene stuff?"

The officer paused, as if deciding what he could say, then sighed. "Well, ah, your neighbor Mr. Sturgensen was killed last ni—I mean, he died last night."

"Killed?"

"I really shouldn't say. I mean, it's an ongoing investigation type of thing." The officer appraised Morty more carefully. "You're absolutely sure ya didn't see or hear anything? No gunshots or nothing?"

"Gunshots? No." *How could I have slept through that?*

The officer peered at him. "What happened to your hands?"

"Last weekend I was up at Bad River. With my girlfriend. We went to an archaeological dig up there, and I tripped and fell onto an elk skull with sharpened antlers." He held up his bandaged hand. "Swear to god. Right in front of her dad, too. Not one of my finer moments. Got cut all over."

"Cripes, that sounds terrible. And, uh, your girlfriend? She can verify this?"

"Yes. She's coming back in a few minutes. She just went to get me my prescription. My stomach hasn't been too happy." The officer nodded, glancing at the spatters of upchuck at the bottom of the door and quickly looking away again. His green reaction would have been amusing if Morty wasn't still trying to process all this. "Seriously? Sturgensen's dead? Killed? Not just dropped dead from all the fatty foods he ate?"

"Can ya think of anyone who would've wanted to hurt him? Have ya seen anyone hanging around who wasn't supposed to be here?"

Morty shook his head. "He didn't have any friends or family I knew of, no enemies either that I could tell. Nobody ever visited him."

"What kind of neighbor was he? Ya mentioned his TV was loud. Ever go ask him to turn it down?"

"Once, yeah. Received a lecture on the general irresponsibility of the younger generation for my trouble." Morty shrugged. "Most of the time, if it annoyed me, I'd just turn up my music. I just assumed he was hard of hearing." Jesus. Someone had murdered the old man. Sturgensen didn't dress like he had a lot of money, though. And this wasn't a bad neighborhood. Morty looked at Sturgensen's door. The jamb wasn't splintered; he had no idea how to tell if a lock had been jimmied. Or if the downstairs door had been broken open.

"He was a crotchety old guy. I really didn't know anything about him."

The cop nodded. "Okay. I'm thinking maybe you should go lie down. Mordecai, right?" He checked the notepad. Morty was sure his landlord had provided more information than was necessary.

"Yeah. How do you know he was murdered? Was his place torn up like someone robbed it? And you said gunshots. Was he shot?" Though exhausted, Morty clung to his doorway. "Any idea why? I mean, the old man was your garden-variety elderly asshole, but who would kill him?"

The cop frowned, scribbling on his pad. "Really can't say much. It's an ongoing investigation. Oh, your landlord doesn't allow dogs. Ever see a dog in Mr. Sturgensen's apartment? Anyone here ever sneak in a dog?"

"A dog? No." Confused, Morty watched as one of the crime techs emerged from the next door apartment, carrying a sealed, clear plastic bag. It contained plaid fabric, possibly part of a shirt, completely caked in something rust-colored and crusty.

"You should probably just get back to bed there," the cop said, offering a sympathetic smile. "If ya think of anything else, you call us, okay? We'll talk to your girlfriend when she gets back."

Morty nodded dumbly and watched the officer glance once more inside the old man's apartment, then turn and clomp down the stairs. Morty remained a moment longer at his door, replaying last night in his mind. This made no sense. Morty edged closer to the neighboring door, peering inside.

Sturgensen's living room had the same angled ceiling as in Morty's apartment. The layout mirrored his on the opposite side of the house. Same dormer windows, and a similar kitchenette area off to one side. The main difference was the blood. Dull red spattered the kitchen linoleum. A huge dark area resembling a map of Lake Superior stained the old shag carpeting. The recliner had been slashed open, and its foam stuffing was also streaked with dark crimson.

Another cop, an older man standing just inside the door observing the crime scene techs, noticed Morty. "Sir, you can't come in here."

"What happened?"

The cop advanced on him, and Morty shuffled back. "Sir, I can't let anyone in here. Officer Thiel spoke to you already?"

"Thiel. The young guy. Yeah. I guess." The cop nodded and grabbed the doorknob to pull the door shut. Morty took a step forward, clutching the blanket tighter around himself. "What the hell did this? It looks like *The Cabin in the Woods* in there."

"We're thinking some kinda vicious dog." The officer squinted at him. "What happened to you, there, buddy? You seem pretty torn up yourself. You live next door?"

Morty repeated all the answers he'd already given. The cop relented when Morty felt dizzy and guided him back to his own door.

Once inside, he dropped to the sofa, weakness washing over him. The only way Sturgensen's death made any sense was if he was Appleton's version of Walter White. Doubtful. Morty's head hurt. His throat felt rough. Water, he should get some water. He stared plaintively at his kitchen sink, then at the front door. Darcy didn't miraculously pop in. With a groan, he hauled himself up again and shuffled to the kitchen.

As he drank from a glass of cold tap water, the smell from his entryway filtered through his grogginess. He remembered throwing up at the door. *Great. You know, a good boyfriend would clean that up before she comes back.*

The idea held zero appeal. However, Darcy was supremely caring to him, better than he deserved. She'd held back any comments about his general lack of organization and had gone off to the pharmacy without his lost insurance card, intent on paying for the prescription herself.

Determined to at least clean up the mess he'd made, he plucked a dishrag from the sink. Shitgoblins, he must've been completely out of it. Never heard the alarm, or his phone. Darcy had told him she'd called the store this morning to see if Morty wanted to have lunch with her, and when told he hadn't shown up for work and wasn't answering his phone, she'd come over to check on him. Morty winced at the crud on the ugly brown carpet. She'd gone out of her way today. The least he could do was scrub up the icky stuff so she didn't have to deal with it. Or smell it. Reluctantly, he set aside the comforting blanket.

He moved slowly, with purpose, fetching a bucket and a bottle of carpet cleaning fluid from under the kitchen sink. He lowered himself to sore knees and used the rag to gather up handfuls of upchucked meat. It looked as though he hadn't even half-digested it. Feeling dizzy, he plucked a thick bone from the rug; it hit the bottom of the bucket with a solid thunk. Gristle stuck to the rug fibers, and he wrinkled his nose in disgust, glad he'd been given a dose of anti-nausea drugs at the hospital. If they hadn't, he'd be throwing up again just smelling this. Instinctively he breathed through his mouth; the driblets of skin smelled especially horrible mixed with the bile from his stomach. He kept picking and plunking, dabbing the rug, until all that remained was a spatter of dark spots. Hopefully, the stain would fade when it dried. If not, oh well. Not as if the landlord had replaced the carpets in forever. He'd have to next door.

Morty emptied the bucket into the kitchen trash, then paused, exhausted, dizzy again. He carefully bent over to knot up the trash bag, doubting he could carry it out to the dumpster without collapsing. *Good enough if I can just toss it outside the door; screw the rules, I feel like sh*—He paused, staring at the shards of white mixed in with the gunk. *Did I eat that many wings? Wait. Bones? How would I have eaten the bones too?*

He doubted the paramedics had noticed, intent on navigating him through the cramped upstairs hallway, and they'd doped him with something to counteract the nausea so he wouldn't throw up more at the hospital. He peered more closely at the mess. At least one of the white chunks seemed too big. *That's not a chicken bone. What the fuck.*

The bone glistened. A tendon clung partly to it. It was round, smooth, and large. Morty touched his throat. It felt as though he'd purged a softball. What was that? A thigh? Couldn't be, chicken thighbones weren't that big.

He stared at it, taking in the other bones and bits of things heaped in the trash. Things he'd thrown up. Things he couldn't possibly have eaten. Something dark and wetly matted showed under a tangle of meat and bone shards. It resembled nothing so much as a drowned rat, except it had a pattern on it. Plaid, maybe. Plaid flannel. Like an old man's shirt.

Darcy burst through the front door, swirling dust and anxious chatter. "I'm back. I hope generics are all right for the suppositories, they were out of the—Sweetie! You shouldn't be up."

Hurriedly he yanked the trash bag closed and tied it off. "Just trying to clean up."

"Want me to take that out for you?"

He knew it was a chore she wouldn't normally do. The Muellers had people for that. Morty found his voice finally. "No. You know what, screw it. I'll just leave it in the hall. Tell Mr. Malnar I'm sick; he'll drag it out." He lifted the bag. The wet, slithery sounds the shifting contents made turned his stomach. He swallowed hard. "I got this. I'm good."

Darcy murmured token protests, stepping out of his way as he swayed toward the door. He clutched the neck of the bag so hard his wounded fingers hurt. He willed his legs to keep moving. He tried to ignore the sound the trash bag made hitting the hallway floor, lurched back inside, and made straight for the bathroom. Darcy followed him as far as the door, turning away when he fell to his knees and heaved into the bowl. "Oh, Morty, I told you, just rest! Why do you have to be so stubborn."

Morty hugged the cool porcelain, unable to produce anything but sour bile and then dry, choking gasps. His whole body trembled uncontrollably. Darcy touched his shoulder and he startled. "Baby, here, come lie down. I'll bring you some ginger ale."

He nodded, unable to speak. He waved her out, shut the door, and pulled himself to a sitting position atop the toilet. He ran cool water in the sink, rinsed his mouth with sloppy handfuls of it, and sat there shivering.

He felt feverish. Dizzy. Drugged. Everything was slightly out of focus. The gunk in the trash can had probably been just a chunk of meat. And carpet fibers. The rug was old. That was just a piece of the rug.

Darcy knocked softly on the door. "You okay? There's an officer downstairs who says he needs to talk to me about your neighbor being robbed. I told him I'd come down as soon as I had you settled."

"Yeah," he choked out. His voice sounded terrible, rougher and higher edged than usual. "Give me a sec."

After a few seconds, he heard her footsteps walking back toward the kitchen. The water gurgled in the sink next to him until he shut it off, hating the sound. Morty stood, staring at his reflection in the mirror. Shadows ringed his frightened eyes, and his face seemed longer and more drawn than usual, his hair mussed and matted with sweat. He lifted his shirt and then pulled up the bandage they'd put on his stomach in the hospital. The new wound on his rounded belly appeared very like a small hole. And he hadn't seen any gravel near his door, or loose tacks. As he looked at it, his stomach growled. As if it wasn't at all deterred by the moist, glistening shards of bone that had come out of it earlier.

He gagged, gripping the sink tightly. Darcy called, "I picked up some finger Jell-o for you. Do you want lime or strawberry?"

Morty sounded hoarse and strained to himself. He forced his words so they'd carry. "Strawberry sounds great. Thank you." He hoped she'd attribute his voice breaking to his illness. He stared into the mirror at the dark red spot below his ribs and the bandages on his fingers, until Darcy timidly opened the door and coaxed him back to bed.

12

Wind whistled in the swaying treetops as Marie padded through the wintry forest, heading for the area where Henri said the bear attack had occurred. She kept low, avoiding bare branches which might snag the sleek fur over her shoulders or scrape the scales along her flanks, pausing every so often to sniff the air.

The scent of motor oil was easy enough to follow. As she came to a wide clearing, odors of *gitchi-mookomaanag* and the grumble of a generator confirmed she was in the right place. She remained at the edge of the trees a long while, studying the corrugated-metal shack and the thick cables running under the door, the smells of several humans strong even under the oil and gas. She growled quietly. They were always so dirty when they invaded the wild places. They should all keep to their cities. Then again, if no hikers or campers ever ventured alone into the Northwoods, she'd be hungry all the time.

Cautiously, keeping a close eye on the shack, she crept over to the large yellow plow which sat on wheels as big as boulders. As she neared it, her whiskers twitched at the metallic scent of blood. She looked at the splash of crimson-brown on the side of the machine, and peered at the ground beneath it, sheltered from the snowfall, where pink spots remained. The claw marks gashing the side of the machine worried her. She stood on hind paws, placing one massive front paw alongside the gouges for comparison. It was tall, whatever it was. Leaning in, she inhaled the scent left by the claws, and jerked back in disgust at the distinct odor of carrion.

She retreated to the clearing's edge again, glowering at the claw marks. Clearly, whatever beast had invaded her territory had no qualms about making its presence known, despite the markings she left on trees all around. She had its scent now. She quailed at the very idea of tracking it, so rank was that odor of decay, burnt ash, and blood. Since a few days had already passed, and the air smelled like new snow approaching, her best chance of locating the interloper was to follow the trail. Bracing herself inwardly, she took a strong whiff, and climbed away from the ugly *waabishki-iwed* things, up a small bluff among the pines and firs. A flutter in the dead brambles caught her eye. Approaching it slowly, checking around her for any sign of life, she noticed the scent of a white man, and saw boot prints half-obscured by the wind sweeping the snow around. Those were fresher than the intruder's scent. Henri did say the game warden and the county sheriff were poking around. Undoubtedly this scent belonged to one of them.

Ignoring the human smells, she squinted in the dim moonlight at the shred of fabric snagged on a thorny blackberry stem. *B...vampire? Merde. For all the evil devils of the underworld, Wiisini!*

She recalled the last time her youngest brother had accompanied her through the streets of Sault Ste-Marie in Michigan on All Hallows' Eve. It had been over thirty years ago, but the memory was as sharp as ever.

Marie had attended her share of costume parties, but never gone door-to-door. She'd heard of the practice of costumed children going through the streets on this night, begging for sweets, and had entreated her brother, Wiisini Namegos, to join her for an outing. He'd been dubious that their natural forms would attract no undue attention on such a night, but when she challenged him to catch and eat more of the silly white men's offspring that night than she could, without being detected, he rose to the bait.

On every street they prowled, Marie had seen children with faces painted deathly white, sporting sharp teeth and often with tracks of false blood down their chins. "What are these meant to be?" she asked her brother. "Are they some sort of white man's *windigo?*"

Wiisini had laughed at her. "I thought you were the family expert on the white men, sister. How do you not know about the *vampire?*"

"It's clearly meant to be a blood-drinker corpse," she sniffed, watching another such character run by with its friends, all clutching bags or fake pumpkins reeking of chocolate.

"Come on," Wiisini said, "I saw something near here that will show you. Also, we should be able to catch dinner there." He led her back a few streets to a movie house. The sign over the entry advertised:

HALLOWEEN DOUBLE FEATURE LOST BOYS FRIGHT NIGHT

They went around the back of the building, and in the alley put on their paler, flatter faces before creeping in through the rear door. Marie had enjoyed the films far more than she'd expected, so much so she nearly forgot the purpose of their expedition. Her brother beat her to their goal, silently nabbing a drunken teen girl during one of the climactic scenes of the first film. Marie had been highly annoyed at his sloppiness when she exited the theatre to find blood in the alley. Wiisini, however, was elated at his success, and thereafter had teased her with quotes from the films every time she visited.

She glared at the torn shirt, printed with the word she'd come to dislike. Wiisini must have grown bored because she hadn't visited him in months. So he'd come here to annoy her. Stupid boy. She thrust her nose at the fabric, smelling that same decaying rot, and the fear-sweat of whatever *mookomaan* – witless white man – had worn it before her brother had ripped it, and him, apart. Ash and iron lingered in her nostrils and across her tongue along with the carrion and disgusting essence of *mookomaan*. The combination was strange, offensive; certainly not one she'd encountered before.

Though all this felt like the sort of prank her brother would play, she couldn't smell him anywhere. Perhaps he'd used the carrion to mask himself. She remembered one autumn when he'd bragged to her about eating several homeless people, able to sidle up quite close before pouncing due to the garbage he'd rubbed on himself. Marie grimaced. If he had any sort of real skills, he wouldn't need scent to cover his own. She studied the ripped shirt, sniffing once more, unsure about the human odor mixing with the carrion. She had enough confidence in her nose to decide she'd be able to identify either again, if her brother was playing at hide-and-scent.

What really irritated her was the direction the combined smell went, as she followed it through the woods. The trail led right back to the Bad River Resort. Her private retreat. Whether this indeed was Wiisini or some other creature, they were hunting right where she most needed the least suspicion aroused. Hackles bristling, she paced around the darkened main lodge building and the newer cabins, searching for further evidence until it occurred to her she was being careless, leaving tracks in the snow. With an angry huff, she resumed her less frightening, less beautiful form, and stalked inside to demand a nightcap.

13

Soft, sweet music brought him slowly to full consciousness. Morty blinked, focusing on Darcy. She stood facing away from him, her long hair in a loose, honey-blond braid, her violin tucked under her chin, her fingers moving gracefully. Reclining on the couch under a throw blanket, Morty simply listened while she played. He didn't know the tune; she usually practiced at home, in her parent's attic. They'd converted it into a music room when she was a child. The melody was beautifully sad and familiar, though he couldn't place it. Tired and with a dull ache in his stomach, he began drifting off again when Darcy hit a wrong note and cursed softly.

"Sounded good to me," Morty mumbled, and Darcy turned, startled.

"Sorry. I was trying to be quiet, but I really need to practice," she apologized, at once setting the instrument down and coming to him. She touched his forehead. "You're still clammy. How are you feeling?"

"'M' okay," he sighed and, with effort, sat up. Darcy wrapped the blanket over his shoulders. He didn't object, although he didn't feel cold. If anything, his head swam in drowsy heat. "You're so good to me. What song was that?"

"'Ashokan Farewell.'" She offered a wan smile. "You still seem pretty sick." She glanced back at her violin, biting her lip. "Maybe I shouldn't go tomorrow."

Morty frowned. "You kidding? The chance to play with the Chicago Symphony as a student? This is a great opportunity. You have to go. You've been looking after me for two days now. I can make it through the weekend on my own. I'm feeling better. Swear it."

She stroked his hair back from his forehead. *She's so pretty. She played a beautiful melody for me.* He caught her fingers and kissed them. She tasted so sweet. Maybe it was a new lotion. He nuzzled her palm, and she giggled. "You smell good. And you play wonderfully."

Darcy shook her head. "I don't think anyone in the audience is going to care how I smell. And I keep making a mistake in that solo. And you're feverish. I think I should stay here. I mean, we have the state tour coming up next month anyway; I can always just—"

"No." Morty stared into her eyes, holding her attention. "Darce, you're amazing. You go to Chicago tomorrow and wow that conductor. This could be the start of your music career. Come on, even this fever shouldn't stand in the way of that." She still appeared doubtful, so he kissed her fingers again. "You're talented." More kisses, and a lick along her right index finger. She squirmed but didn't pull away. "You're a goddamn Swedish goddess." She laughed as he nibbled up and down her fingers. "You smell amazing."

"Ow!" Darcy snatched her hand away, shaking the sting from it. "Morty!"

"What?" He blinked at her, baffled. She cast him a worried look, rising from the sofa.

"You bit me! That hurt, you goob." She laughed lightly, uncertainty lacing the sound.

"Oh," he said, "sorry." Dizzy, he caught himself licking the taste of her skin from his lips. He reached for the glass of water on the coffee table, his brain fogged. And then the previous day came back to him in a rush: the pain in his guts, the hospital trip, the clotted things he'd seen in his own vomit, his neighbor murdered.

Morty reeled. He clutched at the sofa cushions while the room swayed dangerously. When the furnace kicked on a second later, he felt perspiration across his brow and chest. He swallowed dryly. He reached again for the glass and managed to pick it up and drink a little of the water without spilling it.

"You should take some more meds. It's been five hours," Darcy advised, concern showing plainly on her face. He suddenly felt very sick at the thought of her staying overnight.

"Five hours? What time is it?" He checked his phone. "Darce, you should go home, get sleep. Important day tomorrow." He tried to smile at her, unsure how genuine it appeared. "Go on, I'll be fine." She hesitated, and he grabbed the anti-nausea pills and took one, washing it down with water. He needed more ice. Too hot in here. "See? Took my meds, got my finger Jell-o, got my blankie. I'm all set. Plus, I don't want you to catch this."

She touched his forehead again. He gently brushed her hand away. "I'm fine. I promise. Don't catch my germs. Be sure to wash your hands. Go

home, rest up, and text me from the road tomorrow, all right?" She nodded, though reluctantly. He reached for her hand, then thought better of it.
"Is someone going to record the concert? If so, I'll still get to hear it."

"I think Janice is." She sat down next to him, her eyes searching his face.
"I guess, if you're sure you're all right."

"I'm sure. You are a very thoughtful nurse, and I have everything I need
right here. Doc said bed rest for a couple days and I'll be fine. So I'm resting. You get out there and show the Windy City that pretty girls from Wisconsin have mad violin skills."

She snorted delicately. He didn't know how she managed that sound,
but he loved it, especially because it usually meant she was acceding to
whatever ridiculous argument he was making. "You're just trying to flatter
me."

He gave her his patented puppy dog eyes. "Is it working?"

"Goob." She punched his shoulder gently. She laid her hand on his
forehead. "You're burning up. Take more Tylenol." He obeyed, while she
fetched him a clean washcloth soaked in cold water. He sighed in relief
when she laid it carefully across his brow. "Promise me you'll rest. And if
you need anything from the store—"

"I'll call Kim and whine at him," Morty assured her. He kissed the tip
of her nose. Her scent filled his nose, his mouth, and for the barest instant
he had the urge to taste her skin, her neck, her breast, hot and soft against
his palm. He pulled his hand away, frightened suddenly and for no reason
he could explain. "Sorry."

"I think you're still running a fever." Both of them heard his guts growl.
"Are you sure you're not hungry?"

Morty closed his eyes, forcing himself to sink into the sofa and not look
at her, her shining hair and smooth skin and the scent of her and the taste
of her. He swallowed and shook his head. "No, not really. I'll eat something
later if I feel like it."

"Okay, well, drink lots of water. And no beer."

"Got it."

"Are the police going to hang around for awhile? I mean, they still don't
know what happened to your neighbor?"

Morty paused. The cops must not have told her the full story. "Oh. They said someone tried to break into his apartment. Guess it was too much excitement for the old guy. Keeled right over, hit his head. Pretty bloody."

"Jesus, how awful." Darcy shivered. "Sure you're safe here alone?"

"Yes, I'm absolutely safe here. Please, go home and get some sleep, so you can be sharp and ready for tomorrow night." He stared at her, pleading silently, until she nodded.

Morty rubbed his eyes as she stood and packed her instrument and her tablet away. Hypersensitivity had to be a symptom of the fever. Smells and tastes more acute. This was just illness playing happy hell with his brain. He watched her bundle up. "How cold is it tonight?" he asked.

"Really, really cold. Like negative twenty with the wind chill." He almost asked her to stay, to not go back out. Dread stuck in his throat. "Don't worry, the car has a new battery, and it's a short drive home." She shook her head. "I can hear the wind coming through the cracks. You stay warm, babe. Maybe I should bring your comforter out here, if you're sleeping on the sofa."

"No, no, it's fine. I'm fine." He felt too hot. "Hey Darce?" She looked at him, waiting, and he struggled for words. *Stay, I need you. Don't stay, I'm not safe.* "Have a great trip. Knock 'em dead."

She smiled, and something tightened in his chest. "Get better, you goob. I'll be back Sunday and I'll come straight over to check on you. I'll text you tomorrow. Love you, Mordecai." She gave him a hug.

"Love you too," he croaked. The door closed behind her, and fear struck him. He started to get up and go after her, when memory of the churned hair and flesh washing down the shower drain at the resort suddenly flashed, becoming clearer. The bones too big for him to have possibly swallowed at all, which he'd vomited up in the apartment. With a shudder, he sat back down heavily.

He threw off the blanket and chugged the last of the cold water. His stomach rumbled. He reached for the gelatin blocks; the first taste of one repulsed him. His taste buds were all out of whack. Just a stomach flu, had to be. Not some weird pre-Columbian virus picked up from the soil of a bizarre ceremonial burial. *Assmonkeys, I'm sweltering in here.*

Usually the low ceilings and antique light sconces of the second-story rooms gave him a sense of comfort, of enclosure, and the numerous old double-hung windows let in plenty of light to keep his apartment from being too dark. Now, it felt as if the old walls and plastered ceiling were drawing in around him.

He heaved himself upright and made for the porch. His hands shook, and the door groaned in protest when he yanked on the doorknob. Ice broke away and pattered down on his head when he wrenched the door open with a grunt. He walked onto the creaky boards of the sleeping porch; the sheer force of the cold hit him immediately, and a wind gust staggered him back a step. He grabbed the back of his deck chair and stood there dazed, the sleeves of his tee shirt fluttering.

Snow whipped at his face, his bare arms and legs, wind shrieking through the screens. Dazed, Morty clung to the chair, blinking away the bits of ice continually stinging his cheeks. Movement and light from the house next door eventually caught his attention. Mrs. Hietpas was waving at him from her window. Once his eyes met hers, she gestured sharply at him, scowling. He could see her mouth moving, though with the wind he could just barely hear her yelling. "Go back inside!"

Morty gave her a tight-lipped smile and a wave. "It's not that bad out here. And it's none of your business what I do, you sanctimonious cow," he muttered.

He'd learned her name last fall, when he'd seen her struggling to lift a very full handcart of grocery bags over her front stoop as he'd been coming home from work. She had been dressed in ankle-length dark skirts, and her perfectly curled hair gleamed slightly blue in the bright sun. He'd introduced himself, hefted the cart up for her, and then she'd given him her surname and asked what church he belonged to. "No affiliation," Morty responded, finding that generally less offensive to the city's largely Catholic older folks than offering his view all organized religion was a con game. Mrs. Hietpas had given him a sharp glare.

"Well, you should join First Lutheran. It's not far from here. That's where I go."

"I'll keep that in mind." He smiled. "Do you need any help getting stuff inside?"

She clutched her handbag tighter. "No thank you."

"Okay then. Bye." He stepped away; she called after him.

"Are you that young man in the apartment up there, the one with the porch?"

He turned. "Yep, that's me. Yeah, pretty sure I've seen you around the neighborhood too." He offered a polite smile, though she was scowling. "It's a great place to live, though. I mean, it's old and drafty, but the wood-work is all original. Absolutely gorgeous."

Her quivering chin lifted. "You should take more care to make yourself decent. Strolling around at all hours in nothing but your skivvies." She huffed. "And that girl who visits you, she should be more careful about her reputation. I know full well she has stayed all night at least once."

Morty's mood turned ugly. "What business it is of yours? It's my apart-ment, and I'll walk around butt naked if I feel like it." He looked up at the porch, and across at Mrs. Hietpas' upstairs windows. "Are you watching me all day? Jesus, get a life!" Angrily he strode away. He refused to listen as she yelled after him.

"And stop taking our Lord's name in vain! You'd better not expose yourself again to me, or I'll call the police!"

Standing in the blowing snow now, Morty felt heated again. He was childishly tempted to drop his shorts and moon her. Instead he went to the railing. From the porch, he could see not only the side of Mrs. Hietpas' house and her fussily landscaped back yard, but also the back yards of two other homes from this corner lot. The grass was blanketed in white, swings tied to the top of swing sets for the winter, smaller shrubs protected in tarps, fir branches coated in ice and a few still sporting Christmas lights. With weather this harsh, it would be spring before some people would stay outside long enough to take the decorations down.

He noticed the rip in the porch screening was larger now; he could al-most fit through it, if he felt inclined to go lawn-diving. The wind must have whipped the material completely from its staples. No point in telling the landlord about it until spring. He couldn't see the street from back here; he hoped Darcy's car had started without any trouble. He looked down at his hands. In the cold, dim light from below, his skin was pale as a corpse's.

Snow had begun piling against his slippers. The light hairs on his forearms and shins glistened with ice.

He wasn't cold.

A figure resolved from the gray night. The huge squirrel was back, perched on the porch railing. At least it looked like the same one. It watched him with unblinking black eyes. Morty frowned. "What are you doing out here?" he asked it. "Don't you know you're supposed to be hibernating?" He noticed Mrs. Hietpas had her face pressed to her window, staring at him. Ignoring her, Morty gestured from the squirrel to the snow outside. "It's winter. Go find a hollow tree or something."

The squirrel moved suddenly, darting past him, startling him. It circled him once, leaped onto the back of the deck chair, and thrust its muzzle at him. "Gaahhh. Damn you, crazy varmint, go away!" Distressed, he tried to calculate if he was in any danger. Did the resort nurse give him a rabies booster after his fall? No, tetanus. Waving his hands at it in what he hoped was a threatening manner, he backed away. The over-large, potentially rabid, living on his porch, squirrel made no sound other than the scrabbling of its claws against the wooden chair. Surprisingly big claws.

He could see Mrs. Hietpas was still staring at him through her window as if he'd lost his mind. "And you can get bent as well," he muttered. Fumbling behind him, he found the doorknob without taking his eyes off the squirrel and swung the door open. After he closed the door and ensured it was latched shut, he checked outside to find the squirrel thankfully gone. Mrs. Hietpas watched him a moment longer, shook her head, then sharply yanked her curtains closed.

Morty stood just inside his apartment, dazed, while the ice melted on his skin. Too hot in here. No, he was running a fever, his whole system was out of joint. Sleep on the porch tonight? No, he'd freeze to death. His guts rolled, and he winced. Shitbirds, not more throwing up, please. What did he eat that upset everything so much?

You know what you ate.

Shuddering, he wrapped his arms around himself, abruptly chilled from the inside. His gaze tracked over to the carpet by the apartment door. Though it was reasonably clean now, he envisioned hunks of glistening bone. Clumps of hair and fabric. Blood. His fingertips tingled at the memory, as though every finger had been needle-pricked.

Next door was completely silent. He wondered if the forensics crew had cleaned up all the blood.

He wanted to see it.

No one was in the upstairs hallway. The wind moaned under the eaves and through the attic overhead. Not a sound from downstairs. A single lamp lit the stairway. Morty peered around the bend, seeing no one downstairs, not at this late hour on a gloomy winter night. He slowly crept the few feet to Sturgensen's door. Yellow tape crisscrossed the frame. He tried the knob; it opened. Gently, slowly, he eased the door wide enough and ducked under the tape barrier.

The smell hit his nose right away. Iron bloomed on the roof of his mouth and the back of his tongue; sharp gunpowder made him sneeze. He froze, listening. All remained quiet. *What am I doing? This is the worst idea.*

He stepped carefully past the kitchen area toward the armchair. *Shouldn't get near the windows, someone might see me.* His eyes swept the room. *Jesus, his TV is trashed; I can't see anything not wrecked in here.*

He took a deep breath and felt faint; he grabbed at a nearby bookshelf before remembering leaving fingerprints at a crime scene was probably a terrible idea.

It smelled like metal and smoke and—and raw meat. In the gray light through the living room windows, he saw the dark blotch on the rug by the armchair. Black spatters on the furniture. Bits of whiteness that picked up the barest light on the torn chair cushion. Something white and chipped. He knelt for a closer study. Bone. It was the old man's bone, a tiny piece of it, anyway. His blood soaked into the rug. That was the smell.

When Morty licked his lips, he realized he was drooling.

He jerked back, stumbling, landing hard on his ass. He scrambled up again and fled to his own apartment, paused just inside with heart pounding, and then hastened on tiptoe back into the hallway just long enough to gently pull shut Sturgensen's door. Seconds later he collapsed onto his own sofa, panting, staring wildly around. *Did anyone see me? Did anyone hear?* His skull throbbed. He touched his forehead. *Is that a bump? Two bumps. Where do you get plague buboles? Aren't those under the arms?*

He rushed into the bathroom, wincing when he switched on the light. He turned his head to one side and the other, peering at his reflection, fingers searching through his hair for the hard lumps he thought were just there. Nothing. He was fine, just hallucinating, it was the fever and the powerful stuff they gave him for the nausea, it was making him all woozy and— He checked his tongue. It was pale, and his incisors pricked his hand when he lifted his lips to check his gums.

He didn't recall his teeth being that sharp. Certainly not all of them.

With a whimper, he jerked away from the mirror. His own frightened blue eyes stared back at him. Trembling, he opened his mouth wide, slowly. His teeth were fine. Tiny chip on the upper bicuspid from the bicycle accident four years ago. They were normal teeth, not fangs. He had absolutely not just seen fangs. And he hadn't been salivating at the smell of one entire human body's worth of blood soaked into a carpet. Well, a body's worth, minus what had been coating him from chin to legs yesterday morning.

He couldn't recall whether they'd tested any of the blood on his skin at the hospital. They'd probably assumed it was his. Fingers were bleeding, everyone knows fingers bleed a lot, all those capillaries. *It wasn't my blood. It. Wasn't. My. Blood.*

"No," he groaned, shaking his head, backing away from the mirror until he bumped against the wall of the small bathroom. He suddenly remembered, with dreadful clarity, the drinks and nibbles he'd shared with Darcy's father the evening of his clumsy accident at the dig site: several glasses of expensive single-malt, tasty ten-year cheddar and crackers, and crudités with a fancy dip. There had definitely not been any red meat. He remembered the globs of flesh he'd puked into the shower later. Chunks of uncooked meat, red and tough.

Morty huddled in his blanket on the sofa. Now he couldn't stop shivering. He searched on his phone for any news stories involving the Bad River or AmShale. He was about to click on an Ashland newspaper article about tribal objections to the proposed drilling, when a link below it popped out at him:

SASQUATCH ATTACK AT BAD RIVER!

Am I seriously reading this? He hesitated. He touched his tongue to his incisors. He couldn't tell if they were too sharp or just regular-sharp. He clicked the sasquatch link.

Garwood Quell's blog was written in a pseudo-scientific style, about the most sensational monster stories imaginable. Morty read through the top post about a laborer for AmShale who was attacked at the site where the oil company had set up a winter camp. Quell asserted that on the same night Morty had awoken in the shower at the resort, cuts bleeding and stomach roiling, something huge and savage had come roaring out of the woods and bitten the AmShale worker's foot clean off. He'd escaped only by honking the horn of the snowplow, which brought the dig workers out to investigate. No one had seen what attacked the man. Quell posited it could only have been a 'squatch, given the ferocity and the size of the claw-marks it left. Quell promised a new post after he'd interviewed the victim. He asked all readers to submit any stories they'd heard or any evidence they'd seen of Bigfoot activity in the Bad River area. There was a photo of jagged marks cutting down the side of a big yellow plow. Morty clicked to enlarge it, bringing his phone closer to study the details.

The photo didn't appear faked. The gashes weren't paint, he could see shadows inside them. The snow underneath the plow appeared stained pink. He moved down to the next photo of a clearing in the woods with the plow parked to one side. At the edge of the frame was a familiar-looking building. The next picture showed the shanty built over the ancient mound's dig site. Morty recognized the heavy cables leading under the flimsy door, and the sign pasted on it:

ARCHAEOLOGICAL EXCAVATION IN PROGRESS
DO NOT DISTURB

AUTHORIZED PERSONS ONLY

Trembling, he kept going. The next photo was of a low bluff. Morty saw nothing odd about it, then noticed it had been tagged with a comment:

"Directly overlooking the clearing. The beast came from this direction, indicated by angle of claw marks." That seemed specious. He felt momentarily relieved, the spell of the Northwoods tall tale broken, until he saw the next picture. The camera's flash revealed part of a tree and a deer track, a bramble bush of some kind, and a ripped fragment of white fabric. The word *vampire* was clearly visible. Morty's breath stopped in his throat. He knew that font. He knew that shirt, even shredded and caught in thorns. His missing shirt.

Oh, fuck me.

He sat there a long while, staring in shock.

It didn't help that he'd seen *An American Werewolf in London* at least a half-dozen times. Or maybe it did help. He tapped the "contact me" link before he'd really thought about it. A blank message window opened. He hesitated, considering cursed burial sites foolishly desecrated by white men, and the awful things he'd cleaned from his rug, and how nothing tasted right to him. Swallowing down his fear, he began typing in the requisite fields. Normally he self-edited ruthlessly, alert to any error of grammar or awkward phrasing; he made himself rush through it and clicked the webpage's *send* button. He sat back, feeling perspiration all over his skin, mouth dry. He was halfway to the kitchen for a fresh glass of water when his email pinged.

He picked his phone up as if expecting it to lunge at his face. Quell had replied surprisingly quickly; maybe he'd been online already. *Who knows what hours monster hunters keep. Nothing better to do while you're staking out a Bigfoot den than browse Twitter, I guess.*

Morty opened the reply.

"Well hello, fellow enthusiast of crypto lore! I am thrilled to hear from you, as no other witnesses have come forward for that vicious attack. No, I am not aware of any werewolf stories native to the area, but I am open to whatever information you have. I have spoken with the victim, who thank God is well as can be expected and recovering nicely, however I would be interested to hear if your observations corroborate what he experienced. Are you still in the area?

I'll be at Happy Hettie's roadhouse tomorrow afternoon; it's outside Mellen if you don't know it. Would you consent to a formal interview as to what you saw and heard?

Best,

Garwood Quell."

Morty frowned. Wavering with indecision, curiosity won out, and he searched the internet for the town, seeing it wasn't far from the resort. Or the dig site. Where the only clues to what was happening to him were probably even now being packed away for transport to a museum, or reburied. The archaeologist, Lightfoot, had said the ceremonial Ginsu-antlered corpse was going where no one would disturb it again.

He pressed his palm to his forehead; everything felt cold now. He tugged the blanket tighter around himself, tucking his legs up on the sofa. Chills coursed through him. Whether this was an undiagnosed brain virus or worse, something bad was undeniably happening. And it started with that viciously sharp skull in the creepy burial mound. His guts growled, pain creeping from stomach to kidneys. Morty huddled tight, panting through it until it eased. *Well, I guess a Bigfoot hunter can't screw me over any worse than I already am.*

He sent an affirmative reply to Quell, then brought up Kim's number. It was almost three in the morning. He couldn't remember Kim's schedule this weekend. He knew this was asking too much, but without a car he was dependent on friends. He needed to go back to the dig and figure this out. At the very least, get a sample from the creepy skull to take to the hospital, run some tests. Soil samples. Anything. He took a deep breath and thumbed the call button. He waited, anxiously, five rings before Kim's sleepy voice answered.

"Morty. You okay?"

"No. No, I'm not." Before Kim could process that, Morty plunged ahead. "I'm really, really sorry, man. I need your help."

"Dude, hey, whatever you need. Of course."

"Don't say that before you hear what it is. Can you drive me up to Bad River tomorrow?" He felt his teeth with his tongue again. They seemed normal. He shivered, looking out at the treetops bowing in the fierce wind. "I know it's colder than a frost giant's butthole out there, but there's something I really need to do."

Kim sleepily agreed to pick Morty up in the morning. Morty hung up, leaned back into the couch cushions, and stared out at the night. Morty hoped Kim would remember the conversation once he woke up again. After a while, he turned off the lamp. In the darkness, the howl of the wind was the only sound.

14

The bar reeked of stale beer and used oil, and of white men. While Marie found many of them too revolting to eat, hunting them and listening to them scream was always an enjoyable sport.

Marie paused inside the door, fluffing the snow from her coat while she surveyed the room. A few men lingered at the bartop at this late hour. Most were dressed in heavy vests and ballcaps, most likely loggers working the surrounding forests. The frozen ground made transporting cut trees much easier. The only thing that had changed about the industry in two hundred years was oxen-drawn sledges had become heavy trucks; the men doing the work were as hardy, as crude, and as intolerant of tribal residents as they'd ever been. However, since they were in the woods nearly every day throughout the winter, if anyone had chanced to see the intruder on her lands it would be them. Her brother, though a perfectly silent hunter, was not a careful one. It was entirely possible he'd been spotted if he was lurking anywhere near. One of the men was cleanshaven, unlike the loggers, and younger. He seemed to be arguing with the man on his left, who was ignoring him. Marie focused her ears and picked up on their conversation as she slowly approached.

"I know the difference between a goddamn bear track and what I found," the young man said, thumping his mug on the counter. Fortunately, it was empty. The bartender cast the youngster a wary glance, though he didn't notice, completely intent on his speech. "I hunt plenty; I've seen bear and lynx and cougars. And I'm saying this print didn't belong to any of 'em."

Encouraged, Marie sat next to him and signaled the bartender. When she ordered a beer, the young arguer took notice of her. She smiled at him, settling her derriere more comfortably on the barstool, and watched as his eyes flicked over her. He ordered another drink, then sat in silence, fidgeting with the mug handle. The man on his other side said, "No such thing as Bigfoot, is all I'm sayin'. Whatever kinda track you found, it wasn't that."

"Yeah, well, you'll be laughing out the other side of your mouth once it's in the papers," the younger man insisted. "I just gotta get it verified, and then I'm gonna sell it and make a ton of money. Don't expect me to buy you a round when I come in here after I'm famous." He glanced at Marie, his face reddening. She turned to him with a bright smile.

"You're famous?" Her gaze slid from his painfully short hair to his skinny arms, loose in the sleeves of a flannel shirt. She grinned. "Should I ask for your autograph?"

The older logger chortled, then set his mug on the bar along with a crumpled ten-dollar bill. As he shuffled toward the exit, the younger man shot a glare after him, then shook his head at Marie. "Nah, not yet. I mean, I will be."

"What's this about Big Foot?" She always felt awkward speaking their silly term for the *rougarou*. The whites were so ignorant, always treating the big hairy forest tribe like trophies for their lodges. If one of the *rougarou* walked right up to any of these imbeciles, they would ruin their trousers and run. The hairy men avoided her territory, and she respected their lands farther north. As long as enough game remained to go around, she saw no reason to disturb boundaries laid down centuries back. Not like these fools.

The young man played with his mug some more. "Do you believe in them?"

She glanced left and right of the youngster, as if to make sure no one was within earshot. She forced her nostrils not to cringe at the scent of his sweat and spilled beer as she leaned toward him. "Oh, yes, I do," she said, her voice low and reassuring, inviting his confidence. "There are far too many stories of people who have seen things moving in the forest. Or of hikers gone missing." Always too stringy; at least they were easy to catch. She gave him a fervent nod. "I believe. What did you find?"

"Well," he said, licking his lips nervously, "I was out marking trees, you know, for cutting." She nodded, and he continued, "I found this track in the snow, and it was kind of weird, so I followed it for a while. It was right over some deer tracks; I think it musta been hunting the deer. Looked like a big hand, but with claws, maybe like a huge gorilla? You know how they have feet like hands?" Marie gave another nod, her mind puzzling over the description. "Well, I tried to take a picture, but it was so cold the lens on my phone kept fogging up. Then I got to a place where sand had been laid down, for a clear road, near that fancy hotel. You know, over by the river."

"I have heard of it," Marie said.

He took a long drink of his beer; Marie ignored hers, her attention completely on this idiot spewing nonsense. *Rougarou* hunting deer? *Très ridicile.* Even if any of them were out of hibernation at this time, they would be foraging for garbage and carrion before they'd become desperate enough to go hunting.

"Anyways, I had yellow tape with me, for marking the trees, and I marked the spot. And I came back the next day with some plaster, and I made a cast right there in the mud. Got it back at my place right now, and tomorrow I'm going to meet an expert who can confirm it's a real Bigfoot print."

"An expert?"

"Yeah, you know, one of those monster-hunter types. He's written a bunch of books about Bigfoots. Bigfeet. Whatever." He gave an embarrassed chuckle. "I guess I'm sort of a newbie to all this. I can promise you this, those tracks I found weren't from any kind of natural animal." He leaned in, breathing heavily. "You wanna see it?"

Marie stifled the urge to slap his reeking face away. Instead she smiled and touched his thigh. "I truly do."

He gawped, unable to believe his luck. "I live just a couple miles from here. You, uh, you want to go now?" He swallowed hard as she continued smiling. "I mean. Ya know. Just to see it. Before it goes viral."

"I'll be able to say I knew you before you were famous," Marie agreed, stroking up his jean-clad leg a bit further. She watched his entire body tense and chuckled softly. "Yes. I would very much like to see your big...foot."

He hesitated a moment, frozen, then laughed aloud. "Well heck yeah! My name's Brian, by the way."

"That's nice," Marie purred, sliding from the barstool and slipping her arm around his. "Show me what you have. I find things such as this exciting."

"Sure," he said, walking with her toward the exit, a little wobbly in his mud-encrusted boots. "Hey, you maybe want to grab something to eat, too? I know this pancake house not too far from here. They, uh, they open in the morning." The stare he gave her as he pushed open the door was full of naked need. She was always a little disappointed when the hunt was this easy. No fun at all.

She sighed to herself and turned a full smile his way. "Why don't you show me your find first, and then afterwards, I am sure I will want a bite."

She climbed into his truck, hanging on tightly to the door as he drove too fast along snowy back roads. Whatever this imbecile had found, she wanted to see. She would recognize her brother's fat feet anywhere, and it was like him to be careless enough to leave tracks. The boy's "expert" might be worth talking to as well, if he knew anything about the man mauled near the resort.

And, she mused as they pulled up to a trailer surrounded by dark pine woods, if everything this simpleton had turned out to be useless, she could always use a snack before resuming her hunt.

15

The whistling irritated him; he brushed a hand over his ear, and nerves fired, prickling his fingertips. The noise didn't stop. Morty cracked open his eyes, having to rub away the sleep limning his eyelids before he could see anything. Everything was too bright. In growing anger, he brushed what felt like cobwebs from his face and hair, sitting up. He blinked several times before his porch came into focus. Snow had blown in, piled against the deck chair and the side of his body. It looked as though he'd been out here for at least an hour. *Assweasels, I fell asleep on the porch again. What the hell.*

Wind whistled through the screen, flapping the torn section wildly. Dim gray light reflected off every white-coated surface.

He was naked except for his shorts. Though they'd sagged loosely around his waist last night, right now the boxers felt tight and his belly overly full. And his skin was coated in crimson, a dark crust under his fingernails when he lifted his hands before his eyes.

Shocked, Morty lunged from the chair, snow clumps falling from his shoulders. Across the side driveway, he saw the upstairs window in Mrs. Hietpas' house wide open, one curtain billowing out in the wind. Morty took a step toward the railing, and acid washed up his throat and out. He dropped to his knees, gagging. Something stuck in his throat, tickling, horrendous. He coughed, choked, and frantically reached into his mouth. His finger snagged slimy, soft hair. He yanked it out, his stomach convulsing again, and at last was able to draw a ragged breath. Gasping, he retched twice more, and metal bits plinked onto the boards of the porch. Morty crouched, shivering, and stared at the partially flattened metal lumps and the blue-gray waves of hair together in a bezoar clump with half-digested chunks of wet, red meat. One piece still had skin on it.

Morty's stomach clenched; he heaved only droplets of bile and saliva. "No...no, no," he whimpered. He wiped his chin, scrambling backward, his hands leaving pink prints in the snow.

He looked at the house next door. No way would fussy Mrs. Hietpas have left her window wide open on a night this cold. Mrs. Hietpas, the shrill-tongued religious woman with the perfect curls of hair. His stare dropped to the matted mess he'd just thrown up. Bits of a wig. Like Mrs. Hietpas' blue hair. The metal bits reminded him of bullets, like the gunshots reported the night Sturgensen was killed. Morty turned his gaze upon his hands, his legs, spattered and smeared in red, frozen dry on his pale skin.

Oh fuck me.

Forcing himself up, he left the mess where it lay steaming in the chill air and peered over at the open window. "Mrs. Hietpas?" he called, his throat ragged and his scratchy voice weak. He coughed and tried again. "Hey, Mrs. Hietpas? You all right over there?" No answer, no sound but the wind in the trees, branches scraping the siding. Suddenly Morty noticed the sky had lightened more. It must be close to morning by now. And he was standing on his porch, covered in blood, in full view of any neighbor who happened to glance out their back windows.

Frightened and shivering, he shouldered open the door and stumbled into his apartment. He locked the porch door behind him and yanked closed all the curtains. A lamp was on in the living room. His blanket lay on the sofa, empty water glass and untouched gelatin on the table. The tee shirt he'd been wearing lay ripped in half on the rug. Morty picked it up. The redness coating his hands contrasted unpleasantly with the heather gray fabric.

He fled to the shower, weak and nauseous. He scrubbed at his skin before the water heated up, desperate to clean off the dried blood everywhere. He panted as the room steamed up, dizziness threatening to overcome him. Leaning against the tiled wall, he wrung out his washcloth over and over and rubbed his skin until the water around his feet turned clear. He didn't realize he was crying until he'd mostly dried off. He searched his memory. In between Darcy leaving last night and his awakening this morning on the porch again, all he could recall were vague shadows, a forest at night, wind howling. He touched the scars on his belly and just above his collarbone. They'd almost healed, even though he'd just scrubbed off the scabs. All the cuts on his body were mere scars now, the bruises mostly faded on his shins. The only wound still bright crimson was on his left palm, where the antler had pierced his flesh.

He rinsed his mouth out several times, but the taste of bitter iron remained. Morty shaved with trembling hands, nicking himself twice before finally giving up. For the next ten minutes, he stared at his reflection, checking his teeth, fingers feeling his scalp through his wet hair. He appeared as he always did, except more haggard. No one was banging on his door yet. Maybe Mrs. Hietpas was perfectly fine, just airing out a stinky room or something. In zero-degree weather plus wind chill. The knocking on his front door made him jump.

"Hey man, I'm here, you up?" Kim called.

"Just a second," Morty yelled back, trying to keep his voice from shaking. He spotted the bloody shorts on the bathroom floor, and quickly tossed them into the hamper. He tripped over his duffel bag again on the way to the closet. He pulled on clean boxers and sweats. Though he wasn't cold at all, the layers felt normal. He needed normal badly right now. When he swung open the door, Kim handed him a convenience store paper cup.

"Okay. I'm here," Kim said. He glanced at the shared wall; Sturgensen's apartment remained silent. "So, hey, the cops called me like four times, asking if I saw or heard anything weird. They wouldn't tell me what happened except your neighbor was attacked." Morty nodded, gulping the coffee. "Did you notice anything?"

"No. Nothing."

"Maybe someone thought the old geezer had gold bars stashed away. I'm sure he listened to the pitch for them often enough. 'The gubment's gonna fail! Invest all your savings in a ridiculously heavy metal to boost our stock prices and then get robbed by a junkie in your own home!'" Kim joked. Morty tried to chuckle, ending up coughing. He sipped the coffee. It was bitter and burnt, but that was normal. Wonderfully normal. Kim frowned. "So, what, he was attacked right here? Right next door? Is he okay?"

"He's dead." Morty turned away, hunting for his wallet and phone before he located them in the couch. Kim stared at him.

"Whoa. For real?" His grin faded as he saw Morty wasn't kidding. "He's dead dead?"

Morty swallowed, tasting blood. He grimaced. "He was killed. Some kind of animal tore him up. Dog, maybe. Cops don't know why."

"Jesus!" Kim looked at the apartment door. "Morty, you gotta start locking your door. That's crazy."

"Yeah. Yeah, it is." Morty stood awkwardly, wanting badly to end this conversation and just get on the road. "Thanks for coming over so early. I really appreciate it."

"Yeah. Of course. Damn, dude. What kind of sick asshole brings an attack dog to a robbery?" Kim stared at the adjoining wall a long moment, then shook his head as he turned back to Morty. "You look significantly less healthy than your usual sparkly-vampire-wannabe self. Even whiter than mayo on Wonder bread. You're still sick, I'm assuming? Darcy texted me yesterday and told me about your trip to the emergency room." Morty nodded, trying to pull on his snow boots standing up. "You sure you're up for a road trip?"

"Yeah, yeah, I'm fine." Morty glanced uneasily around the room, hoping Kim wouldn't notice the ripped shirt on the other side of the sofa. "I think that's everything. Let's go."

"Whoa, hang on," Kim protested, sounding worried. "It's approximately negative ass out there. If we're really doing this, at least put your coat on." Kim, Morty finally noticed, wore a heavy dark green woolen scarf and sherpa-lined parka, black touchscreen gloves and snow boots.

"I'm not really feeling cold." Morty tried to laugh. "Just got outta the shower."

"Darcy will string me up by the balls if I let you get sicker," Kim argued. "Come on, man. Hat, scarf, coat. And why again are we driving for four hours in this horrible weather to some backwoods town?"

Morty didn't want to stay in the apartment one second longer. He shrugged his coat on and motioned Kim toward the door. "I'll tell you on the way. Promise."

Kim stood in place, unmoving, eyeing him suspiciously. Morty grabbed Kim's hand and pressed it to his forehead. "See? No fever. All good."

"I can't feel you through the gloves. Come on, what the hell is this about?"

Morty glared at his friend. "You going to drive me or what? Last night you promised."

"Yeah, I promised you half-asleep at ass o'clock this morning. Stop for just a second and talk to me. Why do you need to get to the Northwoods so badly?" Morty couldn't speak, his throat raw when he swallowed. Kim shook his head. "Come on, Morty, you're acting really weird and you're starting to worry me. Tell me what's so important up there."

Morty tried to compose his thoughts, tried to ignore the patter of *get out get out you killed them you ate them get out now* running like a horror-movie soundtrack behind his immediate consciousness. "Something really bad is happening to me," he said, hearing his voice trembling. He struggled to master it. "Something really fucked up. And it started when I slid into that bizarre grave in that creepier-than-Ed-Gein ancient burial mound and cut my hand on a prehistoric razor-sharp antler." He gulped. "I don't know if I'm infected with an incredibly rare, weird disease or going crazy. The hospital didn't find anything wrong. Just a virus, they said. But I've been experiencing really weird shit, and I need better answers than 'we have no idea, here, have some suppositories for the nausea and call us if you hack up your pancreas.'"

Kim stared at him, his face unreadable. Morty took a breath and continued, "So I found a guy online who investigates this kind of stuff, and he wants me to come talk to him. And I need to go back to the dig site and figure out what's happening to me. Maybe take soil samples or something. And if this monster hunter guy can help me at all, then I need to talk to him."

"Monster hunter?" Kim shook his head slowly and pulled his cell from his pocket. "Hey, let's call Darcy first."

"Kim, I'm not feverish, and I'm not losing my mind!" Morty shouted. Kim flinched. Morty forced himself to lower his voice. "Okay, maybe I am. Maybe I am going insane. I still need to find out exactly how and why, and the only answers are up north. So please, will you take me there? Or if you don't want to, I get it, it's freezing, so can I borrow your car then?"

They stared at each other a beat. Kim's shoulders relaxed slowly. "If it's that important, sure, I'll take you. I really don't think you should be driving right now. And I think you should have someone around." Morty's gaze dropped to his feet; he knew he sounded like a lunatic. "You say something is wrong with you. Can you spell it out exactly?"

The image of entangled hair, meat, and shining bullets flashed in Morty's head, and he cringed. He passed a hand over his face and took several slow breaths. "I'm not sure. I feel like crap and I can't keep anything down and nothing tastes right. I've been having really freaky thoughts and frankly I'm scared as hell I've—I'll do something awful." He met Kim's worried gaze. "I need to find out what's happening to me before it gets worse."

"And you really think you'll find some kind of answers back at the burial mound?" Kim asked. Morty nodded. Kim pulled his hat off and ran his gloved fingers over his sleek hair, frowning. "Monster hunter, like the guys on that show, tromping around the woods looking for Bigfoot and stuff?"

"Exactly like that."

Kim stared hard at him, his forehead furrowed in concern. "You've been sick. Running a fever and puking your guts up. You're probably dehydrated. Dammit; I'm regretting I brought you coffee now." His voice lowered. "Morty. Is Darcy okay?"

"She's fine. She's getting on a bus to Chicago in an hour. Jesus, do you really think I'd hurt her?"

"You tell me," Kim said, eyeing him. "You said you were having scary thoughts...."

"No!" Morty snapped. His gaze darted to the closed curtains. He couldn't tell if anyone stirred in the house next door.

Kim asked quietly, "Do you remember anything from the other night? I mean, you just crashed after I left, right? You acted like you were on the verge of dropping."

"Look, I'm not—I'm not going to go into everything right now. Not yet. Not until I know exactly what's happening. And how to stop it." He swallowed hard and drank the rest of the repulsive coffee, hoping it would help clear his head. Morty coughed and managed not to retch. Kim didn't say anything. "I realize this all seems a little whack. I'm sorry. I really need to go find answers. You coming with me or not?"

Kim sounded offended. "Of course. I'm just worried about you, dude."

Morty nodded, and gave Kim their buddy salute, tapping his chest twice and then offering a fist-bump, which Kim returned. "Thanks, man. I mean it."

Kim sighed. "Guess we better go, then. Gonna be a whole day driving up there and back. You have directions?"

"Yeah." Morty held up his phone. "Course already laid in for North BFE. Make it so." Kim nodded, and waited for Morty to zip up his coat and pull on his ski hat.

When they trudged out into biting wind and shin-deep snow, Morty looked back at Mrs. Hietpas' house. Her front door light was still on. The interior was dark, curtains drawn, except for the one fluttering from the open upstairs window. Morty chewed his lip, trying to recall anything he'd observed of the old lady's schedule. She had a nurse who visited sometimes, and her biddy friend stopped in on weekends. He pictured her fragile body, housedress bloody, throat ripped out, eyes staring at the ceiling while her blood froze, a few steps away from the open window she used to spy on him. Shuddering, he shoved the image away. *No. She's fine. I'm sure she's fine. No. She's not fine. I'm not fine. Nothing is fine. Someone will come by and find her. Find her dead on the floor. Or whatever is left of her. At least she'll never have to see me in my skivvies again.*

He clenched his hands to stop them shaking. He couldn't stem the flow of horrible thoughts. He barely kept the tears and gibbering despair from taking over. *I have to stop this. The blood. The throwing up pieces of—*

Morty shook his head to clear it. He slid into the passenger seat of Kim's waiting car, warm and with the local metal station playing a forgettable bar band. Seated, he soaked in the atmosphere of normalcy. Everything would be, had to be, okay. He had to find out what had really happened, prove this was all some sort of weird fever-induced hallucination, get better. He buckled in. He felt a bump in the pocket of his sweatpants, and after a moment of fishing around he pulled out a slightly bent joint. *Oh. That's handy.* He held up the joint and asked Kim, "You mind?"

Kim looked at it a long moment, and Morty was about to apologize and tuck it away. Kim muttered, "Yeah. That'll do pig, that'll do. Think it's gonna be that kind of a day." He took the joint from Morty's fingers, lit it with the dash lighter, and took a long drag. He handed it back to Morty with a nod before pulling out into early morning traffic.

Morty filled his lungs with sweet smoke, suppressing a cough. He leaned his seat back as Kim plugged in his phone and selected an Infected Mushroom track. Morty pulled up his navigation app and put his phone in Kim's cell cradle. He closed his eyes, continuing to take hits off the joint, his jangled nerves easing a bit. He was going to listen to the music and re-lax. And he absolutely was not going to think about waking up in the snow, covered in blood and sick to his stomach, for the second time in a week. Nor was he going to imagine the scene behind an open window, where the curtains blew in a bitter cold wind.

16

The drive north was excruciatingly slow after the mellowness wore off. A fierce snowstorm slowed their progress. They were forced to reroute around road accidents. Twice they were stuck behind a snowplow crawling at fewer than ten miles an hour. Frozen lakes which would flood cranberry bogs later in the year gave way to tiny towns. Morty's knee jigged at every two-bit traffic light along the narrow state highway. When the plains and bogs turned to forest, he kept checking their travel progress on the navigation app on his phone. Kim, with an exasperated sigh, had tossed Morty's phone at him and set his own in the cell dock.

Darcy texted him she'd arrived in Chicago with her strings group, and Morty made himself send back a cheerful reply. She promised to text again after the concert. Hopefully by then he'd have better answers. He couldn't keep going like this.

When Kim needed to stop for a pee break, Morty paced in the gas station, eyeing the rack of cigarettes behind the register. *Assweasels, I want a smoke.* It took all his willpower not to buy a pack. The growls his stomach made at the raw hamburger in the store's small freezer case didn't help matters. He left with a couple of summer sausage sticks. As Kim pulled out of the gravel lot, Morty ripped a large bite from the first stick and chewed determinedly. Kim side-eyed him.

"You gonna do this the whole trip?"

Morty shot him a glare. "Do what?"

"Act like you stole Ganon's favorite dildo and you have the entire horde of Guardians chasing you down for it."

Morty bit off another hunk of dried meat. It wasn't satisfying in the least. It tasted old, overdone. He thought about Mrs. Hietpas' smashed window, a curtain blowing in a vicious wind. Uneasily, he tried a web search on his phone, looking up Appleton TV stations. He never bothered with local news much, far preferring online international or political journals. Figuring out which news site seemed to be the least crammed with ads was tedious. The one he picked still loaded too slowly, and Morty smacked the door. "What is this, dial-up? Come on."

"Would you please tell me what's going on in your head? Are you in trouble?"

"No, Ma, I'm not preggers." Morty sighed, exasperated. "Just let me check something."

"Whatever." Kim lapsed into silence, eyes on the road. The flurries from earlier had passed, and as they continued north by northwest, weak sunlight glistened on the snowbanks to either side of the plowed highway. Morty yanked down the blinder on his side, scrunching down further into the seat to keep the light out of his eyes.

The day felt too bright. He watched the trees sliding by, birches stark against pines, and suddenly wanted to seek refuge in their shadows. He shivered. Checking his phone, he saw the site had finally loaded despite the poor signal out here in north BFE. He searched for breaking news first, skimming past the latest skirmish between the governor and the legislature. Nothing about any murders in Appleton. He was about to close the browser when he spotted an update halfway down the page:

POLICE CONFIRM SECOND BIZARRE MURDER IN THREE DAYS

He read quickly. Mrs. Hietpas wasn't named, but the address given screamed out at him even in a small font: North Street and Bateman.

He fumbled his phone trying to zoom in, cursed aloud, and read through the blurb twice. There was a video clip as well, with a pretty reporter in a coat that looked more fashionable than practical standing in front of a familiar, turn-of-the-century house.

"Dude, come on, what the hell. I am your best friend, for fuck's sake. Why are you acting like one of those antsy meth-heads that come into the store trying to pawn shit they stole?" Kim sounded worried.

Morty raked one hand through his hair, feeling a cold sweat on his brow. "I told you, it all started with the burial mound AmShale uncovered.

There was some seriously disturbing stuff in there. Remember I told you about the elk-headed guy? I need to learn everything I can about it."

"So, this dude you emailed, he knows all the Northwoods monster legends? Like the thing in Lake Superior, and the Hodag?"

"Hodag. Sure. He's investigating an attack that happened up near the burial mound." Within spitting distance of the creepy-ass ceremonial thing in the grave, if it had any spit left.

"Okay," Kim said, eyeing him uncertainly. "You couldn't just keep emailing? What about the old Indian guy?"

"Ojibwe. Or *Anishinaabe*."

"What about the Ojibwe guy you said was running the dig? Why not email him? I'm sure he's a more reliable expert than an idiot chasing Bigfoot."

Morty bit his lip, his right foot tapping, waiting for the damned video clip to load. "I don't know his first name. Nothing on the tribal or AmShale sites about the dig at all. And even if I knew how to contact him, I doubt he'd have anything to say to me. I mean, I'm the dumb white asshole who nearly wrecked his best archaeological find. No reason for him to bother with some ignorant chucklehead asking about werewolves and—" He trailed off, realizing how fantastically stupid it all sounded.

"Werewolves? Does this have to do with your neighbor getting murdered? Because, you know, I can understand how that would freak anybody out. Old guy gets wasted just a few feet away from you, and you slept through the whole thing. I mean, you hardly ever lock your door."

Morty cut in, his stomach cold and clenched. "There was another one."

"Another what? Another murder?"

"Listen," Morty said, and played the news clip.

The reporter spoke in a sharp, serious tone. *"The second bizarre murder in just three days has taken place right next door to the first one. Police were called this morning to the home of an elderly woman in the historic City Park district when her caregiver arrived to find her dead, apparently the victim of a savage animal attack. You may recall that just Tuesday night, retired US Army sergeant Olaf Sturgensen was attacked and killed in his apartment here in this quiet, historic neighborhood."*

Kim glanced at Morty. Morty stared out the windshield at the road. The reporter continued. *"Sturgensen may have tried to defend himself, as investigators found a small-caliber revolver which had been fired. Neighbors heard what sounded like a car backfiring around two a.m. So far the police have no definite suspects."*

An image sprang too easily to mind, of the metal lumps tangled in the wet, bloody mess of fake hair he'd upchucked. Morty resisted the urge to scratch at the scars on his belly and collarbone. His throat closed, and he swallowed dry air. *"The first attack Tuesday night was thought to be an isolated incident until this morning. Exclusive sources inside the Appleton PD tell me the murder last night does have characteristics in common with the first killing. Is Appleton being hunted by a serial killer? Police are asking anyone with information about these savage attacks to contact them."* Morty tapped the browser closed and shoved his phone onto the dash.

"Holy shit," Kim said.

Morty nodded. He clenched one fist at his lips, the other grasping at a fold in his sweatpants, to keep his shaking fingers calm. "Two people murdered, right where you live," Kim said. "That's messed up. Did you see anything last night?" Morty shook his head quickly. "And you slept right through the first one since you were sick," Kim continued, casting a worried glance at his friend. "You think maybe the killer thinks you saw them?"

"No," Morty said, choking on a laugh.

"Okay, that's still scary." Silence fell between them. Even the upbeat house music playing did nothing to enliven the atmosphere. "You said you were asking the Bigfoot guy about werewolves, right?"

Morty glanced at him, silent, waiting for him to ask the crazy question.

Kim seemed as though he were going to speak; instead he checked the navigation app. Morty put a hand over his eyes, feeling washed out and starting to question this whole trip. *Way to reassure your bestie, dumbass. Keep babbling about murder and monsters like we're in a cheap knockoff of 'The Howling'. Better yet, why not tell him I've been throwing up bits of what looks like old people?* Sickened, he took a swig of lukewarm water. He could still taste the bile and blood.

Kim slowed for the next turn, obeying the calm, polite voice of the navigation app. "Hey, dude, you know I'll stand by you. No matter what. If something's wrong with you, I'll make sure you get whatever help you need, okay?" Morty glanced over and saw concern and loyalty in his friend's eyes. He nodded, and Kim gave him a small smile. "I think we're getting close. Just saw a sign for Copper Falls, and I know I saw that on the map when I checked the route earlier. What's the name of this place?"

His voice only a bit rougher than usual, Morty answered, "Happy Hettie's. Just outside Mellen."

"Happy Hettie's. Why do these back-country places always sound like something out of an alternate history, where the fifties never ended and white people went on their merry way without ever seeing a brown person?"

Morty shrugged, unable today to pick up the riff where Kim left off. He didn't realize he'd made a sound until Kim looked sharply at him. Clearing his throat, Morty tapped Kim's nav app. "Yeah. Turn left here, and it should be four hundred feet up on the right."

"Pretty hard to miss." Kim gestured out the windshield. The sign for the diner where Quell had specified they meet was old flickering neon, with a chicken outlined in red. As the lights cycled, the chicken raised its wings as if startled or excited, or maybe just happy about being eaten. The building was a large A-frame chalet of rough wood. Old blue gingham curtains lined all the windows. A fair number of cars were parked outside in a frozen, rutted dirt lot; apparently the place was a local hot spot. As they pulled in, a single lamp flickered on in the parking lot, and glaring neon colors advertising Leinenkugel and Pabst Blue Ribbon shone in the front windows. Morty stared up at the sky, where solitary flakes drifted lazily, and the light was fading in the short winter day. Kim yanked up the parking brake and killed the engine. "Your lead."

Morty sat for a moment. Kim waited, watching him. Morty sighed. "Thanks, man."

Kim spread his hands. "No judgement. I mean, you didn't give me any crap when I came out to you as an omnisexual sumo crab wrestler with a walrus penis fetish." Morty looked up; Kim maintained a perfect deadpan gaze until Morty eventually cracked a smile.

"Walrus penises, huh?"

"Once you've had blubber, want no other lover."

Morty laughed. It was a halting, choking sort of laugh, but his tension eased a degree or two. Kim punched his shoulder. "Come on. Let's go meet your Bigfoot scholar."

17

Two hours past the time the logger kid was supposed to have shown up with the plaster cast from a 'squatch's ugly foot, Quell admitted he'd been stood up. Not the first time, probably not the last, at least until he could nail one of the blasted buggers. Hopefully, the second fella supposed to meet him here would show. Quell had given him his cell phone number as well as his email after their exchange through his blog. If he truly knew something about this local attack, waiting here half the day for him wouldn't have been a waste.

Quell had already used most of his petty cash for lunch, and then kept coffee coming steadily to justify his remaining at the booth near the window while the place filled up with happy-hour patrons. With dining and drinking choices severely limited on the edge of the state forest and the reservation, Quell wasn't surprised the roadhouse was growing noisy and crowded. He lifted his empty cup to signal the waitress for a refill. She nodded at him from across the room. When he turned back around, a petite, dark-haired woman was smiling at him. She bore high cheekbones and lips he could only describe as sensuous. "May I sit down?"

Quell hesitated, surprised. "Well, ah, miss—"

"Bois du Nord." Now he placed the accent: French Canuck. She had on a fur-cuffed wool coat and leather gloves, and her eyes never left his face.

Quell smiled. "Good evenin', Miss Bois du Nord. I am truly sorry, ma'am, but I am expecting someone fairly soon."

She glanced at the empty booth seat across from him, then indicated the rest of the room with a lazy flick of her hand. "It is so crowded, and I will only be a moment. I just wanted a cup of hot coffee before setting out again." She leaned forward, placing one hand lightly on his arm. "Forgive me for the imposition. I promise I will leave as soon as your friend arrives. Would that be all right?"

Her soft smile didn't falter. Quell shrugged, smoothing down what was left of his hair, and obliged her. "I guess that'd be all right. It's a free country. And you are right about it being crowded. Is it like this every night?"

"Just on weekends," the woman replied, sliding smoothly into the empty seat. "Hettie makes a marvelous fish fry."

"Oh, yah. It does smell pretty good there. I might just order that."

She cocked her head to one side. "I don't think I've seen you in before. Here for the ski season?"

"Oh heck no. I'm awful on skis," Quell chuckled. "I'm just meeting someone here. Just swapping information." He offered his hand; she was daintily pulling off her gloves, one long finger at a time. "Garwood Quell, ma'am." She accepted his handshake, delicately.

"Mr. Quell." She rolled his name across her tongue as if deciding how it tasted. She flashed him a grin. "Swapping information? That sounds like a spy novel."

"Nothing like that, no," Quell said, his chuckle a bit forced this time. "I'm actually a little bit of a writer. And a hunter."

"How splendid. I knew we had something in common." The waitress arrived, bringing a cup of coffee for Miss Bois du Nord as well as a refill for Quell. The dainty Canadian murmured a thank you, sipping from her cup. Clearly the staff knew her.

"Listen, this may sound kind of strange, Miss Bois du Nord, but have you heard lately of anything out of the ordinary happening around here? Any wild animal attacks?"

Her eyes widened. "What sort of wild animal?"

"Well, I'm up here investigating an incident from last weekend near the resort. That oil company, AmShale, has a drill site a little north of here, and one of their workers was attacked by what the game warden thinks was maybe a bear. Bit the poor fella's foot clean off." Suddenly he realized this was maybe not the best way to approach the subject with a lady. Blushing, he apologized. "Sorry, ma'am. Guess you don't really want to hear all the gory details."

She sipped her coffee, her gaze steady on him, and Quell started, feeling himself falling into those deep eyes. Some pretty girl sat down just for a cup of coffee, and he was made all stupid. To his surprise, she said quietly, "I don't believe it was a bear."

He leaned in, lowering his voice, though the clamor all around them likely masked any conversation. "You heard different, then?"

She gave a light shrug. "I have hunted around here all my life, and never seen a bear." She frowned, tapping one finger to those full lips. "Quell. Where have I heard your name? You say you are a writer?"

"Well. Just a few books, and a blog. I don't expect you'd have heard of it."

She blinked at him. "Wait. You are that man who hunts the Sasquatch!"

"Well knock me over with a feather." He laughed and scratched his head, aware his ears were turning beet red, though he was pleased as punch. "You've heard of me?"

"I read your internet site." She laughed, delighted. *"Mon dieu!* And here you are in the flesh." She quickly leaned toward him, whispering, "Do you think one of the hairy men of the forest truly attacked that poor worker?"

Energized, he scrunched closer over the table as well. The scent of her perfume was heady and unusual, like flowers and warm cattails. What a sophisticated lady, and golly, she knew his work. "Well, at first, of course. I mean, what bear comes up to a man right next to heavy machinery in the middle of the winter? Even if there were a bear or two around here, they're all denning right now."

"Naturally," she agreed.

"I talked to the guy that was attacked, and what he told me has kinda sent me on a different track."

She shook her head, eyes unfocused in thought. "Not the Sasquatch?"

"Ya know, I'm not sure what it was," Quell said, glancing around to be sure no one was paying them any attention, "but whatever tried to kill him, had horns."

"Horns?"

He nodded. "Now, this might sound crazy: I'm thinking Hodag! I mean, that was supposed to be big and ferocious, gored people with its horns and such. Folks up here thought it was just a made-up critter."

She quirked one delicate eyebrow. "I thought the Hodag was a myth. A false creature, dreamed up by some charlatan last century? A frog's head with horns and an elephant's face, body of a dinosaur and a tail with spikes sounds quite fanciful to begin with."

Quell nodded, gulping his coffee. "Well, that's what they say, sure. But what if, after all the expeditions to capture the beast, what if that guy, Eugene Shep-something-or-other, who claimed to have invented it as a hoax to drum up local business, was in fact lyin'. He could've realized all those people trompin' around the woods lookin' for the danged thing might scare off the critter, or worse, hunt it to extinction just like the wooly rhino or the Eastern buffalo. Maybe he made up a story about it just being a story."

Miss Bois du Nord tapped her fingertips against her coffee cup, mulling this over. Quell shrugged. "Well, it's a theory, anyway."

She frowned. "Have you any evidence? Tracks, or scat, or anyone else who can confirm the Hodag exists?"

Quell sighed. "No, not yet. I checked out the scene of the crime, and let me tell you, those were some impressive claw marks it left on a snowplow. As far as anything more concrete than that, no. I have a possible source comin' here today who says they were at the resort by the river there when the attack occurred, and they might have more information." He gestured at the booth seat. "That's who I'm waitin' for. There was another guy supposed to meet me here, too, but he stood me up, so I guess that was nothin' but a prank. You know, a lot of people don't take this science seriously, ma'am. I've received insulting emails and crank calls and been the subject of all kinds of ridicule. It's possible this other source is just messin' with me too. I hope not." He took a breath. Dang, it felt good for him to talk freely with someone who understood all this stuff. She was easy on the eyes, too. "I have to say, Miss Bois du Nord, you are a breath of fresh air."

She smiled. "As amazing as it would be if the Hodag were truly real, perhaps we should consider other creatures as better suspects. Did the man who was attacked have any other description of the animal?"

Quell nodded. "Said it ran on all fours until it reared up to attack. Had some kinda mangy fur, moved very fast, had horns." Miss Bois du Nord looked thoughtful, biting her lower lip. Distracted, Quell completely forgot anything else. "I mean, I never heard of a 'squatch with horns, but the poor fella insisted, so I don't think we're dealing with a Bigfoot here."

"Have you perhaps heard," Miss Bois du Nord murmured, one finger circling the rim of her cup, "of the water panther?"

Quell squinted harder at her. "The mee-shee-pee-shoo? Well, heck, ma'am, if you'll excuse me for saying so, I did think to myself you must have some Indian in you. It's the cheekbones."

She smiled. "A bit. Yes. So you have heard of them."

He pondered. "Hmm. Thought they lived under the water, in lakes and so on. There's supposed to be a biggun in Lake Superior. I never heard of 'em coming on land, just stories about upending canoes, draggin' braves under the water and what have you." He shook his head, chuckling. "No, I don't think so. Those things are water monsters. No reason for 'em to be out in the middle of the woods, jumpin' out at a construction worker."

She shrugged lightly. "I suppose not."

Quell looked at his empty coffee cup. He knew too much of it wasn't good for his blood pressure. This unexpected windfall of running into a fan, and such a pretty one to boot, had got him all worked up. And dang it, now he really did need to take a piss. He didn't want to be rude, though, and definitely didn't want to give up the table. He gave her an apologetic grin. "Sorry, ma'am; I really need to visit the restroom. Would you mind waiting for just a minute? I'd love to talk some more, if you have the time that is."

"Of course."

Quell stood slowly, his back creaking. "Back in a jiff."

*****

The instant the skinny old man turned his back on the table, Marie left a little money under her cup. After all, one mustn't alienate the staff at one of her more productive hunting spots. She slipped through the crowd and out the front door before Quell had reached the restroom.

She paced to the edge of the overhanging roof, unwilling yet to leave the warmth of the building completely. *Horns. Damn you, Wiisini.*

This had to be her brother. Had to be. None of the rest of them would bother stirring a fin out of water during the long, frozen winter; however, her brother always did have a competitive streak, and he knew where she would be hunting this moon.

Marie remembered the logger boy had smoked and patted the coat's pockets. As expected, she found a pack of cigarettes and a lighter. She withdrew one from the pack, lit it, and let it sit between her lips as she inhaled and pulled her gloves back on. Nasty. The *waabishkiiwewaad* had ruined the practice of offering pure tobacco to the spirits of the lakes. The *waabishkiiwewaad* were worse white people than the *gitchi-mookomaan*. They offered no tobacco, no fish or meat to the old spirits or even to their own gods, polluted everything; they deserved their hunted fates. Still, the nicotine calmed her anger. She needed to be clear-headed, to consider what her brother would expect her to do, and then do the opposite. Pity the hunter of Sasquatch was so useless. A Hodag, for rivers' sake! She snorted. *Wiisini, I am wise to your foolishness. You will regret messing with my hunting grounds.*

Wiisini was a silent hunter, but he was not good at the catch. Nor was he adept at covering his tracks. If that fool logger boy could find tracks, surely anyone could. Lazy brother. Continuing to smoke, she wished she had brought along the plaster cast the boy had shown her; the elongated fingers and broad palm captured in relief could have been made by her brother. Possibly. It had not been a clear track.

Her eyes narrowed, gazing out at the falling dusk, the treetops swaying in a growing wind. At least he had not stirred up a complete fracas yet. It sounded as though this attack wasn't attracting too much attention; certainly no large hunting parties were beating the bushes with over a foot of snow on the ground and more on the way. Her concern was her brother might kill the game warden, or someone of higher status, and draw more hunters to the area, searching for the "rogue bear." The very thought of so many people tromping around in her private, quiet hunting grounds made her growl. *All right, brother. If it is a fight you want, I will indulge you. And you had better not trouble my Henri.*

She finished the cigarette and took out another, staring off into the dark forest as more people arrived at the diner and the outside lights flickered on.

*****

"Told you this was better than the fish hatchery," Cory said, with a mouth full of food.

Dr. Sam Lightfoot gave a noncommittal grunt to his intern and continued chewing his trout. The breading on it was too heavy for his taste. At least the beer was cold and good. And only twenty-five-per-cent or so of the patrons were giving him dirty looks, as opposed to some of the logging towns where the prevailing opinion echoed Andrew Jackson, in that the only good Injun was a dead Injun. His two interns had insisted on dragging him along to this night on the town. Sam had only agreed in the interest of fostering better team morale. Everyone was a little on edge after that clumsy visitor, Mueller's daughter's boyfriend, nearly ruined the most important artifact at the site. And then a bear attack, mere yards from the dig.

Sam had sat silently in a meeting of the tribal council yesterday. A few of the council wanted to call off the deal with AmShale. Others argued, as they had months back when the deal was proposed, the money the oil company brought would lift the tribe from its hardscrabble existence outside of casino season. Though only one of them spoke of the bear attack as a spiritual omen, Sam knew many of them were thinking it.

He'd always regarded the *Midewiwin* medicine society as more of a cultural guide, there to teach societal mores. He hadn't believed in spirits guiding his life since he was a young boy. Not for one minute did he accept that an actual turtle had directed the ancestors to move west, seeking the food growing on the water. Hairy men and ice giants definitely did not roam the frozen forests. And a man buried ages ago with the skull of a prehistoric elk was not a dead god, no matter how superstitious some of the old folks persisted in being.

"What do you think? Come on, Doc, admit it: it's nice to get out of the dig once in a while," said Cory. He grinned when Sam gave him a nod. "I know it's loud and it's crowded, but Hettie's is the best around."

Jenny, the other intern, snickered. "More like the only place around, unless you count the resort. Which I don't. That place is too snobby."

Sam shrugged. He'd long ago determined *snobby* or *not snobby* depended a great deal on the shade of your skin. If he'd come in here on his own, he had no doubt he would've been ignored by the waitress, or come outside to find his tires slashed, with no witnesses among the crowd of white faces. He half-wished he was in South Dakota, or maybe the French Alps, examining finds far from the prejudice of his home state. When the mound had been discovered right on the doorstep of his family, so to speak, the council had reached out to him personally, asking him to oversee the excavation and relocation of the ancient elder and his grave goods. Sam knew the whites would make a mess of it and, with a little reluctance, he'd accepted the job.

His university was thrilled and expected him to publish a paper, nay, a book, once the find was fully catalogued. So far, he thought his assistant prof's theory was the most probable: this burial was an effigy, an appeasement, to some malign deity of the deep winter, worshipped by the first inhabitants of this wintry land before the recorded history of the Anishinaabe tribes. He had yet to speak to the tribal elders in more detail, to determine if he'd overlooked any old stories which could possibly explain this ceremonial grave and its lone occupant. He wanted to talk to historians of the Menominee and Ho-Chunk, as well. Their history went back farther than the Ojibwe in this area, and they might have some story to explain the wealth of grave goods and the unusual symbology of the burial. It would have to wait, however; he was too busy at the dig. The frozen ground had to be thawed, dug, and every tiny artifact removed as carefully and quickly as possible.

As soon as the earth warmed in the least, AmShale would start drilling. So instead of waiting until late spring to begin this excavation and then working through the summer, Sam and his team toiled in freezing conditions, during shortened days, racing to conserve the find. He didn't know the exact figure the council had accepted from AmShale; blackmail money in exchange for not making a legal fuss over drilling right on their doorstep. Figured he didn't want to know. It would probably just make him angry. And he knew the whites wouldn't tolerate an angry Injun.

When the waitress dropped off the bill, Cory snatched it up, and Sam felt guilty. "No, let me get this."

"Doc, this is our treat."

"The hell it is. You guys can barely pay for gas to make the trip to town. I'll get this one." Sam reached into one of his coat pockets, then the other, then shifted to feel his jeans pockets. "Damn it, must've fallen out in the truck. You two wait here, so it doesn't seem as though we're cutting and running. I'll be right back."

He strode out the door, head down, keeping his face expressionless. Great. Now he looked like a freeloader, making excuses. It wasn't the first time his wallet had fallen from a pocket; he really should put it on a chain, the way some of the loggers did. He headed for his truck in the back of the parking lot, hoping no one would pay him any attention, just wanting to fetch his wallet and make a point of paying the tab.

*****

The country roadhouse was packed. Morty stopped at the entrance, the scent of fried foods and cheap cologne wafting out when he opened the door. Immediately he felt nauseous. Kim nudged him. "Do you know what this Bigfoot chaser looks like?"

"His pic's on his blog."

"Because of course he has a blog. Do you see him?"

Morty tried to scan the crowd from the doorway, dizzy. "No."

"Pretty full in there. I don't see a table free."

Morty backed up. "You see if you can get us a seat. I'll try texting the guy, see if he's still here."

Kim studied him a moment. "You look like you might hurl. You feeling okay?"

"No. I'm really not." He took a deep breath; that only intensified the scents making his stomach churn. "I'm just gonna step out for some air real quick."

"Okay," Kim agreed. "Want me to find your guy?"

Morty shook his head. "I'll text him. Could you maybe get me a glass of water?" Kim nodded, and Morty retreated. He dragged in lungfuls of cold air, clinging to a support post for the overhanging roof. A familiar smell drifted his way. At the far end of the wooden porch, a figure in a hooded coat stood gazing out at the growing dark beyond the spill of the diner's lights, smoking a cigarette. Morty caved.

"Hey, excuse me. Could I bum one off you?"

Her head turned, and with a light shrug, she silently proffered a smoke. When Morty hurried over to accept it, she handed him the lighter. "Thanks." The first drag was horrible, and he coughed. He admitted, "Quit years ago. Been a stressful week."

The woman nodded, looking away again, her face shadowed. Morty coughed again, handing her back the lighter. "Pretty cold night, huh?" His fingers were freezing. This going from fever to chills stuff was beginning to really, really suck. Remembering his mission, he took out his phone, and numbly typed at the number the cryptid hunter had given him: *"Hi it's me, the guy who messaged your blog about werewolves and the attack up near the Bad River Resort. I'm here at Hettie's. Are you still here?"*

He waited a moment, watching the screen, receiving no reply. "Damn it." Feeling awkward, he explained, "I'm supposed to be meeting a guy here, but I think I'm kinda late." He offered a weak smile as her head turned toward him. Suddenly she flicked her cigarette into the snow and strode away, quickly out of sight around the side of the building. Morty stared after her, then huffed to himself. "Fine. Damn. Thanks for the cancer stick, at least." He didn't feel much like smoking any more of it. He ground it under his shoe, blowing out the last of the smoke from his lungs. Stupid. This was all incredibly stupid.

Through the nearest window, chatting, laughing people chewed fried fish and washed it down with cheap draft beer. Morty didn't think he'd be able to go back in there. Something was deeply amiss with his nose; the cooking smells had immediately nauseated him. He checked his phone. Nothing.

The cold was starting to permeate his clothing; he should've listened to Kim's advice and dressed in more layers. He wasn't feverish right now, but the chill washing over his skin wasn't an improvement. And he really needed to take a leak. That would mean wading through a crowd, which he intensely disliked on a good day, and standing on an undoubtedly disgusting floor in front of an equally disgusting urinal. *Yeah, I'm sure that smell would turn the tide.* He hesitated, beginning to feel this as somewhat urgent. It was frigid out here, with the temperature dropping.

The tree line might at least offer protection from the wind, as well as privacy. Morty groaned softly, turning first toward the diner door, then looking out at the nearest trees. Freezing his dick off was slightly preferable to upchucking and fainting in a grimy backwoods men's room. Unhappy with his options, he hurried toward the woods.

*****

Quell returned to his table to find it occupied by a family of four, and the lovely Canuck vanished. Well this was downright inconvenient. He flagged down a waitress as she hurried by. "Did you happen to see where the young lady who was here went?" he shouted. It took him a couple more tries to get his question heard, and the waitress shook her head and pushed on to her next task.

Annoyed, Quell moved toward the bar, but it was full up too. Some young Asian-looking guy was there yelling out an order for a glass of water, of all things. The barkeep was busy tending the other end. Shaking his head, Quell decided to step out for a smoke. Danged laws changed so much, a man couldn't even enjoy an after-dinner smoke in peace indoors anymore. He went outside, relieved once he was free of the noisy surroundings.

He wasn't so old he didn't recall similar nights out with his lumberjack buddies. When there was no town within fifty miles or more, a roadhouse was good enough if they had steaks and cold beer.

He pulled up his collar, rolled down his hat, and strolled over to his truck. Leaning on it, he dug his lighter out of his pocket. His cell phone tumbled out. He bent stiffly to retrieve it. He'd taken the trouble to memorize the number, so he could give it out to potential sources of 'squatch information, hunters and guides and what have you. Thus far he'd had no luck. His thumb turned on the screen. A text notification flashed at him. Quell read the message, surprised. That fella that had wanted to talk about the Bad River attack was here.

Quell glanced back at the diner. The loud rumble of conversation and a country jukebox penetrated through the log walls as one continuous muffled roar. No way any kind of serious conversation could be had in there now. Well, maybe he could persuade this fella to come outside. Anyway, there were no seats to be had. He sighed, tucking away his battered pack of smokes. He played with the screen a moment, his fumbling fingers having a hard time typing out his reply, until, finally, he gave it up. "The heck with this," he muttered. "I'll just go back in and wave and holler 'til someone hollers back, I guess." He smiled, purpose renewed. Might be a good day yet, even though that pretty lady up and ran.

*****

Marie crouched in the dense brush just past the roadhouse's cleared lot, so furious she unintentionally shifted forms. The scent of death remained in her nostrils, despite the deep breaths she took of the winter air. Not her brother. Not unless he'd suddenly learned how to change his human appearance. She had been completely unprepared for the appalling smell she'd found at the site of the attack to come walking right up to her here. She had managed to curb her instinct to lash out at the creature, barely, choosing to flee a short way away to gather her wits. Not her brother, not *mishibizhu* at all.

With narrowed eyes, she watched the awkward white man. He ground out the cigarette she'd given him—*aha, it was a ruse*—and hurried into the tree line. Her ears perked; she heard the zipper and then his groan of relief. *Or not.* Puzzled, she crept closer.

The *waabishkiiwed,* or whatever he was, paid no attention to her, leaning against a tree while he marked his territory. Marie growled, then silenced herself when his head jerked up. She kept motionless although her anger grew at the brazen insult. How dare this pathetic, soft preything presume to hunt on her land. She took a long sniff. The creature's scent was definitely the same she'd caught where the knife-spirit man had been attacked: the same strange combination of carrion and wood, blood and anger. Never in a hundred years would she have thought that scent would belong to a simple, stupid white man. He had no claws, no fangs; yet something that smelled just the same had tried to take a meal on her land, by her river. This would not be suffered.

He zipped up, shivering, hesitating as he stared back toward the diner. He wasn't looking in her direction. Marie tensed, the tip of her long tail lashing, teeth bared. *Oui. I need to teach this creature a lesson it will not forget.* Briefly, she considered the chance she was wrong, that this imbecile with his hands stuck in his pockets on the edge of the woods was not the same entity which had presumed to hunt her prey.

If she was wrong, she was a little hungry. That logger boy was all skin and bones.

She launched herself at the intruder, claws first.

18

Morty glanced at the roadhouse, reluctant to go inside, although he knew Kim was waiting for him. Hopefully, so was that Quell guy. He checked his phone again; still no reply. Morty grimaced, steeling himself for the assault on his nose and ears, and took one step away from the trees.

Something sharp slammed into his back, and he sprawled headfirst into the snow in agony. He wheezed, breath knocked from his lungs, and something heavy and velvety slapped his head. Stunned, he forced himself to roll, to try to find his attacker. He had a startled impression of luminous eyes, glinting scales, and a loud snarl.

He kicked at it frantically, and when his foot connected, the thing, huge and almost black against the pines, yowled like a mountain lion. Morty scrambled to his feet and ran for the nearest cover, a pick-up truck with a camper top. He stumbled when the thing grabbed at his ankles and tripped him; his head crashed hard into the side of the truck as it broke his fall.

The creature advanced on him, growling. In the dim amber light of the parking lot, all he could see was something large and feline in the way it stalked toward him. He glimpsed glimmering scales on its sides, jutting short horns on its catlike head, and a long, lashing tail. Its enormous paws were velvety black against the snow. Sharp-looking claws gleamed under the one lamp overhead. Morty tried to blink past the red blurring of his vision, gasping. Pain throbbed in his skull and shot down his spine. The agony swiftly changed to fury that burst up and out of his mouth in a screech. A voice in the back of his head began screaming. *How dare you. How dare you touch me! You are nothing!*

He rose, stretching to his full eight-foot height, flexing his claws. The black-panther-thing snarled at him, ears flattened behind its horns. With a roar of outrage, he charged.

The scaly black panther dodged him, claws slashing at his leg. His broad feet skidded in the slush. He swung his antlers down at it and the sharp tines slashed its scaly flank; it hissed. The creature shot a paw under his reaching claws to slap at his knee, gashing his flesh, though it didn't bring him down. The pain enraged him more. He slammed both his clawed hands down onto its back, overpowering it, and swung his head again, aiming for its eyes. The panther-thing jerked its own head up, its smaller horns locked in his antlers a moment. Angrily he shook his head, breaking free, and it growled and spat at him.

"Holy mother of God!" The scream right next to him disturbed Morty's outraged rampage. He whirled, letting go of the panther-thing, snarling at the horrified face staring out at him from the cab of a pickup truck. Its flesh-scent filled his bare nostrils. Hunger overwhelmed him. He grabbed the prey's shoulders; his claws snagged in its coat, and he pulled the squirming food out through the open window of the truck, his toothy jaws opening wide to bite and rend. Before he could sate his raging hunger, the panther-thing slashed his leg. Roaring, Morty spun to face it. The terrified pale flesh-thing tried to pull free of his claws. Hunger growled in his guts, commanding all his attention. Morty lifted the struggling prey and sank his teeth into its neck. He'd meant to crush the head in entirety, but it was wriggling too much. The immediate gush of blood into his face was still very satisfying. The flesh-thing screamed again.

A loud boom echoed in his skull, and fire shot into his back. He whirled, screeching, fear flushing through him at the sure attack of his ancient enemy, the thunder-bird. No great wings swooped down on him. The panther-thing had also vanished.

Confused, angry, and hungry, he turned back to his meal. In the side mirror of the truck, he saw a long elk skull with fangs, curling massive antlers, and cold fires blazing in sunken eye sockets, atop a decomposing ribcage half-covered in mangy fur. The woman caught in his claws sagged, blood spurting out from the gash in her neck, spraying him from nose to chest.

Morty suddenly understood he was staring at his reflection.

Panic hit.

He dropped the woman and staggered back. Someone ran forward to press their scarf to the gash, gaping at him. Morty backed away, hands shaking, looking down at himself. His clothing was shredded. Tufts of brown fur dropped from his coat. Hot blood dripped down his chin and neck, steaming in the frigid breeze. *Oh fuck no, that can't be me, can't be me—*

Finding his footing, he turned and ran. A shovel swung right at his face knocked him cold.

*****

What the ever-loving Lord above, two of them! Quell yanked open the cab of his truck and grabbed his trusty Winchester rifle, hastily checked to be sure it was loaded and flicked the safety off, and lifted it to his shoulder. What in God's name was that thing? He stared at the elk-headed monster with half-exposed ribs and long clawed arms. It whirled, and he ducked out of sight. As he moved downwind of it, toward the back of his truck, he caught its stench full on: rotted carrion, hot iron, and pine ash. Quell peeked around the side of the vehicle. The other monster was just as terrible, but at least it looked fully alive, like a great black-furred panther, but with lynx ears, and distinctly un-catlike scaly sides and small horns. It whipped itself around like a snake on speed to avoid the powerful lunges of the other beast.

He realized both of them had horns. He paused, unsure which to target first. Dang it, this was exactly why he should've brought a shotgun, primed for bear, with enough kick and spread to maybe get 'em both at once. And maybe some grenades.

He glanced at the gas cap on the truck next to the monsters, teeth clenched in indecision. Was it far away enough from the roadhouse and the gas pumps to avoid hurting anyone? Would the owner mind if he blew up a truck in order to kill two fiends at once?

"Holy mother of God!" A woman's shout pulled Quell's attention to the cab of said truck, which was in fact occupied, and the danged fool had rolled down their fogged-up window to see what the commotion was. Quell flinched when the elk-thing roared and yanked some poor woman right out the truck's window. He aimed at its head, but then the monster jerked back when the scaly lynx-thing slashed its gangly leg. Suddenly the woman screamed and a spray of blood shot into the air.

Quell shot straight into the elk-thing's back, immediately cursing his aim. He chunked the rifle's bolt back and forward again. The lynx-thing fled, bounding off the side of his truck and swinging the entire vehicle against him. He stumbled, almost dropping the gun; clutching it, he fell instead.

"God dangit," he panted, scrabbling to his feet, "Hellfire!" He raised the rifle again, shaking, seeing only someone kneeling to help the wounded woman and someone else running away. Quell hurried to the woman, realizing it was probably too late. A guy gawked at him from inside the truck, stunned stupid. "Call for help! She's gonna bleed to death," Quell yelled. Startled, the man pulled out a phone, and started mashing its screen with his thumbs.

No sign of either monster. Demons. Outright demons! He ran, limping, between the parked cars. People who hadn't seen the clash of beasts came out of the diner, yelling, pointing at him. Well, he was holding a rifle with obvious intent to use it. "They attacked her," he shouted, pointing back at the woman on the ground. "Look out! Watch yourselves!"

He checked wildly in all directions as he hurried between the cars and trucks in the crowded lot. Movement caught the corner of his eye. He swung around to see a tall Indian armed with no more than a shovel, standing over someone on the ground. Their eyes met. Quell caught the barest flicker of movement, black on black, and planted the butt of the rifle against his sore shoulder. "Get down," he hollered, and the Indian hit the ground. Quell shot at the glowing eyes just past him. A yowl of fury told him he'd at least nicked it. With a swish of pine branches and a crashing noise off into the dark forest, the creature was gone.

Quell wasn't prone to swearing, but he did now under his breath, and ran after the retreating monster. He doubted he'd be able to catch it; with any luck, it was leaving a bloody trail in the snow. However, a minute or so into the absolute blackness of the forest, unable to see more than a few inches ahead, he stopped, breathing hard, listening.

The wind creaked in the branches overhead. All else was silent and still. He didn't have his flashlight; must've left it in the truck. Dang it. Quell took another step, hearing how loud his boots were in the snow. It might double back, like a wounded panther. He kept listening, unease growing at every snap and groan of branches in a chilling wind. Deciding it would be saner to resume tracking in the morning light, he cautiously retreated before he lost all sense of direction in the dark. There would be time to mull over what on the Lord's green earth he'd just witnessed once he was safely back at Hettie's.

*****

Marie slowed when she reached the bank of the Bad River, panting. She looked over her shoulder. The *waabishkiiwed* hunter must have become lost; no one pursued her. She hissed as she punched through the ice of her home river and slid into its cool, comforting depths. Though it was barely wider than a creek here, it was her river, and the water nourished her and eased her pain. Curled at the bottom, she began licking her wounds closed, every scrape of her tongue over cut scales and aching muscles building her determination to kill the territorial interloper, and the old, imbecilic white hunter as well if she encountered him again. Ever.

She was not entirely sure what had happened, why her challenger had abruptly abandoned the fight, or why he had reverted to his weaker form. And then that Anishinaabe had hit her opponent unconscious with a simple garden tool! She sneered. Coward. Foolish child.

The creature reminded her of stories her older brothers told on cold nights, when she'd been a tiny cub, intending to scare her. Vicious antlers, sharp teeth and reaching claws, just like the tales she'd been told of the *windigo.* That creature surely couldn't be one. *Windigook* were giants, with hearts of ice. This thing that smelled of rotting flesh was bigger than its human form, but it certainly was not a giant. Her nose wrinkled. It had looked and smelled half-dead, and it wanted to eat more than it wanted to fight.

She'd spotted her opportunity to finish off the intruder when the Anishinaabe strangely dressed as a white man had stopped the fleeing coward in his tracks. The Anishinaabe didn't notice her as he bent over to check the pulse of the man he'd just brought down with a shovel. Marie had crept almost close enough to spring when the Sasquatch-obsessed imbecile with the gun burst in. Her teeth bared in a grimace. Though his shot had barely grazed her, it had ruined her stealthy approach, and the shouts and lights of more *gitchi-mookomaanag* coming their way had been more attention than she wanted.

Now she knew its face, the ugly *windigo* pretending to be a white man. She had its scent and would recognize it in either form. She'd make it pay dearly for setting foot in her territory. Brooding completed for now, she curled into a tight ball to rest and recover. She relaxed her mind and drifted into pleasant dreams of ripping the intruder limb from scrawny limb.

*****

Sam rose to his feet with effort, the cold numbing his joints. The man lying at his feet remained motionless. Still alive; Sam had felt the man's erratic pulse at his wrist. Even in the colored, flashing light of the diner's sign, he was positive this was the same man who'd fallen into the ancient elder's grave. And he was covered, mouth to stomach, in someone else's blood.

The old fellow with the rifle had foolishly charged into the trees, chasing a scaly panther-looking thing Sam could only identify as a *mishibishiw*. Never mind he knew no such creature existed. Everyone else was clustering around the woman bleeding out, screaming, shouting. "Doc!" yelled Cory, spotting him. Damn it. As his colleagues ran up to him, Sam pointed at the unconscious man.

"Help me get him into the truck. I'll drive him to the hospital," he ordered, opening the door to the camper top.

"What the hell happened?" Jenny asked, eyes wide at the sight of all the blood. "Oh my God."

"There was a bear," Sam said, getting his arms under the unconscious man's shoulders. "Maybe it was rabid. It attacked him and that woman over there." Cory immediately bent to take up the feet. Jenny looked in horror from him to the yelling, crying people gathered around the woman a few yards away.

"I'm calling an ambulance." She took out her phone. Sam shook his head, grunting with the effort of hefting the bloody man into the back of his truck.

"They'll never get here in time. I know these roads. I'll take him to Ashland." Cory helped him quickly settle the white man in between boxes and knapsacks in the covered truck bed. The man groaned softly. Sam checked his memory; had either of his interns been present when this clumsy *noon-*

dezhi had tripped headlong into the grave? He glanced at Cory, who didn't seem to recognize the man.

"Doc, that's a half-hour from here. I'll go with you," Jenny offered. Sam held up his hand.

"No, you two stay and see if you can help. I'll call you from the hospital."

Across a couple rows of cars, Sam saw a young Asian man searching the milling crowd, yelling "Morty? Morty, where are you? You okay?"

Grimly, Sam shut the back of the truck. "And be careful. That bear looked crazy, and there's a lot of people running around with guns." In shock, his colleagues nodded, and drifted back toward the crowd. Sam jumped into the cab, grateful when the engine started right up. He checked the rearview as he sped up the highway, hoping the unconscious man would stay that way until Sam could figure out what to do with him.

He wasn't sure what he'd seen. Campfire tales from his childhood were just that, stories invented to keep little kids from wandering too far from home. *Mishibishug* didn't swim in every deep river and lake, waiting for foolish people to venture too far from land in their canoes. *Wendigook* didn't prowl frozen lands, hunting whole villages in the dead of winter. Whatever the man lying in the back of his truck was, Sam prayed to a half-forgotten Great Spirit he wouldn't wake up yet.

At the state road juncture, he veered right, away from Ashland and the only hospital for fifty miles. He put the pedal to the floor, hoping like hell no cops came this way. He drove at top speed on the black road, heading for the rez.

19

The red pounding behind his eyes wouldn't stop. Morty lifted a hand to his face, only to find his progress restrained. Squinting, he fuzzily made out a small table, a glass of water, and then the handcuff chaining his wrist to a vertical pipe. "What the fuck?" he muttered.

His other hand was free; he tugged ineffectually at the steel cuffs, then rubbed his eyes. Was he missing a kidney? A tentative touch to his belly revealed no new scars. But his hands were stained red, with dark gunk under his nails that smelled strongly of iron. His chin and neck felt sticky.

He was half-naked, his sweatpants ripped in numerous places, his shirt and jacket barely hanging onto his arms. He could see his pale stomach and the outlines of his ribs. Peering around, eyes adjusting to the fluorescent light, he saw he was in an unfinished basement. A sump pump cover was set into the floor a few feet away, water pipes ran next to the cot on which he lay, and electrical conduits crossed the ceiling. Tiny windows at the top of a wall ten feet away were covered in snow, so he had no idea what time of day it was. His gaze focused on the motionless man sitting across the room, watching him.

"Dr. Lightfoot?" Morty attempted sitting up, though it brought fresh bolts through his skull. "What the hell is this? Please don't tell me I'm going to find my internal organs in a cooler or my leg sawed off for your dinner."

Lightfoot shifted, eyes narrowed at him, expression impassive. "What do you remember?"

"What?" Lightfoot didn't say anything else. Morty tried to piece together the fragments of memory bouncing in his aching skull. "I—My friend Kim and I drove up here. I was supposed to meet this monster hunter guy at some local dive. Happy Hettie's." Lightfoot made no reply. Morty sighed. "I remember staying on the porch. It was crowded inside. I felt horrible. Bummed a smoke off somebody." A splash of red burst up in his mind, screams; the hot taste of iron across his tongue. Gleaming huge eyes in a catlike head. That had to be an hallucination. Maybe his joint had been spiked; it wouldn't be the first time.

"This'll sound crazy, but I think some kind of creature attacked me. It was incredibly fast." The image of a long, toothy skull with wicked antlers appeared in his head. "Something scared me, and I ran." He frowned. "Why am I here? What's this for?" He yanked on the cuff.

Lightfoot leaned forward, a light frown creasing his heavy brows. "You don't remember attacking that woman?"

"What? No! Why would I—" He swallowed, tasting blood. He did remember: the groaning hunger tearing at his guts, the scent of fresh meat, the luscious spray of blood in his face, drinking greedily. A terrible image rose up of his fingers – no, his claws – tearing into an old man's ribcage, ripping out the heart, slicing down the bulging belly to free the steaming entrails, gulping them down only to regurgitate pieces of it all later. A chunk of flesh breaking up in a shower drain. Morty shuddered. "No. No, I didn't. I couldn't."

Lightfoot studied him in silence a moment, then sighed heavily. "Damned if any of the other stories my grandmothers told me are real, but after what I saw tonight, you're a *wendigo,* son." Lightfoot gave him a slow nod. "I can't let you kill anyone else. You understand that, right?"

Morty gaped at him. "Run that by me one more time?"

Lightfoot stood and walked closer, though Morty noted he was still well out of reach. "You're turning into a cannibal. A monster that eats people. *Wendigo, windigo, wintiiko.* Scariest thing in all the old tales; stories exist in all the northern tribes of entire villages consumed by these things." Lightfoot sighed. "It's a documented psychosis, the *wendigo.* People starve during a long hard winter, they start believing the old horror stories, they go crazy. Eat their families. Last *wendigo* killer on record was back in Nineteen oh-six, a man known to the whites as Jack Fiddler who was reputed to have killed fourteen *wendigook,* including his own sister-in-law. Of course, the whites hung him for murder. They didn't understand the only sure way to stop someone becoming a cannibal was to kill them."

Morty stared at him, frozen. Lightfoot shook his head. "I always viewed those stories as examples of how insanely difficult it was to survive up here through the long winters, how it could easily drive someone stark raving crazy. Never once thought the *wendigo* was real. Not like that." He stared hard at Morty. "Not like you."

"What—what about me?" Morty gulped. He tugged desperately on the cuff again; it clanked dully against the pipe. "Come on, you can't be serious."

"I saw you," Lightfoot insisted, "Saw a thing that looked like a walking corpse with an elk skull. Like the elder in the burial mound had just walked on over to the roadhouse for a bite. Hell, I thought that's exactly what it was, at first. I saw you fight with a water panther, a cross between a big cat and a snake, a monster I also never thought was real, then watched you pull a woman right out of a truck and tear open her throat." Morty stared at him, desperate to deny all of this, overwhelmed with flashes of gore and the numbing, deep certainty that his neighbors were dead because of him. "That fella with the shotgun wounded you, hit you in the back; startled you, I guess. And you changed from a monster back into yourself. You panicked and ran, and I happened to be in the right place at the right time to stop you." He glanced at the ceiling and sighed. "Didn't know what to do with you, though. I'm no murderer. Brought you back here to figure out how to stop any more deaths." He rubbed his nose, seeming uncomfortable. "I hope you understand you've given my entire world-view a jolt."

"Given you—What do you think this is? My worldview is shit. You've told me I'm a murderer. You've kidnapped me and chained me in a filthy basement! I don't give a fuck about your world view!"

Morty rose, frustrated by the cuff chaining him to the pipe. He leaned toward Lightfoot, who backed away. "How dare you. Do you know who you're dealing with, you flesh-bag? You pitiable vermin, I'll rip your belly open and feast on your—" Shocked at the aggressive snarl in his voice as much as the words spewing from his mouth, Morty's entire body jerked in terror. His hands shook. He saw them curling into claws, sharp finger-bones slowly pushing through his skin, splitting his fingertips open, blood dripping to the cement floor. He stumbled backwards, the edge of the cot catching his knees and tumbling him onto his ass upon it. Breathing hard, he stared up at Lightfoot, who stared back at him in silence. Morty held back the bile suddenly wanting to crawl up his throat.

Lightfoot lowered the crowbar in his hand; Morty hadn't noticed it until now. "You believe me yet?" he asked. Morty kept staring, twitching, as his finger-bones gradually retracted under the skin again, needles prickling through his hands.

It's real. That thing in the mirror. That thing's inside me. The creepy winter deer god from the burial site. Nauseated, he nodded.

Lightfoot let out a breath. "Okay then. Let's take a step back. This started at the dig, didn't it?" Morty nodded again. He grabbed the glass of water, taking deep swallows, the chill of it soothing. Lightfoot paced across the floor, careful not to veer too close to the cot. "The same night after you nearly fell into the elder's grave, a man was attacked outside. One of AmShale's contractors, out here surveying. His foot was bitten off. He'd have died if he hadn't thought to sound the horn in the snowplow. We didn't see what attacked him." He paused. "You do that?"

Chunks of half-digested meat breaking up in a shower drain. Morty shook his head. "I don't know."

"You notice anything weird then?"

Morty closed his eyes, the memory too vivid to shake. "I woke up in the shower. In our room at the resort. I threw up—something. Blood. There was a lot of blood." Tremors sputtered through his limbs; he curled tightly into himself. "I thought it was just from my wounds. Your ceremonial elder cut me pretty badly."

Lightfoot nodded. "Then what?"

Morty shrugged, angry and helpless. "I don't know. We went home. I felt kind of sick, like I was coming down with stomach flu. Ended up in the hospital. They couldn't find anything wrong with me. Just a virus, they said."

"Why'd you come back here?"

Morty leaned against the wall, eyeing the cuff on his wrist. "I was supposed to meet with this guy who calls himself a cryptid hunter. Has a blog about sasquatch. He said he was investigating sightings of a monster up here. And I needed to take another look at the burial mound." He stared at Lightfoot, pleading. "I have to understand what's happening to me."

The older man gave a light shrug. "Pretty sure you're turning into a *wendigo*."

"So how do I stop it? Do you have some magic cure, or shamanic herbs I can take or something?" Morty's volume raised with each syllable he spoke.

Lightfoot scowled. "Don't come to me for that garbage. I'm a scientist."

Morty groaned. "Oh, fuck me. Come on, fine, all of this is crazy but I need to make it stop. I don't want this! Whatever this is. I don't want this thing inside me." He swallowed dryly. He could still taste the blood. "I left my friend at the restaurant. I should call him, make sure he's okay." He checked his pockets.

Lightfoot nodded toward a bench, laying well out of Morty's reach. A cell phone and an open wallet were the only two items on it. "Don't think that's a good idea. I turned your phone off. Making calls to anyone may not be your best move right now." At Morty's shocked gape, he said, "If this is your last known location, that's not going to look too good for me, especially if I end up having to—" He shook his head. "Besides, you really want anyone else to know? You tore that poor woman's throat out. She bled out well before an ambulance reached her. Guess we owe that hunter; if he hadn't distracted you, who knows how many other people you'd have killed?"

Morty reached around to feel his back. His shirt and the remains of his jacket had huge holes. The pain he felt wasn't in his spine, and he was able to twist around without much effort. "Some hunter shot me? Why can't I feel any wounds?" Old man Sturgensen had shot him, though. Those bullets had gone through his system like bran muffins, no harm done.

Lightfoot gave him an odd stare. "What do you feel, right now?"

Morty shrugged. "My head hurts. And I'm scared. Terrified, actually. No other pain. Just..." He swallowed and said helplessly, "hungry."

"And it doesn't feel cold down here to you?"

"No," Morty said. Then he noticed the white puffs in the air when Lightfoot exhaled. He looked slowly around, seeing the ice glinting on the window edges. He couldn't see his breath. The ambient temperature, if anything, was comfortable.

"*Wendigook* are supposed to have ice in their veins," Lightfoot said.

Morty stood, trembling, heart racing. "No. No, I can't—no. You have to help me. Please!"

"I don't know how. Every story about fighting a *wendigo* ends with the monster being killed. Occasionally a brave person had to turn themselves into a *wendigo* to fight another one."

"Well how did they turn back?"

"They asked a family member to slaughter a dog or a bear, and to pour the boiling fat from it down their throat, to melt the ice and turn them back into a human." Lightfoot frowned. "You really want to try it?"

Morty gestured with his free arm, increasingly panicked. "I don't know. If it'll work, I guess? What's the worst that can happen?" He choked on a laugh. Yeah, he'd just gulp down searing oil like some poor bastard storming a castle, what could go wrong.

Lightfoot regarded him dubiously. "In the old stories, the good *wendigo* was transformed back into a human from a monster. If you're going to try it, I think you need to become the monster again first."

"Are you out of your mind? I'm not doing that!" Morty tugged at the cuff on his wrist, fighting panic.

Lightfoot watched him. "Could you not do that? Not that I don't trust you, but..."

A sick laugh bubbled up in Morty's throat. "But you don't trust me. I get that. Are you sure the woman I attacked is dead?" Lightfoot didn't answer, gazing stonily at him. Morty sagged. "I didn't mean to. It's all a blur."

Lightfoot frowned. "I've been thinking about this while you were unconscious. I dug into the old stories, and I was reminded of another local myth. Maybe there's another way. If *wendigook* and *mishibishug* are real, maybe other legends have some truth to them as well."

"Meaning?"

Lightfoot sat down, rubbing his hands, brief clouds coming from his nostrils. Morty again noticed his own body felt no chill at all. Somehow that was more disturbing than the growling hunger in his stomach. "Not too far north of here, there's a spit of land that stretches out into Lake Superior. It's abandoned, just a long scrap of rocky beach and gorse. Not even fishermen bother with it. A century ago, a traveling folklorist talked to one of the tribal elders, a man at least ninety years old by that point, taking down our stories before our culture was subsumed by the white settlers. Before the complete Christianizing of the area." Morty stayed silent, listening. Lightfoot continued after a long, thoughtful pause.

"The elder said that strip of land was cursed. Generations back, when the *Anishinaabeg* first arrived in this place, not everyone was content to fish, hunt, and gather wild rice. Although this was a place of plenty then, not everyone was satisfied. One man in particular was greedy. He always had to have the biggest sturgeon from the lake, more wives to cook his meals and more children to put to work. One day, he was spearfishing along that strip of land, when he speared the tail of *Gitchi-mishibishiw,* the great water panther, the father of all water panthers to come. The monster roared up out of the lake and would have killed the man, except he offered to give the lake monster one of his sons instead.

"*Gitchi-mishibishiw* accepted the bargain, and told the man he was very fortunate, since if he'd had nothing to give, the water spirit's magic was so strong it would have easily overpowered the entire village, destroyed them for the insult." Lightfoot paused to shove his hands into his coat pockets. Morty held onto the water pipe for support, feeling sick. He had the fuzzy impression that the panther-thing which had attacked him sported horns and scales, though to his knowledge, they'd been a few miles from the Bad River and much farther from Lake Superior. If it hadn't jumped at him... He grimaced. That woman would still be alive.

Yeah? What about Sturgensen? No water panther around when you did that, you sick bastard. He paled, clutching the pipe. Lightfoot went on, "The greedy man was intrigued. He asked to learn *Gitchi-mishibishiw's* magic. The monster agreed to teach him, but every lesson would cost him a child." He gave a thin smile. "Sounds bad. Gets worse.

"When the man ran out of his own children, he took some from the village. People were scared of him. He could summon wild game to him, so he never went hungry. He could call down fire from the sky. He had the spirits build him a home right out on that cursed stretch of rocks, and he became known as the shaman of the black lodge." Lightfoot fell silent, thinking. Morty waited impatiently.

"What happened? Did he turn into a *wendigo?*"

Lightfoot shook his head. "No. Eventually the people couldn't stand it any longer. They couldn't bear for all their children to keep going missing.

No one person was brave enough to challenge him. At last, they banded together, took oil and arrows and fire out there to burn that evil place to the ground, preferably with the shaman inside." His voice lowered. "However, when they reached the place, there was nothing. Not a twig, not a pot, nothing to show a lodge had ever been there. Just some bones. Tiny bones. Like a child's."

Morty shivered. "Okay. That's terrifying. What's the point of this story?"

"The people moved away. Nobody goes near it, not even the sturgeon fishermen."

"Cursed land, scary shaman, got it. Maybe the lake monster ate him. Whatever," Morty said, irritated.

Lightfoot shot him an affronted glare. "I can already see you're white. You don't have to prove it to me."

Morty blew out an aggravated breath and leaned forward. "Cut to the chase! How does this help me exactly?"

"I was getting to that. The shaman of the black lodge was supposed to have many special powers, things he'd learned with the magic given to him by *Gitchi-mishibishiw*. Not all of it was evil. In fact, at first, he wasn't suspected of stealing children, because he'd done good things for the village as well, to impress them with his power. Including curing a man of becoming a *wendigo*."

"How?"

"No idea. The story doesn't say." Lightfoot shrugged. "I assumed the tale was about an Ojibwe version of John Wayne Gacey. Gacey was known and liked in his community, performed as a clown for children in the hospital, murdered thirty or more kids in the process. Tonight, I saw two legendary creatures fighting. So did that hunter. Almost makes me wish I'd had a gun too, instead of a shovel. I didn't imagine it, didn't hallucinate it in a sweat lodge. You're as real as the ancient skeleton at the dig site. And if monsters are real—"

"Maybe the shaman was too," Morty whispered. He licked his lips, ignoring the rumble in his stomach. Whether it was hungry or about to hurl up more offal, he didn't want to know. "But this was centuries ago, right? I mean, the Ojibwe settled here in what, the sixteen-hundreds?"

Lightfoot shrugged. "Likely earlier. However, it's not the only time the black lodge has popped up. Others have claimed to see it from time to time. My grandfather saw it once." At Morty's surprise, he nodded. "Yep. Ice fishing. He was tromping around with his dogs, seeking a good spot on the lake where none of the yahoos making a ruckus about Indians getting too many muskies would run into him. There were lynchings, you know."

"Have I mentioned my mother was part Menominee? I spent a couple weeks every summer as a kid on the rez."

"Whatever, blue eyes. At any rate, the old man thought he'd found a great spot. Setting up camp when he noticed his dogs all growling, hackles up, staring at a point of land a few yards away. He saw a lodge there. An old one, birchbark and willow lashings, black as soot. And smoke rising from the center hole. And he swore it hadn't been there a moment before." Lightfoot gazed at one of the snowed-in basement windows. Morty abruptly felt the walls had pushed in closer, as if the snow would bury him down here, and no one would ever know. He shivered.

Lightfoot continued, "My grandfather hightailed it out of there. He knew it was a cursed place. And he said he felt eyes watching him the whole way home. Someone was there, in that lodge."

"You think the shaman could still be alive?"

Lightfoot frowned at him. "You ever grow out your fingernails that long before tonight?"

"That wasn't me."

Lightfoot's gaze was stony. Morty swallowed hard. "Point taken."

"Your choices are pretty much death, boiling oil, or a trek out to the black lodge. If it exists." Lightfoot shrugged. "I'm leaning toward believing. It's been a weird night."

"Yeah," Morty laughed weakly. "That's one word for it."

"Problem is, though I think I know a way to get you out there, I don't think letting you go is a good idea."

"I'm not a monster," Morty argued, yanking at the cuffs again. "I won't hurt anybody. I won't hurt anyone else."

One dark eyebrow raised. "You won't rip open the belly of the next pitiable flesh-bag you meet?"

"No! I didn't mean that. I was angry."

"Bullshit."

Morty glared at him, though his limbs trembled. His stomach gurgled. He felt horribly thirsty. A glance at the glass of water told him it wouldn't satisfy him. With a shudder, he lowered his head to his hands. The metal cuff clanged softly against the pipe. "Then can you get me something to keep me from flying off the handle? Every nerve I have feels as if it's being twanged, like a sadistic country musician is playing me like a steel guitar. I need some insulation from whatever this is."

"Like a medicine bag? For protection?"

"I will take anything at this point, but I was talking about weed."

A surprised laugh rumbled from Lightfoot. "That I can probably procure. What's your name again? Wending?"

"Morty."

"Sam." They stared uncomfortably at each other a long moment.

Sam offered, "I have an idea, but I'll need to go get something from the dig. No guarantees. Frankly, I'm way out of my depth here. If I tell anyone else in the medicine lodge, they're going to immediately choose the death sentence for you. Plenty of people here who still believe in the old ways, no matter how often they attend church or do their shopping over in town instead of harvesting their own crops. If there's a chance you can be cured, I'd rather do that than kill you. Even if you did nearly ruin my dig site."

"Oh, right. Good thing I didn't destroy the *wendigo* skeleton before it stuck me with its filthy antler spikes," Morty snapped. He forcibly calmed himself. "If I can get mellow enough to go meekly along with your plan, how am I getting out to the cursed spit of land? There's, like, two feet of snow on the ground. You have a skidoo?"

"No, but the lake is frozen solid, at least in the shallows. Ever hear of the ice race up here, Book Across the Bay?" Morty shook his head. "Every year, they mark a course across the lake from Washburn to Ashland. Bonfires every kilometer, and ice luminarias showing the route. The snow on the lake is groomed for skis. It's a big charity event; tons of people show up for it. It's run at night. And the course veers reasonably close to that spit of land. You can ski, right? Or walk in snowshoes?"

"You're serious?"

Sam shrugged. "Easiest way to get there, and I know one of the organizers. We could get you in as a last-minute volunteer. It's tomorrow night." He glanced at his watch. "Tonight." He gave a nod at the snow-covered window. "In the dark, volunteer steps out to check for stragglers, who's gonna ask questions?"

This was batshit. "So, what, I just waltz right across a nicely groomed course to the black lodge, and see if the evil shaman is in and willing to cure me?"

"Or I could skin a dog and start boiling the fat."

Morty stared hard at him. "You are inscrutable, you know that? I can't tell if you're kidding."

"One dog versus a *wendigo* going free to slaughter who knows how many people? Bye, Fluffy."

Morty sighed. "You realize this is crazy, right? Fine. If it works, I'll do it. I'll do anything." Before Sam could reply, he amended, "The ice race thing, not the oil of dog, please."

Sam sighed. "Well, first thing, I need to go take an artifact from the dig site; I think a medicine bag we found there may have been designed to protect people from the *wendigo,* or to contain the dark spirit inside you. And you need to get so mellow that you couldn't possibly hurt anyone."

Morty gave him a lopsided grin. "This is the kind of plan I can get with, Chief Broom."

Sam stepped closer, then thought better of it and stepped away again. His glare was so fierce Morty shrank back. Sam raised one finger to him. "No."

Morty winced. "Yeah, that was rude. Sorry."

Sam walked to the stairs across the room, threw one last glare at Morty, and climbed upwards. Morty yelled after him, "I promise I'll make amends for the stupidity of my race if you'll just help me out, okay?" He heard the steps up the creaky wooden stairs pause.

"And not eat anybody," Sam admonished.

"And not eat anybody," Morty agreed. He heard the other man open the cellar door, and then footsteps above.

Morty sank down on the cot. He looked across at his phone. Damn. Darcy. She must've called by now, must have left him texts. Her big concert was over already, if it was already Saturday morning. She'd be home tomorrow. He wanted badly to hear her voice, to tease her and hear her delicate snort. Wanted to feel her cuddled against him. He shuddered. She smelled so delectable. *Assgoblins, I can't go back to her until this is finished.*

Kim would've alerted the authorities by now. Morty had no idea how he would explain any of this to anyone, let alone the rangers or cops. He could claim he was frightened by the gunshot in the parking lot, fled into the woods in blind terror. He was a dumb city joker to the locals anyway, that should work. But describing things to Kim and Darcy?

He took a deep, shuddering breath, checking the cuts his own fingerbones had made to push through his fingertips. At least Wolverine had the satisfaction of messing up assholes who deserved it. These weren't superpowers. This is what turning into the monster of the story felt like.

Staring at the cuts, at last he felt cold. Bone-chilled, and deeply, crushingly afraid.

20

The local law was about as helpful as a busted snowshoe, and insisted the man who'd just lost his ladyfriend was in shock, babbling about deer skulls with glowing eyes and catamounts with scales and what-have-you.

Quell was saddened to hear the woman the elk-thing had yanked from the truck had died before the ambulance arrived. When the sheriff had established that someone else was missing, Quell had joined in the hunt for the missing tourist. Sheriff's deputies and a handful of local men had beat the bushes and searched for tracks, working by flashlight in the increasingly blustery wind. Blowing snow quickly obliterated any trail. One of the deputies remained behind with the missing fella's friend, the Asian kid. Hettie's stayed open late just for them and the search party. When Quell returned from the unfruitful hunt, only Hettie herself remained, distraught that a wild animal attack in her parking lot might hurt business.

The deputies would search again once it was daylight. The tourist's friend had been sent home. Quell was beat. While he'd hoped to find any sign of the missing man, maybe a blood trail if he'd been carried off by either frightful beast, he'd also searched for any small sign of the one he'd winged, the lynx-thing with scales and a long tail like a whip. Checking for bent twigs was nigh impossible in the wind, and no tracks remained.

Sighing heavily, he eased his sore frame into a motel bed. He'd try again in the morning, if he could get up again. As he pulled his jeans off, something plunked to the floor. With a tired groan, Quell fetched it: his cell phone. They made the danged things unwieldy and bigger every year. He missed those old flip-phones. He had to admit, though, being able to pull up research with the touch of a finger was mighty handy sometimes. If he was anywhere he could get a signal. Even so, he wasn't sure it was a good thing the places without cell service up in the Northwoods shrank every year. He checked the screen again and reread the text from the fella that was supposed to meet him this afternoon, the one who'd asked about werewolves. Felt like a week ago. He realized in all the commotion he never had located the guy, or even learned his name.

.

He considered calling the number. It was going on five in the morning. Guy probably left when things went all crazy, anyway. Who knows, maybe he'd seen those monsters too.

Hope rising at this thought, Quell pressed call on the unknown number which had texted him hours ago. The line rang once, then immediately went to voicemail. "Hey, it's me, I'm busy carrying out my nefarious plan to conquer the universe. Or at least the bookstore. Speak at the beep." The voice was scratchy and full of cheerful confidence. Sounded like some college Joe who never had to face down a 'squatch in full butt-kicking mode. Quell was weary-brained and unprepared for the message tone.

"Uh, hiya there, this is Garwood Quell. We were supposed to meet at Hettie's this afternoon, but I never did find ya. If you were there at around four-thirty, and you saw anything, give me a call 'cause I'd love to talk to ya," Quell said, and hung up.

Maybe the whole thing was a prank. He stared at the number on the screen. A reverse search for the phone number, with fumbling fingers and muttered expletives, turned up no result, though it did disclose where the area code originated: Appleton. All righty then. If he didn't hear back from him, Quell would go ask at the resort, see if anyone there saw or heard anything about the attack last week. Heck, maybe play county agent and ask at the oil company site. One of those monsters was responsible for biting that poor fella's foot off. He thought of the snarl the lynx-thing had given him before it bounded into the trees, and the deer-headed thing's fangs across an innocent woman's throat. He shivered. Whatever their fight was about, the world was best rid of them both.

Sighing, he let the phone drop, and curled under the thick blankets, his bones aching even with the rattling room heater turned up full bore. "Get right on that," he mumbled. "Soon's I get up."

His phone remained on the last text of his mysterious Appleton informant for a few more seconds. Then the screen powered down, and all Quell saw was white snow blowing in his dreams.

21

By the third kilometer, Morty was winded. This was stupid. Smart would be to come back in the daylight on a snowmobile. Granted, it might draw more attention.

He staggered to an ungainly halt a few feet from the bonfire. A volunteer greeted him and pushed a cup of hot cocoa into his mittened hands. Morty nodded thanks, and tried to sip it, burning the tip of his tongue. Wind whistled through the wooden bonfire frame, making the flames dance wildly, but the fire proved too large to extinguish. Morty panted, blinking at the orange light. He turned and looked back; the tent on the shore in Washburn shone like a welcoming beacon.

Though the snow-covered ice to the north faded into darkness not far past the bonfire, glimmering candles in luminarias of ice marked the route gently curving behind and ahead for those willing to push on across the frozen bay. Clusters of people moved past in the moonlight, neon plastic glow-rings around their wrists or on their hats, the joyful murmur of families and friends audible despite the erratic gusts of wind. Morty had already been passed by parents on skis pulling their toddlers on sleds, the kids bundled up like fat little snowmen in multiple scarves and hats. The skiers determined to make a race of this were far ahead by now, probably near the finish line in Ashland. It did all seem festive and fun, if one was willing to call anything done in single-digit temperatures fun.

The clothing Sam had loaned him fit, more or less; though he was overheating in the heavy, oversized coat. The wind against his exposed cheeks hurt. He wasn't sure whether his skin feeling cold was a good thing, or whether it just meant he was edging into frostbite. This vacillating between fever and chills really sucked.

Shielding his eyes from the nearby flames, he peered ahead at the bonfires marking the next major checkpoints. The route curved south; if he went through with this foolishness, he'd have to veer east instead. He hadn't really thought about an excuse for his deviation from the course. He hoped the volunteer bib draped over his coat would serve to discourage any questions. He patted his chest, reassuring himself the worn, dry leather medicine bag Sam had brought him was snug against his skin. It was ancient, filled with who knew what; Sam had refused to tell him. Morty hoped it would keep the ravenous thing inside him quiet. Especially since his earlier toking had worn off. Had to admit, though, it had been potent stuff. Stoned, Morty had been grateful Sam did all the talking at the volunteer tent. Less thrilled the archaeologist hadn't come with him on this fool's venture.

"Beautiful, is it not?" A woman asked, mere inches from him. Morty jerked back, startled at the sudden closeness of another person. He barely avoided spilling the scalding cocoa on her. The woman, dressed in a long, fur-trimmed coat, turned dark, thoughtful eyes to him in the firelight, and smiled.

"Yeah. Sure. If you don't mind even the snow thinking it's too cold to stick around," Morty answered, recovering. He motioned at the light snow flurries as they were whisked away by another windy gust.

The woman chuckled, a throaty sound. Unlike most of the participants he'd seen, she hadn't covered up completely; a noble nose and deeply curved lips accentuated her high cheekbones. With the furred hood framing her face, he couldn't decide if she resembled more a beautiful Ojibwe maiden or a haughty Quebecois. When she spoke again, her accent pointed his impression toward the latter end of that spectrum. "Everyone else looks at the pretty snow lights or the stars. Why do you stare off at the darkness?"

"Uhm." Flustered by her steady gaze, Morty gestured around him. "Well. You know, first time, just kind of taking it all in."

She nodded. "It is quite the spectacle. I join in every year."

"By yourself?" Morty wanted to take back the words the second they left his mouth. He should be out here with Darcy. This was exactly the kind of thing she'd love. The thought brought a pang of worry. While Sam had returned his phone to him, Morty hadn't quite dared to reply to her texts. He didn't know what he'd say to her if this failed. Hell, he didn't know how to spin this if it did work and he returned home free of this curse. It took conscious effort to drag himself back to his present company. The woman watched his face closely, and Morty tried to smile at her.

The woman made a dismissive gesture: *comme çi, comme ça.* "Not always alone. What about you? It can be a tiring walk if you have no companion to share stories with on the way."

"I'm a volunteer. Have to keep the lights lit," he said. A smile teased the corners of her lush mouth, so he foundered onward. "Someone has to make sure the ice is safe, watch out for stragglers."

"Of course," she agreed pleasantly. "There will always be one or two who lag behind. It is a long course, and very cold." This woman didn't seem perturbed by the vicious chill wind. Her gloves were slender and graceful, unlike the rounded mitts Morty wore. His gaze flicked down her form, more to get away from those direct eyes than anything else, and he noted the way her coat flared over her hips and how her boots showed off the curves of her calves. Jerking his eyes upward again, Morty nodded reflexively.

"Yep, sure is cold. A cold night." No one else had passed while they stood there; the sponsors of this checkpoint stood on the far side of the bonfire, barely visible as they watched the next group approaching. He peered along the rest of the course. The family who'd paced just ahead of him so far had vanished, having elected not to stop at this comfort station, pushing on to the next. It was do or die time; he might not get a better chance to veer east. He needed to ditch this strange lady.

He squinted past the lights, out across the ice. Swirling snakes of wind-blown snow twisted off into the darkness. If there were any lights on the shore to the east, they were too far for him to see. Walking into the dark, across a potentially treacherous snow-covered, frozen lake, just because there might be a legendary shaman who could help didn't seem like such a fantastic idea now he'd sobered up.

He sipped his cooling cocoa, hoping the woman would sense he wasn't interested and move on. Instead, she simply watched him. Annoyed, he pointed at the people shuffling from foot to foot on the other side of the fire. "They have hot cocoa, if you want some."

"How very nice." She didn't look in their direction.

Morty thought about turning back. Or just staying here and claiming a sprained ankle, waiting by this nice hot fire with watery cocoa until the lag team swung by on their skidoo to give him a lift to Ashland. It would make much more sense than this. He reflexively touched the spot on his coat where the medicine bag rested, pressing it gently against his skin. The woman's gaze dropped to follow his movement, then met his eyes again. Her smile had faded. Morty sighed and grinned weakly. "Umm. Have a great night. I need to inspect the ice." Swiftly he stepped over the boundary between the lighted trail and the pristine snow, forcing his legs into a faster gait than his skill with snowshoes could really manage. He hoped the woman wouldn't mention his odd behavior to the checkpoint hosts, or to any of the actual course volunteers.

His breath came hard, every inhalation drawing chill air into his throat and lungs. His knees ached with the effort of hiking step after step. The snow was growing deeper the farther away from the course he went. Nobody had packed down the trail out here. Each snowshoe crunched into the dry snow so loudly he wondered why he hadn't drawn the attention of everyone on the lake by now. He paused, panting, looking back, surprised at how much distance he'd covered. The flickering bonfire appeared the size of a lantern now. His solitary tracks pointed the way back to relative warmth and safety. He felt for the bag against his chest again, trying to convince himself to turn back, to give up this ridiculous quest.

He remembered the flash of reflection in the mirror, the elk skull glaring back at him, long teeth stained red. Remembered coming out of the nightmare to feel blood spurting onto him, hearing screaming, heat washing down his jaw and chest. How all of it—Sturgensen's death, vomiting up bones and hair, awakening on his icy porch covered in blood—had suddenly clicked into terrible clarity.

And then Sam had clobbered him with a shovel. It still ached, especially now the weed had worn off. Morty winced, reflexively rubbing his head, forgetting he was clutching a half-full cup of cocoa in the other hand. It spilled onto his shoes and pants. He threw the cup into the darkness. "Goddammit!" Now he could add littering to his list of crimes. A helpless chuckle wheezed in his throat. At least chocolate stains weren't as bad as bloodstains.

He fought the urge to sink down right there. Outside the racecourse, with snow blowing in to cover his tracks, they might not find him until daylight. Or next spring. If anyone thought to check. No one knew where he was except Sam. Behind, lights twinkled in the darkness. Above, the moon provided just enough illumination to distinguish the surface of the frozen lake from the shoreline if he squinted hard. Ahead, darkness and the rocky coast which had claimed more than one ship's final moments. And, possibly, a black lodge where a shaman's ghost might know a cure for his condition.

Morty swallowed what little spit he could muster and braced his feet against another fierce blast of Lake Superior wind. He remembered his flashlight; they were forbidden in the race, though he figured he was far enough away by now to safely use it without attracting attention. When he switched it on, something dark fluttered away from his right side.

He turned, nearly going ass-up in the unwieldy snowshoes. Wildly he swung the light around, seeing only more snow, swirling flakes, and his own tracks. He'd just screwed up his night vision. Of course he'd see shadows that weren't there until his eyes adjusted. He willed his pounding heart to slow. Having a heart attack out here would just be the funniest ending to this trip. He could envision the tabloid story already: *Man Becomes Monster, Dies Spooking Himself on a Lonely Arctic Tundra.*

The woman was standing a foot in front of him.

Morty's shriek was choked by the wind. The snowdrift rose to meet him as he fell backwards; he flailed around for a moment, then froze at the sight of a gloved hand extended down to him. He blinked and, realizing he was shining the flashlight straight into her face when she raised a hand to shield her eyes, he tilted the light down. His right ankle hurt; how ironic an actual sprain would be after all this. "Christ, you scared the hell out of me."

The woman smiled, continuing to hold out her hand. Morty waved her off, struggling to stand on his own, and after a few tries managed to get up. The unceasing wind didn't seem to distract her. Morty brushed the errant snow from his face disgustedly. He looked back uneasily, then glanced down, getting a nagging feeling something wasn't right. "Hey, you're not supposed to be out here," he said, trying to sound authoritative.

She merely gazed at him, appearing mildly amused. Morty took a deep breath and pointed at the distant fires. "Miss, I'm going to have to ask you to go back to the trail. It's not safe out here."

She regarded him steadily for too many seconds. Just when he was about to express his growing irritation at her presence, she spoke. "Are you looking for stragglers?"

"Yes. Yes, I am. And we don't need any more people to wander off, so please—"

"You are hunting in my territory," she said, her tone so firm and brusque Morty felt himself gaping at her.

"I what?"

The woman stepped closer, slowly, her eyes locked on Morty's. She was not smiling. "I have hunted here far too long to give any prey up to a *nouveau manitou* who thinks he can just tromp in and take what he pleases. Get out."

She took another step. Morty shuffled backward, noticing her feet made no sound in the snow. Then it registered she was standing on the surface of the snow. In boots. Not sinking in. And not making any tracks, as though she were snow Jesus.

Hellacious assferrets. Could there not be another fucked up thing in my life right now.

He pointed over her shoulder. "Hey look, rescue patrol!"

The woman sniffed contemptuously, her eyes flicking to the side for an instant. Morty took advantage of her distraction, shoving her roughly, and ran. Pumping his legs as hard as he could, he chugged over the snow in ungainly *flumphing* leaps. He braked, arms windmilling to keep from tumbling over, when she bounded in front of him. "I see you need manners beaten into you, like all men," she hissed, her shoulders broadening, the fur trim of her coat fluffing outward like a deranged kitten's hackles rising.

Morty struggled to regain his momentum in a different direction. She cut him off. Her voice deepened, speaking a language he didn't know, her face turning feline, her body becoming sinuous and scaled. She raised a furred paw, sharp claws unsheathed, to his face. In desperation, Morty lunged straight at her and head-butted her stomach.

She skittered backward with a snarl; Morty saw a long, lashing tail and huge, dark paws dancing across the snow. He dodged and tried to run.

He didn't make four steps before tripping over his own snowshoe, going down with a cry of terror. He rolled clumsily onto his back to face the snarling monster. He kicked helplessly at the deep snow. She lunged toward him on all fours, whiskers bristling and ears back, claws stretching toward him. Morty screamed the only thing he could think of, "I don't want your prey!"

To his shock, she froze. For an instant they stared at each other. The wind brought tears to Morty's eyes, chilling his exposed cheeks. Slowly, like a clock spring coiling, she eased into a crouch. Though shorter than he was, especially in this scaly panther form, she was built far more powerfully. Her claws withdrew into furry black paws, and she stared unblinking at him through narrowed pupils. "Why will you not fight?" she growled.

Morty tried to regain a little strength in his voice, or at least to sound less terrified. "Because I don't want your damned hunting grounds. I don't know what those are or where they are. I don't even know what you are!"

She continued to stare for several seconds. She blinked. A gurgling growl arose from her muscular throat until she burst into a deep laugh. Morty's breath hitched. Great. The last sound he'd hear would be a furious monster laughing at him. The laugh continued, increasing in volume until the whole lake must've heard it.

Her face was an inch from his before he could react, the echoes against the near shore dying away. Her voice was a low rumble. "*Windigo,* go back to your little settlement and eat your neighbors. Stay away from my river and stay out of my forests." Her breath smelled of cocoa, with an undertone of iron. She sniffed at him, then just as abruptly withdrew. "What a shame. I have never met a *windigo* before. I had hoped for a little fun. There is too much white man in you."

"You're not going to kill me? I mean. Right. Of course not. Because you know I'm a big nasty *wendigo.*"

She blinked again. Suddenly she was just a woman again, in a fur-trimmed coat and boots. And she was laughing at him, the sound deep and musical. Morty sat waist-deep in snow, watching her hold her hand to her chest the longer she laughed. His heart slowed its thudding, the fear gradually giving way to the realization his ass was freezing and his ankle had gone numb. *Now my body decides cold is a bad thing. Great timing, flesh.*

When her laughter died to giggles, he began to feel irritated. When she stumbled forward weakly and gripped his shoulder to keep her balance as she wiped tears of mirth from her eyes, he angrily brushed her hand away and flailed about until he could halfway stand. She turned away, bent over, gasping as she recovered from the giggle fit. "Yeah, this is hilarious," he snapped. "Thanks so much." She looked up at him sharply. *Oh shit.*

Then she dissolved into whooping, helpless laughter again.

"Screw this," Morty growled. He cast about with his flashlight, trying to see more than five feet in any direction. Squinting, he could see the faint lights of the bonfires marking the Book Across the Bay event, off to his left. West. Escaping this crazy, heckling woman wasn't an option. He felt sure if he retreated now, he might make it almost there before she changed her mind and ate him anyway. He rubbed the spot over his breastbone, feeling the medicine bag pressing into his flesh. He could take it off. His tongue squirmed; he thought he could still taste blood, even after the mouthwash at Sam's place and the cocoa. She continued snorting laughter.

Morty scowled. "I did not. Come all the way out here. In the middle—of the night—just to be laughed at by a, by a—"

"*Mishibizhu,*" the woman said between hiccupping laughs. She raised her face to the sky and he heard her take a slow, deep breath. Straightening, she returned her gaze to Morty, grinning at him. Her teeth appeared very sharp. "What about this, *windigo.* I saw a child wandering away from the line earlier. Shall we go search for it? If you beat me to it, I will let you eat it."

Morty recoiled. "Eat a kid? What the hell is wrong with you?" He wasn't completely sure he'd even seen a serpent-panther-thing chasing him. Now she was talking about kid food. The whole night was falling into something far beyond surreal.

She tilted her head to one side, teeth hidden behind full lips again. "I would ask the same. Why are you not changing? I know that was you back at the roadhouse."

This was the same monster that triggered his change. The woman in the parking lot would still be alive if this feral creature hadn't attacked him. Anger rose, and a strange prickling against his chest surprised him. He put a hand to his breastbone, feeling the lump of the medicine bag. Morty attempted to wrestle his panic under control; he needed to get his emotions in check. *Whatever else happens, I have to stop this, I don't want to be that, Christ, I don't want to be that thing again.*

"I'll make you a deal," he said, summoning up his best bluffing skills. He wanted nothing more than to dig into a snowbank to hide, but he knew this woman wouldn't let him be. "I'll leave your hunting ground if you'll show me where the black lodge is."

"The lodge of shadows?" She sounded surprised. "Why?"

"Reasons," he said. He held his ground as she took a dainty step closer. She viewed him as a monster, too. He tried to project more confidence. He was fierce. He was fearless. Claws and teeth and blood dripping down his chin. Morty checked his instinctive wince. No. Just a monster looking for the black lodge, no big deal, nothing to see here. He forced a smile. "So, hey, help a fellow freak out."

She chuckled. Her gaze roved over his face, and he had the uncomfortable impression she was reevaluating his entire *windigo* status. "Why is a savage creature not rejoicing at the chance to fight me, and why search for a place that does not exist?"

His stomach dropped. "The black lodge doesn't exist?"

She sucked on her lower lip. "Legends say there used to be such a place." His breath caught in hope. "Maybe five hundred years ago." His guts twisted.

"I have to find it," Morty argued. "It has to be there. Evil shaman, lots of power, knows all about curses?"

"Curses?" Enlightenment dawned in dark eyes. "You want to not be *windigo.*"

"No, I do not. I mean I want to not. I mean—" Frustrated, he pointed the flashlight beam toward the coal-black distant shore. "I want to stop whatever is happening to me before I kill someone else, so yes, either eat me, or point me in the direction of the black lodge and then fuck off!"

She eased back on her heels, studying him. When she didn't respond, Morty wanted to tear his hair out. "Gaaahh! Fine. Whatever." He lifted a foot over the snow, crunched it down, lifted the likely sprained one, and trudged forward. Though the snow shifted underfoot, the wide webbed shoes supported him, and he didn't sink as badly as when he'd run. *Fuck this. Fuck my life. Fuck this ridiculous nightmare and fuck monsters in general and this bitch in particular.*

He'd find this mythical lodge and barter his entire comic collection if he had to. As long as there was a shaman who could keep him from turning into a cannibal, he'd barter damn near anything.

He kept his eyes on the treacherous whiteness just in front of his feet, not trusting the thickness of the ice this far away from the established trail. Maybe it would be best, though, to just sink under. He'd probably freeze before he drowned. Nobody else would be in danger. Kim would stop looking, eventually. Darcy might think he'd left her. That brought a pang of guilt; he shoved it aside. If this was the weirdest wild goose chase ever, at least it was cold enough if he just stopped, he wouldn't feel much at all. He glanced up at a swirl of snow. The woman stood right in front of him again.

This time, he didn't fall on his ass. Barely. "Stop doing that!"

That brought a smile. "You know you are *très ridicile.*"

Morty's chest heaved. "Still not helpful."

"You will never find it that way."

He leaned toward her, too exasperated to be afraid. "Then how exactly should I go about it? Do please illuminate me, ice princess."

"Ice princess—oh, I like that."

"I have had more than enough of this insanity for one night. If you know how to find a magic lodge that isn't there anymore, tell me."

"It might be more amusing not to," she purred. Fury shot through Morty. He swung at her; she ducked easily. *"Hii!* Now this is more fun, windigo."

He advanced on her, fists clenched. "It's your fault I killed that woman at the roadhouse. That one is on you. And I. Am. Done. With. You."

With a delighted laugh, she darted aside, swirling past him in a flash of scales as her form shifted again. Morty turned; she slapped his back hard with a tiger-sized paw. He stumbled, trying to grab her. With the flick of her tail she slipped around him. "You have something wrong with you," she said. He could swear she was purring, but it didn't sound comforting to him.

"Really, I hadn't noticed," he shouted, trying to reorient using her voice. She moved impossibly fast in the darkness.

"Something is on you," she continued in a throaty rumble, evading his half-hearted grab. "It stinks of *Gitchi-manitou*. Keeping you tied, like a hobbled horse."

He put a protective hand over his chest, giving up on trying to touch her at all. "And your point is?"

She was a slim, dark-eyed woman again, pacing around him, commanding his gaze with her own. "Could you at least stop doing that?" he groaned.

"They say the lodge of shadows draws bad medicine to it like a whirlpool draws ships," she said, walking to stand behind him. Morty felt his shoulders hitching up, the hairs on the back of his neck prickling under his scarf and hat. He fought the urge to turn around; all cats enjoyed playing with their prey and she didn't seem to be any exception. "Only dark spirits may cross through the veil to find it. Not even the *mishibizhug* can see it, though it is right on the shore." He felt her fingers touching his shoulder, and grimaced. Her whisper on his cheek made him shiver. "Do you really want to see the black lodge, *windigo*? Do you really want to meet the madman who sits by the black fire, and ask him to help you?"

Morty turned, expecting to see those terrible teeth again. She was petite and serious-eyed, no fangs in sight. The wind ruffled the fur at her collar. He nodded, glaring at her. "Yes. Yes, I do. It's the only way I can stop this."

She studied his face, her expression serious. He was about to explain to her all that had happened; the burial mound, the winter-god depicted there, the dreams. Everything. But in the next instant she slipped one slender hand inside his coat and jerked the medicine bag from his neck.

"Wha—hey!" He lunged at her; she danced back, the crisp snow unbroken under her feet. "Gimme that!"

"The only way to find the black lodge," she growled, "is to let it drag you in." She flung the bag hard. It arced out of sight. Morty gaped at her, horrified.

She slapped him.

Fire rippled across his face; he staggered back. Before he could recover so much as a step, she changed again and her claws slashed at his chest, ripping through his coat and shirt. He shrieked when she whipped behind him and tore through his coat and skin, from his neck to his buttocks.

He attempted a swipe at her; she ducked it gracefully, her claws screeching on the ice beneath the snow as she braked and reversed course. Through the pain, he finally understood the purpose of her taunting, and recoiled. She swept his feet with a whip of her tail, planting him on his ass again. She bounded backward, slowing her momentum with another ear-burning screech of claws on ice. "Stop it," he howled, hearing his voice deepen, roughen. "No no *no!*"

"You want to find the black lodge?" she hissed, darting in to smack his face again. Morty snarled, and she quickly leapt out of reach. "You think the shaman who never dies would waste his time on you? A silly ass of a white man too afraid of his shadow to claim this gift?" Another slap, claws drawing blood across his nose, scampering out of the way when he reacted with a fruitless kick.

"It's not a gift!" Morty shouted, struggling to his feet. His bones hurt. His head hurt. He'd lost his mittens somehow. His fingers curled into bony claws, stretching, sharpening. "No!" His shout turned into an angry, painful groan; he felt his spine cracking, stretching. She was on his left, his right, darting and slashing, a whirlwind of dark fur and gleaming scales. He threw the flashlight at her; it bounced off her flank. He leapt at her, teeth bared, and his long, bony nose met her strong paw. His head rocked back, disorienting flashes shooting through his skull.

"You really want to get to the black lodge, you imbecile?" she roared, her face next to his.

Rage burst free. "*Yaaaassss!*" he roared back, grabbing her by the neck, squeezing.

She cried out, twisting away, and slashed at the ice between them. "Then go to it!"

Too late, Morty heard the cracks of ice giving way. "No! Wait!"

Darkness sucked him down, pulling him and his fury to its depths.

22

Crackle. Rustle.

Morty ached everywhere. Except for where he was numb. Kind of hard to tell which was which.

Crackle crack. Plunk.

The ice, the ice was closing over him! His limbs moved sluggishly, weighted down, warm and heavy and—

Wait. Warm?

He blinked, shadows slowly coming into focus, dancing around him. He blinked again. They brightened into dim, warmly lit surroundings. A log crackled, sap popped, and the wood on the fire resettled with a crunch. Morty's gaze traveled up to rough-hewn beams. Eyes gleamed back at him and he froze, then realized he was staring at a mounted deer head on the wall. It looked old and a bit mangy.

Tall bookshelves ranged on either side of the trophy, holding tattered paperbacks and dusty cloth-bound volumes. The only title he could read from here was *LAKE SUPERIOR FISHING TRICKS vol III.* One of those asinine rubber singing-fish bass trophies was propped on a bookshelf.

He tried to move again, his fingers tingling. He rubbed the hem of an old wool blanket between thumb and forefinger. It was draped over him from toe to chin. That explained the warm heavy thing on his arms, at least. He moved his jaw. It took a moment to force any sound out. "What, what is this?" Coughing seized his lungs. His skin prickled, ice and warmth fighting across his flesh.

"Ah, you're awake." An elderly man stood from a chair by the hearth, and hobbled closer to the sofa where Morty sprawled. "Well heck. Worried you wouldn't make it the night there, son." He beamed at Morty, laugh lines crinkling around his eyes. A neat white beard framed his face, and his accent was one hundred percent Upper Midwestern.

Morty looked around, eyes adjusting to the illumination of the fire. The log cabin walls appeared old and patched, but the room was warm. Buffalo-check curtains were drawn over the small windows. "What happened?" Morty croaked. He carefully pulled his hands from under the blanket. His knuckles were bruised, but they were hands now, not claws. Hands good. Claws bad.

Coughing wracked his body again. When he was able to uncurl a bit, the old man held out a steaming stoneware mug. Morty accepted it; chicken broth wafted to his nostrils. He sat up with a groan.

"Just take it easy there," the old man advised. He limped a few steps to the chair and dragged it closer to the sofa before settling into it. His slow movements bespoke one well acquainted with the aches of arthritis. "What happened, is you were danged lucky we found you, ol' Naabesim and me." He stretched out one hand, and a large black lab pushed his furry head under it. The man scratched the dog's head, watching Morty cautiously sip the broth. "Jeez, what a night, huh. What were ya doin' so far out on the ice?"

Confused images of claws raking at him and a *femme fatale* swirled in Morty's head. Feelings of rage, the sound of breaking ice. It all seemed unreal now. A cuckoo clock ticked quietly next to a doorway, through which Morty could see a narrow cot. Coiled rag rugs in faded colors covered most of the floor. The stones of the chimney went up through the roof, solid and firm. Though older, this place was a comfortable haven on a midwinter's night. Morty shook his head dumbly. "Not really sure."

The old man chuckled. His dog gave one low woof and lay down next to the chair. "You part a' that danged fool ice race across the bay? What a sight. Never been. I can see the lights from the jetty." He sighed. "Every year, seems like, some idiot drinks a few too many and veers off course somehow. Can't see how they manage it, with all them bonfires and candles, but they do." He cast an appraising look at Morty.

Morty only shook his head again. Impossible to explain anything that had happened. If any of it had. What if he'd slipped on the ice, hit his head, and the woman-panther-snake-thing was just his brain starving for oxygen? He drew the blanket more closely around himself, only then noticing he was nude beneath it. "What—where did my clothes —"

"Found ya in the water," the old man said. He nodded toward the fireplace. "Got your clothes drying out there. Luckily, I think you were only in for a couple seconds. Was takin' this old feller for a walk, and we heard the ice crack. Naab's faster'n I am. He pulled you out. I hollered for help; I guess they couldn't hear me over there. Thought you might be a goner already. I got ya on the sledge and pulled ya home fast as I could."

"Thank you," Morty said. His chest ached. Hypothermia would explain the numbness and cold fire rippling over him in waves. Hypothermia and craziness. He shivered. He must've walked away from the course, out over the frozen lake; he couldn't recall how far he'd traveled before the ice cracked. A swirl of darkness passed over his eyes as he remembered sinking into the blackness. He glanced at the dog, which appeared content to sleep beside the fire. "How long?"

"Oh, about four hours ago," the old man replied. "Thought about trying to make it over to Route Two, to the gas station maybe; I don't keep a phone here. You were still breathing, if just barely, so figured I oughta get you warm first." He gestured at the mug in Morty's hands. "Warm yourself up from the inside, that's the best way."

Morty nodded. No kid grew up in Wisconsin without learning about hypothermia, and ways to alleviate it. He drank; the broth was salty and rich. "Thank you," he repeated. The old man smiled. "Where am I?"

"Not too far from Ashland. You very nearly made it to the shore, but there's a shipping channel out there, deeper water. Sometimes it don't freeze as solid as the rest of the bay."

Morty nodded again, his breathing calmed. He'd be lucky not to catch pneumonia. "I'm very grateful to you, Mr.—"

"Just call me Winn, son. Glad we found you." He chuckled. "Bet ya won't go drinking and ice-walking ever again, hey?"

"I wasn't drunk," Morty protested, then realized he had no good explanation for why he was so far off course.

"Oh?"

"I was looking for something."

Winn laughed. "Son, there's nothing out here but rocks and ice. What exactly were you trying to find?"

Morty felt a flush rising up his neck. "An old legend," he muttered, and gulped more of the hot broth, unable to meet the old man's curious gaze.

"Really? Oh, you mean the giant sturgeon? Ha! I've lived here years and years and fished that lake more times than you've gone to the store for beer, I bet; and in all that time I've never caught so much as a whisker of that fish."

Morty forced a chuckle. "Yeah, well. Everybody wants to chase a wild goose once in a while. Or a wild fish."

"Except when it puts you in danger of becoming a popsicle."

"Except then," Morty agreed. He finished the broth. Winn leaned forward to take the cup. Morty shivered as he gave it back.

"You need more, I think," the old man observed. "Let me just stoke up the fire, and I'll fetch you another cup." He stood slowly, his back bowed.

Morty felt deeply guilty. He hasn't been thinking straight, coming out here looking for a stupid myth in the middle of the night. He took in a painful breath. He wondered whether he'd swallowed any lake water before he'd been dragged out. He pressed a hand to his chest, feeling a wheeze in his lungs. Frowning, he felt around his bare skin, unsure if he was missing something. Shadows played on the wall as Winn stirred the fire and plunked a fresh log atop the pile. "What's your name, son?"

"Morty." He traced the unbroken skin over his ribs. No claw-marks. Feeling like an idiot, he sank back into the lumpy cushions of the old sofa.

"Short for Mortimer?"

"Short for Mordecai." Morty smiled ruefully. "My parents thought it was a wonderful name."

Winn chortled, using a poker to rearrange the logs. "I think I knew a Mordecai once. You any relation to the Von Snells?"

"No sir. The Wendings."

"Mordecai Wending," Winn mused, and Morty coughed a laugh.

"Yeah, it's distinctive, I guess. I'm sure it's more interesting than I am." He absently rubbed his chest under the blanket, then paused in confusion. Although the light from the fireplace cast the room in a comforting glow, the flames themselves appeared dark, glowing tongues of black velvet dancing over the logs. The old man scratched his beard thoughtfully, gazing into the fire. Noticing Morty's stare, Winn smiled.

"Oh, I wouldn't say that. You certainly caught my interest, Mordecai Wending."

Morty tried to speak; no words would come. He tried to move; his body was frozen in place. Winn ambled over, his smile fading, face thoughtful. "What do you think, Naabesim? We haven't had a guest in so very, very long." Morty fought to blink, to step away. His muscles ignored his impulses. A fierce pain shot through his skull, and he cringed inwardly.

Winn's eyes narrowed, then suddenly brightened. "Well gosh and buckets." He reached down and grasped the antlers suddenly growing from Morty's skull. Morty keened, dragged to his feet by the old man who now displayed startling strength. "Well I'll be danged, a ween-dee-go!"

Morty choked, his skull splitting. Winn flicked his free hand at Morty's windpipe, and Morty sucked in a precious breath of air. "Stop!"

Winn regarded him with the pleased bemusement of an angler who'd thought he hooked a tin can and instead pulled forth a trout. "Why, I don't believe we've had a *windigo* around here in, gosh, when was that, Naab, eighteen ninety-three?" The dog heaved itself to a sitting position, blowing out an annoyed-sounding woof. Morty looked at the dog's coal-black eyes and sooty fur; its outline wavered like fog.

"I'm not a *wendigo*," Morty gasped. He couldn't move. The antlers slowly spread upward like winding thorns, agony shooting down his spine and into his pelvis.

"Well, not quite yet," Winn agreed. "Gettin' there." He chuckled again. "No wonder the lodge pulled you in!"

Morty gritted his teeth. "Stop. That hurts."

"Change always hurts," Winn said. He lowered his hand, guiding Morty back down to the sofa. Winn let go of the antler and dropped with a grunt into his chair, then leaned back and simply studied him. Morty shivered, grasping the bony protrusions as if he could push them back inside. His breath came in staggering hitches. Though the old man seemed to have released his hold, figuratively and literally, Morty didn't believe there was any chance he could overpower Winn.

"You're not just a *windigo*, though," Winn said. He absently scratched the hell-hound's head. The creature grumbled as old dogs do and settled back to the floor. Its outline shifted so much it floated through the floor and the chair. "There's an old, old *manitou* on you. Some sorta spirit. Older than me, even."

"Hard to believe, if you're as ancient as the legend says," Morty said, his voice harsh. His bones stretched, his spine twisted. He bit back another groan.

Winn frowned. "You didn't just get drawn in by the lodge," he mused. "You came hunting for me, didn't you, son? Now why in the heck would ya want to do that?"

"I heard," Morty strained to keep his voice level, though carrying on a calm conversation in present circumstances felt beyond bizarre. "I heard there was a shaman in the black lodge who might know how to get this evil out of me."

"Get it out?" Winn chortled, settling back in the tall armchair. "Why would I? Nothing embodies pure, primal hunger better than a *windigo,* and they're plenty rare these days. Heck, I'm fairly sure we haven't seen one in these parts for well over a hundred years, and that last one, lemme tell ya, she wasn't what I'd call really enthused about the job."

"Can't imagine why," Morty said through gritted teeth. His chest hurt; he could feel the dark spirit inside yearning to burst through his skin. His head swam; he struggled to remain conscious.

Winn studied him a moment in silence, then sighed. "Well, now. What would you give me in exchange for lifting that dread *manitou* off you?"

"Anything!"

"Oh, now. We both know that's not true." The old man's eyes twinkled. "Would you give up your soul? Would you give me someone else's soul? Your child? Your true love?"

"Pretty sure I don't have any of those things," Morty muttered, and Winn guffawed.

"Would you pass it on to another, then? You go free, and a *windigo* roams the Northwoods again."

Morty groaned, clutching the blanket tightly in bony claws. Sure, just pass this on to someone else. Someone stronger. *I can't do this. I can't* ***be*** *this.*

He shook his head. "No," he groaned.

"Well, what then?"

"I don't want to be a cannibal," Morty snarled. Winn raised an eyebrow. Feeling broken, Morty sagged, wrapping his arms around his thinning frame, wracked with shivers. His fingers felt hideous against his bare skin, claws growing longer as his flesh sucked against his ribcage. "I'll do anything else you want if you'll just get this thing out of me. Please. Please make it stop."

"Hmm." Winn sighed again and sucked on his pipe stem. "Well, son, I've mellowed a great deal over the years. Back in my prime, I would've set up all sorts a' quests for you to endure, beasts to fight, trophies to bring back to me. Oh yah, it would've been quite the adventure." He grinned, then sighed softly. "The sad truth is, I'm tired. Making you come back here and bother me a dozen more times would only annoy me." He gazed around at the peaceful cabin which, despite the black flames, seemed about as far from a shamanic lodge of dark medicine as Morty could imagine. "Yeah, as much fun as it would be to make you run all over creation and back, my heart's just not in it anymore. Besides which, it's incurable."

Morty stared at him, all pain momentarily forgotten. "What?"

Winn shrugged, rising tiredly to his feet. "Like I said, that's one really old *manitou* ya got there. It's way more than your average *windigo*. There's something strange and beautiful about it, something ancient. I could no more get it to go away and leave you living than you could breathe water."

"You're fucking kidding me!"

Winn frowned at him. "Language, son."

Morty rose, fury welling up his throat. "I come all the way out here looking for the legendary shaman in the black lodge, and all I find is an old codger who can't even—*urk!*" Morty choked as Winn gestured at him. Unable to breathe, he clutched at his throat, discovering the whole Vader gag wasn't all that amusing when one was on the wrong end of it. An invisible vise tightened around his windpipe, and he struggled to grasp it in his claws. The old man stepped closer, remaining just out of Morty's reach.

"Let me tell ya about winter, and about balance," Winn said, and began refilling his pipe from a small leather pouch. He lit the pipe with the tip of his little finger, a black flame kindling a puff of gray smoke reeking of slimy lake algae, dead fish, and stagnant water.

Morty continued to fight for breath with whatever force held him upright on his feet like a marionette. Winn's movements were slow and deliberate, his voice thoughtful. "You know how the *windigook* came to be? The Starving Moon, that's how. The place between the end of winter and the beginning of spring, when nothing is growing yet, the lake is still iced over like a cloudy mirror, and there ain't nothing moving in the woods. If there's more mouths to feed than food to put in them, that's when your neighbors start looking sorta tasty there, don't they? Or you start thinking you don't really need your new baby, after all. It'll probably die of the cold anyway, and why should such a juicy morsel go to waste?"

"Stop," Morty gurgled, unable to free himself, unable to halt the bony growth from his skull, the antlers' tines curling outward. His guts drew tight against his backbone as if pulled inward with sinew cords. With a sickening shredding sound, the skin below his ribs split open, exposing squirming intestines that writhed under their own volition. He didn't want to know what his lower regions were doing; searing ice streaked from his groin down to his toes.

Winn puffed his pipe, unconcerned. The shadow-dog sat, watching Morty's agony, alert and unmoving. Winn pointed the stem of his pipe at the window. "That's what winter is, though, real winter, not the jingle-belling, ice-skating nonsense you children think is meant for you to play in. I'm talking about the true cold, so cold it gets right into your bones there and ya never really warm up again. The desperate hunger that stretches a man out past the limits of his morality. Oh, it's easy to listen to the *Midewi-win* teachings when you have a belly full of rice and fish, and the sun is warm, and all kinds of wonderful things are growing. Now, when the wind howls and everything is buried six feet deep in snow, that's when people re-alized they might do better to offer up prayers to the jealous *manitou*. The god of Winter. The ancient one who they say destroyed the people who lived here long, long ago, before the Anishinaabeg came here following the Turtle spirit. Before the Menominee and the Ho-Chunk settled here."

He tapped the tip of one of Morty's antlers with his pipe-stem. "Every creature has a hunter, son; every living thing fears some larger, meaner ani-mal keeping them in check, so they don't over-populate the earth. The rab-bit is hunted by the fox. The frog by the crane. The deer and even the moose by the wolf and bear. Man, ya know, he don't have a natural predator. So they say that long, long ago, when the First People lived here, and grew too many, and the summer harvest wasn't enough to sustain them through the bitter winter, that was when the first old Winter *manitou* came into being.

He checked their growth. He brought balance back to the earth, by un-
leashing his children, the *windigook,* into the forests and the dark places in
the snow. He sent them into the lodges of the First People who had grown
too numerous. To right the scales of all that the First People had taken from
the earth."

Morty strained for speech. "They found a burial mound—"

Winn raised both eyebrows. "You are very possibly the stubbornest
white man I've ever met, and that is saying something. Now, listen: Winter
doesn't give a good gosh-darn about any man's idea of right and wrong.
Winter kills because that's its entire purpose. Putting life in check. And
that, Mordecai Wending, is what you have freezing your blood right this
minute. Not any ordinary cannibal spirit; I'm betting you didn't become
this by craving the flesh of your neighbor during a hard, starving month.
The *manitou* on you is the jealous, hungering spirit of the dead of winter,
or I'll eat my hat." He gestured to a fishing hat hung on a wall-hook by the
doorway; it was old and water-stained, festooned with trout-flies. "I don't
make that boast lightly. It's a danged useful hat."

Morty growled, at last managing to catch his breath. "I don't care what
it is. Get it out of me!"

Winn sighed. "Even if I wanted to, I couldn't. That spirit is far too old
and too powerful." He flicked his thumb at the pipe, and it vanished. He
stood gazing thoughtfully while Morty strained to hold in the tremors rippling through his flesh. "Very, very old spirit. Still, a spirit. A *manitou,* a
mystery, a god, possibly." He grabbed Morty's antlers by their knobby bases.
"This thing is *manitou;* you're definitely the more carnal sort of creature.
Now I wonder." The shaman quieted and closed his eyes, still holding onto
the antlers.

"Please," Morty groaned, his voice deepening, sounding more guttural.
"I will do anything you ask. Just make this stop!"

"The *manitou* is going to keep fighting ya, and it's probably going
to win," the shaman said. Morty cringed, trying to blink his vision clear,
though everything was tinged red now. "Spirit against flesh. I wonder, what
if the two were one?"

"What? No! Fuck no!"

Winn cackled, releasing Morty. The shaman gleefully rubbed his hands together. "Oh, my. Let's just see how this goes!" Winn's form wavered, shifted. The dog barked, circling Morty. He didn't spare it a glance, terrified by the black form rising in front of him. The old man's shape became indistinct, eyes glowing, shadow flowing around him like a cape of raven feathers. He began chanting in a low, resonant voice, and fresh pain shot through Morty's entire body.

Morty slashed at him, panicked. His claws sailed right through the old man's chest. Smoke trailed from his fingertips as if he'd tried to catch a cloud. Darkness seeped out of the fireplace, engulfing the room. Morty could barely see the old man as something *other,* vaguely humanoid and insubstantial as mist. The dark shaman grasped Morty's antlers and forced him to his knees, chanting old words from an ancestor's tongue, the voice reverberating in his bones, striking him like a bell again and again from crown to feet in waves of agony. Something dark fought to pull out of Morty, ripping his skin as it thrashed wildly and tried to flee. Ice filled his chest; he gasped, his heart thudding erratically. Wind screamed past his ears. Morty felt millions of icy needles thrusting into his writhing flesh. And then it all became too intense for him to think anything. He threw his head back and screamed; the cold rushed down his throat and up into his brain as blackness yanked him under once more.

23

Uncomfortable wetness seeped into his awareness. Something brushed Morty's eyelids and he panicked, thrashing himself to a sitting position, before he saw gently drifting snowflakes all around him. He blinked up into a gray dawn, scrub pine the only feature of the landscape surrounding him. His entire body was numb. He flexed his fingers, looking down at his chest. Naked. In the snow. What the fuck. His gaze traveled farther and he started at the coarse fur covering his legs and his elongated feet with broad, pointed double toes. "No," he moaned.

The claws didn't seem as long, nor his arms as bony, but these weren't his hands. He reached up with his not-hands and confirmed the antlers hadn't vanished. "No, no, no." Touching his face carefully, he felt his nose and chin where they should be. And no fangs. "What the shitgoblins," he whispered. He sat there in the snow, taking stock internally.

He clambered to unsteady feet as broad and flat as a caribou's. He studied his right hand, unnerved by the claws jutting from his fingertips. Concentrating, he was relieved to see his form obeying, fingerbones pulling in, claws shrinking back under fingernails, leaving drops of blood and prickling nerves on his fingertips. It hurt like hell.

Wincing, he focused on his feet, gasping as the bones twisted back into more familiar structures. Trying to revert his hips into a fully bipedal stance shot agony through him, and he fell to his knees, breaking the thick crust of snow. The wet snow felt unpleasant against his shins, but not cold. At least they were shins again, not hairy elk legs. Panting, he closed his eyes, one hand on an antler. *Okay. Crazy obvious antlers are next.*

"I do not think that is the best idea."

Morty jerked away from the voice, toppling over, his naked ass landing with a smack on a rock under the snow. With a yelp he rolled off it, scrambling to get hands and feet underneath himself and stand. He cupped one hand hurriedly around his most tender parts. The woman in furs gazed steadily at him. A slow smirk lifted her lips.

"Thought I was done with this hallucination," Morty growled.

The woman toyed with the end of her cashmere scarf. "Did you meet the dark shaman? What did he say?" Her eyes darted to his groin, and Morty shivered, discomfited.

"Yeah, I met him. He stole my clothes," he said. "Can I borrow your coat?"

She blinked slowly at him. "No. Why do you not simply change? It seems you are becoming more the master of your beast."

"I don't want to become that thing!" To emphasize the point, Morty concentrated, eyes clenched shut, willing the antlers to shrink away. His skull throbbed. When he hesitantly touched the top of his head again, all he felt was his normal hair and sticky blood that quickly froze. He sighed in relief, though dull pounding continued behind his eyes.

The woman tittered, circling him daintily. Morty turned to keep her in view. "For a start, it would keep you from freezing your skinny, pale *derriere*. Unless your intention is to make your grave in the nearest snowbank."

Morty shook his head. "None of this is real. This is a bizarre hallucination caused by hypothermia." He pointed an accusing finger. "And you! You're the one who cracked the ice and sent me into the damned lake."

She leaned toward him, grinning. The glimpse of gleaming, sharp teeth behind her rosy lips unnerved him. "Ah ha! So, you admit that was real."

"You know, the only thing worse than being taunted by a hallucination is being taunted in that ridiculous accent," Morty snapped. He stumbled a step over the uneven terrain below the thick snow.

"My mother was the daughter of a *voyageur*, you ignorant *waabishkiiwed*," the woman returned, eyes narrowing. "Your nudity does you no favors. You are not appetizing at all. Put your fur back on."

"What, you don't want to eat me when I'm helpless and stranded in the middle of nowhere? What kind of monster are you?"

She sniffed. "One with taste. Besides, you have not answered my question. If you found the black lodge, what was the old shaman like?"

Morty squinted at the sky. It appeared lighter in one direction; could be east. He assumed he was still far north of everything. He began walking south, one hand cupped protectively around his privates. "Yeah, I found it, and the shaman was there. Figuratively pegged my ass better than one of your *voyageurs* with a two-dollar whore, too."

She swept alongside him, no longer a woman. Dark eyes glared at him from a panther's face. Her sharp horns glinted in a brief ray of light before the clouds closed the sky off again. "I have killed smarter men than you for breakfast, pale-rump. Do not insult me." Morty gave her a sideways glance; she made no move to attack. Yet.

"What are you, anyway?"

She lifted her chin, reminding him for a moment of the most royal housecat ever. "I am *mishibizhu,* of *Gichigami* family. Your people called us water panthers. My family have ruled the lakes for thousands of years. I was born when no roads crossed these marshes, before the French trappers and loggers died off, before your father's grandfather was even whelped squalling into the dirt. You are merely a *windigo.* Do not presume to talk to me as you would one of your dirty human friends."

"First off, I'm not a *wendigo,* or *windigo,* or whatever," Morty said, stopping to face her. Her enormous paws rested atop the snow; Morty was shin-deep. "That vicious old bastard in the black lodge—which, mind you, was about as far from an Ojibwe medicine lodge as I am from a body-builder—said whatever this thing is inside me, it's way older and meaner than your garden-variety cannibal monster." He kicked at the snow, irritated. "He said he was going to bind it to me. And I just woke up wherever this is, looking like a half-deer freak, so what say you cut me a little slack." Arguing with a water panther in the snow while naked didn't seem any weirder than anything else in the last forty-eight hours.

She tilted her head to one side, one ear flicking at a drifting snowflake. "You looked more like an elk to me. Except with claws. And still half-*waabishkiiwed.* Definitely not as handsome as the *windigo* from earlier."

"Handsome." Morty shook his head. "Lady, you have seriously weird appetites."

"Whether you are *windigo* or something else, you had better change back before you freeze to death. Now hurry up! I want to hear the whole story and that will be impossible if you are dead."

Morty gritted his teeth. "I'd rather die."

"You will die if you don't put your fur on."

"I don't know if I can change back to me again if I do! What if this binding the old man did—what if it means I get stuck in that form?"

She shrugged. "At least you would be better company."

"Screw you," Morty snarled, and resumed walking. The *mishibizhu* grumbled, and suddenly whipped her tail around and slapped his legs out from under him. Morty hit the ground hard. Roaring with pain and fury, he leapt to his feet, slashing at her. She skittered nimbly out of reach. "How the hell do you move so fast?"

Mid-slash he saw his claws. "Oh shit." He watched the fur grow from his torso, and his legs lengthen. "No!" His fists clenched as he tried to marshal his thoughts, to send the transformation away. An enormous paw smacked him sideways into the snow.

"Stop this ridiculous denial at once," she growled.

Panicked, he touched his face. "Oh god. Am I a skull-faced thing? Ow!" His claw pricked his flesh. He jerked his hand away from his cheek.

"You are completely foolish," the water panther huffed. Her form shifted, and the woman stepped forward, cupping his chin in her gloved hand. *"Noondezhi.* Such an idiot." She brushed his small scratch with a finger, then licked it from her glove. "Hm. You do not taste like one of the whites. You taste..." She spat out the droplet. "Like something rotten. Yet you are not as fierce as you were on the lake."

Warily, Morty eased away from her. "This can't be real."

She sighed, then quickly slapped him. "Does this feel real?"

"Hey! Stop that. Do you even know how to have a non-violent conversation?" Morty pulled his hand from his stinging cheek; only a tiny smear of blood showed on his palm. His fingers were long again, with sharp curving claws. Taking a deep breath, he focused on drawing his finger knives back in. Being butt naked was preferable to being that awful, half-dead-looking thing. The *mishibizhu's* eyes narrowed again. He held up a hand, palm forward. "Okay, for fuck's sake, don't hit me again. I'm not going to be a monster. You can deal with me as I'm supposed to be, or not at all."

She sniffed. "I will make you a very sensible proposition, then. You must tell me everything about the black lodge, since I believed it to be an old ghost story."

"And you'll what? Refrain from eating me or fighting with me?"

"I will guide you to the world you call home." At Morty's dubious glance, she laughed, and offered him a hand up. "Or at least to the nearest rangers."

Her smile seemed almost genuine. Morty eyed her hand. "Are you going to keep changing back and forth? Because it's really playing hell with my brain."

She thrust her hand at him impatiently. "Get up, imbecile."

Morty grasped her fingers carefully. She hauled him up faster than he'd anticipated; he wobbled, legs weak. She laughed. "You are like a moose child trying to stand for the first time."

"Thanks. You look like a snake had a torrid affair with a mountain lion and a cow," he replied. Large eyes and sharp horns were suddenly an inch from his face.

"Are you calling me a cow?" the water panther growled, teeth bared.

"No," he said, lifting his hands toward her. "Step back a second, okay? What do I call you?"

"Marie. Are you going to tell me about the shaman or not?"

"All right, don't get all slappy."

"This way. And talk."

He tried to match her pace, though she glided along the snow, paws barely denting the crust, while he took difficult, plodding steps. "The lodge looked like a fishing cabin. Bookshelves. Trophy deer on the wall. Curtains. There was this old guy, with his dog, and at first I thought he was normal."

"The shaman appears harmless, to trick his victims," Marie agreed, nodding.

"Guess so. He said he and his dog pulled me out of the lake when the ice cracked and I slipped."

She frowned. "You know that is not what happened."

He shook his head. "Rampaging noseweasels, give me a break. It's not as though anything this crazy happens to me. I've experienced some unlikely events in the past year, but nothing close to turning into an old Northwoods monster. So, yeah, I was much more willing to believe I'd somehow gone out on the ice too far and fallen through than to accept the last thing I remembered, which involved me changing into the George Romero version of Bambi." The dark, scaled panther gave a low growl of confusion, and he waved her off. "If you attack me again, swear to god I'm going to bite you."

"At least you are talking more like a *windigo*."

Trying to ignore her, Morty continued, lurching from step to step beside the pacing beast. His balls swayed uncomfortably, and he kept one hand over his exposed parts. *I definitely do not want literal blue balls. Kim would never let me hear the end of it.* "As I was saying, he appeared perfectly normal. Just an old man, holed up in his cabin, maybe up here for a little ice fishing. He gave me a quilt and hot broth to drink, and—"

"You drank what he offered?" Her eyes widened. "That was foolish."

"Right, old stories, don't drink the fairies' wine, I know. I wasn't exactly thinking along those lines, more concerned I'd nearly frozen to death." That brought out nasty ideas. The shaman could have planted some dark mission in Morty's head. He might not have a choice; he might suddenly turn into the skull-faced cannibal thing and not be able to change back. *He said it was spirit, and I'm flesh; is it flesh now, fully? Is it fully me? Am I fully me?*

A rough nudge nearly toppled him. "I want to hear the story," Marie growled.

"I'm still trying to figure out the story," Morty snapped. "I don't really know what he did to me."

"If only you had someone around who has heard every legend there is to tell, north or south of the great lake." Despite her growly voice, her tone was light and mocking, and Morty glared at her as he trudged along.

"Pardon me, I didn't realize I was in the presence of a folk historian. Do please shed light on my ignominious transformation."

"Tell me the rest of it, idiot. What did he say to you?"

Morty took a deep breath, beginning to feel heated. "He tricked me into telling him my full name. Yes, I know, stupid me, your commentary is not required. That was when I realized something was wrong. Guess the black flames in the fireplace should've been my first clue. I was too absorbed in contemplating my brush with death to pay attention at first. He made me change."

Morty paused, his steps slowing, then forced himself to continue. "He said the spirit on me was ancient, way older than your average *wendigo*. Some kind of winter god. A *manitou*, he said. He said if he was younger he'd

have sent me on all kinds of useless quests, pretty much for his own entertainment, but he was old and tired, and anyway there was no way he could
get the spirit out of me without killing me." He felt Marie's gaze upon him
as they walked. He kept his own eyes on the snow in front of him. "Then
he said he was going to make the two become one; flesh and spirit. And he
cast a spell, I think. I'm not sure. I was in a lot of pain, and I blacked out."
He took another long breath, looking at his hands. His fingertips bore red
lines where the bony claws had shoved through. "And I woke up as a monster, out in Satan's ass-end of a winter slough, and you know the rest."

Marie was quiet for awhile. They passed through larger brush, and into
a copse of scraggly pines just tall enough to swallow the sky from view. The
trees blocked the wind gusts, though their whispering needles lacked the
usual peace Morty associated with forest sounds. Was he now the avatar of a
cruel and hungry deity? One likely to go on a bloodthirsty rampage and eat
more of his neighbors. Sick, he stopped, grabbing a tree for support. *Please
no. That wasn't me. That was the* manitou. *Old god. Whatever this thing is.
Not me.*

The image of the winter deity on the shield loomed in his mind, with
animals struck down at its feet and icicles dripping from its massive antlers.
He felt faint.

"Come on, tell me the rest," Marie insisted. "What did he look like?
Did he have a cloak of night, as the legends say? You said he had a dog; was
it more of a hound or a wolf?"

Morty shook his head, eyes closed for a moment. "It wasn't really there.
A shadow, or something, in the shape of a dog. I don't know. The shaman
looked like an old fisherman. Like a harmless grandpa. Except when he
started chanting, right before I passed out, he didn't appear as an old man
anymore. He was darkness. Darker than the room." The darkness in his
memory cackled, and Morty shivered, casting it away. "What am I? Do any
of your old lake stories tell you that?"

The *mishibizhu* regarded him with serious eyes. She gave a slow shake
of her head. "If this is truly an ancient *manitou* upon you, as the shaman
said, then perhaps. I have heard very old tales of the father of the *windigook*,
stories my older brothers used to tell us younger children, to frighten us into staying beneath the water all winter."

Morty saw a flicker of movement behind her; a large gray squirrel paused at the edge of the trees. Dully he wondered if she'd eat it, or if it would prove too insignificant for a snack.

"The shaman told me something similar," Morty said, dread in his stomach. "I think this all started at that burial mound, near the resort." She tilted her head, puzzled. He elaborated, "Inside was a skeleton with an elk head. Lots of baskets of food and weapons, jewelry, a big painted shield. I thought at first it must have been a chief or a shaman. A person made into an effigy of a god. Now I'm thinking it was definitely not human."

Her eyes widened. "The old hill of the dead god? You went there?"

"Hill of the dead god. Great. Yes. To my complete mortification. AmShale unearthed the grave while excavating for a fracking site." Seeing her frown, he explained, "An oil company is about to tear up this part of the Northwoods for a quick profit, never mind that it'll ruin the groundwater for decades and poison the watershed. Huzzah for all the state congressmen putting a few dozen 'jobs' before the welfare of the entire region."

She scowled. "You knife-spirits have always treated the lake and the forests as things to benefit only you. This is nothing new, whatever name you give it."

"Yeah, preaching to the choir here, and please don't count me among that crowd. Point is, they brought in an Ojibwe scholar and a team of archaeologists to dig everything up and remove it to—"

"Remove it!" she hissed, tail lashing. "Not even we would disturb such an ancient grave." She cursed long and fluently, in what sounded like a mix of French and a Native American tongue, pacing back and forth in the small clearing. Whirling back to him, she growled, "It is fitting that a white man is suffering the curse of the dead god."

"Hey, I didn't dig it up! I'm not the one killing the land for a few bucks. Do not pin this shit on me, princess." Morty clenched his fist and felt a shift in his jaws and skull. Frightened, he jerked back, willing himself to remain himself. He panted in relief upon touching his face and feeling the fangs receding.

She eyed him with contempt. "There must be a reason the winter *manitou* cast his darkness upon you."

"Yeah, you want to know the reason? I'm clumsy as hell, I slipped and fell almost on top of a creepy-ass elk-skulled thing, and its goddamn antler cut my hand." He held up his palm to show her the scar. It remained red and obvious against his skin. "And ever since, my life has been one insane thing after another! I've been shot twice, I've fought a big cat-monster and met the most evil old grandpa ever, and I'm pretty sure I've eaten a couple of my neighbors."

Marie sniffed, stopping in front of him, her gaze traveling up and down his trembling form. "According to the stories my brothers would tell, the people could not kill him, the father of the *windigook*. The villagers tricked him into drinking a bark tea which made him sleepy, and he lay down in his lodge. And there, the Lake People, who lived long before the Ho-Chunk and the Anishinaabe, they buried him in his slumber. They put many offerings of food in his lodge, in case he awoke and was hungry. They covered the whole thing with rocks and mud and let the summer sun bake it solid as stone. Over time its location was lost." She nodded at him. "If the grave of the dead god is truly what the *waabishkiiwewad* uncovered, after so many centuries, it is no wonder he woke up angry, and hungry."

Morty noticed a large gray fox sitting quietly near the squirrel. The squirrel didn't seem to have seen the fox yet. The fox approached the squirrel quietly, stealthily. Morty wondered if Mrs. Hietpas had seen him coming. Maybe she didn't even have time to try and whack him with her Bible. Sickened, he asked, "So you think the shaman was right: this thing I accidentally stabbed myself with is a dead god? One so awful that people buried it alive centuries ago?"

She made a dismissive gesture with one paw. "Dead only in the sense no man worships it any longer, so ancient and forgotten it has become. I am speaking of *manidoog*, spirits. They cannot be killed, only driven away. They do not die, they hibernate, like the bear, until they are awoken."

"Speaking of critters which should be hibernating," Morty whispered, slowly looking around. An unusual number of surprisingly large hares, foxes, badgers, and squirrels gathered on the edge of the clearing, all silently watching them. Marie followed his gaze and startled, rearing up on hind paws.

"The *Bagwajinini!*" she snarled, tail whipping.

A monster scared of squirrels? Okay, they were big squirrels. And they were all staring at Morty. He glanced from one creature to another, disturbed to see each pair of huge, black eyes focused on him.

A chorus of flat, buzzing voices slammed into him, the wave jarring his brain instead of his ears: "Abomination. Unclean. You may not continue."

Morty staggered, grasping the trunk of the pine for balance; his free hand went to his skull, successive tremors of agony pinging off his bones. He cried out. Marie stayed upright, claws out, her head swinging and eyes frightened. "What—I don't—" Morty gasped.

The horrible buzzing racked his brain again. "Unclean *manitou*. You should have remained asleep. Now we shall destroy you."

24

"Wait!" Morty yelled, hands shooting into the air. "Wait, I'm not what you think." The assemblage of creatures stared at him, silent. Breathing hard, he strained to control his panic, to force his bones and sinews to keep their more usual shapes. The effort left him kneeling in the snow, shuddering. He reached one placating hand toward the nearest chipmunk. "Wait, see, I'm not a monster," he panted.

Unblinking eyes stared at him. "I'm just a geek," he pleaded, "Just an idiot who was in the wrong place at the wrong time and just happened to get possessed by the wrong *manitou*, okay? I'm not a monster. I promise."

Marie shifted into her more womanly form. She gestured at Morty, addressing the staring animals. "This is true. He is just a sad *waabishkiiwed*. He will not even go hunting with me." Morty didn't get more than a moment to wonder if she was insulting him or sticking up for him; a huge gray badger stepped forward, cutting a glare at Marie.

"You will leave us. We must examine the abomination."

Marie stared at it, then at Morty. Her body shimmered, as if she was unsure which appearance to take. He shook his head at her, desperate, but with a flick of her tail she bounded off and was lost to his sight in the trees. "No, please," he begged, hugging himself. "Nothing to see here. She's taking me back to civilization, and once I get there I'll be more than happy to never come out here again. I don't even enjoy camping."

He never saw them move. They surrounded him, so close he could see the utter lack of light in each pair of eyes. He cringed. "Gahh! Really, I promise, no need to destroy me. I'm nobody. I'm just a schmuck who's been through way more than I can handle in the past couple of days, so if it's all the same to you, I'll—"

"Be quiet, *waabishkiiwed*." Morty flinched at the reverberations through his skull. His eyes darted from fox to squirrel to rabbit, all of them leaning in to study him. He realized none of them were breathing. Or blinking. Just like the one on the porch.

Well, shit.

He swallowed thickly. "I take it none of you are really gentle little forest critters."

Light rippled between him and them, and abruptly each animal was a short, hairy humanoid. Tiny horns poked out on either side of their rounded heads. Their black, round, lidless eyes hadn't changed. Thick gray fur covered their torsos. Several carried simple bows and bark quivers full of arrows; the arrowheads appeared disturbingly sharp. One of them had a tall staff topped with the skull of a snapping turtle. Squirming back a bit, his ass uncomfortable in the wet snow, Morty searched his memory frantically. Uncle Vern used to tell him stories about little men in the forest, who could only be seen by children. *Mimakwisi?* Pukwudgies?

These weren't friendly little gnomes, given how fast Marie had fled. He ventured a smile, slowly raising his hands again to show how harmless he was. "Hi. Whatever that might have looked like, I promise I'm not a monster or whatever it is that really pisses you guys off."

One of them inhaled sharply, then grimaced. "It has Anishinaabe blood."

"It smells more *waabishkiiwed*," another said. Their mouths didn't move, but Morty had the impression the emotionless, wracking speech he felt rather than heard originated from different creatures in the semicircle pressing in on him.

The stories about Pukwudgies Uncle Vern had told him usually involved them teasing hunters in the woods, loosing canoes from riverbanks, springing traps. He had difficulty envisioning any of these menacing gnomes playing silly pranks. Sticking a spear up his ass and roasting him over an open fire seemed more their style. "My mother was part Menominee," he said. "I'm sorry; I don't really know much about proper behavior in the forest. No one in my family really talks about—"

"It is the *manitou* of the Starving Moon. It is weak. We must kill it before it regains strength."

"No, hey, wait a minute. So maybe I have an evil *manitou* in me, but I can control it now." Morty desperately hoped that was true. He tried not to think of the implications of the spirit of a dead winter god bound to his very terrified flesh, just in case they could read his thoughts. "I'm no threat; I'm just a stupid white guy freezing his ass off in the woods."

"*Wendigo,* you do not fool us."

"I am not a *wendigo!* Maybe the thing that used me to do some really bad stuff, maybe that was the *wendigo.* That's not me. I swear."

"Have you not eaten the flesh of your kind, *waabishkiiwed?* Have you drunk the blood of babes?"

"What? No, I haven't eaten any babies." He could barely speak, his tongue thick with fear. *Assturkeys. Don't let them be mind readers.* Desperately he tried not to think about Sturgensen. Or Mrs. Hietpas. Or the woman in the parking lot. "Hey, maybe you can help me."

"We will help the world by ridding it of you."

"Can we just stop with all this kill-the-*wendigo* stuff for a second? I don't want to be a monster! I just want to go back to my old life, my friends, my crappy apartment and my middle-management retail job." He glanced between them, unable to read any sympathy, any compassion, any emotion at all in their faces. "The shaman in the black lodge did something to me, and I'm not sure yet what, but if you folks could help me un-bind the ancient *manitou* from my flesh I'd be eternally grateful."

He sensed a shift then, a ripple of uneasiness. "You found the black lodge? How?"

Though their lips never moved, he thought that a different one replied. It felt like separate voices in his head, at least. "The darkness only attracts the darkness. The creature is not *waabishkiiwed* or Anishinaabe; it is abomination."

Morty huddled in their center, sheer panic alone keeping him from collapsing into the snow. "Stop with the 'abomination' stuff, please. I went there hoping to get rid of this thing. The shaman said he couldn't pull it out of me, and instead he bound it to me, whatever that means. I'm still me, though." He gestured at his nudity, desperate to convince them. "I mean, look at me. No threat here. Right now, I'm really, really needing to get home, so respectfully, if you guys can help me, fantastic; if not, could I maybe just go on my way?"

"It is abomination. Bring it forth and we will kill it."

Morty started to protest again; his words turned to a shriek as antlers burst from his head and his spine wrenched. He didn't have a chance to fight it as the change overwhelmed him, stretching his arms and legs, yanking his belly taut against his pelvis, claws splitting his fingertips in sprays of blood. Forced to all fours, he struggled to stand, managing only to crouch. Coarse fur matted with dark blood sprouted from his skin like thousands of needles all over, and the flesh split below his ribs, exposing wet organs. Red blurred his sight, fangs cut his tongue as he cried out. He fell forward, gasping, and dimly saw the hairy gnomes drawing arrows. "No, wait! Stop!" he shouted, his voice raspy-deep and strange to his ears.

To his surprise and relief, the nocked arrows didn't fly. The one with the staff regarded him in silence a moment, then knocked it against Morty's head. He heard the dull *thunk* of bone hitting bone, and winced. "Stop, please. Don't do this," he begged.

Straining, he willed the elongated nose and jaw of his skull to withdraw, to regain some semblance of humanity. "I'm not this thing, this dead god or whatever. I don't want to hurt anyone. I don't want to be a cannibal."

The gnomes' heads turned to look at each other, then as one all eyes returned to him. "It speaks. How does it speak?"

"Of course I can speak," Morty panted, groaning as he drew in the claws. His fingers were on fire, blood dripping into the churned snow at his feet. "Because—I'm not—a *wendigo*." He dropped, exhausted, unable to complete the transformation back. "Don't kill me. I'm not the one who disturbed the grave, all right? This was an accident. I don't want this."

"The *gitchi-mookomaanag* unearthed the sleeping *manitou*. This is known by all here. You are a fool to have woken it."

"Are you not listening to me? I didn't wake it up!" Morty shouted, his voice startling an owl into flight from the trees nearby. He felt a dull ache between his eyes, where the bridge of his nose wanted to stretch out into a hungry muzzle. "The idiots who dug into the mound and disturbed the old god are selfish assholes who destroy the land for their own greed. They don't care who they hurt in going after their profits. I'm not one of them," he pleaded, staring into the blank, black eyes of the one with the staff. "If it was up to me, I'd put this thing right back in the ground and bury it for another few thousand years, and I'd sabotage all their digging machines. Because I respect the earth." He fell back in the snow, panting. "Thank you for coming to my TED Talk."

Silent moments passed. With surprise, Morty watched as the bows were lowered, creepy stares were no longer focused on him. He had the impression they were talking amongst themselves. Ripples teased at the back of his mind, putting the hairs all over his skin on end. It felt like the worst possible goosebumps, and he shivered. He glanced from one creature to another, unable to read their faces. Slowly, he coaxed his limbs to revert, his spine unwarping kink by painful kink. Unsure if he should say anything else or just make a run for it, he glanced toward the trees where Marie had vanished. If she was long gone, he was never going to find his way to civilization.

Telepathic gnome speech slapped him in the brain, knocking him back. "You may be useful, abomination. Do you swear on all the sacred *manidoog* you will fight the white men who have angered the spirit of the Starving Moon?"

"Ow," Morty muttered, shaking his head once to clear the echoes out. "Can you please not project your thoughts so loud?"

"Do you swear you will fight all those whose greed overpowers them?"

"Will I what now?" Morty blinked at them, confused. "Guys, not sure exactly what you're asking here..."

"You say you are not with the *waabishkiiwewaad* who overburden the earth. Those who take more than they need. The ones who awakened the winter *manitou* must pay the toll, or else all will suffer."

"We stop their rifles. We steal their tools. We can cause their metal beasts to rust where they sit. Yet they do not stop. Every year brings more destruction to our forest." Every pair of soulless eyes stared into his, and Morty shrank back from them. "You are not truly the spirit of the Starving Moon, nor are you only a man. We cannot tell if you are flesh overflowing with *manitou, or manitou* made true flesh. You are abomination. You are new. Perhaps you can be honorable. Perhaps you can stop the *waabishkiiwewaad* from destroying our home."

"Stop the drilling?" Morty thought about it. These claws could probably rip through metal, if the photos Quell had taken at the dig site were any proof. Dread knotted in his stomach over whether, if he took the monstrous form again, he'd be able to change back.

"Punish the greedy ones who would destroy us all. In these acts you would prove yourself a creature of honor."

"Wait a second," Morty protested, "I'm not going to kill anybody." He swallowed down sour bile. *Else. I'm not going to kill anybody else.*

"If you devour the ones who have lost their spirits to the darkness, we will not hold you to blame. You will bring balance. If you stray one step off the path of honor, we will know you are consumed with greed yourself." Their eyes bored into him. "We will watch you, *wendigo.* Take care how you act."

"Wait just a minute, I'm not going to—" Morty blinked. Nothing was in the clearing. A brief swirl of wind spun the falling snow, then settled. The rustling of the surrounding pines and the sharp, dry air in his nostrils filled his awareness. The creatures had vanished.

He stood carefully, peering all around. Nothing moved except the branches. He took a cautious step forward, half-expecting to see a squirrel darting away or a fox watching from the undergrowth. The voice behind him made him leap several inches into the air. "They're gone? They let you live?"

Morty glared at the water panther, watching her pick her way delicately between the trees. "Apparently, yeah. Thanks for abandoning me to the mercy of the Seven Psychotic Dwarves."

Her eyes were wide and scared. "Did they make you promise anything? Did they bind you?" Morty opened his mouth to reply, then stopped when he realized he had no idea what had just happened. Marie stared at him. *"Sacre bleu, windigo,* what did you do?"

He gave her a helpless shrug. She shook her head.

"You thought you were 'fucked' before, *windigo?* Now you have really done it."

25

Marie's nose was still bothered by the *windigo's* odd scent, though less than before. He trudged alongside her in silence, again appearing as nothing more than a simple, pale *waabishkiiwed*. No simple human would have been able to go naked a hundred yards in this frigid weather, much less a few miles as this man had. He kept one hand cupped around his loins, head down, huffing a bit as he paced her. For a creature bearing an ancient winter spirit within his skin, he was singularly awkward in the deep snow.

Marie's wide paws slid across the surface easily, leaving only the barest of tracks. The white man plodded heavily, step by step, and again she was annoyed that he refused to let out his stronger form. "You are making this more difficult than is necessary."

He didn't look up, brown hair damp and matted over his brow. "How much farther."

She snorted. "Not far. However, you do not seem as though you are in any condition to reach the rangers' station."

He gave a small shrug. "Do they have a phone?"

"I assume. If the wind has not blown the lines down again." She chuckled. "Once, when only one of them was there, I pulled a tree down onto the line, and then went about the building, scratching my claws." She smiled at the memory. "For two days I frightened him, until he could stand it no more and ran into the sloughs. He was easy enough to catch then. Perhaps the others who arrived the next day thought he had abandoned his post."

The *windigo* cast her a sour glance. "Hilarious."

She shook her head. "What exactly do you expect will happen next, foolish *windigo?* Do you really believe you can just go back to your life in the city?"

"That is exactly what I'm going to do."

Marie scoffed. "With the dead god inside you?"

He slowed, glaring at her. "As long as it never comes out again, damned straight I am. I'm going back to my life, my bookstore, my apartment and my girlfriend, and I'm going to pretend the past week was nothing but a bad acid trip."

"You know this is impossible."

He stopped, panting, and jabbed a finger at her. "You're part of my problem, you know. If you hadn't jumped me at the roadhouse, I never would've attacked that woman, and I'd have met up with the monster hunter and figured out a solution. Instead he shot me, and if I run into him again I have to assume he's going to try to kill me. I would, if I were him."

"Had all of that gone differently, you would not have found the black lodge."

He barked a laugh. "Right, because that worked out so well."

Marie shrugged. "And how would the idiot with the gun have helped, other than to shoot you as soon as he knew what you were? You should thank me for forcing you to confront your *manitou* and the shaman."

"No, this is your fault. Now I have this thing bound inside me!" He looked around at the thick snow over the land as if any answers could be found there. Shadows under his eyes made him appear older and haunted. "I only want to go back to my normal, uneventful life. Thanks to you and Sam and that utterly insane shaman, I'm apparently going to have a ravenous undead god in me for who knows how long, just waiting for me to stop paying attention so it can slink out again and eat more of my neighbors."

Marie tapped her paw, scowling. *"Plus ça change, plus c'est la même chose.* All I see is a whining pup of a white child, throwing a fit because life is not going his way." She sniffed, her tail swishing. "You can find your own path. I am tired of you." She turned and stalked away. She had taken but five steps when the *windigo* was running after her, calling her name. Marie kept walking. Spoiled, stupid creature. He had experienced so much more than most humans already in a very short time, and lived. Yet he griped and fussed like a child. She knew this imbecile would never find his way anywhere without her, and she was tired of his complaints

"Marie, wait! Please, wait. I'm sorry!"

A teething child. Unused to catching his own food. After years of having it brought to him, already dead and burnt by fire, this must be new for him. And frightening. She could smell his desperation, fear wafting from his pores even though it was too cold for him to sweat. She slowed a little, uncertain. He was so frightened of the old god he would rather struggle through the snow with no protection than become the antlered creature again. The *windigo* had been largely quiet since the *Bagwajinini* had departed. He would not say what bargain had been struck with the dangerous little men of the forest.

"Wait, Marie, please."

She could hear he was out of breath. She stopped, looking back. His expression brightened, and he put on a burst of speed, hoping to catch up to her—and tripped on a hidden stump, sprawling face-first into the snow. Marie sighed. After all, this *noondezhi* was barely more than a child, and based on what she knew, a *windigo* for only a week. She padded back to him. She shifted to her less threatening form, and grabbed one of the antlers starting to grow from his head to haul him back to a standing position. "Aaagh! Hey, stop!" Flustered, he waved his hands over his head, then scrunched his eyes shut, panting, until the antlers disappeared. He had left himself exposed; he quickly cupped one hand down. Marie rolled her eyes.

"If you cannot control when you change, you are never going to make any of this work, your plan for going back to normal life. Idiot." He glared at her only a second before his eyes dropped. He stood there in the snow, flushed with effort. How had her big brothers taught her to control the changes, so long ago? She frowned at the memory. This way.

She slapped him, fast and hard across the face. He staggered back, then surged toward her, snarling. Marie calmly slapped him again, harder. He fell back a step once again, then rose tall with a deep bellow, thorny spikes shooting from his skull, flesh melting to expose vicious teeth, claws stretching for her. "No," Marie said firmly, as one would to a disobedient cub, and slapped him again, driving his muzzle down and away from her. "If you cannot master the *manitou* in you, there is no point in me taking you back to your people!" she shouted when he growled at her.

That seemed to hit him harder. He trembled, and his bony ribcage heaved for breath. Marie waited, unmoving, watching him regain control. When he stood before her again as a simple human, she nodded. "Good. Again."

He ducked this time, making Marie grin. She whirled, catching his long nose with her open palm on the return trip, and then swept his feet from under him for good measure. He sprawled gracelessly. She stood and folded her arms, waiting. The *mookomaan* and the *manitou* wrestled in him for the better part of a minute before he groaned and clambered to his feet, pale and shivering. Marie studied his face; he grimaced, showing sharp teeth, then he forced the *windigo* back inside. Marie started to raise her hand. He held up his palm toward her. "Stop! You're killin' me, Smalls."

She frowned. "If a slap feels like a killing blow to you, you must be weaker than I thought."

He shook his head. "Look, I don't—this is new and weird and I don't like it one bit." He ran a hand through his hair, blowing out a frustrated breath; Marie felt it as a cold breeze. "You flip between monster and human like you're kicking your shoes off! How long did it take you to learn that? Which form is your real one?"

"They are both real. What sort of foolish question is that?"

He threw his hands in the air, turning away, and sat down on a snow-covered fallen log. Marie considered his meaning. He was not born to this. As the *Bagwajinini* said, he was abomination, unnatural. Spirit made unwilling flesh.

She sat down next to him. He eyed her as if expecting to be slapped again. She folded her hands in her lap over her pretty fur-trimmed skirt, thinking she really ought to get new clothes. It was so difficult these days, finding pretty skirts and coats made of real leather and fur, not as when she was younger. The synthetics simply would never work when she shifted form. Her clothes had to still have something of the spirit of their animal imbued in them to change with her.

"My mother was Odawa and French. My father is *Gitchi-mishibizhu*, the most powerful underwater panther in all the lakes. I have been able to take whichever form pleases me from birth."

He nodded, shoulders slumping. "Great. So you never had to worry about turning into a monster if you sneezed too hard."

Marie laughed. "You are so full of gloom! Of course I had to train to move easily between the Anishinaabe world and the *mishibizhug*. It was very difficult for me not to simply attack my prey at first. I had to learn patience. Discipline." He opened his mouth; she touched his lip to silence him. "I mean for this. To take one form or the other. Not to give away my nature to the prey. After all, you humans are suspicious creatures, and if one saw my ears a little too pointed, or my teeth a little too sharp, they might become *en garde*." She pushed her long hair back from her face, showing him her completely soft, round ears.

"If I slap you, you'll kill me, right?" he asked warily.

Delighted, Marie bounced to her feet with a laugh and grabbed his hand; reluctantly he stood. "Let us make a game of it. You see if you can provoke me, and I will do the same to you."

"Again, why does everything with you turn out violent."

"Blah, blah, blah," Marie said, and headed toward the rangers' station less than a mile distant. "Do you want to go home or not?"

"Yes," he said, and she clearly heard his clumsy attack coming, and side-stepped it. He stumbled, recovered, and glared at her.

"And if you want to hunt well, you will have to do much better." Grinning, she continued forward. He caught up, able to pace her a little better since she remained in human form.

"Didn't we discuss this already? I don't want your territory because I don't want to be a *wendigo*. Christ, I've already..." His breath hitched, and his unhappy gaze dropped. "I've already done some awful shit."

They walked in silence awhile. His panting as he slogged through the snow and the wind in the trees were the only sounds. The sun must have been nearly at its summit, though the overcast sky gave no clear sign of where it might be. Marie loved days such as this; she especially loved them curled by a fire at the Bad River Resort, with a foolish businessman hanging on every delicate lick of her lips above a lushly spiced drink. Which reminded her this pathetic imbecile was keeping her from all her winter delights. And yet, it was sad they would never know which of them would have won that fight. Her lips twitched upward.

Shifting suddenly, she slammed a paw into his chest, knocking the wind out of him as he fell. He lay in the snow, grimacing, sharp bones pricking from his fingertips. It was bloody and painful-looking, and Marie almost changed her mind.

Almost.

She clawed him deliberately, gouging flesh from hip to thigh as he tried to regain his feet. He yelped, the sound changing to a snarl, and the *windigo* braced his feet and charged her, his body audibly creaking as limbs and spine stretched. A long muzzle of bone snapped at her, faster than she had expected, his antlers grazing her flank as she leapt aside. Marie growled, skidding to a halt and reversing direction; his lunge missed her by mere inches.

He was on all fours, long claws splayed and hooves digging to stop his momentum. Marie saw the perfect opening. She leapt onto his back, grabbing his ragged pelt, and he wheezed like a wounded buck. Marie shoved her claws in, her teeth bared in distaste at the carrion-iron smell. "*Imposteur. Amateur,*" she growled, hanging on as he tried to reach back and pry her off. She loosened a paw enough to swat away his questing fingers, and he cried out again.

She squirmed over his hipbones, holding tight with her hind paws, and smacked his skull hard as she could. A noise like a dying trumpet came from his open jaws, and he staggered, forced down. "Coward. *Imbecile!* Is this all you can do?" she shouted, taking advantage of his weak footing to kick at his flanks and slap his head down again. He tossed his skull backward, and she flattened herself against his spine to avoid the sharp, wide-spreading antlers. He bellowed, twisting and turning, trying to snap at her. Marie snagged the eye socket of his elk-like skull with a claw, and yanked it closer, glaring right into the burning coal she saw deep within. "You are a fool! *Windigo,* go back to the woods and cry some more, because you will never go home like this!"

She slapped his head, so hard this time she heard the echo of it from the trees nearby. He roared, rearing up, and just as suddenly dropped onto his back. Marie failed to unhook her claws from his ragged fur in time; she slammed into the snow, her body finding the unyielding ground beneath it. To her shame, a cry escaped her.

Snarling, she twisted herself, bringing all four paws up to slice him, and felt his hand on her chest, the other raised before his face. "Stop!" he yelled. Wide blue eyes stared into hers. She halted, her claws just shy of his soft, unprotected stomach. They both lay there a moment, out of breath, hand and paw poised in the air. Slowly, he eased his weight off her, trembling. Marie lowered her paw, and he collapsed beside her, one hand going to his shoulder where she'd sunk her claws in, the other to his forehead.

"Hellmonkeys. That hurt," he gasped.

Marie felt bruised, and her tailbone ached. Seeing the blood smearing his body was terribly satisfying, however. She rolled to a sitting position, studying the exhausted white man. He was breathless and those might have been tears at the corners of his eyes which he quickly knuckled away. He showed no trace of having been a skeletal, antlered *windigo* just moments before. She nodded. "Much better."

He raised his head to glare at her, then dropped back into the snow, eyes shut and brow creased. "Can't we just do wax on, wax off? I am really not cut out for this predator versus predator crap. Ow. Holy wolverines on steroids, that really hurts."

"You are in pain?"

He opened one eye. "No, I love having the flesh shaved off my bones. Best massage ever."

"And you were extremely angry with me?"

He panted, one hand self-consciously covering his testicles again, the other pressed to his chest. "You know, I've read the phrase 'white-hot fury' but I never really grasped the full meaning of it before now." He touched the pulsing vein under his jawline. "If your intention was to make my heart explode, great job, nearly there. B-plus."

He jumped when she nudged his shoulder with a soft paw. "And you managed to rein yourself in anyway."

He stared at her, then nodded. "Yeah, I guess." She smiled, and he winced. "Are you happy or about to eat me? Because I'm never one hundred per cent sure, with all those teeth."

Marie laughed, and shifted form to offer him a hand up. He accepted after a moment's hesitation. "Are we done here?" he asked.

She appraised him carefully. His scent had changed, smelling more *waabishkiiwed* and less of carrion. She'd no idea whether the other white men would notice he was different at all; for her, a whiff of iron and spoiled meat remained.

She wrinkled her nose. "I would advise you to buy a good cologne, but I think maybe you are ready. As long as you can stop the change before you start, if you are angered or if someone attacks you."

He held his wounded shoulder, long face morose. "Marie, I am the least angry guy you'll ever meet, thanks to my naturally easygoing demeanor, and regular infusions of sweet cannabis."

She chuckled. "You are a silly *windigo*. Perhaps you will not allow the *manitou* to take charge so easily now." She began walking again, and he fell in step with her, limping a bit.

"Silly *windigo*, yep, that's me all over." He glared at the blood on his hand and the spatters across his thigh. "Great. Thanks for making me look like Hannibal Lecter's foray into abstract expressionism. That really hurt, since I don't think you heard me the first two times."

Marie shrugged. "I will be sore for days, so we are even. Of course, we both know who is the weakling here."

He halted, staring at her. "Are you seriously trash-talking me right now?"

"I am only saying you are right. You do look like a Jackson Pollock piece."

He paused, then caught up to her again. "Okay, setting aside for the moment the idea a water panther knows anything about mid-twentieth-century art, I think we both know if I hadn't reined in the undead angry god that my next move would've been to gore you while you were down."

"Oh?"

"Damned straight. Right for the kill move." He gestured with one hand, plunging his fingers downward as though they were antlers, and Marie laughed. He glanced at her uncertainly, and she patted his cheek.

"I am happy now I didn't kill you before, *windigo*. You are *très amusant*."

"Live to serve," he grumbled. He glanced up at a power line crossing in front of them, and changed direction with Marie, going around a hidden slough she knew well. "Civilization?" She nodded, her smile fading.

When he returned home, there was no way he'd be able to hold in the winter *manitou* forever. His determination was almost beautiful in its futility, but eventually his best efforts would fail. What use would be his amusing words and soft body, once the winter spirit gained more strength?

If the old tales were true, then with every slip of control, every human he devoured, the father of the *windigook* would become more powerful. She studied his face as he stared hopefully toward the snowy, rutted road which would lead them to the ranger's station. He struggled in the deep snow with renewed drive towards the place that would return him home. A home he still believed in, where he thought he could still fit in, taking up his old life as one might resume a card game after dinner.

Marie stopped. He walked on a few steps before he noticed. "What?" he asked.

She shook her head. "Follow that trail. You will find the rangers there. They will clothe you and take you home, if that is what you wish."

He looked at the snowy trail, then back at her. "You're not coming? I'm supposed to just walk naked up to their door, smeared with blood, and—hey!" He recoiled when she slapped a handful of snow against his shoulder.

"Stand still, imbecile." She rubbed the snow against his clotted wounds, scrubbing the sharp coldness over his skin to remove the blood spatters. He moved away after a few seconds, and scooped up a handful of snow to work on it himself. Marie watched, occasionally gesturing at a spot he had missed. "There. Tell them you fell in a thorn bush. There are plenty of black-berries around here."

"And my clothes?"

She shrugged. "You fell in a creek and became so chilled you removed them."

He quirked a brow at her. "And the fact I haven't frozen to death?"

Marie snapped, "Then just eat them, if this is so difficult!" He blanched, and she lowered her voice. "You have some sort of brain, possibly, *waabishkiiwed*. Make something up. They will help you. It is their purpose."

He nodded slowly. "I guess this is it."

She smiled, though part of her wanted to grab his hand and pull him into the forest hedging the road. Take him deep into the trees and show him how to creep up on a logger and share the kill with him. Coax him into accepting the spirit he bore and enjoy a hunt together. His eyes were too wide and fearful, his posture too uncertain. It was obvious he would never accept the *manitou* within him, even though he had little choice. "Good luck, *windigo*," she said, and shifted as she bounded away. She could smell his confusion, his dismay. She did not look back, leaping effortlessly over the snowy ground, returning to her silent river. Alone.

26

"See if I ever stay here again," Garwood Quell shouted as the door slammed in his face. He groaned, levering himself up from the raised flower beds at the resort's entrance. "Oughta sue you, too, for injuring an elderly person." Wincing, he limped back to his truck. Though he'd become accustomed to nonbelievers asking him to leave when he asked too many pointed questions, it had been a long while since anyone had physically tossed him out of anywhere. Who would've thought that skinny little front desk fella had the strength. Quell shook his head, relieved when his truck started on the second try. Going back in to request a tow would've been terrible.

He sat pondering while the engine warmed. No reply yet from that Appleton guy. Straight to voicemail. And no sign of the missing tourist in Mellen.

He'd found a sympathetic ear in one of the county deputies while they'd been beating the bushes after the parking-lot attack. Deputy Bill had texted him earlier today to let him know there was still no sign of the missing man, but they'd keep hunting for him and had put out his description to neighboring stations. He was presumed dead at this point. Unless the man had excellent survival skills, with nights dipping below zero even before you tacked on the windchill, there was little chance they'd find him alive, if at all.

Quell had begun to wonder if the missing tourist and the man who was supposed to meet him at Hettie's might not be one and the same. He could've sworn the guy who'd texted him was named *Mortimer,* and he'd spent hours tromping through the brush with the search party yelling for a *Marty,* but still... He hadn't had much time to ponder the two fellas who never turned up to meet him at Hettie's. Too busy hunting with the deputies. Quell had been peering at the trees, hunting for claw marks or bent branches as much as for any sign of a stray tourist. He couldn't be one hundred per cent positive he'd found anything at all.

And this sure was a dead end. He glared at the resort's front entry, now barred to him forever, just for asking the folks hanging around the lobby if they'd heard any odd stories going around. *'Harassing the guests,' my foot. Not like they're doing anything important. They're just rich people sitting around being rich in a ritzy resort. At least they have wi-fi.*

He thumbed through a map of the area on his phone, intent on the local businesses in particular. There was a Bart's Bar and Grill listed, just up the road; that sounded more like it. As he turned the truck around, he didn't mind driving straight over the snow-covered garden beds lining the resort's main approach. Served 'em right if it left a rut. Danged snobs.

The highway had been plowed, at least, and he made decent time to the bar. Backwoods taverns were the best places to catch a little gossip or tall tales. Not that he could just walk in and ask about Bigfoot or those two randy monsters that had torn up Hettie's and killed a woman. No, he'd probably have to buy at least a couple of drinks for someone first. In the muddy lot next to the bar, Quell checked his wallet, dismayed at his dwindling resources. Those terrible beasts killed one person and maimed another, and would keep at it until he could bring them to heel. No one up here was safe until those monsters were killed. And that was worth the price of a couple drinks, for information that might lead him to them.

He assessed the small crowd of patrons as he settled onto a barstool. A handful of men were drinking this afternoon, all loggers by the look of them, bearded and burly and wearing variations of flannel and camouflage. These were his people, once.

Quell nodded a greeting at the man nearest him, accepted his mug of beer from the barkeep, and sipped quietly. Since he was dressed the same, right down to the battered ballcap, after one glance the patrons ignored him. Quell drank slowly and listened to the conversations around him. They were normal, local. Sage predictions about snowfall and early spring, speculation on the price of timber, griping about the wasting disease spreading through deer in the area, making it hard to find a good buck worth hunting any more. Quell was trying to decide which topic he might jump in on when one of the loggers spoke up. "Hey, old-timer. You ever cut timber?"

Quell turned and nodded at the younger man. "In the U.P., sure. Why?"

The man nodded back. "Thought so. You care to settle a bet for us?" He indicated the two men sitting next to him at a small table. Quell picked up his beer and joined them.

"What sort of bet would that be there, then?"

"Judd here says logging's gonna become a hard industry soon. Says we're running out of good stands. Less birch and hickory out there than there was even ten years ago." The logger lifted his bearded chin in the direction of a red-haired companion. A skinnier man, one with a full mustache, snorted.

"How he can walk out in those trees and claim there won't be enough of 'em soon is beyond me," Mustache said.

"Well, the way I see it, all depends on the housing market, ya know," Quell offered.

"See? Housing, that's what I said," Judd agreed loudly.

Quell nodded. "When people need new homes built, the demand for fresh timber goes up. Last I saw, more people leaving this state than coming into it." He smiled. "Now over in the Upper Peninsula there, they got vacation cabins going up, more every year. If things get tight around here, I recommend you try your luck up there awhile."

The men nodded. "I ain't seen nothin' to indicate the market here's slowed down all that much," the first logger stated, and downed the rest of his beer. Quell beat him to signaling the bartender, and pulled a twenty out. The logger nodded, "That's very kind of you, old-timer. I'll spot the next one."

Quell hoped so; it was his last twenty. Judd asked, "You been over to the U.P. lately? Still plenty of timber?"

"Oh, plenty. No matter how many rich folks up from Ann Arbor build their condos on every dadburned lake," Quell said, and the men chuckled. "Sure, there's work to be had there, ya know, if you know your way around a loading truck or a saw."

Warming to him, Mustache asked, "What brings you out this way?"

"Well, I'm writing a book."

"Like a memoir of your glory days?" Judd asked, grinning.

"Now son, I just bought you a beer there. Show a little respect for your elders," Quell chided, but he grinned right back. "No, not about my logging days, interesting though they were. I'm actually collecting tall tales of the Northwoods." He glanced between them, gauging how they received this proclamation. "You know, legends of Paul Bunyan, stories about monsters in the woods. Bigfoot. That kinda thing."

"Too bad Brian's not in." the first logger said, and they all laughed.

"Haven't seen him in a couple days. I figured he finally got famous and left us all behind," Judd chimed in, to more derision.

"Who's this now?" Quell asked.

Mustache snorted. "Dumb kid who thinks he's gonna get rich selling a fake footprint from Bigfoot."

Now this was unexpected luck. "Bigfoot? No kidding."

The first logger shook his head. "He's kind of a special snowflake, that Brian. Too busy huntin' for weird stuff in the woods to be any use on a crew, if you ask me."

"Thought he found a real Bigfoot track and he just won't shut up about it."

"Though looked like that woman in here the other night was interested." Judd chortled. "Nobody else is, that's for sure."

The first logger grimaced. "I will believe these tall tales about an actual, live-blooded woman going home with Brian when one of you produces a photo of it and not before."

"Well, that's what you get when you go home early, Kurt. Miss all the good stuff!"

Quell's gaze flicked over each of them, intrigued. "You say this fella believes he's found a print made by a sasquatch? Is he in here much?"

Judd chortled. "Trust me, man, you don't want to open that can of worms. It's all he talks about. Insists he made a plaster cast of it that he's gonna sell for thousands of dollars, just as soon as he gets it 'authenticated.'"

"Though where in the hell he'd find anyone to judge it is beyond me," Mustache said.

A nasty suspicion crept into Quell's head. "Did he say where he found an expert to authenticate his print?"

Judd shrugged. "Some fella he found on the internet. I'm sure whoever it is, they're probably charging him an arm and a leg just to take a look. Brian ain't exactly the sharpest knife in the drawer, there."

"Well, sharp or not, that might make a funny story for my book," Quell said. Sadly, it was obvious these boys were skeptics. He sincerely hoped none of them ever ran into something they couldn't explain out in the woods. Something that might bite them first and tell them its name later. "You know, a bit of modern interest among all them dusty old tales. Anyone know where I can find this Brian?"

He sat with them for another round, so as not to call too much attention to himself, chatted about the unusually cold and wet weather even for northern Wisconsin, and excused himself as the bar became more crowded. Leaving the tavern with rough directions in mind, he checked his phone; no signal penetrated this corner of the woods. He'd just have to get there the old-fashioned way. He slowed down the truck and took the next turnoff. The loggers didn't have an exact address for this much-maligned Brian. They'd told him to watch for an old yellow trailer with a new SUV out front which probably cost more than the trailer.

In the dying light, with flakes swirling down at the windshield, Quell was hard put to determine the color of his own truck, much less any other man-made object. However, not too far along, he saw a beat-up single-wide with a gleaming hulk of a vehicle parked out front. The snow on it proved it had been there at least a day.

Hopeful he might find the owner of the 'squatch foot cast at home, Quell pulled into the dirt driveway. He'd bet his last few dollars this was the young fella who was supposed to have met him at Hettie's. He'd said he really hoped Quell could authenticate the print, and had asked how much it could be worth. Staring uneasily at the dark, silent trailer, Quell turned off the truck's engine.

Quell walked toward the trailer. A security light clicked on, washing him in amber light. Quell stopped, and waved at the front window. "Hello? Anybody home?" He waited a moment. Nothing stirred that he could see. Coming closer to the door, he called out again. "Brian? You home?"

Silence, except for the icy steps to the trailer door crackling under Quell's tread. He knocked. The loose latch clicked open, and the door slowly swung outward. Quell waited, but nobody appeared. "Hello?" he asked quietly, having misgivings about this. No answer. Quell braced his nerves and reached inside the door, found a light switch, and flipped it on.

The trailer was untidy, pretty average for a young bachelor. Dishes in the sink, cigarette butts in an ashtray by the well-worn sofa, empty beer cans strewn on the coffee table. Quell walked slowly in, peering around. The place smelled of stale smoke and cheap beer. There was an undertone of something else. Quell approached the kitchenette, nose wrinkling. A packet of bacon, unwrapped, sat beside a pan on the stove. The stove itself was cold; the bacon had been sitting out longer than was good for it. This didn't feel right at all. The heater was still on, too.

Quell moved toward the back of the trailer, wishing he'd brought his rifle from the truck. He was gonna see if the place held any awful secrets and then get out quick. Unless, of course, he could find the 'squatch foot cast. He pushed open the bedroom door at the end of the narrow hall, and there it was: white plaster chunk atop a low dresser, looking like a ghostly grub in the security light shining in from outside.

Quell turned on the bedroom lamp. The bedcovers were tossed aside, and a pair of jeans and skivvies were rumpled in a heap next to the mattress. No sign of the man who'd worn them. Quell checked the small bathroom, finding nothing more out of the ordinary than a toilet needing a good scrub. He returned to the bedroom, certain no one at all was home, and studied the plaster cast.

Whatever the heck that was from, it was no Bigfoot. The print, in low relief, looked more like an elongated hand. Narrow claws extended from thin, bony fingers and what might be an opposable thumb. He placed his own hand atop it for comparison; the fingers stretched more than twice the length of his own. It was sort of like the claws on the half-dead deer thing. Now he really needed to find this kid and ask him where exactly he found this print.

He nosed around a little longer, finding no indication of what might've happened to the owner, growing more uneasy by the minute. He should take the cast for safekeeping. He hesitated, then pulled out his trusty notepad and penned a note for the owner. He included his phone number, promising to return the cast as soon as he could speak with Brian about his find. He left the note on the dresser, taking the cast and wrapping it carefully in an undershirt from the floor. Carrying his prize, Quell headed for his truck. A nagging, unpleasant feeling prompted him to check the open crawl space under the trailer.

Old tires and more beer cans littered the dirt. Almost no snow had blown in beneath the trailer. Quell fished his flashlight out of his pocket and turned its thin light on the ground. He was dismayed to see a large, dark stain. He hoped it was oil. He scooped up a bit and sniffed it. Iron filled his nose.

He crouched, trying to ignore the ache in his knees, and pointed the light into every corner under the trailer. No body, no tracks, except for a smooth area that led, like the trail of something heavy dragged, out and into the snow, away from the security lamp. Thinking about going back for his rifle, Quell paused, staring into the darkness beyond his small beam of light. He noticed a hollow between a couple of trees where the landscape fell away from the relatively level area of the trailer. He moved toward it cautiously, listening for any creak of wood, any shifting in the branches overhead. Quell took one step down into the hollow, shining his flashlight around, then another. His third step settled on something hard and slippery. Stumbling back, he grabbed a young pine trunk for balance, training his light down. A white face stared back at him, a crimson collar around its neck like a priest's surplice.

Quell stifled a yelp, quickly swinging the light around. Nothing stirred. Heart pounding, he looked more closely at the dead man. What was left of him, at least. Head and shoulders stuck up out of the snow. The area immediately around him was dug up, and snow piled over the midsection of the corpse. It was tinged pink where the body submerged under it. Like a cache that a bobcat might leave. Big cats up here were prone to bury their kills in the snow, where they stayed preserved for weeks or more. Half-eaten and buried so something could come back later for seconds.

He very much doubted a bobcat would've been able to drag a grown man from under the trailer to here. Possibly a lynx could, but certainly not without leaving tracks in the dirt under the trailer. If it was a lynx, it wouldn't have taken the time to wipe away those tracks. Big cats just didn't do those kinds of things. That smacked of a creature smart enough to hide its misdeeds.

In a panic, Quell fled to his truck. He jumped in, slammed the door shut, and started the engine. The plaster cast fell out of his coat when he reached behind him for his rifle. He stared at it. The horrible deer-thing wouldn't have been able to fit under the trailer. Too tall and rangy. But the other beast, the scaly black-furred lynx that fought the deer-thing; he bet that monster could slink under there easy. He recalled, with frightening clarity, its eyes glowing in the dark, its bloodcurdling yowl when he'd shot it.

He stared from the cast to the trailer. What in the dear Lord's name was going on here? If this was a fight over territory and the monsters killed anyone who got in their way while hunting each other, it was all the more imperative he find and end them.

Quell set his rifle down across his lap, watching the black space under the trailer where nothing stirred, glancing back at the empty highway. He ought to call his friend Deputy Bill. Report this. Get someone out here to dig the body out of the snow. The truck cab heated slowly, too slowly. His bones hurt and his heart beat too fast. How many days ago did those boys last see Brian?

How many days could a big cat go between meals?

His hands trembled. Quell spun the wheel, skidding in reverse, the truck bouncing dangerously over the ruts until the tires hit asphalt again. He sped back toward the motel in Mellen. Best not to do this in the dark. Call Bill in the morning. Cats were cunning; no way that big lynx-thing would chance another fight in the open. And Lord only knew what the ugly deer-thing would do next. Quell passed a hand over his face, cold perspiration prickling his brow.

He knew full well Bill wouldn't believe him. The deputies in Mellen hadn't seen the attack and they didn't believe the witnesses at Hettie's. Too dark and it happened so fast. People never wanted to accept the cold, hard truth: humans were just small prey to much bigger, more hideous things lurking in the woods. Hybrid things, like that scaly big lynx. Or a half-dead deer that walked on two feet. Absolutely unnatural. Shivering, he turned up the truck's heater, its loud rattle almost soothing his frayed nerves. Unfortunately, years of trying to make people grasp that Bigfeet were not only real, but part of a larger conspiracy, had taught him one thing. Most people treated his hard-won information as a joke. A scam. A load of hooey.

No one was going to aid him in this fight unless they saw for themselves what he was fighting. Which meant he'd need to bring at least one of these monsters in. Dead or alive.

Despair crouched at the back of his skull as he drove. He wasn't even sure where to go. And for the first time in years, he thought about having a serious drink, something stronger than beer. Maybe more than one.

The night swallowed the truck's headlights. He switched his brights on. The darkness of the forest and the cloudy sky and the road behind pressed in on him all the same.

27

The ranger frowned, checking the thermometer again. "Still too low. I think maybe we oughta get you over to the hospital."

Morty shook his head emphatically. "I'm fine. I'm warming up. Also, my toes hurt." He watched the second ranger unwrap the blanket around his feet and check. "See? Pink. Not blue. No frostbite." He wiggled his toes to prove he could. The second ranger, a young Ojibwe man, poked Morty's foot with the tip of his pen.

"Feel that?"

"Yes, and you can stop poking me every five minutes. Guys, I'm fine," Morty protested. He drank the last of his second helping of hot broth and set the mug aside on a table.

The first ranger seemed dubious. He was an older gent with a deeply lined face under jet black eyebrows and a patch which read Lemieux on his uniform. "How far back you say the slough was where you fell in?"

Morty shrugged. "Dunno, maybe a couple hundred yards. I could see your lights, and I got all excited and didn't look where I was going, and *sploosh*." He shook his head with a wry smile. "Definitely lucky this place was so close."

"Why didn't you just leave your clothes on?"

"Not thinking very clearly, I guess? I think I heard once, somewhere, it was better to get out of wet clothes in freezing weather. Something about it lowering your body temperature even more. I shucked 'em off and made a run for it." Lemieux kept frowning. Morty made a helpless gesture with both hands. "Okay, maybe that was stupid, but I'm here, I'm warm, and I'm extremely grateful you guys were here to help. Do you think now maybe I could borrow a phone?"

The older ranger studied him a few seconds more, then nodded. "All right. Sheriff down in Mellen was supposed to let your family know, but they'll probably want to hear from you." Morty nodded gamely. *You can call Jed, sure, good luck with that. Fat chance he'd care if I were dead.*

Brown, the younger ranger, laughed. "I think that sheriff wanted to come up here and see for himself. He couldn't believe you walked all this way. I bet it's over twenty-five miles in heavy snow."

"Yeah, crazy, huh?" Morty tried to laugh as well. "Thanks for letting them know I wasn't still missing." He needed to talk to Darcy and Kim, then remembered someone else who'd want to know how his quest had ended. "Could you also look up a number for me? I was talking a couple days ago with someone here on the reservation. Dr. Lightfoot. Sam Lightfoot. He's at the archaeological site near the Bad River Resort."

The two men exchanged a surprised glance. "You work with them?" asked Brown.

"Well, not really. I visited the dig site a week ago, and it really caught my interest. I was actually in Mellen to meet up with Dr. Lightfoot, to talk with him a little more, maybe volunteer?" Morty offered. Not too big of a lie.

He hadn't decided if it was a good thing or not that Sam had been at Happy Hettie's the same night Morty showed up looking for the Bigfoot hunter. He remembered seeing the horrendous thing inside him in the truck's mirror, and everything was a blank after that until waking up in Sam's basement. Sam had told him, after Morty was suitably sedated, how a shovel to the face had been what halted his panicked flight. That ache was now lost among too many others to count. At least frostbite wasn't a problem. No one would believe he'd been out in the snow since last night with no protection at all, and he sure as hell wasn't going to advertise the fact.

He shook the sting out of his fingers, nerve endings prickling uncomfortably as the heat of the wood stove bathed his flesh. He hadn't seen the thermometer reading. He guessed from Lemieux's glum reaction a few minutes ago that it wasn't ninety-eight point six. Morty suspected it probably wasn't going to rise that high. Ever again. *Coked-up Christ on a snowmobile. I just want to go home and forget the last week.*

He turned to Brown, who seemed uncertain. "Could I have that phone now, please? My girlfriend and my best buddy are probably worried, and I'd really like to talk to them."

Brown nodded. "Yeah, sure." He handed Morty a bulky satellite phone. "No cell service up here, and the damned wind tore down the lines in that last storm. Not like we're high priority on the phone company's to-do list."

Morty had to search his memory for Darcy's number, too used to relying on a cell phone. When he was fairly sure he recalled it, he punched the blocky buttons on the sat phone. She answered it after four rings, just as Morty was going to hang up. "Hello?"

"Darce, it's me." Relief and sudden fear swept through him, though he'd rehearsed a cover story mentally while the rangers fetched him blankets and hot drinks.

"Morty! Where are you? Are you okay?"

"I'm fine. Well, fine now, at least. I'm at the northernmost forest ranger station, on the reservation."

"Station Three-forty-three," Brown supplied. "Tell them to stop at the clinic at Odanah. We can drive you there to meet them." Lemieux shot him a frown. Morty nodded thanks and repeated the directions for Darcy.

"I'm on my way," Darcy said. "I set out as soon as the sheriff called. God, I'm so glad you're alive. Kim said everyone was out looking for you; he told me about the gun fight in the parking lot."

Damn. I owe you, Kim. "Yeah, it's all kind of a blur. I don't remember much. I heard gunshots, and I ran, and it was snowing and I guess I got all turned around in the woods," he said.

She sighed. "You shouldn't have left your apartment with that fever. Kim said you just had to see that band you like."

"Yeah. That band, right. Listen, don't be mad at Kim, okay? We've been on road trips before."

"I wish you'd told me you were planning on driving way up north this weekend," Darcy said. He could hear relief mixed with anger in her voice, and grimaced. This would take a lot of apologies. Better go with whatever Kim told her. He had no idea how he was going to spin all this to Kim. He must've heard the screams, at least, and the gunshot. Morty's muscles ached all over but he felt no pain equal to what he assumed being shot should have entailed. Realizing his brain was rambling, he coughed and tried to focus.

"I know. I thought about that a lot, while I was wandering in the woods. I'm really sorry, Darce. I should've texted you, at least, to let you know. It was just a spur of the moment thing."

"Kim said you'd been wanting to see that band forever," Darcy countered.

He backpedaled gracelessly. "Oh, well, yeah. I mean, who wouldn't? They're great live. We only decided to drive all the way at the last minute. You know, just a dumb guy thing, spur of the moment two-hundred-mile road trip." He hoped Kim told her it was a band he actually liked. "Darcy, I'm really, really sorry. I was stupid, thoughtless, inconsiderate..." He heard her soft sigh, and felt even more of a heel. "Idiotic, an asshole, a terrible boyfriend." She gave that tiny, delicate snort he adored, and relief spread through his chest. "Also, a lousy dancer, morally questionable, bad at sportsball, a staunch mocker of golf shorts, anti-cheap-beer-drinker, and the bearer of the tremendous burden of too much astonishing skill at lovemaking." As the words left his mouth, he remembered where he was and felt a flush rising in his cheeks. Ranger Brown winked and gave him a thumbs-up.

"I'm an idiot, Darce. I love you."

She sighed once more. "You are just a goober, you know that?"

"You're breaking up, what was that?" he teased, relieved.

"You're a *goob,* Mordecai."

"I'm a what? I don't know that word, being from a less fortunate socioeconomic strata where vocabulary was rather less constrained by the propriety of—"

"You are such an asshole," she laughed. He wanted to hug her tight, enfold her in his arms and against his body and do all he could to relieve her fears. His eyes closed. "Okay. I'm glad you're all right. I was really worried, Morty."

"Yeah. Me too." He still felt guilty. At least this was normal. This was good. "Please be careful. Are the roads plowed?"

"Yeah. I should be there in about three hours. And I'm taking you straight home with me. No arguments, Morty."

"Okay." He paused, picturing the pout of her lips, the determined frown almost certainly on her face at the moment. "I'm sorry, Darce."

"It's fine." Strength returned to her voice. "It will be, anyway, soon as we get you to a doctor. Do they have a doctor up there? Shouldn't they take you to the nearest hospital?"

"Darcy, I'm fine. Truly. Cross my heart. Just be careful. Oh, hey, does Kim know they found me?"

"Yes. I texted him right away. I would've called your brother or someone, but—"

"No worries." He'd never bothered to share any contact information for his family with her, or with Kim for that matter. Briefly, he wondered how his brother Jed would've reacted to news of his death. Probably mild irritation that he'd have to come claim the body. Good thing he hadn't interrupted Jed's sportsball season. "I'll call Kim next. You keep your eyes on the road, young lady. I swear, kids these days, all hopped up on goofballs and textin' and drivin'."

"Asshole," she said, and then, softer, "I love you, Morty. Be there soon."

"Love you. See you," Morty replied, and Darcy hung up before he could figure out which clunky button ended a call. He took a moment to compose his wild range of emotions, fear and relief winding equally around his brain.

He wanted to toss off the hot blankets wrapped around his shoulders; a glance at Lemieux stifled the urge. The ranger was eyeing him warily. Brown might buy the lost-in-the-woods story, but this guy clearly didn't. He was definitely going to go searching for Morty's clothes in every slough near here. Too bad they were back at the black lodge. Along with his wallet and phone. Not enough that he was repressing a centuries-old cannibal winter god inside his body; now he'd have to get his ID and cards replaced as well. He sighed. "All right if I make another call?"

Brown nodded. "How you feeling?"

"Better. Thanks. I don't suppose either of you have any clothes I could borrow?"

Brown appraised his narrow shoulders. "Well, mine would be big on you, but guess you can't go meet your girlfriend naked." He grinned, and left the room. Morty managed a dutiful chuckle. Lemieux stoked the fire in the wood stove, saying nothing. Tough crowd. Morty took a deep breath and punched in the number for BookStop.

He was passed to at least three different people, all exclaiming in relief that he'd been rescued, before Kim took the line. "Dude where the fuck have you been?"

"Lost," Morty replied, wincing. "I'm okay now. I found a rangers' station. They gave me blankets and broth. I'm lucky I stumbled across them."

"I heard a shot outside, and when I came out everyone was running around screaming, and a woman bled out right there in the parking lot! I looked for you, I kept calling your name. It was awful."

Morty cringed inside. "I'm so sorry. Some redneck just started shooting, and he barely missed me; scared the shit out of me. And I took off into the woods. I just ran, and I got lost, and I ran until I couldn't hear people screaming any more, and then I couldn't find my way back. It was snowing, and I couldn't see a thing."

"The sheriff had search parties out hunting for you," Kim said, sounding pained. "For two days. You never heard them?"

Morty swallowed dryly. "No, I—it's all kind of a blur. I was pretty feverish. I just stumbled around a long time. Slept under a big fir tree at one point. Couldn't figure out where I was. Thought I was going south; apparently it was north." He felt the older ranger studying him, and cut short the elaborate story he'd planned. "Anyway, I saw lights and headed for them, and the rangers found me. Good thing, too."

"The deputy from Mellen called me," Kim said. "And then Darcy texted like five minutes later. I've been trying to find the number for whatever backasswoods place you're at, but nobody would give me any info. I tried the Ashland cops, I even tried the reservation offices."

"Here I am," Morty said, trying for chipper.

"Fuck you, goddammit." Kim sounded close to breaking. "Jesus, why did I agree to take you up there, chasing some completely whack conspiracy theory."

"Hey, this is not your fault."

"I could tell you were sick and talking complete craziness and I drove you up there anyway!" Kim shouted. Morty flinched. "And then I had to make up crap to tell Darcy because I know she'd flip out if I told her any of the weird bullshit you were babbling about. Christ, dude. Werewolves? Bigfoot hunters?"

Morty shrank into his blanket shroud. "I know. I know. I wasn't in my right mind. I'm okay now."

"You better be!" Kim snapped. Silence fell, punctuated by soft static crackling on the line.

"I'm sorry, man. Thank you for telling Darcy whatever you did. The road trip thing."

"Yeah."

"What band were we seeing?"

Kim paused. "Pretty sure it was GWAR."

Morty choked, a laugh startled out of him. "GWAR. In North BFE."

"Yeah. Surprise concert. You know how much lumberjacks love alien thrash metal."

Morty glanced at Lemieux and tamped down his laughter. "Right, right. Naturally."

Kim sounded calmer. "I'm glad you're, you know. Not dead."

"Me too. Thank you. Seriously. None of this is your fault. I was sick."

"You feel better now?"

"Yeah. Guess wandering around in freezing wind blew the fever right out of me."

"Pretty sure that's absolute bullshit. Whatever. Glad you're safe. Darcy coming up to get you?"

"She was already on her way when I talked to her a minute ago." He forced a smile. "I think she intends to lock me up in her parents' house."

"Serve you right, asshole."

Morty sighed. "It would."

"You're really okay? Not still convinced your neighbors were killed by a monster? You know, the cops caught some dickhead trying to break into another house a couple streets up. Just yesterday. They think he's the same guy who killed your next-door neighbor and the old lady. Looking for money, high on meth, freaked out and went psycho when he couldn't find whatever wealth he thought was hidden in the mattresses."

Convenient. Morty doubted the robber's *modus operandi* included savagely butchering and eating his victims. There was nothing he could do to fix what had happened. Morty forced levity. "What a rube. Old-people money is always tucked into their Bibles, in two-dollar increments."

"Yeah," Kim chuckled. "You sure you're all right?"

"I'm great. I'm sitting here by a nice cozy wood stove while the rangers ply me with chicken broth and sultry charm." He smiled at Brown, who'd returned holding up a pair of jeans and a flannel shirt. "I think we're about to play dress-up. I kinda lost my clothes when I fell into a slough."

Kim laughed. "You are the worst. Ask 'em to fix your feet so you don't keep tripping over them." Morty snorted, relieved. "Okay. You want to talk to Leila? She'll probably give you the week off, seeing as how you're the poor rescued village idiot now."

"Yeah, put her on. And thanks, Kim. I mean it."

Morty endured a few minutes of his boss fussing at him. He agreed to let her know when he arrived back home and when he was recovered enough to return to work. If he had a say in it, he'd be back within another day at most. He wanted badly to slide back into normality.

He tried on the clothing Brown offered him. While the apparel was categorically sized for a more muscular man, it fit adequately, if comically, with a belt and the shirt tucked in. He was given clean, thick socks and spare mud boots. He donned his new duds while the rangers argued over whether they should take him to Odanah yet. Lemieux pointed out he'd radioed ahead to make sure a nurse would be waiting at the clinic there, and that settled the matter. Morty put on the heavy coat and hat they insisted he borrow and climbed into the Snowcat with Lemieux. Brown cheerily waved them off.

Despite it being just after noon, the light of day was dim and gray, and the landscape of endless snow over the quiet marshlands felt dead and empty to Morty. He almost jumped when Lemieux spoke. "So...you wandered in the woods, for two days, from Mellen to here."

"Uh, yeah."

The ranger kept his eyes on the road. "You didn't notice when you crossed right over Highway Two?"

"Must've been at night."

Lemieux gave one nod. Morty didn't know what else he could say. He huddled in the oversized coat, feeling overheated in the cramped cab of the Snowcat as it bumped over the trackless snow.

"Been hearing funny things about the shooting down in Mellen."

"Oh yeah?"

"Some people claim a rabid bear tore out a woman's throat. Right there in the parking lot of a bar. Or two bears. Or an elk and a panther were fighting. You see anything like that?"

"I don't remember. Everything happened so fast."

"You have scars on your back that look pretty fresh."

"Just thorns. Tripped into a blackberry patch." *Thanks, Marie; at least one thing coming out of my mouth doesn't sound like a total lie.* He couldn't deny her vicious little lesson this morning hadn't forced him to exert better control over the *manitou* inside his flesh.

Lemieux grunted, though Morty wasn't sure if that implied acceptance or doubt. "You don't remember seeing any wild animals in Mellen?"

"It's all a blur. I remember some asshat shooting at something, and that's what scared me into the woods."

"Sheriff said it was an old hunter passing through. A number of witnesses swore two huge animals were fighting in the parking lot, and he shot at them. Although some of the descriptions didn't sound too believable."

Morty shrugged. "I didn't see anything. The parking lot was pretty dark. Plus, they do serve alcohol, so maybe a few of the patrons were unreliable witnesses by that point anyway."

Lemieux side-eyed him, but said only, "Could be."

They continued in silence another minute. Morty gazed out the window, hot and uncomfortable. How far was it to this town, anyway? Assuming they were headed to a town. The suspicious ranger could be taking Morty out to the middle of nowhere. Slow panic shivered in Morty's guts. Lemieux must've heard the old stories and myths, if he grew up here. Sam had said every tribe up north had *wendigo* stories. Stories so scary they were only told in the dead of winter, when malicious animals such as toads and snakes were asleep, so as not to draw their attention. If Lemieux read any of the actual witness statements, like from the husband of the woman whose throat was ripped out... Morty couldn't repress a shudder. There was nothing he could do about it. Except make sure this thing never surfaced ever again.

"You said you were at the archaeological site."

Morty wrenched his attention back to Lemieux. "That's right. A week ago."

"How much of it did you get to see?"

"Some. Very impressive. I think it pre-dates even the Ho-Chunk, they said. Really fascinating. I still want to talk to Dr. Lightfoot, if possible. I'm sure he was wondering why I didn't show up to our meeting in Mellen."

"Mm." Lemieux didn't reply to his suggestion. After another long pause he said, "Not everyone thinks digging into a burial mound of the Elders is a great idea."

"Oh no?" Morty tried to keep his tone and his expression guileless. He suppressed the urge to start jigging his knee.

"It's disrespectful. We've fought to have sacred bones returned to us after white men took them for museums. Kinda strange for one of our own to be doing it now."

"I was under the impression the new museum was going to be on the reservation. And that only the pots and artifacts would be displayed, not the skeleton," Morty offered.

"You saw the Elder? The skeleton?"

Morty hesitated. "Have you?"

Lemieux shot him a hard stare. "Yes."

Morty shook his head, trying to laugh. "Pretty weird, huh? Very ceremonial, I guess. I was told it was going to be reburied somewhere else."

"Should be burned to ashes," Lemieux growled, surprising Morty.

"Wouldn't that be disrespectful?"

The ranger glared at him a moment, then stared back out at the snow. "They should never have opened that mound."

Morty couldn't argue with that. He shut up, watching icy brushland give way slowly to small groups of fir trees. A couple of trailers appeared, a cabin, a highway. The Snowcat's tracks rumbled easily along the snow-dusted asphalt. Finally, actual roads. His legs ached from the long trek this morning, after tromping across the lake last night. Holy frozen assholes, Batman. This was the longest lost weekend ever. "So this is Odanah?"

"Yep."

Morty nodded. "It's nice."

Lemieux grunted again. He drove the Snowcat past a small gas station, a casino with bright neon signs, and several other buildings before turning onto a side road. Signs directed visitors to the tribal offices. The ranger was quiet until he parked the vehicle outside a larger building, its broadly sloped roof caked in thick snow. Morty checked the sign, writ both in English and what he assumed was Ojibwe. "Fish and Wildlife Commission?"

Lemieux opened the door, killing the engine. "Home office. Come on."

Morty followed him inside, stamping the snow from his borrowed boots before walking after the ranger into a dark room. "Hey, so I wanted to thank you again, you know, for rescuing me." He froze as the ranger turned with a shotgun in hand. *Oh crap. I'm calm, I'm not changing, I'm chill...*

Morty stared at the weapon. Motion-triggered florescent lights flickered on overhead. Lemieux stared steadily at him a moment, then tucked the gun under his arm. "Just wanted to pick this up," he said. "We're going across to the clinic now. Nurse there can check you out."

Morty swallowed. "Right. Cool." Lemieux didn't move. Morty looked at the gun again. He couldn't tell if it was loaded or not; he knew almost nothing about guns. Getting blown apart at point-blank range couldn't be a healthy thing. Not even for a *wendigo*.

Lemieux nodded down at the weapon. "Just a precaution. Mellen's not so far from here that a rabid bear couldn't come this way."

"Right," Morty said, trying to keep his voice calm. "Sure. Rabies is serious stuff."

"Go on," Lemieux said, nodding at the doorway. "Straight across. That big ugly place over there is the social services center. Clinic's inside to the right."

"Sure," Morty said, nodding. "I understand you're just being helpful. And I appreciate it. I'm really fine. I feel fine."

"You weren't warming up very well."

Morty choked out a laugh. "Are you kidding? What is this, down-stuffed? This coat is incredibly warm. I'm great. No frostbite. You guys saved me in time." Crap. If a nurse judged him too cold she sure as hell would send him to the hospital. He just wanted to go home. Lemieux waited; reluctantly Morty began walking where he was told to go. He heard the ranger's soft footsteps behind him, crunching lightly through the snow when they crossed the short distance between buildings.

Please. I just want to go back to my life. Normal, average, boring life. No wendigo, *no water panther, no sadistic shaman.* He sat down in the clinic exam room where Lemieux indicated, waiting for the nurse, closing his eyes. *Just gaming with friends, reading old books, eating more spicy food than is good for me. I want to go back home, go back to Darcy...just want to crawl into bed with her and hold her and be me again. No weirdness, no horrible dietary urges, just plain old average Morty. I just want that.* He took in a slow, deep breath and held it for a beat.

The nurse blew in, clipboard in hand, chattering before Morty could begin his exhale. "There you are, the lucky man. My goodness, what an ordeal! Let's just have a look at you." Morty blinked at her overwhelming chipperness while she turned his head this way and that. She peered into his eyes, felt under his jaw, and pulled off the borrowed boots and socks and gloves to examine his feet and hands. She thrust a thermometer into his mouth. He gamely held it there with his lips while she checked his blood pressure. She pulled out the glass stick and squinted at it. "Ninety-eight point two. Well, close enough, and I don't see any sign of frostbite. Wiggle your toes. Do you feel that?"

"Ow," he said, and she poked the other foot with whatever sharp object she was wielding.

"And that?"

"Ow. Yes."

She looked pleased. "Well. You are incredibly lucky you found the ranger station. There's pretty much nothing else in that area at all. Jim, you've done this young man quite a service." She beamed at Lemieux. He glanced at her, then back at Morty.

Temperature almost normal. He stared at his fingers. The cuts in his fingertips were faded, the flesh pink with healthy blood. Yes. Hell yes. Just an ordinary guy who'd survived a Jack-London-worthy trek through freezing wilderness. Gaining courage, he replied, "Yeah, I would've been up the creek without the proverbial paddle if this man and his fellow ranger hadn't been there. I'm extremely grateful for their help."

Lemieux frowned. "He was at the site of an alleged rabid animal attack, and he says he can't remember much. Could you run some tests?"

"Oh, sure. Of course we won't get the results back for a couple of days, since we have to send out to the lab at Ashland, but I will definitely get blood work started. Wouldn't want to overlook anything. Could you take off your shirt and hop up here for me?" she chirped, scribbling on the clipboard sheet. Morty obeyed, feeling the ranger's eyes on him. The nurse glanced at his bare chest and shoulders. "You do farm work? Dairy?"

"Uh, no. Bookstore."

"Ope, just gonna get in here and tie this." She buzzed around him on the exam table, tying a rubber hose around his upper left arm while she prepped a needle. "Looks like you have a couple old scars there. Thought you might have tangled with barbed wire, ya know."

Lemieux's gaze hardened. Morty gave an awkward shrug. "Blackberry thorns," Morty said.

The nurse clucked her tongue. "Oh, gosh darn it, those things are so prickly. I know how that is. Got a garden in the summer, and every year, those things manage to get me no matter how careful I am." She jabbed the needle into Morty's inner elbow, quickly drawing a blood sample and just as quickly releasing the tourniquet and pressing a small gauze square to the pinprick wound. "Just hold that there for me a sec, 'k?" Morty winced, though the sting died swiftly. The scars Marie had left were thinner, fainter, than they'd been an hour ago. The scar on his left palm was still red. The nurse nodded at it while she strapped a small bandage over the needle hole. "That must've hurt. What'd you do there, then?"

"Oh, that? I fell onto something."

"You get it checked out? What was it, rusty nail?"

"The nurse at the Bad River Resort gave me a tetanus shot," he said quickly, certain this nurse would jab him again before he could blink if he didn't head her right off.

"Well that's good." She examined the scar. "Looks like you maybe could've used a couple stitches, though. What cut you?"

"An antler. A really sharp antler," he added at her dubious expression. He berated himself silently. He should've made up something. Dropped a glass bottle on the floor, tin can that fought being recycled, undead ninja pirates with cutlasses, anything. Lemieux stared at him. Morty shifted around on the exam table, wrapping his arms around his stomach. "Could I get a blanket?"

"Oh, you poor dear. You can put your shirt back on; I just need to listen to your heart and lungs a sec, okay?" He took and released several deep breaths at her direction, and she patted his shoulder. "Everything sounds good. You don't seem to be having any trouble breathing, and it doesn't sound like there's any fluid in your lungs. You can cover up, and I'll fetch you a blanket." She swept out of the room.

Lemieux glared at Morty's bare hand. "Cut by an antler," he said.

Morty's heart thudded. He kept his voice calm. "Yep. Stupidest thing."

The ranger shifted his grip on the shotgun. "You sure seem a lot better than you did an hour ago."

"Thanks," Morty said. A scowl crossed the ranger's face. The nurse bustled back in, wrapping a wool blanket around Morty like a shawl.

"There ya go. Here's some water, drink up. Let's get your socks back on too—there we go. Now is anyone coming to get you?"

"My girlfriend is on her way."

"Oh, that's so sweet. She must be a wonderful young lady to come all this way. You hold onto that one."

"I absolutely will," Morty agreed. The nurse turned and finally spotted the shotgun Lemieux held.

"Jim! Now you know you can't bring that in here. You shouldn't even have it in the building." She shooed him with flapping hands. "I swear. Just because it's fox season doesn't mean you can bring your guns with you everywhere and you know that, Jim Lemieux! Take it outside right now."

Lemieux frowned. "He seems all right to you?"

The nurse huffed. "Didn't I just say what a wonderful job you did rescuing him? Yes, thank goodness, there are no signs of hypothermia or frostbite. You feeling warmer now, hon?" she asked Morty. He nodded, and she smiled. "I'm so glad. Now you just rest here. You can sit in the chair if you're more comfortable, or if you want to take a nap, I'll turn the lights off for you. You must be exhausted!"

Morty nodded meekly. "That sounds very nice, thank you."

The nurse beamed at him. Morty lay down on the padded table, and she fussed with the blanket. "There you are. You just rest a bit, and soon your girlfriend will be here to pick you up." Morty nodded again. She turned off the light and practically pushed Lemieux out the door. "Let him rest, Jim. And get that gun out of here; I am not telling you again."

The door clicked shut. Morty let out a slow sigh of relief, grateful to be in the care of the fussiest nurse in the Northwoods. He closed his eyes, trying to get comfortable on the narrow table. He'd just wait here for Darcy, then go home, and never set foot in this place ever again.

He could hear the low cadence of Lemieux's voice outside the room, and another hushed burst of argument from the nurse. With any luck the nurse would shove the ranger right out of the building. He was far too suspicious. And Sam had told Morty what the best cure was for a *wendigo*. He shivered, curling the blanket tighter for protection from the monsters in the darkness. He was deeply relieved his vital signs appeared normal. He felt completely himself, heartbeat steady, breath calm and assured, not too hot nor too cold. Perfectly human. *Huh. I'll bet that's how Marie does it.*

He didn't expect to doze off. He woke, blurrily, to the nurse shaking his shoulder. "Hey there, wake up, someone is here to see you," she said, voice soft and excited. Disoriented, Morty rubbed the sleep from his eyes and sat up. And then Darcy's arms were around him, her breath hot on his cheek, her forehead pressed to his. He embraced her and felt her breath hitch. Her warm tears trickled against his skin.

"Darce," he murmured, hugging her tight. After a moment, he dropped his feet to the floor, feeling unsteady. She braced her body against his. He leaned against the table, gladly pulling her close again, burying his nose in her hair to inhale her clean, heady amber-and-vanilla scent. The nurse made appreciative "awwws" and bustled around, turning on the light, placing the mud boots by his feet.

"I'm so glad you're all right," Darcy said. Morty stroked her cheek, smiling at her.

"Me too. You didn't have to drive all this way." She opened her mouth to protest, and he added, "But I'm very happy you did. You're the best."

She smiled, wiping tears from her cheeks, mascara starting to smear. "And doing my favorite zombie chick thing, too. You spoil me," he said. She laughed, hugging him tight.

"You're such a dork. Oh my God, you are skin and bones. Did you eat anything? Did he eat anything?" She turned to the nurse.

"I think he had broth at the ranger's station. There's a restaurant over at the casino; I think they're open today for a little while longer," the nurse suggested.

Darcy nodded firmly, going right into practical Midwestern mode. "Sounds great. Babe, bundle up and let's get you some food before we drive back. What would you like?"

The wholly unwelcome image of glistening, crimson intestines surged into Morty's head. He froze, not realizing his fingers had clenched on Darcy's shoulder until she squirmed. "Ow, careful. Are you okay?"

"Yeah," he said, shaken. "It's just been a really long weekend." He had to keep himself from flinching when she touched his face. She gazed solemnly into his eyes, and stroked delicate fingers down his nose and up his cheek, smiling at the scruff on his chin.

"I love you," she said. "And you're safe now. And we're going home. Just as soon as we get real food into you." She glanced at the nurse. "No fever?"

"Nope. He's fine to travel. He's very lucky to have people who care so much about him."

Morty's mouth felt too wet. He touched his tongue to his teeth. They seemed normal. He swallowed the extra saliva. "Yes. I'm extremely lucky." He searched Darcy's earnest gaze for any sign of disapproval, any hint she saw anything at all wrong with him. Her expression turned questioning.

"You'll tell me if you start feeling bad again, right?" He nodded dumbly, and she smiled, taking his hand in hers. He stared at their entwined fingers, his average, clumsy ones in her long slender ones. His fingerbones remained inside his skin. Darcy grinned. "Look at you. You need a good meal. How about if I buy you a fat, juicy steak?"

Her tone was soft and teasing, her eyes bright. She swung his hand lightly in hers as if nothing was wrong and nothing ever would be wrong. Morty swallowed again. His voice sounded raspy, even for him; he croaked out, "That would be great."

"Come on, then. Love you, Mordecai."

"Love you," he replied, and let himself be pulled out of the clinic.

28

Darcy spent the remainder of Sunday night at his place, curled into his arms in bed; eventually Morty slept as well. If he dreamed anything, it was gone in the morning when Darcy handed him a mug of hot coffee and kissed him. After he promised several times he'd stay in all day, she reluctantly left him to attend her classes.

Morty spent Monday cleaning the apartment. Tying a handkerchief over his nose and mouth helped while he scraped up the frozen mess on the porch and double-bagged it in the trash to prevent any odors escaping. He took it to the bin outside for good measure. He lit a candle Darcy had given him at Christmas; it smelled of cranberries and pine needles. The vaguely foresty scent calmed him somewhat. He carried bedsheets down and back from the basement laundry, mopped the cheap linoleum floors, vacuumed the carpet, and scrubbed the small bathroom.

The day turned sunny. Morty opened the curtains, thinking more light would banish the darkness creeping around the edges of his thoughts, but after just a few minutes of squinting, he gave up and shut them again. His rooms were warmly, if dimly, lit, and that would do. He took a shower and carefully shaved, and refused to think about anything except making himself and his place presentable again.

He certainly he didn't think about how quiet it was next door. He certainly didn't imagine he could still smell the blood if he ventured too close to that wall. He lit a second candle.

Darcy took him out to buy him a new phone, overruling his guilty protests until he shut up and picked out the color of case he preferred. She kissed him and twined her arm through his all evening. Dinner at an excellent noodle joint downtown was her treat. Morty grumbled he had money in the bank, though he still needed to replace all his cards. He showed off his chopstick skills by feeding bites of his pork *phở* to her, happy when she giggled at him, and relieved that food no longer tasted strange and burnt. Seeing her happy, he was able to relax a bit. Guilt wouldn't stop romping around in his head, though, and he took both her hands in his. "Darce, I'm really sorry. I should've told you. It was just such a last-minute thing. I still should've at least texted you. Especially considering what happened." He brushed his fingers over her smooth, soft palms, tamping down the dismay he couldn't tell her everything. He felt much better, no more pain or horrible cravings. He stared worriedly into her eyes. "Never again. I promise."

Darcy nodded, and then leaned in to kiss him. Morty hesitated a second, remembering the urge which had made him bite her fingers. *She smelled so delicious. Skin so sweet I wanted to taste her.*

Then her lips were pressed to his, soft and yielding. He closed his eyes, smelling her faint vanilla perfume, and gently touched his tongue to hers. She made an agreeable sound and began exploring his mouth. Morty stroked one hand through her silky hair, doing his best to silence the fear trembling in his chest. *I should just shut up and let the lady do what she wants with me. Stop being an idiot. Everything's fine.*

Darcy pulled back, smiling, a flush creeping up her neck. She squeezed his hand. "You'd better not run off like that again. I'll get a bloodhound and track you down."

He smiled back. "Diana the huntress, huh?" He knew her favorite class last semester had been Feminist Perspectives on Classical Mythology. When she blushed, he added, "See? I pay attention."

She tossed her hair back. She'd worn it loose and unstyled tonight, which he preferred to the salon waves she'd had when they'd first met. "Yeah, that's right. You stray too far out in the woods and I will come after you, you bad beast."

Morty saw the way she bit her lip before smiling at him again. She had to be upset. Going off the way he did had been incredibly stupid. Especially while running a fever. Morty tried to shove aside the guilt as well as the memories which continued to bubble redly just under his conscious thoughts. No. Whatever all that was, it was done. Everything was back to how it should be. He covered his anxiety with another shot of hot *sake*. The heat and immediate pleasant fuzziness helped. "I'm a beast? And what will you do once you catch me, o huntress?" He waggled his eyebrows at her.

She giggled. "Goob." She leaned closer and whispered in his ear, so close he felt the tiny hairs prickle. "I guess I'll just have to tame you."

"I believe I might enjoy being tamed," he agreed, fingers stroking over hers and up her arm.

She gazed into his eyes a long moment, her breath hot against his cheek. "Let's go. I want you out of those clothes." Morty's throat went dry. Without taking her eyes off his, she eased back into her seat and waved for their waiter. Happily, the drive back to his apartment was brief. As he climbed the stairs to his apartment ahead of her, he jumped when she smacked his ass. Damn. He should get lost in the woods more often.

Morty was glad he'd taken the time to clean his apartment; Darcy glanced around approvingly while he hung up their coats.

"Can I get you anything to—whoa!" She grabbed him, pulling his head down so his mouth met hers, hungry and eager. Morty held her close, her breasts rubbing against his chest, giving himself over to the heat of the kiss. "Or," he gasped, "we could skip to the main course," he offered when she let him take a breath. Darcy grinned, tugging him by the hand after her as she strode to the bedroom.

"Strip," she ordered, and he obliged. She ran her fingers over his unimpressive chest and soft stomach as though he were the sexiest man alive, and his blood surged in response. Her breath quickened, and she stroked down his growing shaft, making him groan. He reached for her blouse; she lightly slapped his hand away. "How dare you touch the Huntress."

He chuckled, enjoying the flush of pink all down her cheeks and neck. Confidence was sexy as hell on her. "O, mighty Huntress, your beast is aroused, and he must rut!" He shoved his erection against her, and she backed up, laughing, falling onto the bed. Morty growled, pouncing. Again she slapped his reaching hands away.

"No! Bad beast. You must—" She wriggled out of her jeans and underwear. "You must be tamed!" The delightful sight of her curvy hips and nicely muscled thighs gave Morty extra incentive to grab her. Darcy squeaked in protest, standing on the mattress and yanking up his pillow. "Bad beast. Down! No!"

He laughed, ducking his head as she thwacked him several times. "Oh mercy, fair Huntress. I am only a simple creature of the forest, and all I crave is your touch." Breathless, she tossed aside the pillow, grinning down at him. Morty stretched out on his back, opening his arms wide. "Give to me your blessing, and I will be your loyal beast always."

Darcy chuckled, a low and musical sound which sent pleasurable shivers down his spine. She peeled off her blouse and dangled her unhooked bra in his face. He breathed deeply; her scent was clean and sweet, filling his nose, tingling across the roof of his mouth.

"Well then," she said. She dropped to her knees on either side of his legs and wriggled closer to where he wanted her, skin shining in the warm lamplight. "Submit to me, and maybe I'll spare you."

"Oh, I absolutely submit," he agreed, enfolding her in his arms and kissing her.

"Play with me," she whispered. Morty sucked gently on her lower lip as he slipped one hand between her thighs. When his fingers found her soft folds, teasing her, she sighed, grinding against him. She kissed him deeply, moaning, when he stroked one finger up and into her. "Oh, God, yes. More..."

He gently eased a second finger inside, moving slowly. Darcy rubbed herself into his hand, speed building, kissing his shoulder, her breath hot against his skin. Morty kissed her neck, rising to suckle her nipples gently when she sat up with a soft moan, inhaling rich vanilla bean and amber musk, sweetness and depth. When she gasped he realized his teeth were pressing against her skin, and pulled back in dazed surprise. Darcy stared at him, her eyes full of determination. "Mount me," she said, "be my beast, Morty."

He hardened the rest of the way immediately, almost painfully. "Well if it's a beast you want," he rasped, and with a lunge rolled her so he ended up on top, "then the Huntress will have to give in to the rut."

Darcy stared at him, eyes wide. Then she turned over, spreading her legs. Morty growled, sliding off the bed to stand, and took hold of her thighs. Her muscles tensed. He ran his hands gently up and down her calves until she relaxed, then slowly pulled her to the edge of the bed, lowering her feet to the floor. Her whole body shivered, and she looked over her shoulder at him as she raised herself on her forearms, her breasts enticingly visible with nipples taut. They'd played in bed before; however, this was a new level of role-play. Making sure, Morty asked in a low voice, "Is this what my Huntress desires?"

Darcy gulped, and nodded.

Morty grasped her hips firmly, used his feet to nudge hers wider apart, and thrust deeply. Darcy cried out, and he struggled not to move further though every instinct flared to simply slam himself inside her again. Darcy pulled slowly away and then, delight of delights, pushed herself against him. A deep, only half-conscious moan rolled from Morty's throat, and he began thrusting, pulling her hips toward him each time he rocked forward. Heat welled from her into him, up his stomach and chest, making his head swim. She cried out again and again, her scent filling his nostrils as his whole body tensed, straining to plunge his full length into her each time. His skull throbbed, he gripped her tightly, panting, and something flickered at the corner of his eye. He glanced that way and slowed, ice shooting through his chest.

The squirrel stared in through the slim break between the curtains of the window nearest the bed. The warm light from inside caught the blackness of its eyes. "More," Darcy panted, "Almost there; more, my beast..."

Morty glanced down and saw his long, tapered cock, slick with her arousal, poised at her entrance. The coarse fur of his groin was damp from her. His wide, split-toed hooves were planted firmly just between her feet on the rug. His head jerked toward the bathroom door. The mirror on the back of it reflected the growing antlers jutting from his head. "No," he whimpered, desire fading swiftly. Darcy shoved herself back, taking him inside her again with a moan. Morty choked, staring at the long claws stretching from his fingertips; he jerked them away from her skin. "Fuck," he moaned. *No, this can't be happening, not now, I don't want to hurt her, not her, no please—*

And Darcy pushed against him hard, taking his entire length with a happy cry, and Morty swooned as her heat rushed from his loins to his head.

He clasped her hips tightly and bucked into her, over and over, hard as he could. He threw his head back, a wordless deep-bellied shout bursting from his lungs as he climaxed. Darcy screamed, shaking violently, and collapsed onto the bed, pulling free of him.

Morty staggered back, dazed, frightened. "Oh no," he whispered, "Please no." He strained, trying to focus over the panic, and forced his claws to melt back into his fingers. Pain wrenched his spine, and he clutched at the bedside table, willing his bones to resume their proper shapes and places. He shot a glare out the window. The squirrel twitched its whiskers at him and darted out of sight.

Darcy sighed, curling up in his blanket, pulling it around her. Thankfully her eyes were closed. She was still breathing hard, her face beatific, her smile one of utter delight. Morty took a step toward his robe on the hook of the bathroom door, and she mumbled, "Baby?"

"One sec, just going for a glass of water." She murmured what sounded like agreement, so he snatched his robe and quickly pulled it on, knotting the ties as he hurried into the living room. Morty turned the lock and yanked open the porch door. The squirrel, huge and gray and unblinking, perched atop his deck chair. Morty snarled; it didn't so much as flinch. He came out on the porch, ignoring the fierce wind blowing through the screens. "You utter little shitweasel," he growled, advancing on it, "You did that, didn't you? That fucked-up deer lycanthropy thing in there, just now."

It didn't move, didn't blink. Its speech blasted into his brain, knocking him back a step. "Why do you protest? Your mate enjoyed it."

Morty shook off the shock of its telepathy. "No!" he said, then in frustration lowered his voice. "That," he hissed, "was wrong. That was evil! You have no right to screw up my life like this. What are you doing here? I haven't done anything!"

The *Bagwajinini's* buzzing voice almost sounded amused. "I am here to remind you of your oath, *wendigo*. More and more knife-spirits come into our woods, and they have resumed felling the trees by the mound of the winter *manitou*. You must stop them."

Morty shook his head angrily. "What am I supposed to do? Take down an entire oil company by myself? I have news for you: I'm just an average guy. I have no power in this world."

"That is a lie. We do not tolerate lies. Especially not from you, abomination." Fire shot through his head; Morty choked on a yelp, his hands going to his skull to find the antlers trying to spread upwards again. Heaving for breath, he forced them to dissolve. He wasn't sure if they melted back inside him or just vanished, and didn't care at this point. The squirrel continued calmly, "You will go back to the burial mound. You will make the destroyers stop. You will convince them to go away. This is your bargain."

Morty clutched his robe tighter around himself, feeling naked and judged. "What am I supposed to do, claw the plows and the timber trucks? Hope AmShale doesn't send more of them?" He gestured furiously at the quiet backyards below the porch. "Go forth and eat all of their workers? Besides the fact that's utterly repulsive, it won't work. They'll just increase security; bring more and more people into your goddamned forest, and start drilling as soon as they can anyway. I can't stop all that. I wish I could."

The squirrel regarded him blankly and shrugged, the movement so minute that had it not been so still before, Morty wouldn't have caught it at all. "Our verdict was clear. Even you should understand this. The spirit of the Starving Moon lives in your flesh. This will not be tolerated, unless you turn the dark power to restore balance in our land."

Morty threw up his hands, out of words. *Fuck this. Fuck evil dead cannibal gods, and shamans, and all this weirdness...* He looked back at the *Bagwajinini,* which hadn't moved. "And fuck creepy squirrels that aren't squirrels in particular," he muttered. It twitched a whisker. Morty couldn't tell if it was laughing at him or contemplating killing him where he stood. Or worse. He came closer, fists clenched. Snow blew into the porch. One flake touched his nose, and he brushed it off. He realized he was barefoot. Ice glistened on each thin hair on his bare legs. He wasn't cold at all.

All anger seeped away, replaced by numbness. "What the hell am I supposed to do?"

"Your tribe is inventive, if stubbornly childish. You will think of something. Do it soon, *wendigo.* We are watching." It abruptly leapt from the chair, zipping toward the rip in the porch screen.

Morty snarled at it, "Fine! But don't ever turn me into a sex deer again!"

It paused at the edge of the railing, staring back. "We did nothing." They stared at one another. Morty's whole frame stiffened with shock, and then the squirrel was gone.

Morty started, realizing it had been some time since he left the bedroom, purportedly to fetch water. His fingers trembled when he closed them around the doorknob and let himself back into the apartment. Under the dread, his thoughts raced like panicked rabbits. He filled a glass with water from the kitchen tap, and rinsed off the blood from his fingers. His scalp felt damp; touching it revealed more blood where the antlers had grown from his skull right through his skin. He wiped it off as best he could with a wet rag at the sink, and walked slowly back to the bedroom.

Morty touched his head, feeling no antlers. Everything was quiet and normal. When he set the glass down on the nightstand, Darcy opened her eyes and smiled at him. "Hey," she said.

"Hey."

He sat down next to her; she curled around him, kissing his cheek. "Your scars look a lot better."

"Yeah."

She smiled at him, one hand stroking up his back. "You are amazing." He shook his head with a grimace. She argued, "Babe, that was—wow." She laughed. "Just wow." Morty tried to smile; it felt forced. Darcy leaned in to plant kisses on his bare chest. She started tugging his robe open wider. Morty gently caught her hands in his, and she pouted. "Aww. But I want your cuddly tummy."

He quirked an eyebrow at her, the silliness of her protest pulling him up from the depths. Darcy sighed, and snuggled against him. "I wish you could see how good you are to me. I love you, Mordecai."

An ache pierced his heart. He put an arm around her and kissed her. "Love you too, Huntress."

She snickered, hugging him. "Okay. I'm going to clean up. I'm staying the night. Where's the phone charger I left here?"

Morty found the cord and plugged in her phone. While she stepped into the bathroom to wash up, he looked at the screen. She'd been browsing earlier for camping sites, no doubt thinking about their six-month anniversary, which she'd told him would be "outdoorsy stuff." The picture of pristine woods and a burbling creek sparked a tiny thought. He turned the idea over in his head a bit. He opened her browser and searched for AmShale and the Bad River. He found a public notice of a meeting by the county's Natural Resources department in two days' time. 'Informational meeting.' It sounded like the kind where they simply stated what they were going to do because any chance to protest anything was already swept under the corporate rug.

When Darcy returned, smelling of his sandalwood soap, she tilted her head curiously at him. "What's up?"

Morty swallowed his fear and turned the screen toward her. "You know, after seeing how pretty the woods are up by the resort, and knowing what's going to happen to them once your dad's company starts drilling, I had an idea." She toweled the ends of her hair, waiting. He gathered his courage and managed a small smile. "Exactly how badly do you want to be the rebel in your family?"

29

Morty glanced at the flyer handed to him detailing the health risks posed by fracking. He nodded thanks, then turned his attention to the basement auditorium. He'd done plenty of research already. He was dismayed to recognize a few faces from the Book Across the Bay, but nobody had looked twice at him yet. He hoped the volunteer crew chief wasn't here. He didn't feel like explaining why he didn't turn in his vest at the end. He was surprised to see a small group of Ojibwe sitting off by themselves, and deeply uncomfortable to observe Sam was with them. He jumped when Darcy touched his arm.

"Pretty decent turnout," she said, then frowned at him. "You okay?"

"Yeah, I'm fine. Guess we should find seats before the room fills up," he joked, gesturing around at the small room where only half of the folding chairs were in use.

A couple of space heaters didn't do much to abate the chill, Morty guessed, since he noticed most people had sweaters or coats on. He realized his flannel shirt, open to show off his vintage "Fight the Power" tee underneath, stood out among all the folks dressed more warmly (and conservatively). It was far too late to do anything about it. Besides, he was already warming up. If he went closer to a heater he'd be sweating. He headed for an inconspicuous chair in the back row, but Darcy waved. "Hey, Dr. Lightfoot!"

Morty let himself be dragged over to say hello. "Hi there," Darcy said. She looked around once, pushing her hair out of her face. "It's really good to see people here from the reservation, since this affects you the most." Sam gamely nodded at her, though he quirked an eyebrow at Morty.

"It's very unexpected to see you, Miss Mueller," Sam replied. "Are you here on behalf of your father?"

"Oh, no, he doesn't know I'm here!" Darcy laughed. "He'd give me a hundred lectures if he knew." She blushed a little. "First time I've done anything like this. I've always loved the outdoors, though. The more I've read about all the rivers and streams feeding into Lake Superior, the more I realized this really isn't a good site for his company's drilling project."

"You can just call it fracking, Darce," Morty muttered. "There's no such thing as a good site for that. Anywhere."

"And how are you doing, Morty?" Sam asked, his tone guarded. "I heard you were rescued. Are you completely recovered from your—misfortune?"

Morty met his gaze and held it a moment. "I'm getting by." Darcy squeezed his hand, and he looked at her. Her eyes showed concern, and he tried to smile. "Had a nasty bout of flu, but all good now."

"Well. I think the meeting is about to start," Sam said. "Perhaps we can chat later." Morty nodded. *Yeah, no. All you did was push me into a worse situation. Maybe the boiling oil of dog would've been the better choice.*

The men sitting by Sam barely glanced at Darcy or Morty. One of them stared at a bunch of white men a few rows up. They were currently glad-handing another white man in an ill-fitting suit. Morty guessed that was probably the county official, from the way he stood confidently at the head of the rows of chairs. All of them had beer guts and crew cuts, talking loudly about kids' hockey practice and taxes and how them danged millennials didn't know how to find honest work, not like when they were teenagers.

Morty glanced between the two groups as Darcy nudged him into a chair across the center aisle from the Ojibwe contingent. He guessed the crew cuts were the good old boy network, all in favor of a little friendly fracking.

A silver-haired woman rapped a gavel on the podium at the front of the room. The murmurs of conversation quieted while she looked around. "Thank all of you for coming tonight to this presentation by the Natural Resources Commission. I'm very pleased to see such a high turnout. Thank you, everyone, for braving the cold to join us." Morty took a quick head count; around twenty people had shown up, clumped together in social groups. The good old boys sat with their wives, a few teens with hand-lettered signs and cell phones camped in one row, and the Ojibwe who sat silently and away from the others. "I'll just go right ahead and turn the stand over to our county Natural Resources Officer, Mr. Jim Troelstrup. Jim?"

Desultory applause came from the middle-class crowd. Morty nudged Darcy and whispered, "Nineteen seventy-five called. They want their mustache back." She stifled a snort. "Oh my god, please tell me he's not wearing a clip-on tie. He is. Man. Bet that'll impress the yokels." Darcy elbowed him. They shared a grin, and for a moment Morty wasn't thinking about his discomfort, or why he'd suggested they attend in the first place.

"Good evening, folks," began Troelstrup. "I am here tonight because there seems to be a lot of misinformation and misplaced concern surrounding this drilling project, and I'd like to lay any worries to rest." He beamed at the small crowd. "Now, first off, I'd like to remind you that AmShale applied for their permit to drill over two years ago, and the proposal underwent vigorous scrutiny for its impact to the local community before it was ever approved."

"Approved by a corrupt governor and lame-duck legislature so far up big corporate asses they still haven't been seen by mortal men," Morty muttered. Darcy snorted quietly.

"This project, once it really starts this coming spring, will create dozens of jobs for the local economy. They're going to need both skilled and unskilled labor, and AmShale is already investing thousands of dollars in our community. Some of you may have heard that an archaeological find was uncovered on the proposed site," Troelstrup said, and gestured at the Ojibwe. "Of course, the tribal council were consulted, and AmShale is generously funding their new cultural appreciation center, even though the drilling site is not on tribal land." He beamed again, the most generous man in the world. Morty glanced over; the Ojibwe men sat expressionless. "The site is located far enough from local wells, schools, and farms that the county sees no serious impact at all."

One of the teens said loudly, "It's going to have an impact no matter how far it is from anyone." Morty grinned.

The woman who chaired the meeting called back, "Could we please all remain quiet until Mr. Troelstrup has finished his presentation? Thank you. There will be time for questions afterward."

Undaunted, Troelstrup continued, "Thanks, Miriam. Now, I know some of our young people are only here tonight because they've heard very misleading things."

"Please tell me this asshole's not going to say 'fake news,'" Morty groaned softly.

"I have here a study done by the American Resources Research Institute that debunks the wild stories in the, let's say, the left-leaning news outlets, about the supposed dangers of hydraulic fracturing. There is no proven link between these kinds of energy operations and cancer, our rivers and lakes are not suddenly going to catch on fire, and all waste from the operation will be safely and legally disposed of. I have some pamphlets here for anyone to take with them after the meeting." A hand went up from one of the women sitting alone. Troelstrup's smile thinned. "Let's wait a bit for questions, okay?"

Morty scowled. Unable to hold still, he raised his voice. "Excuse me, do you happen to know who funded that study?"

Troelstrup sighed. Several people turned around to stare at Morty. "Sir, if you don't mind, would you please hold your questions 'til—"

"Oh, that wasn't a question," Morty replied, "It was an accusation. Seems kind of disingenuous to use a study funded by oil companies to claim fracking has no ill effects." Darcy tugged on his shirt, and he looked at her. She bit her lip, and he relented slightly. "Never mind. Oil companies say fracking is the best thing since apple pie, carry on."

"See, there's another piece of misinformation," Troelstrup said, shaking his head as he returned his attention to the white folks. "No oil here. What they'll be drilling for is natural gas. Extracting more gas will make heating your homes and businesses cheaper. Combine that with the jobs this will bring in, and you're going to see an overall economic benefit to the county that will affect every person living here."

One of the men in the middle-class group asked, "Will they be hiring long-term?"

"I have it on good authority AmShale is committed to working with Ashland County for years to come," Troelstrup replied, nodding. "There'll be opportunities both for direct work with the company, and the county, as more road crews will be needed to build and maintain a route for the trucks."

"How come he gets to ask a question?" one of the teenagers complained.

"Brett, you shut your mouth right now, or you can go wait in the hall!" A man in a camo jacket stood long enough to glower at his son across the aisle. His cheeks flushed, he glanced at the county officer, and sat again, shaking his head.

"Ah, to be young and that sure of ourselves again, ya?" Troelstrup said with a chuckle. "Look. I know all of you have concerns. That's what I'm here for. We license fishing and hunting, right? Well, we also license energy exploration. AmShale went through all the proper channels and got all the proper permits, and they've agreed to compensate both the state and the county for anything they take out of the ground. Ultimately this will be to everyone's benefit. Cheaper heating all winter. Who doesn't want that, especially when it's so cold out there, I saw Leonard wearing two beards?" Chuckles came from the good old boy group as one large man with a very full beard grinned and nodded. "This will provide more money in the county treasury, where we can all vote on how to spend it."

Morty forced himself to stay silent, only realizing his fists were clenched when Darcy tentatively laid her palm over his left hand. The permits Troelstrup mentioned meant less than nothing. Fracking was barely regulated. This asshole sounded just like Darcy's father. No concern at all for the water, the land, the poisons left behind after they sucked it dry and moved on.

He felt his teeth prick his tongue. He tasted blood. Immediately he took a deep breath, willing himself to stay calm. He glanced at his hands, white and strained, though not curling into bony claws.

Shivering, Morty eased back in his uncomfortable metal chair. Darcy wrapped her arm around his and snuggled against him. He realized he could hear her quickened heartbeat, could smell her anxiety. He turned to study her more carefully. She gave him a nervous smile. "You okay?" he whispered.

"Yeah," she whispered back. "I've just never done this."

"Never listened to a spiel of capitalist bullshit? That's hard to believe."

"Never spoke up," she said softly. She appeared so shy and guilty he wanted to wrap his arms around her. "I never did do any research before on Dad's projects. I don't know why, just busy with stuff, I guess. Now I feel really guilty I didn't try to do anything about it before." She swallowed hard, looking down at her lap. "My car, all the gourmet dinners at our house, all the show tickets and skiing vacations and Dad's boat." She shook her head, frowning. "All of that is since he took the CFO position at AmShale. All this time, everything he's bought for me, all of it's been funded with projects like this."

"Darce," he murmured, taking her hands in his, "It's all good. You are not your dad. Thank you for doing this."

She searched his eyes as the speaker went on extolling the many ways the county could decide to spend the projected windfall of tax revenue from fracking. "I'm hoping maybe if I talk to Dad about this, maybe he'll see this is a dead end."

"Darce," Morty began, about to express his severe doubt that an oil giant would ever give up a profitable operation, no matter how much damage it did, and stopped. The fragile gleam of hope in her eyes stopped him cold. He swallowed, took a breath, and tried to smile for her. "You know what? I hope he does."

She squeezed his hand again. "You're good for me, Mordecai."

"No, you're good for me. Thanks for coming with me."

She smiled. "Hey, somebody has to be the rebel in my family, right?"

Humbled, Morty managed a grin. "Hell yes."

Troelstrup finished his sales pitch. "Now, are there any questions?"

A woman with long black hair streaked silver stood up. She'd been the one handing out anti-fracking flyers. "Yes, I have a few. First, how can you sleep at night, knowing you're selling these people snake oil?"

Troelstrup's face reddened. The chairwoman at the front rose, frowning. "Miss Wolf, could you please confine your questions to legitimate ones, and leave out the insults?"

"My name is Lana Wolf-Goes-Hunting, and I haven't begun to insult Jim yet." The anti-fracking woman set her hands on her hips among several beaded scarves wound round her waist. Morty heard a low grumble among the good old boy crowd. The Ojibwe were looking at the woman warily. Morty wondered if she was a tribal member or a New Age wannabe.

"This whole thing is a con job." She spread her hands toward the small crowd. "There's no care for how much local freshwater is contaminated with methane, just to get your wonderful gas out." She tossed her hair back, eyes fierce. "Or how that's going to kill the fish, poison the wild rice harvest, and pollute the lake since AmShale sure as hell isn't obligated to clean up after themselves." Troelstrup opened his mouth; she ran right over any response.

Her voice rose in volume and strength. "Tell them how AmShale is getting a big fat tax break from the state and the county for creating all of twenty or thirty temporary jobs, and once they've pumped out all the gas, they'll move on and leave us to clean their mess up, while they reap the profits! None of the gas is even coming back to the county. They're selling it all to overseas markets. Tell them, Jim, how much AmShale paid you to stump on their behalf for a project which will kill this community."

The room echoed with angry shouts; the Ojibwe were on their feet, two of the good old boys were yelling at Ms. Wolf-Goes-Hunting. Morty caught the phrase "half-breed." The teenagers were cheering and waving their signs that read NO FRACKING and AMSHALE = MURDERERS. Troelstrup had turned the shade of a cooked beet, gripping his sheaf of papers tightly.

The chairwoman banged the gavel for order. "Miss, if you're going to come in here and accuse a government official of accepting a bribe, you'd better have proof!" she shouted.

Wolf-Goes-Hunting stood tall, her eyes full of anger, ignoring the men and their professedly Christian wives hurling insults at her. Morty stood to add his voice; Darcy rose as well, though she held onto his arm. "I'm sure if we get a judge to subpoena his bank records we'd find some dirt, but that's beside the point," Morty said loudly, and several people turned their attention to him. "Fracking kills. Period. If you allow this to go forward, it's a death sentence for the reservation."

Troelstrup glowered at him. "I don't recognize you, son. What town are you from?"

Morty could see where this was going. "Appleton. However, I've recently come to feel a connection to this area." He was aware of Sam side-eyeing him. He didn't take his own glare off the resources officer.

Troelstrup pursed his lips. "Then I recommend you take the issue up with your own representatives, if you feel state law needs changing. As you're not a resident of this county, you are attending this meeting as an observer only, son."

"I'm not your son," Morty snapped. His head was starting to hurt. Clenching his fists for control, he added, "And thousands of people visit here every year, for fishing and camping. You're going to see all your tourist revenue disappear. How short-sighted are you?"

A couple of the locals appeared subdued at that. Another yelled, "Why don't you just go back to your big city and stop telling us how to run our county? No one wants you here!"

Morty pointed at Troelstrup. "All he cares about is making his oil-company masters happy. They've probably already promised him a job with them." Troelstrup appeared shocked and Morty knew he'd hit home. "Look how guilty he is. You people honestly want to swallow what this con man is spewing, be my guest. I'll come back here in a couple years to say I told you so. I'll have to wear a Hazmat suit to set foot in the county by then!"

"Sir, you are out of order, and I'm going to have to ask you to leave," the chairwoman shouted, banging her gavel again. "You too, Miss Wolf."

A sheriff's deputy at the door was heading toward Morty. "Fine," he growled. "Just remember, your decisions don't only affect you. Selfish assholes." He held up his hands angrily as the cop reached for him. "I'm going, I'm going." He strode to the door, Darcy hurrying after. Shortsighted rednecks. Real spiffy of them to fund the new cultural center. A couple years from now, that's all that would be left of the reservation.

Darcy tugged on his hand when they reached the lobby upstairs. "Morty, hold up, please." Irritated, he stopped. Her eyes searched his. "Maybe they won't listen, but that was amazing. You're amazing." Morty shook his head, taking deep breaths. His pulse raced, and angry shivers coursed through him. "I never thought about what Dad's company was doing. I don't know, maybe if I'd spoken to him sooner..."

Her expression was so sorrowful he felt guilty. Sighing, he took both her hands in his, resting his forehead against hers. "No, I'm sorry."

She stroked his cheeks and tilted her lips up to his for a soft kiss. "Don't be." She kissed him again. "I'll talk to Dad tomorrow. He'll be home for a few days; there's an officer's board meeting in Green Bay next week. He's not a mean person, Morty. Maybe if he understands what will happen here, he'll do something about it."

Mueller wouldn't care. This was hardly the first fracking project for his company. Morty nodded anyway. He wished he could share her hope, her optimism.

The woman who'd spoken up in the meeting came up the stairs, the deputy's hand on her elbow; she angrily shrugged him off. She headed for Morty and Darcy. The deputy stood by the stairwell, watching stonily. "Hey, sorry they tossed you too. I should've warned you this place is insular as hell," she said, offering her hand to them each in turn. "Lana."

Darcy introduced them. Morty shook Lana's hand. "Yeah, judging by the pitchforks and torches, they don't want us meddling kids."

Lana smiled. "I've lived here ten years, and they don't like me either. You were right about the pollution scaring off the tourists. My biggest clientele is folks up from Chicago wanting the authentic medicine sweat lodge, and that'll dry up fast once word gets out about fracking in the area. Guess I could move; I've got property over in the east part of Chiquamegon. But I prefer it here. Feels more like home. My ancestors have harvested rice up here and fished in the lake for centuries."

"Are you a member of the tribe?" Darcy asked.

Lana laughed. "I've got the blood tests to prove it, but no, the council doesn't like me either. I stir up too much trouble for their taste, I guess. So why did you two come all the way from Appleton for this?"

Darcy shrugged. "We just want to help. We visited the dig site a week ago. The artifacts they found, all the Native American history up here, the beautiful wildness of the whole area—it just made me realize this is sacred land."

"Good for you," the activist said, "maybe you were a Chippewa in a past life."

Morty recalled how he'd had to explain to a college admissions officer that all he had to prove any Native American lineage was a little vague family genealogy. Taking a blood test would prove nothing and be insulting to his family and the tribe to boot. *Blood tests and 'authentic' sweat lodges my ass. Yeah, she's definitely not part of the tribe.* Morty held his tongue.

Nerves at the back of his neck prickled, and he turned. It was Troelstrup over by the stairs. Lana was chatting with Darcy, something about a deep spiritual connection to the land. Morty, half listening, watched the officious official disappear around the corner. "Back in a sec," he said, and strode after Troelstrup.

Morty found Troelstrup standing at a urinal, head down. Morty walked up behind him. All the arguments in Morty's head faded as he glared at the man who was willingly condemning everyone here for personal profit. "How much are they paying you?" he asked. Startled, Troelstrup spun, then cursed as piss spattered on his shoes.

"You need to leave," Troelstrup grunted, turning back to the urinal to finish up. "Goddamn city slickers have no right to come up here and preach to us. Appleton, huh? Home of the paper mills. Fat lot of nerve you have telling us 'don't pollute.'"

"Do I look like I support paper mills?" Morty snarled, closing in. Troelstrup zipped up and turned to him, eyeing him angrily.

"Back up, son, before I call the deputy."

"Coward," Morty growled, "selling out your fellow humans for your own benefit."

Troelstrup took a step toward the sink, though he didn't take his eyes off Morty. "The AmShale project isn't going to affect Ashland at all, or the farms around here. As to the lake, hell, worse crap than this flows in from timber logging and copper mining all the time. Nobody's gonna suffer due to a little gas being pumped out of the ground."

"What about the reservation? They're directly downstream!"

"AmShale is giving them a very generous grant, not to mention it won't even be on their land, so legally, they have no standing at all. And that's definitely not your business." He snorted. "Unless you've got some Indian in you. You look white, but I know you never can tell who might'a slept with who back in the day. If you're a half-breed, take it up with the tribe, son."

"So that's it. Doesn't matter if the tribe gets poisoned, since they're not your white neighbors who go to your church and your kid's football practice?" A fierce chill fractured his skull. Morty snarled, "So what if the rice is ruined? So what if the fish die? So what if the wells on the rez are full of methane, as long as you get paid?" He advanced, and Troelstrup's eyes widened. "Your kind has plagued the earth too long, taking everything, sucking up all the life around you. High past time for you to give back." He snagged the man's collar in his claws, yanking him closer. Troelstrup stared up at him in abject fear, jaw slack, hands limp. Morty's vision turned crimson. "Murderer. Vermin. Empty crawling thing."

The scent of Troelstrup's sweat, breaking out in cold beads across his forehead, made Morty salivate. "This is all you're good for," he rasped, lifting Troelstrup off his feet. Morty opened his jaws wide.

"Oh fuck," said a familiar voice behind him.

Morty whirled. Sam and one of the other Ojibwe stood just inside the bathroom, frozen in shock. Morty realized he still held Troelstrup, and opened his claws; fabric ripped as the county officer dropped to the floor.

"Windigo," the man next to Sam gasped, "Windigo!" He fled.

Troelstrup wheezed, face chalk-white, as he scrambled to get his feet under him. Morty caught his own reflection in the bathroom's solitary mirror. An elongated skull full of sharp teeth and thorny branched antlers stared back at him. Horrified, he took a step back, and the fearsome visage shrank into his own haunted face, pain rippling through him as his bones scrunched back into their usual dimensions. Troelstrup pulled himself up by the edge of the sink, panting, staring.

Morty tried to summon strength into his shaky voice. "Call off the drilling, or I'll find you. Understand?" Troelstrup gaped at him, then staggered to the door and pushed past Sam. "I'll find you!" Morty yelled after him.

Trembling, he checked his hands, his chest. The seams at the shoulders of his shirt had ripped. "Shit," he muttered. He passed a hand over his head, feeling no antlers, though his fingertips and scalp were bleeding a little. He stepped to the sink to wash up. The cold tap water felt warm to his flesh.

"What the hell," Sam said quietly.

"That wasn't what it looked like."

"It looked like you were about to eat him."

"No," Morty said, his breath hitching. "No, I was just trying to scare him. Bet he'll think twice about accepting AmShale's deal now." He laughed weakly.

Sam shook his head. "I was afraid of this, when I heard you'd gone home, without coming back to talk to me."

Morty snapped, "What, to thank you for sending me to the crazy-ass old shaman who screwed me over worse? Gee, thanks. At least I have it under control, with no help from you." He pulled off his flannel shirt, dismayed at the rips. "Dammit."

"That was you in control. Not a monster about to eat a man alive. Interesting."

"The shaman bound the *manitou* to me," Morty growled, glaring at Sam. He stepped towards Sam and felt the sharp satisfaction of seeing him flinch. "The thing you uncovered in the burial mound is a god. I found your black lodge and your evil shaman, and he bound the dead spirit to my flesh. Do you get what that means? Because so far, all I've been able to tell is I still have this creepy winter death god inside me, except now at least I'm conscious when it comes out."

"You were going to eat him, if I hadn't come in."

"I was not!"

"Yes, you were! And now Mike is going to spread word to everyone there's a *wendigo* around. Christ." Sam ran a weary hand over his face. "Everything is going to be crazy. You'll have the whole rez in an uproar. Some of the elders were already saying disturbing the burial mound was going to bring evil upon us, and now they'll use this to shut down the dig. Run me out if I refuse."

Morty threw his arms in the air. "So? Good! Shut it down. Bury this monster again. Maybe then it'll leave me alone."

"It's not that simple. Shutting the dig down will cost me my job, and not just mine; all the people working on it. Believe me, as much as I want to just cover the mound and pretend none of this ever happened, I can't. If the council demands the dig stops now, there will be lawsuits and a big academic fuss. And none of this will stop AmShale from drilling as soon as the ground thaws." He glared right back at Morty. "Nice work, white man. All you've done is stir up a maelstrom of political infighting and scared the piss out of one corrupt county administrator."

"Well, at least he'll revoke the drilling permit, right?" Morty argued, checking his appearance in the mirror. He wiped away the smears of blood from his scalp where the antlers had been with limited success. The scent of death lingered in the closed room. "I mean, I definitely scared the hell out of him. You saw his face. Bet he's hurrying to pull the paperwork right now."

Sam snorted. "That weasel is probably packing a bag for Bermuda."

"Oh yeah? Where's he live?" Morty started for the door; Sam caught his arm. Morty stared at the hand on his forearm, slowly raising his eyes to the other man's. "Don't," he growled.

Sam released him, hands palm up, backing away a careful step. "You don't act like you're in control. Slow down and think about this."

"I'm done listening to your advice," Morty snapped. "This was your idea!" He gestured at himself, though no trace of the *wendigo* showed now.

Sam held up a placating hand. "Why didn't you come find me?" He shook his head. "I've been worried something went wrong."

"Oh, so now you want to hear about it? I was at the reservation clinic for three hours. I even told an incredibly suspicious ranger there I wanted to talk to you, and I would've tried to call if I hadn't been so wiped out. I fell asleep there, after walking naked through the snow all night and all morning." Morty glared at him, grimly pleased when Sam took another step back. "You know, you had my phone and wallet, when I was chained in your basement. You could've written down my contact info. You could've called me. I have a new phone, same number, since I lost everything on me at the black lodge. I guess you figured if I survived my visit there, then everything must be wonderful. Or did you think I wasn't coming back ? Anyone else you've sent out there come back at all?"

Sam stared at him. "I've never sent anyone else out there. Until a few days ago, I thought all of the old legends were just legends."

"And in any of the legends about the black lodge, did any of them have a happy ending?" Morty yelled. Sharp stabbing at his temples made him wince. "Assbadgers, this hurts." He glared at his reflection, willing the budding antlers to subside, breathing hard. When they melted into wisps of darkness, he turned back to Sam. "See. Under control. Even with no medicine bag. Which, by the way, was no deterrent for that crazy *mishibizhu*."

"You encountered the *mishibizhu* again?"

"You could say that. She pushed me into the lake. Right into the black lodge." Morty took a breath, calming the tremors in his fingers. The digits wanted to stretch into claws. "Guess she's not all bad, though. She brought me back to the rangers' station afterward. Now the *Bagwajinini,* those were scary little bastards."

Sam shook his head, eyes wide. *"Bagwajinini* too." He let out a low whistle. "All the old tales are real. I can't begin to imagine what you're going through. Come back with me, and let's talk to the *Midewiwin* elders. Let's think this through. Maybe there's still a cure."

"Drink boiling oil? Thanks, but no thanks. I got this." Morty headed for the doorway. Surprising him, Sam stepped in his way.

"Do you?" Their eyes locked, and Morty saw genuine fear there. He subdued his own rising terror, forcing himself to stay still a moment. He nodded.

"Yeah. I'm fine. I'm conscious, I know what I'm doing, I won't eat anyone." He swallowed hard, hoping Sam didn't know about the previous murders in Appleton. "I won't hurt anyone. I give you my word."

Sam studied him, then gave one slow nod. "I'll try to do damage control. See if I can stop the whole rez from going into a panic. *Windigook* are serious stuff; everyone grew up hearing stories about them, and it wasn't so long ago that people were put to death for the merest suspicion of turning cannibal in the worst winters." He sighed. "I guess if the reservation fights the universities over the dig site, I can argue it's no fault of mine. I don't have any political standing here. Maybe I can still write the book they want me to publish."

Morty shrugged. "Let 'em panic. Let the whole county panic. Maybe that'll get them to fight, send AmShale packing."

"You really have no idea how this works, do you?" At Morty's irritated glare, Sam explained, "The only way AmShale is prevented from fracking here is if the county says no. AmShale already has the permits, and I don't think one scared pissant of a county administrator is going to swing the balance."

"Fine." Morty grimaced. "If I have to personally scare the crap out of everyone involved, I'll do it." He rolled his eyes at Sam's wary expression. "Yeah, yeah, no eating people, promise."

"I hope that was a terrible attempt at humor." Sam shook his head. "Let's wait and see whether anything happens." His eyes flicked to the doorway. "I'd better go see if the guys are coming back with guns and flaming arrows, and you'd better return to your girlfriend." He peered worriedly at Morty. "Does she know?"

"Hell no. And I'm keeping it that way." Something else struck Morty. "Troelstrup knows my face now. He could pull security footage, ID me, find out where I live." Sam laughed. "How's that funny?"

"Security footage? Look where you are. No cameras here; this isn't a bank. Nobody's going to believe Troelstrup, even if he does tell anybody what just happened. My concern is the guys from the rez storming in here any second now."

"Wouldn't do any good," Morty muttered. "I've already been shot."

Sam raised a brow. "Well, this room is too small for a shootout, and I don't want my guts punctured by ricocheting bullets. We should leave. Promise me you'll call me as soon as possible. You need to keep yourself in control." He searched through his wallet and handed Morty a business card with well-worn edges. "We need to discuss this further." Morty took the card and shoved it into his pants pocket. *Discuss this later? Nope. I'm done. Scared the oil-company shill, did what I said I'd do for the creepy little squirrels.*

As they emerged into the hallway, running footsteps could be heard approaching. "They didn't see you," Sam hissed, and shoved Morty toward a side door.

"That one guy definitely—oh." Luckily, the side room wasn't locked. Morty ducked below a desk inside and listened to Sam telling the men who arrived, apparently including the sheriff's deputy, he hadn't seen a thing and didn't know what all the hubbub was about. It didn't sound as though anyone believed him, but after a few minutes of arguing in the hallway, they all left.

Once it was silent again, Morty eased open the door, double-checking before he headed back to the lobby. He gazed glumly at his ripped shirt, then folded it over his arm. He couldn't think of an excuse to give Darcy as to how it had been damaged. Clearly this required more planning ahead. Except he never wanted to do this again.

Shivers ran through him. For just a split second, there in the men's room, with the terrified official caught in his long claws, all Morty had been able to think of was how succulent his pink flesh would taste, how hot the blood and savory the fat of his belly. Only for a fraction of a second. He'd never say a word to Sam or anyone else about it. He ran through an excuse for Darcy in his head, desperate to think of anything else. Anything, except how hungry he was. And how tasty that greedy Troelstrup had smelled.

Only for a split second. And never again.

30

The phone went straight to voicemail again. "Hey, it's me, I'm busy carrying out my nefarious plan." Quell hung up without leaving a message, irritated. He knew someone was checking these, because just yesterday it said the mailbox was full. He slouched in the truck's well-worn seat, sipped from a bitter cup of gas-station coffee, and considered what options he might have left. All trails had gone cold.

Nosing around the local casino had earned him nothing except stony glares from the tribal employees. The only folks willing to return his friendly hellos had been a couple of drunk tourists, and they claimed not to have heard a thing about any animal attacks, natural or otherwise. Security had asked him, politely but firmly, to either play the slots or move along. Quell was broke and never had a taste for gambling anyway. He'd returned to the site of the original attack, only to find more trucks and earth-movers, plowing a roadway and hauling out timber. Whatever they were clearing land for, they seemed eager to get the trees out of the way before a good blizzard hit. At any rate, all this activity meant it was impossible for him to get back into the site.

Not that he didn't try. When a man in the orange vest stopped Quell's truck well away from the actual area of the attack, he rolled down the window and gave him a friendly smile. "Hey there, what's all this?"

The heavyset man in his deer-flap hat eyed Quell suspiciously. "You one of them protestors?"

"Protesting what exactly?" Quell chuckled. "I'll protest this dad-burned wind for sure."

"Yeah, you got that right. No, there's been some ruckus around here, is all. Indians saying we're tearing up a sacred site or somethin' like that. Was a meeting in town over it a couple nights back, and ever since, we got all kinda Indians wailing out here like they were being massacred."

"Really. Huh," said Quell. "A sacred site, you say?"

The man pursed his lips a moment. "Look, mister, if you don't have business here, I have to ask you to turn around. This is AmShale's property, and we got a lot of work to do to get this timber felled so's they can start drilling in the spring."

"Is that one'a them new skidders?" Quell asked, nodding toward a large timber harvesting machine he saw moving toward the standing trees. "The kind with the computerized whatnots? Man, I sure wish we had those back in my day."

The man's voice softened a bit. "Oh yeah? You used to work timber?"

"Long time, 'til my leg got clipped by a—well, it's a long story. Could I just go have a peek?"

"Can't," the man said, shaking his head. He stepped a little closer to the heat wafting out of Quell's open window. "Regulations. You know how it is. What's your business out here?"

"Well, I wanted to find out if there was any news about Randy. Randy Lamer, the fella who got attacked out here."

"You know Randy?" At Quell's serious nod, the man sighed. "Shame what happened. That's why we're all supposed to carry these now, in case the crazy bear comes back." He patted a rifle slung awkwardly over his coat. "Though I seriously doubt any bear would come at us with all these machines working all day."

"Oh, no doubt." Quell studied the snowy trail ahead, where plows had cleared a path for the timber trucks. "What's all this about a sacred Indian site? Randy never mentioned it."

The man waved a dismissive hand in the general direction of the clearing up ahead. "I don't really know; AmShale broke into some old mound on accident while they were surveying, and the tribe up here claims it's some kinda ancient god. I don't know, you know how they are, every rock and bug is an old spirit or whatever. There was supposed to be a team of archaeologists excavating it, moving all of the pot shards to the reservation and what have ya. Yesterday morning a bunch of Indians in full war paint came out here and shut it all down. There was a huge fuss with the night security, right as I was coming on site, too." He laughed. "I'm not superstitious, now, but a couple of the boys are, and they got all antsy. Some nonsense about a cannibal and a curse." He shrugged. "Whatever. Deputy come over from Ashland and got everything quieted down enough so's we could work. Keeping the crazy Indians away from our site and on their own damned land. That's all I care about."

"Well I'll be," Quell said. He hadn't seen anything like a mound the last time he was here. "All right then, don't freeze your hinder off out here."

"Yeah, you too," the man said. He returned Quell's wave as Quell turned the truck around and headed back to the county road.

Indians all riled up, and monsters fighting in a parking lot. He'd bet his gun there was a medicine shaman somewhere on the rez who knew something.

Back at the tribal offices no one he had asked had any comment at all for a scruffy-looking white man. Even the handful of white employees in the clinic didn't know anything about anything.

Hours later, forced to accept no one was going to talk to him, Quell sat in his truck, parked at a solitary gas station in a tiny town. Frustrated, he sipped from a cup of terrible coffee he'd paid for with one of his last three dollars. Hearing that cocky fella's voicemail again, with no answer, really rubbed him raw.

Dang this whole thing to heck. Knowing something more involved was going on than he'd first suspected was close to driving him nuts. He could try talking to the folks who were there in the parking lot again. No, that was no good. He'd had the best view of any of 'em. Blast it, he should've had better aim. He could've proven these creatures existed and rid the world of at least one murderous beast all in one go.

Tired, he rubbed a hand into the deeply lined skin of his eyes. He could go back to the trailer, set a trap. A shiver passed through him. No. If that poor boy died at the claws of the same horrible lynx-thing he'd shot in the parking lot, and it caught a whiff of him, he didn't want to bet it wouldn't remember him. He said a quick mental prayer for the dead young man half-buried in the snow. The jangle of his phone made him jump so bad he nearly spilled coffee all over the dash. "Hello?"

"Garwood, it's Bill."

It was his deputy friend from Mellen. "Hi there, Bill, any news?"

"In fact there is. I was out sick the last few days and so I only just found out this morning, but I knew you'd want to hear it. They found that lost tourist. The one who went missing after the incident at Hettie's."

Quell sat up straight. "Really? They found his body?"

"No, they actually found him alive. Wandered naked into a darned ranger station on Sunday, up on the north end of the reservation. Can ya believe it."

"I'll be danged." Quell knew the weather conditions. Not dyin' in it was miraculous. "How in the heck did he survive in the woods? And how far is that from Mellen?"

"Near about twenty-five miles. I can't imagine how he managed it. Seems like he just wandered up that way after having the piss scared out of him by all the commotion, ya know. Fell in a slough and got soaked, but managed to reach the rangers in time before freezing to death."

"Uff da," said Quell, "wonder why he didn't hear us beatin' the bushes for him. I'm glad he's all right. Hey, is he still at the reservation? I sure would like to talk to him for that book I'm writing. Sounds like quite a story."

"He went home to Appleton. No sign of frostbite, if you can believe that, so off he went. They said his girlfriend drove all the way up there to get him. I'm thinking maybe he has some, you know, mental issues," Bill confided.

"Appleton, huh?" That sealed it. The fella that emailed him and was supposed to meet him at Hettie's and the missing tourist surely must be one and the same. "You know, maybe I'll go look him up, if he's amenable to talking to an old fart. You happen to have his name and address?"

Bill did. After promising the deputy he would indeed give best regards to the rescued tourist, Quell hung up and opened the browser on his phone, searching the address to see how far away it was. A news article about that very same address caught his attention immediately:

SUSPECT QUESTIONED IN MURDERS OF ELDERLY NEIGHBORS

Quell clicked on the page, fumbled to enlarge the text, and read slowly, with growing unease. Two older folks murdered, and one lived at the same place as that guy who'd been lost. The other, right next door. A picture of the suspect, who'd been arrested while allegedly threatening another old lady with a gun in her bedroom, made him pause for study. This criminal sounded ordinary to Quell, if no less despicable. What kind of jackass waves a loaded gun in an old lady's face. One hopped up on goofballs, no doubt.

There was a link to an earlier article about the murders. Quell clicked it, and upon reading the details known to the press, felt a deep chill in his bones. Savagely attacked by an animal. In their own homes. No eyewitnesses, but another tenant in the rental house heard screams and gunshots. He went searching for something with more details, and soon found a tabloid site less picky about repeating neighbors' hearsay.

The downstairs neighbor heard gunshots and yelling...called the police...the room was like a horror film, all covered in blood. Quell felt numb as he read, eyes wide. The story said the other neighbor upstairs was unavailable to talk to the reporter, having gone to the hospital the same morning.

Struck by an awful idea, he brought up his emails and quickly found the one from the man who'd been supposed to meet him at Hettie's, the one who'd asked questions about werewolves, of all things. Oh no. It was bigger than he'd thought. Much bigger and much worse. The attack by the resort, the monsters at Hettie's, the cast of that footprint, the mangled man in the snow; this fella asking about werewolves, the lost tourist whose address matched the very place there were horrible killings... A pattern began to form in Quell's mind. Shaking, he sank back in the seat. He had an urge to turn up the rattly old heater in the truck. He knew it would do no good. The chill he felt came from inside.

It was all connected. The Indian mound, what was it that logger said; some kind of god and something about a curse. This was bad juju for sure. Trembling, he looked up the dates of the murders in Appleton, and checked the calendar on his phone. The killings there happened in between Randy getting his foot bit off, and the crazy fight at Hettie's.

Quell tossed back the last of the terrible coffee with a grimace. Guess he knew where he was headed. He gazed up at the darkening sky. Driving at night, with snow maybe on the way; not his druthers. Regardless, he had to talk to this man, find out what he saw that made him reach out to Quell. And he had to find out what in heck a monster was doing in Appleton, Wisconsin, of all places. He really hoped it wasn't the big lynx-thing. Though the deer one wouldn't be any more preferable, seeing as how it enjoyed ripping out people's throats.

The needle on his gas gauge was only at about quarter-tank volume, and the gauge itself was unreliable. He needed fuel, or money for fuel. The gas station behind him had already closed for the night, so he couldn't go in and put his last two dollars in the tank. He'd driven so far west he was closer to Ashland than anywhere else; surely there'd be something open in Ashland. Maybe even a bank teller machine where he could get a little cash from his account. If he had much left to take. Cash was always, always preferable to using a slick plastic card; a card wouldn't grease the palm of a kid working behind the bar at a local dive. A card wouldn't soothe the hesitation of a witness who'd seen more than they could believe. Yeah, best head to Ashland, get funds and fuel, and maybe food as well. Anything would be better than that last pre-packaged trash he'd eaten. And then straight down to Appleton if the weather cooperated. People were gonna die, if those vicious beasts were roaming around. And if there was one loose in a big city like Appleton it was gonna be bad.

He eased off the clutch and goosed his old truck westward, peering through the flurries swirling at the windshield. There was no time to lose.

31

The night proved colder than Marie expected. By the time the chocolatier closed shop and Marie strolled out with a precious bag of truffles, the wind nearly tore it from her hand. Annoyed, she flipped the furred hood of her coat up and tightened the drawstrings. Flurries blew ahead of her along the main street of Ashland. Her feet were soundless in the snow, in her cute little boots. It had been near-impossible to find actual suede ones with real fur trim and lining. She really ought to procure more of these. Not that she was hunting tonight. She had not been in this quaint little burg in ages, and had been delighted to find jewelers, clothing boutiques, and the chocolatier. How nice to discover pleasant changes to what had been just a lakeside fishing town on *Gitchi-gumi's* south shore.

A couple of young men passed her going the other way, and she smiled at them. She could hear them turning, making comments behind her. Marie smiled. She had not intended to hunt tonight, but if the prey came to her, she would positively take advantage of their offering. She listened to them a moment longer as they dared one another to say something to her, and sighed. She was not truly hungry, and she did not wish to dirty these boots. She wanted a pedicure. And cucumber water. There were two day-only salons on this street, but both were closed. Marie pouted as she picked up her pace against the chill wind. She could always return to the resort. Perhaps there was a fat businessman with an adventurous side who needed a bit of play. And it was always amusing to make them think she had agreed to one sort of playtime, when what she had in mind was far deliciously bloodier.

She sighed again, looking up at the pretty fairy lights strung up and down the street, illuminating the storefronts. There would be more snowfall within a day or two. A real snow, to coat the trails and silence all sound. The best kind of snow. *I wish the* windigo *had stayed.*

She pictured him learning to hunt beside her, crouched low in the forest just by a ski trail she knew, one with dark, looming trees which made for very entertaining stalking. She smiled. He was so clumsy. Such big foolish eyes, which observed so little. The instinct to kill was there, however. He could be taught.

It had been almost a week since she'd left him at the rangers' station. Such an imbecile. *Certainement* he had killed again by now. Her brothers said a *windigo* was always hungry, always eating.

She paused by the window of an oddities shop, intrigued by an antique lamp: it portrayed a lithe, limber woman in gauzy drapery, holding a lantern aloft. She bit her lip, unexpectedly overcome by nostalgia. It had been a long, long time since she had been with a woman. The long arms and legs of the copper-hued beauty reminded her of a dancer she had known, that one winter in her excitable youth, in Montreal.

Suddenly angry, she strode away. She crossed the street and entered a bar. Warmth and noise rolled over her, slowing her as she crossed the threshold. She took down the hood of her coat and made her way through the crowd to the bar top. "Whiskey, neat, the best you have," she yelled at the bartender. She slid onto a seat the instant it was vacated by someone, tossed back the first shot, and tapped the glass with a long fingernail. As the second shot was poured, she peered around more carefully. She still was not hungry, though now she dearly wanted to kill something.

It took another half-hour of sipping liquid fire before a muscular young man with a ginger goatee bought her a round. Her head swam while she made conversation with him, unwillingly, giving prickly answers to his questions, smirks to his compliments. When he leaned close and suggested they go somewhere else, she gave him a direct, dark stare, and he fumbled with his wallet. *Imbecile.* As she started for the door, he took her upper arm in a very firm grip and steered her toward the back instead. "Outside," he breathed in her ear. "I know what a slut like you needs."

"Oh really," she murmured as he propelled her ahead of him. "Which is?"

"You need a real man to take charge of you."

She widened her eyes in feigned surprise. Then they were outside, in the alley. Marie glanced left and right; it was pitch back here. A slight noise in a dumpster a few yards away caught her ears. Before she could determine the source, the man slammed her against the brick outer wall of the bar. Marie winced, not resisting as he shoved her skirt up and pulled her woolen tights down. His hands on her were coarse, probing and squeezing. He held her against the wall with one splayed hand while he unzipped his pants. Marie sighed. Ah well. At least there would be one fewer of these in the world, molesting girls in bars. Right as he made to thrust into her, her claws speared his throat. He gurgled, eyes bugging in surprise. Marie stared into his face a moment, dispassionately watching the life leave him. Then she retracted her claws and shoved the body away from her. It fell with a solid thud into the slush of the alleyway.

She glanced both ways again to ensure no one had seen, then licked the blood off her fingers. She straightened her tights and skirt, smoothing down her coat, composing herself enough to go back in for one last drink.

A movement over the dumpster startled her. Her hands went up, ready to slash if need be. The intruder was only a fat raccoon. She relaxed, sniffing a laugh. "It is all yours, if you're hungry. I am not in the mood tonight." She toed the corpse with her boot, chuckling. "Not in the mood at all, a pity for him."

"You hunt in their city? Strange for a *mishibizhu*." The mental words kicked her back a step; her hand went to the wall for balance, startled.

"*Bagwajinini,*" she whispered, then straightened her back, glaring at it. "I hunt where I please."

"You should at least eat your kill. To kill and not eat is wasteful. It is more like the knife-spirits who hunt only to hang a head on their wall."

Marie ignored at the dead man, his blood darkening the snow in the dark alleyway. "He insulted me. He paid for it. I am not hungry. What is one of the forest tribe doing in a city? Are you here to check on the trees they keep prisoner, or to shepherd their small cubs across the street?"

The raccoon waddled closer, its stare black and unblinking. Distasteful little beasts. She'd encountered far too many of the *Bagwajinini,* and all in the past week. She disliked the way they watched over the human young who became lost in the forest. As though there weren't already too many men spreading over the earth, like vicious ants. She was unaware her contempt showed until its telepathy slapped her brain again. "Do not mock us, water panther. You are out of your element here. Every place trees grow and creatures live, we observe and care for them."

"Fine," she snapped. "What do you want?"

"More and more destroyers tear down our trees by the old hill of the winter *manitou*. This should worry you as well; they will be expelling their waste into your river."

Marie considered. "If you wish me to kill them one by one, that is easy enough." She sniffed. "Apparently it has been too long since the *waabishki-iwewaad* learned to leave my river alone. They brought their saws and their shovels last time, and all they left with was coffins."

"There are too many. They work too quickly. The abomination should have stopped their destruction by now. He hesitates."

"You told the *windigo* to chase the white men away?" She laughed, incredulous. "Have you seen him? He is a helpless cub."

"He has the *manitou* of the Starving Moon in him. It could easily destroy all their works and punish the greedy ones who poison the water." The raccoon came closer, its beady eyes staring up at her. Marie stifled the urge to back away from it. Something about their black stare always disturbed her.

"The abomination was told to make these men go away and leave untouched our trees and waters. My brothers report all he has done is speak loudly at them. The *waabishkiiwewaad* loggers have not stopped." It pointed at the end of the alley, where streetlights cast a wan glow. "Go find the *wendigo,* and persuade him to use his powers. The winter *manitou* will strike at anyone if his rage is not directed. He trusts you; go and speak with him. Insist he do as he has promised."

Marie stared at the raccoon. "What powers? I have spent time in his company, and I can promise you he is a fool. He will no more unleash any fury against his species than a baby otter would." She remembered the last fight with the *windigo,* how she easily bested him and could have killed him if she'd intended. "He is quick to anger, *oui,* but only if provoked."

"The fury is not the man, but the *manitou*." The *Bagwajinini* clasped its forepaws together, although its toneless mental voice expressed no emotion. "He resents being tricked so long ago, and resents more being woken, his grave plundered, and greedy mortals overrunning the wild places. His role was always as the forceful bringer of balance, through blood and cold and terror. Sooner or later the *manitou* will burst free of the man, and he will not distinguish between friends or enemies. He will attempt to destroy all people, no matter their role in this."

"And what if he does?" Marie argued, "I know your tribe recalls a time when the lakes were full of fish, and the forests free of two-legged hunters. Perhaps this whole area needs to be balanced." She lifted her chin at the raccoon. "I think you very much over-rate the *windigo*. The white woman he killed at the tavern practically threw herself into his jaws. It was simple luck, and I have seen no evidence of any medicine power in him, unless you consider tripping over his own feet worthy of awe."

The *Bagwajinini* didn't move a limb, yet suddenly it perched atop a crate right next to her, inches from her face. Marie froze. No one really knew exactly what one of the little forest braves was capable of; Marie did not especially want to know. Not right this second, at least. "He will gain strength with every kill. Go find him. Make him direct his anger at those destroying our forest. He must be made useful, else he lose all control and call forth the deepest howling winter as he did centuries ago. Know this, *mishibizhu*: if you fail, we will not forget. Even if you hide in your father's deepest lake, we will find you."

It took her a moment to recover; she was disgusted with herself for recoiling from the raccoon's threats. "I do not know where he is. Do you have a map? A scent trail? He is among his own kind, who knows where."

"He has no kind. Not anymore. And if the *manitou* regains strength, no common blood will stay his claws." The raccoon darted into the alley, then stopped, so fast Marie blinked to reorient on it. "My brothers have been watching him. He returned to his home. You can find him at the sprawling city of the *mookomaan* downriver from the old Ho-Chunk village, near their great temples of learning. You must persuade him to return to the place of his death and put an end to the destruction. If balance is restored, perhaps the *manitou* will be satisfied."

The implication didn't pass by her. "And if the dead *manitou* is not satisfied by killing a few greedy white men?"

"Then we are all in danger, sister *mishibizhu*. Even you." It vanished before she could think of a retort.

Marie stood there a minute longer, wondering how·in blazes she was expected to travel so far, and then find the white *windigo* among a whole city of the knife-spirit people. She cast a glance back at the corpse. The heady scent of blood had faded, and now the strongest smell was of the emptied bowels. She had no appetite at all now.

She began walking, pulling the hood of the coat up again and shoving her hands deep into the pockets when she turned the corner into the wind. This was all *très ridicile!* Enough with the little forest tribe and their proclamations of doom. She could go back to the resort. Henri could be massaging her calves right now. She could be eating truffles in a luxurious bath. She growled at the last thought, realizing she'd left the bag of truffles in the alley. She had lingered too long as it was; sooner or later someone would stagger out back for a cigarette and discover the body.

She stomped a delicate foot. Stupid, horrid little creature. She could have coated all those wonderful truffles in that idiot's blood for later, if that awful little monster hadn't turned up to lecture her.

She cursed it under her breath for a good half-minute, striding along the sidewalk under the twinkling lights. Slowing, she saw her reflection in a dark shop window, and halted to tuck her hair under the hood more artfully, and to fluff the hood's trim around her sharp cheekbones. "Idiotic little furbrains," she growled as she straightened her coat over the skirt, and tugged a wrinkle out of the woolen tights over her left thigh. "I was having such a nice night."

White men overrunning her river again, the raccoon said. She should go kill them. Pluck them from their ugly machines and cut their throats, let them bleed out hidden in the trees where their people would never find them. Their diggers were too heavy to move. Not like the skiddoos. She recalled the claw marks the *windigo* had left in the massive plow. He could, perhaps. Or shred their engines. Perhaps that strength of limb was what the *Bagwajinini* meant by powers; the *windigo* looked far too skinny in his human form to be so strong. Marie huffed. *Fine. I go find him, somehow, and talk him into coming back north, somehow, and then he can destroy the machines while I hunt every last one of the fools operating them.*

Assuming she could succeed at parts one and two of this plan, part three sounded fun. He could hunt with her. Well, once he learned how not to be so graceless. It could work, the two of them removing all the *gitchi-mookomaanag* from the territory around the river. That should please the annoying little forest tribe. The blood would please her. *If I can find a way to get to him.*

The Ho-Chunk village was miles and miles from here, south by the inland lake. The lake where the whites had killed cousin Wakshexi Te Xeti. She had only met her cousin once, at a great family council, when her father had summoned every underwater panther and lake serpent together to discuss what to do about the white men whose numbers on the lakes had increased to concerning levels. They should have broken all their boats, sent all the whites to the depths to drown and be consumed.

Her distant cousin had been a mighty warrior in his day, terrorizing the tribe living alongside the lake of stagnant water. He had ultimately perished when the white men had dammed up the lake so tightly, he had to hunt deer and elk just to keep his belly full. An antler had gored him from within his stomach. He'd be alive yet and taking Ho-Chunk young right out of their wigwams, if those arrogant knife-spirit men hadn't moved in. If the old winter *manitou* was truly in that silly fool of a white man, she hoped he did emerge to get his revenge on them all.

She sniffed, catching the scent of people running from a nearby tavern toward a lot full of their smelly vehicles, laughing in the cold. If she were to travel so far just to find the *windigo* again, she could use a car. And a driver. She grimaced, seeing the speckles of blood on her clothing. *And now I will need new boots, damn it.*

To commandeer a ride, she would need to find a lonely truck driver. She checked the wad of paper in her pocket. Canadian money and American bills mingled, a mixture of large and small denominations. It should be enough to get a trucker's attention. *That, and this body of mine.* She smoothed down the black tights over her shapely legs. They were truly such predictable animals. No fun at all. The *windigo* was fun.

Marie walked away from the lit main street, heading for the outskirts of this small town. She remembered seeing a gas station with a diner not too far away. Farther than she enjoyed walking as a human, but shifting form here would be too risky; their streets were too flat and open. She increased her pace, hoping she'd be able to find a ride quickly. She needed to find one willing to take her all the way to the city by the stagnant lake. And then find the *windigo* somewhere in that city. And then, if he would not come with her, she would hit him so hard he would come roaring out of his white face and chase her wherever she led him.

Her feet ached in these tiny boots. She truly hoped the *windigo* would listen to her, and do what the forest tribe demanded. If he refused, maybe she could just make the dead *manitou* so angry he decided to kill all the *waabishkiiwewaad*. She was sure even if she couldn't outrun the *windigo* in full fury, she could easily outrun any white men who got in the way. All she needed was to be faster than them.

She grinned and, despite the tight boots, picked up her pace again.

32

The afternoon shift was busy, and Morty was tired. He hadn't slept well after the meeting in Ashland three days ago. He awoke each morning staring at his hands in raw panic until he was certain his fingers weren't actually claws, and that his skin wasn't coated in someone else's blood. He'd been back at work for most of the week now, eager to bury his worries in routine.

The Bigfoot hunter had called a few times. Morty pressed *Ignore* to send him straight to voicemail, and then erased any messages. Involving that guy had been a mistake. On finding the card Sam had given him still in his jeans pocket, he'd debated calling the archaeologist. Sam had said the surest cure was death. And that was no help. Morty had tossed the card in a drawer at home, and thrown himself back into his normal life.

Dealing with rude Karens, potential shoplifters, and the continual slog of retail chores proved almost too much for his patience. By seven p.m. he was on his third mug of black coffee, and had already dealt with a customer who insisted they didn't want Tom Sawyer written by Mark Twain "but the one written by that other guy, Huck Finn I think his name was." Another customer wanted "that book you had over here last month, it had a red cover, come on, you know." And one argued with Kim over the cash value of very old and scratched Playstation discs he was trying to sell to the store. As the "these are rare games and you guys suck!" customer finally stormed out, Morty took a slow, deep breath, massaging the bridge of his nose.

"Thanks," Kim said quietly, wiping the dust and dirt off the trade counter.

"No problem." Morty sighed. "Privileged people gonna privilege."

"You up for a game night?"

Morty hesitated. It would be awesome to get back to routine without worrying about whether any furry little creeps were going to come screw with him again. That asshat official up at the Bad River was surely scared enough to walk back AmShale's drilling permit. Morty felt as though he were going to drop, but hopping onto the Xbox with Kim was so beautifully normal.

Kim offered, "Maybe not, you look ragged, dude."

"Just tired. I'm okay."

"Darcy coming by?"

Morty shook his head. "She has some family thing, relatives in town. I was more than happy to work tonight rather than hold my tongue through caviar casserole and a discussion on how young people need to go back to church."

"Caviar casserole?" Kim laughed.

"Whatever. I have no idea what rich people eat when they're at home. Anyway, yeah. I'm free tonight, after all this blissful interaction with the unlettered masses."

Kim nodded, side-eyeing him while stacking another box of sorted games onto the electronics department cart. "So Darcy is suddenly into tree hugging?"

"Yeah. Go figure. Maybe I've become a bad influence on her after all."

Kim chuckled. "Bet her daddy hates you."

"One has to possess emotions in order to hate."

"He know she's against his fracking project yet?"

Morty shrugged. "No idea. I imagine that's a sensitive subject at the Mueller house. You know, one of those traditional things one doesn't discuss at the dinner table: religion, politics, and exploiting the land while poisoning the natives."

"Hah. Well, we all knew dating you would be the gateway to a slippery slope of anti-establishmentarianism. Next thing you know, she'll be trading her little sports car in for a Prius."

Morty threw his hands in the air. "Ohhhh, the horror!"

Kim grinned. "At least you sound better."

"I feel better." Morty chewed his lip, watching Kim going about his work as though everything was fine. "Hey, man, I'm sorry I bugged out on you up there."

Kim shrugged. "That whole weekend was completely surreal. I'm glad you didn't freeze to death out there. You were out of your fucking skull, if you'll pardon my Chinese. You had me really worried. People searched for you for hours."

Morty winced. "I know. I was feverish, and yeah, I guess I was freaked out. Uh, you know. Given the all the weird shit going on."

"I keep telling you, you watch too much bad horror. That stuff gets down in your reptile brain and comes out when you're sick or stoned. Especially since your neighbors got killed. Surprised you hadn't smoked some spiked pot that sent you on a freakout spree before then, to be honest."

Morty had trouble processing all of this in time to react to it properly. "I—wait what? Reptile brain?"

"You know, like the deep subconscious. Where all your most primal fears and urges live." Kim studied him thoughtfully a moment. "Which in your case, are probably all about worrying when you're gonna lose the rest of your hair, and desperately wanting to obtain the last known copy of Lovecraft's secret porno novel so you can spend your nights rubbing it all over your sweaty loins."

"Stop thinking about my sweaty loins," Morty laughed, throwing his empty plastic mug at Kim. Kim batted it aside.

"Eww, gross! Don't give me your nasty ancient burial mound germs. I don't want to end up flailing around in the woods screaming about Danielle Steele books."

"What?"

"That's how I pictured you, wandering around in the woods. Raving how mass-market paperbacks are the devil's work and calling down serial bestsellers as a sure sign of the End Times."

Morty slapped his hand on the counter. "Blasphemer! How dare you mock the Sacred Words of Wending, book seven, chapter five, verse fourteen. 'For lo, they worshiped false authors who gave them characters of cardboard, and verily could not tell the difference between one book and the next, and indeed there was none. And the people grew stupid, and despaired.'"

Kim laughed. "Dude. I'm glad you're back."

"Me too." They smiled at each other.

"So, you up for anything tonight? It's cool if you're wiped out. You've been through a lot lately. Or if you want, we could go to my place, if being at yours is too weird right now. With all the dead old people and stuff."

"Yeah. That would be good." Morty sighed. "Thanks." Kim nodded, tapped his chest twice over his heart and then offered a fist bump. Morty returned the salute, relieved. *Yes. I don't want to think about the dead old people and stuff ever again. Done with that.*

He deeply hoped his threat to Troelstrup had been successful, and events were already in motion to shut the fracking down before it started.

He turned his attention to a waiting box of books on the trade counter, picking through them to see if there was anything more interesting than last year's sociology textbooks or yet another copy of *The Da Vinci Code*. Nothing excited him about this particular book deal. He tried to always accept at least one or two things for trade if possible, to keep customers bringing stuff in regularly. He could take one more paperback copy of the latest Nicholas Sparks; it probably had another week or two of life in it with the book-club crowd. Oh hey, there was the new Joe Hill, that could go on the New Release shelf. He rifled through the rest of the stack. *Meh*. Well, two things, not a total loss. It was Saturday night anyway; hardly anything interesting came in when it was dead. All the cool kids were out partying, families at their kids' hockey games. He should go back to working weekend mid-shifts; that's when the good stuff came in. Making a mental note to ask Leila if he could change around his schedule, he marked down the trade offer on a paper slip and left it atop the books he'd accept for the store. If there'd been another deal waiting, he would've moved right to it instead of looking up at the front door as Cracker Joe walked in.

The homeless man shuffled in, eyes darting around warily, checking to see who was on duty and likely to toss him back into the cold night. Morty was fairly sure Joe suffered some sort of mental illness; he was quiet and unobtrusive most days, on others talking to himself and creating piles of CDs on the floor in patterns which made sense only to him. Not to mention the occasional outburst such as they'd witnessed a fortnight ago. Tonight, he was wrapped in at least two coats and scarves, a thick hat, and gloves. When his eyes met Morty's, Morty gave him a friendly nod.

"Hey Joe," Morty said, "How's it going?" Instead of relaxing and heading for an armchair in the back of the store, Joe froze, eyes going wide.

Joe trembled, his hands clutching his scarves. A low moan escaped his throat as he abruptly turned and fled out the door, running into a customer. She staggered, and Morty hurried over to help. He gathered up the bags she'd dropped, then checked out the front windows. No sign of the home-less man.

As Morty returned to the counter, Kim asked, "What the hell was that about?"

"No idea. He just freaked out and ran."

Kim shook his head. "Cracker Joe. Maybe he thought you were The Man come to take him in for more alien anal probing."

Morty gestured at his current attire, jeans and a Chemical Brothers baseball jersey. "Do I look like The Man?"

Kim cocked his head to the side. "Yeah. I think it's the comb-over."

"Oh, here we go."

"Or just the general level of whiteness going on here."

"That's it. Tonight. It's on. Mario Kart, asshole. Get ready for more turtle shells up your ass than the last time you got pegged by Gamera." More trash talking followed, a new insult cheerfully piled on each time they passed near one another at the counter.

During his break, Morty texted Darcy to let her know he'd be over at Kim's; she made them a date for tomorrow evening. He'd almost forgotten about Cracker Joe until he was up front an hour later, restocking the new release shelves. A wave of fresh air from the entry wafted over him. What made him turn were the exclamations of shock and disgust which broke out nearby.

Cracker Joe shuffled on his knees from the door toward Morty, holding something furry. A thing that left a dripping trail of dark red across the floor. Joe stopped a few feet away, still on his knees, and lifted a freshly killed raccoon in supplication.

The customer nearest him recoiled. A couple of college students at the chess table by the front window stopped mid-move. Cracker Joe swayed, muttering words Morty couldn't understand. Louder and louder, Joe chanted, or beseeched, or proclaimed, and held the dead animal out toward Morty. When Morty took a step back, Joe's strange rant became more ur-gent, and he knee-crawled closer. He stared at Morty with terror-filled eyes, and thrust the raccoon at him. Morty caught a whiff of it, unwashed fur and dark iron and whatever garbage the beast had been feeding on when it was killed. He felt water at the corner of his mouth, and brushed it with his sleeve. He was drooling. Morty stumbled backward, desperate to retreat behind the trade counter. Joe advanced, moaning, still holding out the dead rodent.

Kim strode past Morty, a baseball bat in his hands. "Get out! Get the hell out, you freak!" Joe fell backward, scrambled to his feet, staring wildly from Kim to Morty and back. Kim raised the bat, and Joe fled, stumbling over his scarves, his hands streaking the glass front doors red as he shoved them open. The dropped raccoon lay on the floor. Morty turned away, pressing his hands to his head. He shut his eyes, willing the bumps he felt to vanish. *I am not a monster, I am not a* wendigo, *I will not be triggered by some bizarre animal sacrifice or whatever that was, I do not want to eat a goddamn raccoon!*

He jumped when Kim brushed past him to fetch a trash bag. "That lunatic has really lost his shit this time," Kim complained. "We should call the cops."

Morty gulped down the fear worming its way up his throat, and nodded. As supervisor on duty, that would be his job. He held the phone receiver tightly while he dialed the non-emergency police number. He was peripherally aware of Kim scooping the furry corpse into a trash bag and spraying the floor with bleach. He focused on telling the officer who answered how a disturbed homeless man had just dumped a dead animal in their store and run; he was assured animal control would be dispatched and that officers in the area would look for Cracker Joe.

Joe had never spoken anything except English before, unless schizophrenic muttering counted. Morty could guess what Cracker Joe had been staring at. What he'd seen, under the casual shirt and comfortable jeans, under the pale skin and faint five-o-clock shadow on Morty's jawline. What he'd been supplicating to, in abject terror. He was offering a sacrifice. Offering it to a god.

Kim slapped Morty's arm, startling him out of his unhappy thoughts. "Got it cleaned up. Must kinda remind you of..." He trailed off, and Morty had a split second of panic before he recalled Kim knew his neighbors had been murdered, just not by whom.

"Yeah. Yeah, sorry. Just sorta froze. Sorry I wasn't any help." He swallowed. Kim nodded, glaring at the front door.

"Totally out of his mind. Hope this time the cops get him to a psych ward where he belongs. He shouldn't be roaming the streets." Kim made a sound of disgust. "That thing was still warm! He must've killed it himself. There was blood all over." Morty clenched his fists and pressed his tongue against the roof of his mouth, straining for serenity. "Anyway. Dude, you look like you're gonna faint."

Morty nodded quickly. "I think I'll just go sit in the break room for a sec."

"Good idea." Morty forced his feet to move, heading for the relative safety of the back rooms. "You sure you're up for a game tonight?"

Morty paused, then nodded. "Yeah. Mind if I crash over?" He brushed a hand through his hair, relieved not to feel any antlers. "Guess I'm not such a big fan of blood that's not corn syrup and food dye." He laughed weakly.

Kim snorted. "I'm only not giving you shit because you actually do have a good excuse right now to be such a pussy. Fine, my place. Don't expect me to coddle your sorry ass, though."

"In the game or in bed?"

"Either, dumbass. Go sit down before you fall down." Kim shook his head. Morty started to walk away, then stopped again.

"What'd you do with the—"

"Out front. Animal control can pick it up. I'm not carrying that crap through the store." Kim waved a dismissive hand at him, frowning. "Go. If you faint here I'm not picking you up. Even if you've lost twenty pounds this week."

Morty glanced down at himself. Okay, maybe he had lost a few pounds. His jeans were a little loose this morning, but that was just due to the sickness. He'd eaten hardly anything for days.

Really? Hardly anything?

He tamped down the blood-soaked memories trying to push into his mind. He walked to the windowless break room, drank a glass of cool water, and sat on the beat-up sofa, flipping through an old issue of *Mc-Sweeney's*, trying to focus on it, trying to focus on anything besides the emptiness in his guts.

33

The gas station, with its smelly abundance of sickly-sweet and overly fried food options, proved fruitless; Marie was ready to give up the entire venture. Her feet ached, she was tired of smiling at strangers, and faintly ill at the burned grease-scent of the cheap diner attached to the station. In the past half-hour, she'd considered and rejected a handful of male drivers for various reasons: too nervous, obviously married. One had been too cocky, she might kill him before they reached the city. Another smelled hideous and must own a dog.

She had been hooted at by a car full of young college boys and propositioned by one tourist who took her for a whore. Not a single truck driver had pulled in while she was loitering, and she noticed the clerk inside was beginning to take notice of her. *Horrible little furry men! How dare they impose on me their odious little tasks. I do not need the* windigo. *I will go home and eat the loggers myself.*

Still, the very fact the *Bagwajinini* had approached her in a city alleyway, much less petitioned her to act on their behalf, had her hackles up. The little men of the forest, and their cousins the *memegwesi*, who lived along the riverbanks, were not exactly enemies of the water panther tribe. But neither were they truly allies. Considering the furry forest wards sometimes helped the children of both white men and Anishinaabe, when Marie's family would much rather eat them.

This entire matter was too strange, she mused, watching a battered old truck pull into the parking lot. All this nonsense about the *windigo's* medicine was too much to believe. At best, he might lose himself in the joy of a fresh kill. He could barely keep from changing at the merest slap.

The wind blew her hair into her face, and she turned toward the station to escape its fierce buffeting. Under the garish lights, a familiar, idiotic face emerged from the battered truck. There was nowhere to go to elude the buffoon. He walked towards her, recognition lighting up his face.

"Well I'll be," the hunter of Big Feet exclaimed, shoving a hand at her. Marie forced a smile, and barely touched his welcoming fingers with her own gloved ones. "Miss Bois du Nord! Imagine running into you here. Do you live around here?"

"Not very far away," Marie said, wishing with all her might she'd never set out to find the intruder in her hunting territory. This whole debacle had been a series of distasteful encounters with white men. "And you, Monsieur Quell?"

"Heck, a French title just makes me sound way too sophisticated, Miss du Nord. I'm still on the hunt. And," He leaned in, his face alight with excitement, "I may have a new lead." He paused. "Well, you were there at Hettie's when it all happened! The fight between those two hideous monsters! Did you see anything?"

Keeping her expression mildly confused, Marie asked, "Fight? Monsters? I don't know any of this. I left rather rudely, I know. I hope you can forgive me. My ride showed up and was very impatient to leave." The hunter's face drooped, and she pressed, "Did something happen?"

He laughed, shaking his head. "Miss, since you didn't see it, I'm not sure even you would believe it. Boy, do I have a story for you!" He gestured at the greasy diner. "Care to come in? I may have just enough left for a cup of coffee."

Marie gave him a wan smile. "Regrettably, Monsieur Quell, I have no time to sit. My dear auntie is unwell, and my car is with the mechanic, so I am trying to find a ride out of town."

The hunter's bushy brows went up. "Back to Quebec?"

"No, I must travel south. To Lake Winnebago," she replied, having to search her memory for the name by which he would know it. "My aunt lives in the city there, north of the lake."

His scraggly brows shot still higher. "To Appleton? No kidding." He pushed his old ballcap back to scratch his forehead and nod up at the sky. "Well, I guess someone Up There likes you, because I just so happen to be going to Appleton myself."

Marie gawked at him. "You are going there? Why?"

"It's kind of a long story. Tell you what, let's go inside for a bit, and let me make sure I have enough for—that is to say, just need to gas up the ol' truck, and grab a bite, and then you're welcome to ride with me, Miss du Nord. If it all sounds all right to you."

She inspected him from head to toe, this time truly seeing the clearly worn and mended coat, the scuffed edges of his old boots. She forced a smile. "This would indeed be the most fortunate of coincidences, Monsieur Quell. Please allow me to pay for the gas."

"Oh, no, now I couldn't take money from a lady in distress."

"I insist. And you can tell me your long story on the way."

Quell nodded. "That's truly a lovely gesture, Miss du Nord. You're eager to get on the road as soon as possible, I take it?"

"My auntie may not have much more time. I am quite grateful for your offer, and more than happy to pay my way. Yes, I would like to reach her as quickly as I can."

The old hunter sighed, casting a longing look at the pre-wrapped burgers on the warming rack a few steps inside the glass doors. "Well, you're a loyal niece, for sure. All right. I'll just grab a bite for the road, and get some gas." He tried to refuse the money she held out to him. "Oh, now, I can't allow you to pay for my eats too."

"Monsieur Quell, please; get whatever you need. Is it all right if I wait in your truck?"

"It ain't locked, go right ahead. Excuse the mess, please; I wasn't expecting any company. I'll pump the gas in just a minute, so you don't worry about a thing, just get comfortable if you can. And, uh, thank you, for the gas money."

She pressed his hand between hers a moment, fluttering her eyelashes at him. "Thank you, Monsieur Quell. You are a lifesaver. Fate must have brought you here tonight."

He blushed. "I'm a'tingled I can help. All right, won't be but a minute." He ducked into the gas station.

Marie watched him another moment. An ugly coincidence, to be sure. At least he was unlikely to put his paws all over her. It should prove an easy trip; his truck appeared capable of driving the roads even if it snowed on the way. Though she would have to listen to this fool for hours, at least she would do so in relative safety.

The truck door opened with a groan. She hoisted herself up into the passenger seat, noting the rifle on the rack behind her. With a quick glance at the gas station to make sure Quell was busy at the register, she lifted the gun down and emptied out all the bullets into her lap. She tucked them under her seat cushion and replaced the gun before he left the building. She nudged aside a thing wrapped in a plain white shirt, and a smell she thought she knew wafted up at her. When she uncovered the object, the plaster cast of an odd track gave her pause. This idiot hunter had been to the den of the foolish logger boy. Frowning, Marie tucked the cast on the floor between the seats. She relaxed her shoulders and gave the ridiculous *mookomaan* a smile when he returned to pump the gas. He might have another weapon on him; best to be cautious. She grimaced at the memory of being shot by Quell. *Dangerous ass. I will make you pay for that yet. Perhaps when we reach the city I will dine on you for the troubles you have caused.*

They hadn't traveled two miles before he was relating the attack in the roadhouse parking lot, how a skeletal deer-thing had fought "like cats and dogs" with a beast which was half-lynx and half-snake until Quell had interrupted them with a shot. "And dang it, I dearly wish I had better aim. Gettin' too old for this business, I guess," he lamented.

Marie pretended amazement. "You shot them? Did you kill them?"

Quell sighed, shaking his head. "To my shame, no. All it did was distract the dead deer-thing and spook the lynx one. It ran off, and I looked to see where it had gone, and in that second t'other one must've run off too. That poor woman! I heard later she didn't make it." Quell gave her a sorrowful shake of his head. "When I think how if I'd only taken that shot quicker, and gotten its head, maybe—well, that blood is on my hands."

Marie pressed a hand to her lips. "Oh, no, you cannot blame yourself."

"Miss Bois du Nord, that's kind of you, but no. It is my duty to kill these horrendous things, and I failed. I ran all through the parking lot, and saw some other fella that must've been attacked as well; hope he ended up all right. I saw the lynx-thing again, stalking someone who was trying to help, and by God I put a shot right into that sneaky bastard!" He smacked the steering wheel with his palm, then coughed. "Excuse my French there. I just get so worked up when I replay that night in my head, ya know, thinking about what I shoulda done different. Whether that woman might've lived if I'd acted sooner." He fell silent, his hands gripping the wheel tightly.

Marie stared out the window. Blackness raced by, dotted with flurries which caught the lights of the truck like shooting stars. "What do you think they were, these creatures?"

Quell shrugged. "Not 'squatches, that's for sure. One of them had to be the monster that attacked that worker up near the resort, the AmShale fella. And here's the thing," he said, his tone turning quiet and serious, "There've been attacks in Appleton that sound disturbingly the same, just within the last couple weeks. A whole lot enough alike that I have to go investigate."

Not having to fake interest this time, Marie asked, "The same types of attacks in both places?"

"From the reports I saw, yeah, but very much worse. Two elderly people flat out butchered. Geez, miss, my apologies You don't want to hear all this. I get so caught up in wantin' to stop people from gettin' killed."

"Tell me," she urged, touching his arm. "Please. My aunt is also very elderly; do you think she is in danger? Are these creatures hunting older people?"

"Hard to say. I'll know more once I get to Appleton and look up someone who might know."

"You have an inside source? That is what it is called, no?"

"Yeah, could be. See, there was this guy who was supposed to come talk to me at Hettie's the very night those monsters showed up. Apparently he was in the parking lot, and got frightened so bad he run off into the woods and got lost. But somehow, he made it two days out in the snow, and turned up at a ranger's station, physically all right from but couldn't remember a thing." Quell sighed. "He went back home to Appleton. According to the address my deputy friend gave me, that fella lives right in the same place these old folks got murdered. He must've seen something or know something." Quell paused to wet his throat from a styrofoam cup of coffee. "I've tried calling him but he won't answer. I think he's scared." He glanced at Marie, seeming abashed. "I know, I'm probably assigning too much intelligence to these vicious things. What if—hear me out—what if this fella witnessed one of those monsters committin' one of the awful murders in Appleton, and it found out he was comin' to tell me about it, and tracked him up to Mellen?"

"You think one of these creatures followed your Appleton person up to Mellen, to prevent him from talking to you?"

"Now I know how it sounds, believe me. That monster would have to be a whole lot smarter than your average 'squatch. But my money's on the lynx-thing. Cats hold grudges, ya know. It might not be too smart, but cats are cunning as heck, and I'll bet that thing is no exception." He sighed. "So, I need to find this fella, and see what he knows. I really hope he'll talk to me, scared out of his wits though he is. I absolutely have to stop these ugly beasts from killin' anyone else."

Marie sank into her seat. "You are a brave man, Monsieur Quell." *'Not too smart'? You will see how smart I am, you staggering old fool. Smart enough to dupe the very cretin who dared to point a gun at me.*

His words startled her out of her furious musings. She realized she was digging her fingernails into the armrest of the truck. Fortunately the hunter was oblivious, gazing out at the road. "Anyway, that's my mission, and a dire one it is. I'm sorry to hear about your aunt. You just give me the address, and I'll take you right to her doorstep."

"Thank you, but my cousin is going to pick me up from the bus station. I had thought I would take a bus, then found none were running from Ashland in this weather."

Quell nodded. "I hope you're able to visit with your family, then, before... It's good you're going to visit her. And I'm certainly grateful I could be of some help."

She smiled thinly. "As you said, someone must have been watching out for me."

"Oh, no doubt. I'm glad I ran into you before some old truck-driving pervert tried to pick you up. Miss Bois du Nord, you wouldn't believe just how awful some people are, especially to young pretty ladies such as yourself. I shudder to think about the stories I've heard."

Marie returned her gaze to the window. "Not all monsters appear so on the outside."

"That is the God's honest truth." He paused, then fumbled open a bag of chips. "You sure you aren't hungry?"

She glanced at the greasy fried tubers. "No thank you. Perhaps I will eat when we reach our destination, depending if it is still dark, or if the sun is up."

"Good point; you never know what'll be open when you get into a town you've never been to."

She planned on slitting Quell's throat for his transgressions; eating him, however, would not be an appetizing experience. He was all gristle.

Road closures delayed them. What should have been a five-hour trip, according to Quell, turned into seven. The sun was well up by the time they reached the Appleton city limit. Far too bright out to attempt killing him; too many humans around.

She alighted from the truck at the downtown bus station. The smells of gasoline and sodden clothing hovered in the air, a miasma of *mookomaan*.

Quell called out the open truck window, "You sure you're all right here? I don't mind taking you to your aunt's house."

Marie turned, forcing politeness. "Thank you, no. My cousin will come get me soon. This is a family matter, and I must talk with him before I see my aunt." She gave him her sweetest smile. "I will remember all you have done to me, Monsieur Quell."

A puzzled look passed over Quell's face, then the hunter chuckled and shook his head. "I will miss your accent and your way with words, Miss du Nord. Buh-bye now." He shut the door, waved, and pulled away. Marie stepped inside the bus station, watching Quell depart.

He would be hunting for the man who was 'rescued' by the rangers. The *windigo*. Thankfully, he was too stupid to realize they were one and the same. She frowned. Unless he did something to provoke the angry *manitou*. As Quell turned east, Marie strode across the station, ignoring the stares of a few patrons lingering in the plastic seats, and pushed through the opposite door. She hesitated by an evergreen hedge when she saw the faded red truck turn away from the downtown area onto a residential street just a block away. She followed.

Businesses mingled with homes, all in older buildings, for a short distance, then the neighborhood became all houses, Victorian folk style side by side with bungalows. She was careful to keep to the edges of yards, shielding herself behind trees each time the truck slowed, tracking its turns. It didn't have far to go.

Quell stopped at a large turn-of-the-century yellow house, on a corner opposite a snowy park. He climbed the steps to a small porch, and studied the mailboxes nailed there. Movement caught Marie's eye at the house next door; a small woman in a long skirt and coat wrestled a box out of the side door, and set it down next to a car in the driveway. She fumbled with a set of keys, then slowly bent to pick up the box again.

"Oh, hey there, ma'am. Let me give you a hand." Quell hobbled over to her, and lifted the box into the back seat of the sedan for her. Marie couldn't hear the woman's quiet replies. "You're very welcome. Do you happen to live here? Oh, your sister's house? Sorry if this is a sensitive subject, but did you hear anything about the murders?"

The woman burst into tears. Quell froze an instant, then whipped out a handkerchief and offered his deepest sympathies. After a minute or two of quiet, tearful talk, the woman nodded, and Quell followed her up into the smaller house. Marie watched a moment more. The door remained closed, and the windows all had curtains drawn. She glanced around once. No one else was out. Sunlight glistened off the ice coating every tree branch. The wind was calm.

Marie crossed the street, looking up at the windows in the larger house. Lights were on in one of the rooms on the ground story. She climbed onto the wraparound front porch, placing her feet carefully, testing her weight on each board before committing to it, wary of creaks. Each mailbox, she saw, had an apartment number and a name: O. Sturgensen, M. Wending, N. Malnar, and B. Gordon. Wonderful. She never did bother with the *windigo's* name. She frowned at the large front door. The lock appeared simple enough. Perhaps she might enter without having to trouble any of the residents. Leaning closer, she caught a familiar scent. *Imbecile. He did not take my advice to buy cologne. Feh!* She stifled a sneeze at the top notes of shaving soap and sandalwood; the blood-smell and the faint trace of carrion lingered beneath them. Fresh. Strong enough to follow.

She stepped off the porch, nose up, glancing once more at the house next door where Quell had gone. She began walking along the street edging the park, close to the way she'd arrived, sniffing the air every few steps, gaining speed and confidence as she went. Yes. It was him. Her nose wrinkled as she caught another noxious whiff. She strode on, following the trail, grateful the wind was calm. With any luck, it would remain so until she located the simpleton. She was less sanguine about her chances of persuading him to return north with her. At least, if those furbrained little bastards were watching, they would see she did as they asked. Then she could go home, and set about a bit of proper killing. The mental image of white men in ugly plaid-check shirts, screaming as she clawed open their faces, cheered her. If nothing else, she supposed, she owed the irritating little forest tribe for informing her once again, lessons needed to be taught regarding humans setting foot in her river.

She did so enjoy playing teacher.

34

By Sunday morning, Morty felt calmer. Kim dropped him off at his own place to shower, shave, and enjoy a decent cup of coffee before work, since Kim's idea of coffee involved a paper cup and the corner convenience store. They'd played MarioKart last night until they were both too drunk to recall how many rounds each had won, called it a draw, and flopped down for a few hours' sleep. Morty managed to assuage his hangover in time for work, and walked the few blocks through the neighborhood from his apartment to the bookstore. The day was sunny, and kids played in their yards as he passed. Icicles sparkled in the glinting light. He watched the construction of a snow fort in someone's yard as he walked by. Two girls laughed, chattering together behind the castle walls as they packed snow higher. Everything was light and beauty around him, so he turned his face to the sun and picked up his pace.

The bookstore was busy, and Morty hustled from one incoming deal to the next, ringing up trade credit, moving from one end of the counter to the other to keep up. Leila was in charge for mid-shift today, so Morty was freed of supervisory duties. He dove into box after box of books, digging for treasure, relaxed and in his element despite the hectic pace. The store felt large when empty, but crowded when even a few dozen shoppers browsed the rows of shelves. College rock playing over the speakers wasn't too obnoxious. Morty held onto the thought tonight he'd see Darcy. And hopefully there'd be no interruptions by furry squirrels-that-weren't-squirrels this time.

He grinned when he pulled an old copy of *Callahan's Crosstime Saloon* from a box of dusty paperbacks. "Now that's what I'm talking about," he crowed, and lifted out stacks of well-worn books, taking care not to tug too hard on their covers. "Butler, LeGuin, hey, Zelazny. You have taste, Random Customer. Or your relations did." He noted the words scrawled in marker on the top of the box: *MOM'S BOOKS*. He paused a moment, thinking of how his own mother had taken him to the downtown branch of the library almost every week as a kid. She'd let him pick books from the grown-up fiction section. Smiling, he pored through the box of goodies, absorbed in them until someone cleared their throat right in front of him.

Morty blinked, slowly raising his head. "Oh, hey, still looking; could you give me maybe five more..." He trailed off as he raised his eyes to see Dr. Lightfoot. "Oh." Surprised, he glanced back at the paperbacks. "Is this your deal?"

Sam shook his head. "Not mine. Hoped I'd find you here."

Embarrassed, Morty lowered his voice. "Yeah, I've been meaning to call you. Just been busy."

"Too busy to let me know how things are going?"

Morty shrugged. "Yeah. You know. Life happens. Everything's fine, really," he insisted at Sam's raised brow. "You came all this way just to check in with me?"

Sam leaned close. "We need to talk. Now."

Great. Just what he wanted, a deep probing conversation on all the freaky shit in the middle of what was a perfectly normal day. "Yeah, sure. Just give me a sec." He quickly added up in his head what he felt the books would sell for, and scribbled a generous offer on the trade slip. He looked toward the front counter, where his boss was chatting with a couple of regular customers. "Hey Leila, back in a sec, okay?" She nodded at him, and Morty hurried from behind the trade counter, beckoning Sam. "Come on, we can talk in the back."

Sam frowned, and followed Morty to the corner bounded by Sociology and Political Science. As expected, no customers were in this far reach of the store. Except for students or profs from Larry U, this section usually languished. Morty peered between rows of books to make certain nobody was nearby, then nodded at Sam. "Okay. So what's up?" Sam appeared grave, and Morty's tension increased. "Don't tell me those assholes are still going to drill." Sam merely stared at him. Morty swore heartily though quietly. "Mother fuckers. Thought I'd scared that county official so badly he'd rip up the drilling permits with his own greedy fingers. Shitgoblins. Guess I'll just have to try something else." He paced, thoughts racing. *I can't take time off to go keep "convincing" these bastards. How much more will it take before they leave well enough alone? Before I'm left alone?*

"You'd better do something," said Sam. "You know how those white men are. Won't believe the devil is real until he's breathing down their necks." He grinned. "Their pale, fat, tasty necks."

Morty halted. "What?"

"If you really want to stop them from drilling in the wilderness, you know the best way to do it. So what's stopping you? Why haven't you already ripped their steaming entrails from their fat, jiggly bodies and feasted on their terror?" Sam poked Morty in the chest, punctuating each word.

"What the hell! You told me I had to control this," Morty hissed, quickly checking again to be sure no one could overhear.

Sam cackled. His face shimmered, remolding into that of an old white man with a neat beard. His eyes fairly twinkled with mirth. "I said no such thing, Mordecai. Now what I want to know is why a perfectly healthy *windigo* is skulking around a bookstore, of all places."

"You!" Morty snarled, wanting to slash the smirk right off the shaman's cheery face. He grabbed the nearest bookshelf and held tight, struggling to remain himself, though anger raced through his blood. "You son of a bitch. What the hell are you doing here, in my store. In my life at all. Get away from me!"

Winn giggled, leaning closer; Morty shrank away from him, unconsciously baring his teeth. "Thought I'd come see how you were, son. And I must say I am sorely disappointed. Why, you haven't eaten anyone in over a week. You must be famished by now."

"Fuck off," Morty snarled, edging away from the shaman. "How the hell did you find me?"

Winn pulled familiar objects from a pocket. He turned over the leather wallet in bemusement. "Nice how everyone carries all this information around with 'em these days. And this thing. Funny little device. Oh, and I did really enjoy the pictures on it. Pretty blonde ya got there. Not so much a fan of the music, though." Morty stared at his lost cell phone. He lunged for it. Winn moved back, ridiculously quick; Morty flailed a moment for balance, grabbing at another shelf. "Not the first one I've had a chance to play with. You'd be surprised how even with your eyes in the sky telling you where you are all the time, you white men still get lost up by *Gitchi-gumi*.

The lake's a treacherous thing, ya know. Can't be too careful, especially out on the ice."

"Give those back!" Morty demanded. Winn studied him, smile etched into his wrinkled face.

"Or what? You'll eat me?"

Morty's fists clenched. Sharp claws pricked his palms. He forced himself to take slower, deeper breaths. *No. I will not be played like this. I will not.* "That's theft. Seems kind of low for such a mighty shaman."

Winn laughed. "Son, you never heard stories of *Weneboozhoo?* He stole things all the time. Granted, I hope I'm not as foolish as he was. If you want your things back, you're going to have to take them from me."

"No," Morty growled. The roughness in his throat came with a flash of pain in his skull. He gulped, trying to calm his reactions. "I'm not your trick monkey. I won't dance to your sick tune."

Winn watched him struggle to hold in the changes which threatened to rip through his skin. "Looks like you haven't accepted your role yet. That's a shame. A damned shame. I had high hopes for you, Mordecai Wending."

Morty felt a chill ripple through him; he cringed. He gritted his teeth, ignoring the blood as growing teeth cut his gums. "I am not a fucking *wendigo.* So fuck you and your high hopes!"

Frowning, Winn muttered something, waving a hand at Morty. Morty's hips buckled, and he stifled a cry, struggling to remain upright. He glared at his hands, his claws scratching the paint on the bookshelf, panting until he managed to recover his fingers again. Cold sweat dripped from his brow, but Morty forced himself to stand straight, narrow shoulders thrown back. "You're not doing this to me again," he growled, relieved as he heard the tone of his voice revert to his usual scratchy tenor range. "Give me back my stuff and then ride your broom back to your black lodge and stay there, asshole."

Winn stood back a few steps, all mirth vanished. "Well. Now that is interesting." Slowly he pulled a pipe from a pocket, lighting it with the tip of his finger. Reeking smoke trailed upward as he took a puff.

"And you can't smoke in here," Morty said. He grabbed the pipe from Winn's lips, and crushed it in his fist with a very satisfying *crunch.* "Whatever you thought you were going to do here, you're done. Give me back my things and get out! I never want to see your ugly evil ass again." He opened his hand, letting the bits of pottery fall to the carpet. Small chunks of ice encased the shards. Morty suddenly realized he could see his breath, cold in the warm air of the store, and that the shelf he gripped had frost tendrils spreading out from his touch. He jerked his hand away, staring at it. It appeared normal. Except for the ice crystals spreading across his fingertips as he watched.

"Mighty interesting indeed," Winn said. "The *manitou* become the man. Maybe there's hope for you yet."

Shock reverted to anger. Morty advanced on the shaman. "Whatever you're doing to me, stop it, you son of a bitch! I don't want this! I am back to my normal life, and this town is my home, so you need to—"

Winn chortled, backing away, hands raised and delight on his lined face. "Oh, that's not me this time, son. That is all you. I can't imagine how you've gone so long without a good meal. Just look around this place; it's practically hopping with tasty little rabbits. Don't you want to just grab one of them, and rip open all those silly layers of clothing to get at the good meat way inside? Don't you just about go crazy having them around you all the time? All those petty people, bitching and complaining about their money and their stuff and making you hop to like you're their servant?" He put an empty reading chair between himself and Morty. "And all the time, you can smell all that hot blood, and all you can think about is how good they'd taste, how chewy and juicy between your teeth—"

"Get out!" Morty shouted, grabbing the nearest thick book and hurling it straight at the shaman. He vanished, and the book smacked loudly against a shelf, knocking several other tomes loose. Fire shot up Morty's skull from jaw to crown. *No, fuck me not now, not here, dammit no!* Gasping, he willed the antlers curling upward to retract, to retreat. He stood there a few minutes, heaving for breath, tears stinging the corners of his eyes, until he was sure no trace remained of the claws, or the antlers, or his fury at once again being made to become something horrible.

He picked up the book he'd thrown. His fingers were wet with his own blood. He cursed silently as he wiped the cover of the textbook with a tissue from his pocket. A trickle of moisture down his forehead proved to also be blood. He could taste iron. He crossed the store and strode through the stockroom quickly without greeting anyone. In the employee bathroom, he checked his scalp, dismayed though no longer surprised by the cuts where the antlers had burst from his skull and the claws through his fingertips. By the time he'd cleaned up, the scars were already fading. One of the many perks of being a cannibal monster. His stomach rumbled, queasiness seeping through his guts. "And you can shut up right now," he muttered at it.

Morty made his way slowly through the stockroom, nodding hello at a couple of co-workers. *It's casual. Everything's good, yep, nothing to see here, just your friendly neighborhood* wendigo *getting back to his day job.* Head down, he almost ran right into Kim.

"Hey, dude, watch it. I see somebody had an extra couple of beers in spite of a wiser soul advising them not to," Kim laughed, shoving Morty's shoulder. "White boy lookin' kinda green today."

Morty swallowed back the bile trying to come up, and managed a sickly smile. "That's funny, I seem to recall an overconfident Asian kid having beer after liquor, despite his older and wiser friend telling him that guaranteed a rough morning."

Kim spread his hands, grinning. "And yet here I stand, cheerful as the dew on a honeybee's butt, and there you are, looking like your head just split open."

Morty's hand went to his head; he tried to pass off the gesture as casual, smoothing his parted hair to the right. "That's...because I have a surfeit of brains, and sometimes if I get a really amazing idea, they just burst right out. Genius can't be contained."

"Dork. You on the counter today?"

"Yeah. It's been busy. You're stocking today, right?"

"Nope. I'm the games buyer this shift. Don't you ever check the schedule?"

Morty shrugged, heading toward the front of the store. "See you up there in a few."

"I'll give you ten minutes to brace yourself for my incoming brilliance," Kim said, giving an elaborate rolling wave of his hand as he headed for the break room to stow his coat.

Morty returned to the counter, hoping no one had overheard or seen his exchange with the infuriating shaman. All they'd see would be him yelling at an old codger who appeared to have stepped right out of a Christmas parade, jolly grin and all. He paused before delving into the next box of books on the trade counter, patting his jeans pockets to assure himself nothing was missing. Finding his new wallet, keys and new phone where they ought to be didn't improve his mood much. An old horror movie line popped into his head, and he grimaced. *Santa Claus stole my wallet. I'm gonna get that bastard.*

35

Quell did his best to balance the teacup and saucer on his knee. The end table next to the loveseat was completely covered in china figurines of smiling children, many of them with cherubic wings. Mrs. Evers noticed his gaze. "Margie always wanted children," she said. "She and Roger never had any, though. It was her deepest regret."

"That's a plumb shame," Quell replied. "How about you?"

The sister of the late Mrs. Hietpas waved a hand in a nervous, fluttery gesture. "Oh, Harold's and mine are grown, with kids of their own now."

"Congratulations," Quell offered, smiling.

"What about you, Mr. Quell?"

"Just Gar, please, ma'am. I have a daughter. She married a Navy fella, and they live down in Virginia. I don't see them as much as I'd like, but such is life."

Mrs. Evers nodded, eyes downcast and red-rimmed. She seemed on the verge of tears again, as she had since he'd mentioned the murders. Quell badly wanted to ask more about her dearly departed sister. He recognized a gentle approach was needed. "And thank you again for the coffee. It was a very long drive down here."

Mrs. Evers's eyes darted to the ceiling. "So you came all the way from Ashland to investigate Margie's—what happened to her?"

"Yes ma'am, that I have. Her and her neighbor over there. Did she know the gent?"

Mrs. Evers shook her head. "I don't think so. She never mentioned an older man in that house, just some youngster who paraded around in his skivvies at all hours. She could see him from upstairs."

Quell coughed a laugh. "Well! Honestly, what the younger generation does these days, ya know. It's like their parents never taught 'em how to be decent."

Mrs. Evers nodded. Her hands fidgeted with her teacup. "She complained about that one to me a few times. She never mentioned any of the other neighbors. Other than myself, and the girl from the service who came twice a week to clean and help her with errands, I think she really only socialized with her church group. Since Roger passed, you know, she pretty much kept to herself here."

"When's the last time you spoke with her?" Quell asked, taking out his small notebook and a pen. He hadn't really said why he was looking into the murders, and Mrs. Evers naturally assumed he was with law enforcement. He felt a little guilty. Not guilty enough to correct her.

Mrs. Evers set her teacup aside, clasping both hands together in her lap. "Right after the police spoke to her. Last week. She called them when she heard the shots."

"Two shots, at around four in the morning, was that right?"

"I don't know. I think so." She glanced at the ceiling again. "They told her it was probably a car backfiring. When they hadn't come by after a while, she called again, and then they sent an officer over."

"And when they went next door, that's when they discovered the," Quell checked himself. "The crime?"

Mrs. Evers fluttered her hands helplessly. "I don't know. I suppose."

"Okay, well, you say you talked to her right after that; did you come over here?"

"No, no. I live in Fond Du Lac," she said. "We have lunch together once a month. I should've come right up then; she was so upset. It sounded like the police were handling it, and then Harold had his doctor's appointments, for his back, and I couldn't—"

Quell reached across the coffee table full of half-packed boxes to touch her hands. "I'm so sorry, ma'am. Truly."

Mrs. Evers sniffled, gesturing at the boxes. "And now I'm supposed to— All of this! I don't even know what to do with half of— Excuse me." She stood, hurrying from the room. Quell heard her quiet sobs.

Well, dang it. She wasn't going to be much help, poor thing. He sighed, finishing his coffee in a gulp. Maybe the police left something to see. After all, they weren't thinking a monster killed this woman. He dusted the cookie crumbs from his jeans, and followed the sound of crying to the kitchen. He gently placed the empty teacup by the sink. Mrs. Evers startled, dabbing her eyes with a tissue. "Mrs. Evers. Would it be all right if I took a look around? I know the crime scene folks cleaned up already, but maybe there's something that got missed."

"Do you need more evidence, to put away the horrible drug user who did this?" She blinked up at him, mouth set in anger.

Quell paused. "Truth be told, I don't think he did it. I think the monster who killed your sister and her neighbor is still out there, and I want to make sure they never hurt anyone ever again." Her obvious shock at his pronouncement turned to a scowl.

"Then you do your job, Mr. Quell. You go right on up there and see what you can find. And you catch whomever murdered my sister and see to it they pay for it!"

"I will do exactly that, I promise you," he said. She pointed to the staircase.

"Her bedroom's the one on the right. I can't."

Quell nodded, and mounted the stairs slowly, joints aching. He had no idea whether all the blood had been cleaned up, or the carpets steamed, or really if anything at all was left which could indicate which of the monsters he'd seen was responsible. Since he had this opportunity, it couldn't hurt to check. And then he'd ask next door, see if he could talk to the fella who'd emailed him. Maybe he'd open up once convinced Quell could help. He shook his head, hoping this wasn't the lynx-thing. Either way, past time to put a bullet in both those monsters' skulls and drag their carcasses out into the light of day. Grimly, he flicked on the light in the bedroom, and sucked in a breath. *Holy mother, what a mess!*

A large, dark stain on the formerly pristine textured carpet marked where the late Mrs. Hietpas had been found. One huge area would be forever soaked in a dull rust color, and the wallpaper bore spatters that would never come out. The mattress was bare; he imagined any blankets would have been splashed with blood as well. One of the filmy gauze curtains at the window was torn. Quell walked carefully around the room, examining everything, trying to picture the scene as the police had found it. The tabloid he'd read stated Mrs. Hietpas' throat had been ripped out, and her body disemboweled. He stared at the stain on the carpet. He shuddered.

The heater kicked on, and the vent blew the gauzy curtains. Her sister said she could see that one indecent neighbor from the window.

He pushed aside the curtains. The bedroom window overlooked a shared driveway. A screened porch jutted out from the second story of the neighboring house. One section of screening flapped loosely in the wind. Quell studied the distance between the houses. Twenty, twenty-five feet, maybe. Close enough Mrs. Hietpas mighta seen something, or anything over there could've seen her. His eyes tracked down from the second-story porch, wondering which side of the building housed the other elderly victim's rooms. He noticed scratches in the siding. Deep, long, parallel scratches. Quell stared at them, goosebumps rising on his arms, remembering the gouges on the heavy earth-mover at the site out in the woods. He'd bet anything one of those beasts climbed up and got in through that screen porch.

Maybe that's where the old guy lived. How did the police miss those gouges? Well, they weren't thinking about a supernatural critter climbing the outside walls, that's how. He shook his head, trying to judge how high up the scratches were from the ground. Surely the lynx-thing should be able to climb, though the elk-thing had powerful legs.

He rubbed the stubble on his chin thoughtfully, then peered down at the ground. Too much snowfall in the last week, here too. No tracks remained. He took one more slow assessment of the bedroom, only then spotting the gouges on the ceiling. His pulse quickened. He squinted, then climbed upon the empty mattress for a better look. Directly over the blood-stain on the carpet, a number of deep slashes marred the otherwise smooth ceiling plaster. As if something tall had reared its head back. A thing with huge sharp antlers. He nearly fell getting back down off the bed. The deer-thing! It savaged this poor woman, and must've survived being shot at, if the old guy next door had tried to defend himself. The bullet Quell himself had put into its back hadn't stopped it.

He took a moment to calm himself, and went downstairs. Mrs. Evers was in the parlor, wrapping one of the little cherub figurines in layers of newsprint. She looked up expectantly at him. Quell wasn't sure what to say. He took a deep breath, and firmed up his spine. "Ma'am, what happened here was truly awful, and again, I am so sorry for your loss."

"You think you can find whoever did this?" Her eyes were full of desperate hope. "Bring them to justice?"

Well, just desserts, anyway. "I'll do everything in my power," he assured her. "Listen, you mentioned that next-door neighbor; do you happen to know if she talked to him, or to anyone over there, about the—"

"The only time she spoke to that man was to tell him to behave himself. Parading around in his underwear on the porch where everyone could see, playing un-Christian music so loud she could hear it, and consorting with very loose-moral types," Mrs. Evers tutted, shaking her head. "And the language he used! You know, I told her this wasn't a decent neighborhood any more, but she refused to sell the house."

Quell frowned. "In his underwear, on the porch, you say?"

She fluttered her hands. "I tell you, the young people around here. It's all the influence of those college professors, I'm sure. You know, all those socialists."

Nodding slowly, Quell glanced at the curtained window, wondering if anyone was home next door. "Oh yah, for sure. Well, thank you again for your time. I believe I'll go talk to the folks next door."

She grabbed his hand, giving it a quick squeeze. "Thank you, Mr. Quell. Will you be in touch?"

"If I find out anything, I'll make sure you hear about it," he said. Well, if he tracked this beast down, the whole danged world would know. He'd make darned sure of it.

Outside, he slogged through the deep snow which had blown against the neighboring house to take a closer gander at the gouges in the siding. They were at least eight feet up, and they aimed right at the second-story back porch. Right at the torn screen. He couldn't see into the windows up there. A disturbing idea was congealing in his head. *Younger guy, walkin' around in his skivvies on the porch. Rude and cocky. Just the type of fella who'd put a joke on his answering machine message.* He dug out his phone, and again read the emails from the guy who'd texted him at Hettie's and then never showed. Likely the same man who'd gone missing in the woods, only to turn up days later and return home to Appleton, without ever exchanging another word with Quell, though he'd seemed eager to ask about monsters. What did Quell know about werewolves and shape-shifters, he'd asked. And said he had information about the old man who was killed right in this very house.

With a sinking feeling, Quell called the phone number again. It rang three times, and then the message came on: "Hey, it's me, I'm busy carrying out my nefarious plan to conquer the universe. Or at least the bookstore. Speak at the beep." Sure sounded like the voice of a guy who'd think nothing of walking around in his tighty whiteys and telling off old church-going ladies. Quell looked up at the second-story porch, and the claw marks. He ended the call without leaving a message. He thought about retrieving his rifle from his truck; one glance around advised him it might be severely misinterpreted. This was clearly a high-class neighborhood. Large houses, all more than a century old, surrounded the broad park full of mature trees. Kids ran down the sidewalk, one pulling another on a small toboggan. Someone across the street was starting a snowblower to clear their walk. *No, not yet. Not until I'm one hundred per cent sure.*

Quell climbed the steps to the front porch, studying the names on the mailboxes. Sturgensen, that was the old guy who got killed. Maybe Quell could see his place first; before confronting the tenant who had the back porch. He hesitated, then pressed the doorbell. Almost immediately, the blinds of the nearest front window yanked up, and a suspicious scowl met his surprised stare. A balding fella with a portly build peered at Quell. A heavy robe didn't quite cover his pajamas. "Can I help ya?" he spoke up through the glass.

Quell tried to smile, though his throat was dry and nerves on edge. "Hope so. I'm here about the Sturgensen—"

"You with the newspaper?"

"No, sir, I—"

"You with the cleaners for the apartment? I hope you brought better equipment than the last guys." As Quell stood there, unsure how best to answer, the man made an impatient gesture and the blinds fell. Quell glanced back at his truck, parked at the curb. He thought again about his rifle. The front door jerked open, and the man in the bathrobe gave him a curt nod. "You're not charging extra just 'cause it's Sunday, though. I told your guys on the phone, since you didn't do it right the first time, this time better be free. Being a landlord ain't cheap."

"I'm just here to take a look at it," Quell improvised. The guy peered past him suspiciously. "Didn't bring tools today; just wanted a better, uh, a better idea of what needs to be done."

"And you'll handle it?"

Quell nodded, and the guy opened the door wider to let him inside. "This way. And just so's you understand, I can't show the place until this is spotless. Bad enough all of this was on the news; at least now they've caught the animal that did this, things will settle down again. Soon, I hope." He beckoned, and Quell followed him through a high-ceilinged front hallway. It had been grand in its day. Quell wondered briefly what the original lay-out had been before apartments were sealed off to the left and right of the central hall. "I've had to change the front lock, and that mother with her kids in apartment two is talking about moving out before her lease is up. This place is all I have, ya know. And I'm super careful about who rents here. None of those college kids here, let me tell ya, rippin' up the walls like in some of these places," the landlord declared, pausing to tamp down the carpet runner which had come loose from one stair. "No sir. If they don't have a job, they shouldn't even apply, is what I tell 'em. Of course I was happy to have a fellow vet room here, gave a bit of dignity to the place—and now this! What is the world coming to, when a man like that, served in 'Nam, gets murdered by some drug-crazed bastard right in his own home?" Quell tried to keep up as the landlord led him the creaky staircase. "And if you can make it so's I don't have to replace the carpet, that'd be great, but I think maybe it's a lost cause. At least get into all the cracks your guys missed. Cripes, it was all over the kitchen, all over the walls, just horrible." The landlord unlocked a door with a prominent number three affixed to it and swung it wide.

The kitchenette's linoleum and counters appeared well-scrubbed to Quell. The dark, rust-colored stains on the living room carpet, less so. "Did you see anything or hear the shots?" Quell asked.

The landlord snorted. "There's another thing. The cops couldn't find the bullets. I figure they must be stuck between the wall panels, or up in the ceiling, maybe. If you can find 'em, that would be good. Can't have a new tenant finding bullets in the walls." He glared at Quell. "And no, like I told the cops, I had my earplugs in. I can't sleep without 'em."

Quell stepped carefully around the stain on the carpet. Other than built-in shelves along one wall, the living room of the small apartment was empty. "I put an ad in the paper, but nobody showed up for Sturgensen's things, so I had everything sent to St Vincent de Paul's. Damned shame. I guess if he had any family, they'd maybe have tried to sue me, for not having enough security or something, ya know? Like anything bad ever happened around here before all this. This is a quiet neighborhood."

A quick check showed only windows in both the living area and smaller dormer ones in the adjoining bedroom. No access to the porch. Following Quell, the landlord added, "Oh, and I've already replaced the lock on the window, but it still needs a new coat of paint. In fact, the whole place could use it. I was told your company does that too." He glared expectantly at Quell.

"Window?"

"The window the robber busted to get in here." He showed Quell the scratch-marks around the jamb of one of the larger living-room windows. "Just look at that! Cops thought at first he brought along some kind of dog, but the door was locked, and how the hey would he have even drug a dog in through the window? Absolute bullpuckey, I tell ya. Ya know what I think, the guy was hopped up on that there crack cocaine, and had a knife on him, and just went psycho." The landlord nodded sagely. "Anyway, think ya can fix it?"

"Maybe," Quell hedged. "Hey, is the person who has that back porch at home? I might need to talk to them."

"What for?"

"Oh, well, I noticed the screen's all ripped, and I thought to take a look."

"If it is, he's payin' for it outta his own pocket, then. I replaced those screens five years ago."

"Oh," said Quell. "All right, maybe we can get that repaired, as long as we're out here."

The landlord waved a dismissive hand at an interior wall, presumably adjoining the next apartment. "You wanna take it on, go right ahead. Again, that's on him. I don't know his schedule. He just went back to work a few days ago. You could probably do the repairs over there while he's out."

"Back to work?" Quell asked.

"Yeah, he was up north someplace, got lost in the woods or something, I heard. And sick the week before that. Was in the hospital the day the cops were here about all this." The landlord shook his head. "I let his girlfriend in a couple times; she was over here lookin' after him. Now, it's none of my business what they do, bein' consenting adults and all. I've told him if she's gonna move in here, her name has to go on the lease. It's only right, ya know?"

"Oh, sure," Quell said. A girlfriend. He should find out her name too. Speaking of. He felt certain his guess was correct, but needed confirmation the missing tourist from Hettie's, the man who'd emailed him, and the tenant with the screened porch were all one and the same. "What's his name?"

"Wending. Morty. If he's not here, he's probably at work. At that bookstore on College, ya know, the one near the university." The landlord frowned. "Back to the issue at hand here; how long is it gonna take to clean this here up?"

An old man, a veteran for crying out loud, was murdered right in this house, and all the landlord cared about was the carpet and how soon he could rent out the apartment again. Quell frowned, and gestured at the rug. "Well that stain is definitely not going to come out. You're looking at replacement, for sure, there."

The landlord cursed softly. "What about just removing it? There's wood floors under there, good wood, this place was built to last a hundred years. You could just refinish it."

Quell shook his head. "Now, sounds like we're movin' from just cleanin' to complete restoration here. And that's extra." He studied the dark area on the rug. Just as across the way in Mrs. Hietpas' bedroom, there were additional stains in several areas. That monster ripped them apart, both these two helpless old folks, as if they were chew toys. Vicious, horrible butchery. "You say the old man shot his attacker?"

"Well, the cops said his revolver had been fired, and people reported hearing gunshots or a car backfiring or what have ya, but they never found anything. That drug addict they arrested wasn't shot up, least not that they mentioned on the news, so I'm thinking the bullets have to still be in here somewheres."

"I'm going to have to get my tools and come back," Quell said.

The landlord shrugged. "Does this mean you're gonna start right away?"

"I'll need my tools first," Quell repeated. "But I'll take some notes and measurements here."

"Whatever you have to do. Just the sooner, the better." Shaking his head, the landlord left, thumping down the stairs.

Quell took a deep breath to steady himself. So the fella in the next apartment was definitely who he was supposed to meet at Hettie's, the guy who got lost in the woods. Wending. Went to the hospital the day the cops came to investigate the murder here.

Quell crept closer to the wall, listening, wondering how thick the insulation was between the upstairs rooms. The apartment was chilly; might not be any insulation at all anywhere. Lord knows the landlord was talking loud enough. No sound came from next door. Quell studied the deep scratches in the painted wood of the window jamb. He peered out the window, estimating the distance around the corner. There was about a twelve-foot drop, at least, to the backyard below. The roofline above was steep, the gutter along the edge bent badly in two places, as if a heavy animal had climbed along it. Or used it to swing down from the roof.

Quell thought about his rifle back in the truck. Shooting the deer-thing only made it mad. He grimaced. Best to just see if the neighbor was at home first.

Feeling deeply uncertain, he left the late Olaf Sturgensen's apartment and approached the only other numbered door up here in the huge, Victorian house. Steeling himself, he knocked. Several seconds of silence ticked by. Quell felt perspiration on his brow. He knocked again. He tried the knob gently; it was locked. What did the landlord say? A bookstore? Bookstore near the university.

Quell headed downstairs, checking his phone; only one bookstore showed on the internet map for a College Avenue location. According to the posted hours, it should be open. Quell managed to let himself out the front door without alerting the landlord, and hoofed it to his truck. *All right there, Mr. Wending. Are you avoiding my calls because you're scared the monster will kill you if you talk, just like it probably did to Mrs. Hietpas, or is something much worse going on here? Which are ya there, man or monster?* He started the truck, ignoring the landlord coming out the front door with a confused look on his face. *I tell ya, though, sorta glad it's not the lynx-thing. Cats hold grudges.*

36

The scent was less distinct once Marie reached the main street of the city, with cars spewing their smelly effluence in white puffs as they passed. She pulled her scarf up over her face to ward the stench off; however then she couldn't track the *windigo* at all. To the stinking underworld with this ugly city, and its smells, and its creatures! She hesitated on a corner, her gaze sweeping the street in both directions. No sign of the specific white man she needed to find, nor of any small forest animal which might prove to be one of the *Bagwajinini*. There was no way to track him through this. She scowled. How could these animals live here? How dull their senses must be. She could not tell whether her quarry had turned left or right or gone across the street; even his distinctive odor was lost among the myriad competing stenches.

She debated the notion of returning to the house where he denned. Running into the hunter again would be less than ideal. And standing around for who knows how long would bore her to tears. A few of her brothers were lazy enough to hunt that way, mimicking logs as they waited for their prey to approach close enough to be snapped up in massive jaws and dragged under the surface. Marie possessed no such patience. The avenue, just a block from the university campus, boasted numerous taverns, bars, and eateries. As her gaze traveled along the street, she registered a sign not far down it. Wait. Did the *windigo* not say something about a bookstore? Ha. *It may be worth stopping in. I like bookstores. They are good hunting grounds.*

Marie strode across the street, ignoring the squealing of brakes just as she had ignored the posted crosswalk. She yanked open the large glass door of the book shop. Her pace slowed just inside, and she carefully unwrapped her scarf and took a breath. Low displays of new releases and best-sellers crowded the small front area leading up to a long, horseshoe-shaped counter divided by a wall. The store stretched back on either side of the counter, with racks of colorful plastic cases yielding to taller bookshelves. She glanced at the young woman ringing another one's purchases up at a register on the left-hand side. Then the scent reached her nostrils. She sniffed, and huffed in disgust. The right-hand side utterly reeked of *windigo*. And there he was, hunched over a box on the counter, right under a sign which said

SELL US YOUR STUFF! CASH OR TRADE CREDIT.

Marie approached cautiously. He hadn't noticed her, engrossed in riffling through the pages of a stack of books. He appeared different with clothes on, skinnier. His brown hair was neatly parted to his right, combed over his high brow, and his blue henley shirt hung from his narrow shoulders. It set off his eyes, though, cold like lake ice. She shook her head, untying her coat sashes and pulling off her gloves, a delightful idea striking her. She still had specks of blood on her fingernails. Licking them, she crept close to him along the edge of the counter without him noticing, leaned across it and brushed her finger down his nose.

The effect was better than she had hoped. He yelped, jumping back, hands flailing, eyes wide. He slapped a hand over his nose and mouth, staring at her, and then winced, both hands going to the top of his head, whispering "No, no, stop it, no!"

Marie snickered. "You are *très ridicile, windigo.*"

His surprise turned swiftly to anger. He lunged half-over the counter, his nose an inch from hers suddenly. "You can quit screwing with me, because I'm not going to change," he snarled. He only then seemed to notice a nearby customer giving him a frown, and sank back, though he glared at Marie.

Marie blinked at him. "It was only a silly prank. You are over-reacting horribly." She sniffed, drawing back. "Calm yourself, idiot."

"Why are you still here? Did you really think looking like her would fool me? Asshole! She's much prettier than that." The *windigo* sneered at her, and Marie felt both irritated and oddly flattered.

"I am pleased you noticed me, but it would never work between us," she retorted. He stood back as well, seeming confused. "Who do you think I am?"

"Marie?" He sounded uncertain.

Marie laughed, *"Regardez ça,* he does have a brain. I wasn't certain, since you insisted on coming back to this ugly stench-hole. Who did you think you were speaking to?"

His shoulders dropped. "I thought you were the shaman. Wait. Why are you here?"

"I cannot barge into your territory the way you did into mine? How very hypocritical of you."

"It's not my territory, damn it! This is just—" He took a breath and massaged the bridge of his long nose a moment. "Why are you here. Like right here, talking to me?"

She eyed him more closely, noting his anxious glances, hushed voice, and general twitchiness. "Why did you say you thought I was the shaman? This is intriguing."

"Because he was just here trying to control me," he hissed, again glancing around as if convinced something horrible was just waiting for him to let his guard down. "He showed up looking like Sam—the archaeologist from the burial mound—and then he tried to make me turn into a monster again."

Marie did her best to follow this babble. "The shaman of the black lodge came here and masqueraded as another, to trick you into revealing yourself? *Windigo,* you need to hide better."

He gave her a wounded glare. "Would you please stop calling me that? My name's Morty."

She shrugged. "Fine. If the shaman is here I would very much like to see him."

"Why?" His tone was suspicious. This was becoming very annoying.

"Idiot. He is a legend. One who mastered arts only my father knows, and the only man to ever be allowed to live after trespassing in my father's territory." She sighed, toying with an earring. "Papa never speaks of him. He is the fish who got away, *non?* Of course I am curious! What did he say to you? Did he cast any spells?"

Morty grimaced, and after another glance around picked up the books once more. "Like I said, he tried. I was able to stay me. Barely. Now why the hell are you here? Come to provoke me, or to scratch my back again?"

She chuckled. "I missed you, Morty. You are very silly." He glared at her, and she shook her head, picking up one of the books he had stacked. It was a romance, with a breathless pale woman on the cover, melting into the arms of a dark, broody male. "These dresses were so impractical. Definitely designed by men, so they could see all the *décolletage* popping out like buttered rolls." He opened his mouth; she cut him off. "I am here because our favorite little forest cousins asked me to find you. They say you haven't done what they asked you to do. The whites are still clearing the land for drilling or whatever it is they do."

His eyes widened, and then his long face drooped. "What do they expect me to do? I went back up there, I spoke out, I scared the piss out of one pathetically corrupt county official."

"Did you eat him?" Marie asked, interested.

"No!"

"Ah." She went back to the romance novel, sampling a page. "'Lord Lucifer.' Now that sounds more fun. I bet he eats people."

Morty snatched the book away from her, slapping it down on the counter. "Stop fingering other people's stuff. You'll get blood on it." He glanced at the cover, and added, "Besides, it's a decent series. Darcy reads it."

"Darcy?"

He gave her a very direct frown. "My girlfriend. And we are not discussing her."

She pouted. "You waste your time behind this counter, among all these dusty old things. You are made to hunt, now." She grasped his sleeve. "Come with me. Come back to my river and help me kill all the ugly fools who dare to mess with what is mine. The forest tribe said you have powers; they said the winter *manitou* in you could easily destroy all the men who are tearing up the forest and trying to poison the river. Come help me put an end to their pillage."

He pulled his arm away, shaking his head. "I don't have any powers. Except for this thing in me that just wants to kill. That's not me. I refuse to let that be me. Ever."

Morty straightened up as a young man approached, with lovely *za-awi*-colored skin and deep brown eyes. He smiled at Marie. "Hi," he said.

She smiled slowly in reply. "Mmmm. *Bonjour, mon chérie.*"

Morty frowned. "Hey Kim. Do you know if anyone wiped down the front counter yet today?"

The taller, younger man looked puzzled. "Uh, no?"

"Would you mind doing that, please? I'm kinda swamped in deals right now, and Leila did ask us to be more regular about it. You know, flu season and all, and everyone leans on it and breathes all over it, snotty kids."

The young man hesitated, eyes shifting from Morty to Marie and back. Morty gave him an expectant stare. "Do you mean now?"

"If you're not busy. Thanks, man."

He shrugged, giving Marie a curious glance before grabbing a clean white rag and a spray bottle from underneath the counter and heading for the front. "*Très sexy,*" she observed.

"No," Morty said firmly, holding one finger up. "No, you may not eat him."

"He would enjoy it," Marie purred.

Morty bared his teeth at her, only for an instant. It delighted her. "He's my friend. Lay off." She shrugged, smiling at the friend when he looked back at them. "I'm sorry about your river, but I'm sure a bunch of loggers are nothing you can't handle." He swallowed hard.

She sniffed. "Of course I can kill simple men. I cannot harm their big machines. This is your job, with your big, powerful, manly claws."

"Are you seriously trying to puff up my ego?"

She walked her fingers across the counter toward him, grinning at him. "Oh, I will happily rip all of their throats, but as long as their big machines and saws and plows are there, they will send more men, and I cannot hunt all of them all the time. Some of them will keep sawing and plowing because that's the kind of dirty animals they are. I need you to help me." Her fingers touched his, and he jerked away. Marie tossed her head back with a shrug. "Regardless, the *Bagwajinini* said they made a bargain with you, for you to stop the men clearing the land. What did they say they would give you if you did this, besides the pleasure of the hunt?"

"They're not giving me anything," he muttered. "They threatened to kill me. Keep calling me an abomination. You know, it kinda makes me less enamored of them and their demands. Someone should talk to them about positive reinforcement techniques."

Marie sobered immediately. "Their threats are real, *windigo*. You cannot brush them off and expect everything to come out fine, like in a fairy tale. The forest tribe have powerful medicine." The raccoon had said the *manitou* of the Starving Moon needed to be persuaded, to be turned to a better path. Observing this drawn, pale, frightened-looking white man among his silly books, she could hardly believe they were concerned about what he might do. She was not sure what they might do to her, though, if she failed to entice him to accept this divine quest. "Morty, my river needs your help. Think of the *manoomin,* the rice which will be ruined! All of the animals poisoned. All the people living at the reservation sick. Our dear little forest friends told me you can stop this."

He slammed another book on the counter, not looking at her, writing numbers on a slip of paper. "I tried. I did. I went back there and I tried to get the drilling permit walked back. If it didn't work—"

"They say it has not."

Morty shot her another glare, then dropped his gaze again quickly. "I am not going to kill more people, Marie. I don't care if that's what those creepy little squirrel bastards want." He moved along the counter, checking each pile of books or DVDs, stopping at one which did not yet have a slip of paper on it. He lifted the first book in a heavy stack of them, thumbing through its pages. Marie followed him, gnawing her lower lip as she gave the problem some thought.

He really was too ridiculous. She put her elbows on the counter, crouching slightly to lean toward him. "You have a god inside you, Morty. You know this. The shaman said so, the *Bagwajinini* have confirmed it. The *manitou* of the Starving Moon will not remain silent. How long will you fritter about here, among your silly books, pretending to be a simple idiot? Not that your performance is unconvincing."

He grimaced at her. "Thanks." Turning his back to her, he opened the next book in the stack.

"You know what you want to do. What you crave. Why not kill two *mookomaanag* with one claw? Come back to my river and help me chase away all the dirty pigs who are muddying the waters. You will save the river, save the lives of all the animals and people there. And if a few horrible men go missing while you do, it will not matter."

He gritted his teeth, fingers clenched on the sides of the book. "Hell no. I am not going to kill anyone else."

"Have you not fed since you returned home? You look thinner than I remember."

"No, I have not. And I'm not going to!" A ripping sound made them both look down. His fingers were bleeding, sharp bones piercing the fingertips. The book's spine was torn in two. Cursing, he dropped the book, curling his hands against his chest. He stared into her eyes, his own full of anguish. "Stop this. Please! I'm not a god, I'm not anything. I am just me, and I have a life, and a girlfriend, and a job, and I'm happy, damn it! Or at least I was before all this started. Christ, I wish I'd never heard of the Bad River, or AmShale, or any of this."

Panting, he checked his hands; the claws had disappeared. He started to wipe his fingers on his jeans; Marie caught his wrist. He looked sharply at her. She pulled off the delicate silk scarf from under her woolen one, and handed it to him. After a moment, he nodded thanks, and used it to clean his fingers. Poor creature. He really didn't understand he had no choice.

She thought suddenly of her Anishinaabe mother, how horrified she had been the first time Marie changed in front of her. Marie had been an infant, barely cognizant of the world. Her mother had hushed her growls, gathered her up, and spent long nights whispering to her she must not, she could not, that Marie must only be her little daughter. Her little girl. She couldn't accept the truth. Marie was never going to be one of them. Years her mother spent pretending she did not see the teeth or the claws, did not believe, until Papa returned. It was not so different for this man. He refused to accept the winter *manitou* inside him. "Listen to me," she said, speaking quietly, holding his eyes with her own. "Whatever your life was before, you are not that anymore. You are afraid of your own shadow. And it is only going to get worse. You will make yourself crazy trying to fight this."

His jaw set stubbornly. "So that's your solution. Just give in and eat people. Great."

She smiled, shaking her head. "It worked well for me, however all creatures have to walk their own path. All I am saying..." She sighed. "Everyone living downstream of the men who destroy the balance, who destroy every living thing in their way—they need your help, Morty. I need your help; there are too many of them. The *Bagwajinini* say you have the strength to do this, to save everyone."

He stared at her glumly. "You're painting me as some kind of nature savior, like a tree-hugging superhero. I'm not Captain Planet. Fuck it, I'm not even a Planeteer. I'm just a dumb schmuck who fell onto the wrong evil antlered corpse and now I have to pay for it. Nobody else should die because of me. Not even the ones drilling for gas in what was supposed to be protected wetlands." They stared at each other a long moment. Then he went back to tallying up books, including the one he had ripped, silent.

"Then I will have to kill them all myself," Marie said.

Morty shook his head, his movements tense. "No. Won't work. AmShale will just send more. Trust me, the money they'll make from this fracking project far outweighs a few deaths on the job. They'll just post armed guards, better security, bigger machinery."

Marie folded her arms, glaring at him. "Then what do you suggest, since you seem to know their methods so well?" She sniffed. "I suppose I should have expected a white man such as you would be familiar with such destroyers."

He set down the stack of books, clearly exasperated. "I'm not one of them, dammit! Don't you dare lump me in with those bastards. I've never worked for an oil company; I don't—" She waited as he trailed off, a dumbstruck expression on his face.

"Did you forget how to speak, or have the antlers simply grown downward into your brain this time?" she prodded.

He recovered with a scowl. "Funny. No. I just realized there might be another way."

Marie waited, while he walked to the next pile of boxes on the counter. He opened the top box, which was full of paperbacks, then stood there chewing his lip, lost in thought. Marie leaned forward and blew in his face, startling him. "And?" she prompted.

Morty glanced around; his friend was at the far end of the counter, conversing with a customer. Although no one was nearby, he muttered so only she would hear, "Darcy's dad works for AmShale. He's their CFO. He's the whole reason I was at the dig site in the first place, the mound of the dead god. He thought it would be nice for Darcy and me to view the artifacts. He's at least indirectly responsible."

Marie nodded. "Kill him in his sleep! Very good."

"Galloping fucknuggets, why does everything with you have to be about killing?" he hissed. "No. I was thinking I could talk to him, try to get into his good graces, and then persuade him it would cost less to pursue other projects."

She blinked at him. "Do you believe that will work?"

He shrugged. "I can try. He already sort of angled for me to take a job with AmShale. Maybe if I go in there all humble, I can get him to listen."

"Or you could eat him," Marie suggested. At his scowl, she made a light gesture with one hand. "I am only saying, it tends to end an argument very easily."

"I am not eating my girlfriend's father."

"And what if he will not listen?" she pressed. "How likely is he to let go of all the money you say these horrible men crave? What then, *windigo?*"

"Then I'll threaten him. I'll scare the crap out of him." He appeared very unhappy with this idea.

"You tried this already. Yet they continue to cut the trees."

"This is different," Morty insisted. "He has real authority. If I can convince him, he can make up some numbers showing the company would take a loss by continuing the project, or something. He's supposed to be in the office this week; maybe Darcy can set me up a meeting."

"You must be quick, then, for your own skin as well as for my river. That hunter is searching for you. He is probably on his way here any minute."

He gaped at her. "What hunter?"

She poked his shoulder with a long fingernail. "The one who shot you." Morty went dead pale, eyes widening. It would have been comical if she had not been proven right; that very instant, the scent of the other imbecile blew through the front door, putting her teeth on edge. She glanced back and saw the doddering fool wandering around the front section of the store. He had not yet spotted her. Marie quickly slipped over the counter, looking for a hiding place or an exit out of the hunter's eyesight. *"Merde! He is here!"*

"Hey, you can't—" Morty protested. Marie grabbed his arm and yanked him behind a cart full of boxes, crouching. She clapped a hand over his mouth and peered around the edge of the cart. The hunter was veering toward the counter now, squinting in all directions. Morty was gaping at Marie as if she had lost her mind. She released his jaw, but shook her head, warning him to remain silent.

"Whatever plan you have, do it soon," she whispered. "I rode here with him, and all the while he talked of killing monsters. He said two elderly people were murdered here, and he thinks one of us did it. I assume that was you." Morty gulped. She smiled briefly. "Good for you! Now he wants to kill you. As soon as he realizes you are *windigo,* he will almost certainly try to end your life. I suggest you kill him first. I need to get out of here; show me the rear exit."

Morty regained his voice, sounding overwhelmed. "There's a back door through the stockroom, that way," he nodded toward the rear of the store, "but you can't go through there."

"He must not see me," she hissed, pulling the hood of her coat up. "I am here visiting my dying auntie as far as he is concerned. Talk to your mate's father, or eat him, or whatever it is you're going to do. Do it fast, or I will take the matter into my own claws." She gave him a pointed glare, then leapt over the counter, dodging between customers, putting tall bookshelves between her and the hunter. She blew through the stockroom door, ignoring the sign reading

NO CUSTOMERS BEYOND THIS POINT.

She gave a flirtatious wave to the employees who tried to confront her before she kicked open the back door. The alley was colder than she expected, with a vicious wind. Moving swiftly, she headed for the next corner, turned out into the avenue, and checked to be sure she wasn't followed.

Her feet ached, slowing her down. *Ugh, these boots. What was I thinking? And this coat is too obvious now.*

She eyed a young woman passing by, heading away from the bookstore, wearing practical leather mukluks and a long black suede coat. She looked perfect. Hello, *mon petit apterif.* Falling into step behind the oblivious female, Marie checked ahead, watching for any convenient side passage. First, a change of clothes. Second, leaving this horrible place.

The *windigo* could keep his filthy hunting grounds. She was going back to her river. She'd done as the *Bagwajinini* had asked. It was now up to Morty. Marie would give him exactly three days to do something, then she would begin slaughtering the intruders. They would pay for their insolence. She smiled, wrapping her thick scarf up over her mouth and nose. Perhaps Wiisini would want to share the meat. There was likely to be quite a feast along her river.

37

Kim finished ringing up trade credit for a customer, and walked the few steps to the cart full of incoming merch to dump in a pile of videogames. He found Morty crouching behind the cart, eyes wide and wild. "Dude, what—" Kim began. Morty shushed him and beckoned him to come around the corner. Morty appeared pale and anxious. A knot started to form in Kim's stomach.

"Do you see that old guy?" Morty hissed.

Kim shook his head. "What's up with you?"

Morty peeked around the corner, quickly pulling back again. "The guy in the gray coat and red flannel shirt. Don't let him see you," he warned.

Kim eyed his friend in dismay. "Yeah, I see him, what about him? Why are you hiding?" He reached for Morty's forehead. "Are you feverish again?"

Morty shook him off, standing slowly. "I'm fine. Look, I really can't deal with him right now. That's the Bigfoot hunter I was going to talk to last weekend." Morty's eyes begged Kim for help. "I need you to distract him."

Kim placed both hands on Morty's shoulders; Morty's back was pressed against the wall, and he kept glancing toward the corner of the counter as if expecting an axe murderer to lurch around it at any second. Kim tried to hold Morty's attention. "First off, calm down. You are acting weird again, and it's starting to freak me out." Morty met his gaze, nodded quickly, and stared at the edge of the counter again. "That's the guy you told me about, the Bigfoot hunter with the blog." Morty nodded again. "Why is he here? You didn't email him again, did you?"

Morty shook his head. "No. No idea why he's here. I can't let him see me."

Kim tried to make any sense of this. "Does he know what you look like?"

"I don't know. I don't think so. If he asks for me can you please, please just tell him I'm not here?"

"Only if you go right to the back room and take some Xanax or something!" Kim snapped.

Morty blew out a breath, and relaxed his shoulders. Kim let go of him. "Sorry. I'm just really trying to put all that weirdness behind me, and the last thing I need is this guy dredging it all up."

Kim nodded warily. "Okay, but you're not gonna freak out and you're going to stay here."

Morty nodded in agreement. "I'll wait in the back 'til he's gone. I'll sort and price books. Get a cart ready for the bestseller rack; that needs doing anyway. I'll send Richie up to the counter to fill in."

"You're the book boss." Kim shrugged.

Morty clapped him on the shoulder, then gave their salute, and was gone. Kim watched him sprint toward the back of the store and blow through the swinging door to the stockroom as though every demon in hell was hot on his tail. *Morty, you are freaked like I've never seen you freaked before.*

With a frown, he returned to his duties, keeping half an eye on the grizzled white guy who kept peering around the store as if searching for something. When the man veered closer, Kim spoke up. "Hi, can I help you find anything?"

"Hope so," the older guy said, squinting at Kim. "I actually came in hopin' to find someone who works here, Wending I think his name is? I need to follow up with him about the incidents in his neighborhood."

Kim assessed the guy's dirty clothing and graying stubble. "You with the cops?"

"Not exactly." The man gave him a polite smile. "It's very important that I talk to him. Is he here?"

"He's off today. You can leave a message for him if you want."

The scruffy guy frowned. "Well, I already checked with his landlord, and he wasn't home. If he's not here, any idea where I might find him?"

Why would a Bigfoot hunter be visiting Morty at home? None of this felt right. Kim shrugged. "No idea. I can give him a message next time I see him."

The man's eyes suddenly widened, and he pointed a finger at Kim's face. "Wait just a gosh-darned minute. Aren't you the kid who came up to Hettie's? Saw you waiting inside when I come back from the search party."

"Don't know what you're talking about," Kim said.

The man nodded firmly. "Yes you are! You're the Asian kid who was with the fella I was waiting on, the one who run off into the woods and got lost."

Kim gave him a pointed glare. "Never been lost in the woods, man. Maybe I just look like some other generic Asian kid to you."

The man came closer, leaning toward him. Kim frowned but didn't retreat. "Don't you give me that, son. You know darned well what I mean. And I'm sure you heard about the old folks here being killed; the ones who lived right next to your buddy."

Kim shrugged, picking up a price gun and starting to tag a pile of games. "They caught the guy who did that. Read a newspaper or something." The scruffy guy kept staring at him through red-rimmed, squinty eyes. Kim raised his head to glare directly at him. "Now is there anything else I can help you with, sir?"

"Just back down a second here, son. I am not the enemy. Did you hear exactly how those poor people were killed? Butchered, in the most horrible way possible! And I'm sure you musta heard how a woman had her throat ripped out in the parking lot at Hettie's."

Uneasily, Kim studied the older man. Though clearly in need of a shower and a few hours' sleep, his hands were steady and his gaze didn't waver. "Yeah, a bear or something. Nature is lit."

"No way. No bear would walk into a lot fulla cars outside a noisy roadhouse and just pull a woman right outta her truck, son. I've hunted a lot of critters all up through the Northwoods and I'm here to tell ya, that just doesn't happen."

"What does that have to do with anything?" Kim argued. He gestured at the shelves of DVDs and CDs behind the old man. "No wild animals here."

"Well I reckon it doesn't look like an animal right now," the old man said. He gave a grave nod, lines deepening around his mouth. "Name's Garwood Quell, son, and I came here tracking the very creature that killed the woman at Hettie's. The same thing killed those two elderly folks here in town as well."

Kim stared at him. "Why would a wild animal break into an apartment to kill some old Army vet? In the middle of a city?"

"See, you're making the wrong assumption here," Quell said. "It wasn't an animal, per se, I mean not in the way you're thinking." Before Kim could muster a reply, the old guy asked, "Your friend Wending ever mention werewolves to you?"

Kim glanced around uneasily. Though Leila, the manager, was nowhere in sight, the phone was only a couple of steps away. "Look, dude, whatever your deal is, unless you have stuff to trade, or you want help finding a book, I'm gonna have to ask you to leave."

Quell leaned closer, glaring hard at Kim. "You musta heard how the old man was torn apart, guts ripped right out, how he shot the thing attacking him and was slaughtered anyway. I heard your friend Wending was at the hospital when the cops arrived; any idea why?"

Kim snapped, "Yeah, he had a nasty virus and was running a fever so bad it messed with his head for days. And he was so screwed up he actually contacted some nutjob Bigfoot hunter, and wanted to drive four hours in a goddamn blizzard to talk to him." Quell scowled, and Kim leaned on the trade counter, lowering his voice. "Now I'm sorry; either buy something, or leave, or I'm going to have to call the cops."

"You do that," Quell growled, "And you ask 'em why there's claw-marks on the wall leading up to your buddy's back porch."

Kim shook his head. "You are out of your mind, boomer. Leave. Now." He saw Leila at the opposite end of the counter, writing in her planner notebook. She'd back him up. This guy was absolutely insane.

Quell shook his head. "It is critical that I talk to this Wending fella. Because one of two things is going on: either he saw something, and is so scared of it he's ignoring my calls, or else—"

"Or else what?" Kim demanded, then corrected himself. "No. You know what? I'm not playing this crazy shit any more. Get out of here or I'm calling the cops. This is harassment."

"Has he said anything to you?" Quell persisted. "Did he say why he ran into the woods? Has he remembered anything about what happened up there, or about the nights when his neighbors were murdered?"

Kim grabbed the phone. "I'm not kidding, old man. You are crazy and you're freaking out the customers." The one shopper within earshot stared at them curiously. Undaunted, Kim poised a finger over the buttons. "Get out. And don't come back."

Quell lunged at him; Kim clutched the phone receiver, backing up. "You have to ask him what he knows!" Quell shouted. Heads turned; Leila looked up. "Ask him why he won't answer his phone. What's he afraid of? What's he hiding?"

Leila strode over, fire in her eyes. "Sir, what's the problem here?"

The man's head jerked toward her. "Ma'am, I'm sorry for the disturbance, I truly am, but this is important. Is there a fella named Wending here?"

"This guy's crazy," Kim said. "Ranting about murders and bears. I've already asked him to leave."

"Sir, I need you to calm down," Leila said. She exchanged a glance with Kim. Kim dialed 911. He couldn't tell if the older man's thick coat might conceal any weapons; best not to take any chances. Some of the customers were already edging away, or flat-out hurrying out the door.

"Now, I said I'm sorry," Quell told Leila, gesturing at Kim, "but this kid is being downright unhelpful. And this could be a matter of life or death. I need to talk to this Wending fella. Five minutes. I just need to ask him some questions about the murders last week."

"Hi, there's a disturbed man here in our store, and we're concerned he may try to hurt someone or himself," Kim said to the dispatcher on the phone. "We need the police here right away. BookStop on College."

Quell appeared pained. "Son, I am not your enemy. You had better start asking your friend some hard questions."

"No, I don't know," Kim replied as the dispatcher asked if the man was armed.

Quell backed away, yelling over Kim. "You ask him about the monsters in the parking lot. Ask him what made him run into the woods and get lost. Ask him why these killings seem to follow him around!" Kim stared at him, barely hearing the dispatcher say officers were on their way. Quell pointed at him, trembling. "You better make sure you do it with a big gun though, because a thirty-three didn't help that old neighbor of his one goldang bit." Quell stormed out the front door. Kim stared after him a second before he realized he was still holding the phone.

K.A. SILVA

"He just left. Could you send someone over anyway? He didn't seem too stable." Kim swallowed. "Thanks." He hung up.

Leila blew out a breath, touching Kim's shoulder. "What the heck was that about?"

"No idea. Dude's nuts."

Leila shook her head. "Cops on the way?"

"Yep."

"Okay. You go take a break. I'll send the officers back to talk to you when they get here. What did that guy want with Morty?"

"No idea," Kim repeated. "He was just ranting about crazy stuff. Murders and wild animals."

"Uff da. Right after the homeless guy freaked out last night, too." She sighed. "It's like we're suddenly a magnet for every crazy person in Appleton. I've never seen that guy before. You or Morty know him?"

"No, never seen him before."

"All right then, Morty in the back?" she asked. Kim nodded. "Tell him to stay there a while. Go on, you take fifteen. And however long you need to talk with the cops. Poor Morty. He really is having the worst year."

"No doubt," Kim agreed. "Sure you want to stay up here by yourself?"

She dismissed him with a light laugh. "It's fine. I doubt he'll come back. Seemed like he didn't want to stick around to talk to the police." She shook her head. "Well, that's just sad. I hope they get him help."

Kim walked to the stockroom, tense. He found Morty at the book sorting table, picking through hardcovers from a pile of full boxes. "Hey, so your Bigfoot hunter friend is a complete whackjob," Kim said. Morty's head jerked up.

"Is he still here?"

"No, he started yelling about murders and we called the cops. They're on the way over. He ran out the door."

Morty relaxed a bit. "I owe you."

"Damned right you do," Kim said. He leaned against the sorting table, studying Morty while he continued to price books. "Tell me what's going on."

"What do you mean?"

Kim huffed, "Come on, man, don't. You've been acting freaked out all day." Morty hesitated, and Kim prodded, "Ordering me to clean the counter earlier. What the hell. Pulling rank on me, Mr. Supervisor? Really?"

Morty winced. "Sorry about that."

"Who was the chick you were talking to? And that crazy Bigfoot hunter went on and on about bears and the old-people murders."

Morty set down his pencil, taking a deep breath. He braced his palms on the table as if seeking strength from it. "He keeps calling me. Emailing him when I was feverish was a really bad idea." He swallowed dryly. "And that woman was, uh, just a customer."

"Bullshit." Kim glared at him; Morty could barely meet his eyes. "You're gonna tell me everything. You know, me, your best friend. The friend who drove you up to north BFE when you were out of your skull with a fever, and who is now seriously reconsidering the decision not to tell Darcy why you really wanted to go up there."

Morty cringed. "I honestly don't know what the Bigfoot hunter is doing here. I haven't replied to his emails or his calls or his texts, but he keeps harassing me. He seems to think I know something about that bear mauling, in Mellen." Kim waited. Morty looked at the table, his voice uncharacteristically quiet. "And the woman was someone I met up there. At the reservation, when the rangers found me. She's in town visiting her aunt. Total coincidence."

Kim spread his arms, frustrated. "You couldn't have just said that? Instead of pushing me off like the hired help?"

"It's embarrassing," Morty countered. "I'm trying to forget last weekend ever happened but it's a little hard when people won't let me!"

Both of them fell silent. After a moment, Kim nodded. "Fair enough."

"Thanks."

Kim stood there. Morty seemed calmer, at least, but Kim couldn't shake the feeling something was still very out of whack. Morty sighed, and picked up a book and his pencil again. "It's been a really weird couple of weeks."

"You still don't remember much?"

Morty paused. "No. Not really."

"That guy was asking about you going to the hospital. Did you tell him about that?"

Morty glanced at him, frowning. "No."

"You sure?"

"Pretty sure. I know I asked him about really weird stuff, but no. Didn't mention the hospital trip at all."

"He said he went by your place looking for you."

Morty straightened, giving Kim his full attention. "The hell?"

"Did you give him your address, or tell him your full name?"

"No and no," Morty said, rubbing his jaw.

"Well, maybe you better ask the cops to stake out your place for a few days. Just to be sure this creep doesn't try to break in. He was insistent on talking to you. Said he had to ask you about the murders." Kim watched Morty begin pacing in a tight circle, alternately rubbing his jaw and running his fingers through his hair. "I mean, if you need to stay at my place for a few, it's cool. This guy had stalker written all over him."

Morty didn't seem to hear his offer. "How'd he find me?"

"Don't know. I don't get the impression he's giving up yet." Morty's agitation unnerved Kim. He tried to project more confidence than he felt. "At any rate, the cops are going to want to talk to both of us; Leila said we can take as much time as we need."

"Why?" Morty asked, a panicked look in his eyes.

Kim frowned. "Because I was the one who had to deal with the crazy asshole, and you are the one the crazy asshole is obsessed with. Dude. Calm down, please."

Nodding, Morty pulled a wooden stool closer and perched on it, huddling into himself. He looked awful; Kim had never seen Morty this shook.

Kim touched his friend's shoulder, hating that Morty flinched. "Hey. It's all good, man. I'm sure the cops'll keep an eye on your apartment for a couple days to make sure this stalker doesn't bother you. I promise, as soon as they hear the crazy things he was saying, they'll definitely look for him."

Morty's wide eyes fixed on Kim's. "Why, what was he saying?"

Kim shrugged. "Just insane conspiracy babbling about how you know something about the murders and about that woman killed by a bear. Animals that aren't really animals. Crazy-ass bullshit."

Morty choked on a laugh. "Wow. Yeah. Pretty crazy."

"I mean, I assume you haven't seen any bears breaking into your neighbor's apartment."

"Ha, no. No bears."

Kim studied him a long, quiet moment. "Maybe you should move."

Morty shook his head. "Can't really afford it right now."

"Your girlfriend drives a sports car and lives in a huge mansion in the swanky neighborhood. Ask her for the goddamn deposit."

"I can't do that," Morty argued. "She already bought me a new phone. She drove all the way up there to get me. I'm not going to be a leech, Kim. I won't do that to her."

Silence returned. Morty's phone buzzed. He pulled it from his pocket and checked the text. "Darcy," he mumbled. "I'm invited to dinner tonight."

Kim nodded. "Staying with her tonight?"

Morty shook his head. "Her parents are kinda uptight. I mean, it's obvious their daughter's been sleeping with me for months, but they don't want any hanky-panky under their roof."

Kim chuckled. "Did you seriously just use the words 'hanky-panky'?"

A grin touched Morty's lips. Only for a second, but Kim felt better upon seeing it. Anything was better than Morty acting spooked and being evasive. "Oh, ya know, them kids these days, with their naughty dancing and oral sex and what have ya."

Kim laughed. *There we go. There he is.* "You mean you're not going to just throw Darcy down on the table and bump uglies right on top of the Jell-o salad?"

A full laugh burst out of Morty, and his shoulders relaxed. "Uh, no."

"So just dinner and then they kick you out into the cold?"

Morty shook his head, reading Darcy's texts as more came in. "She says I can stay in the guest wing. Not just the guest room, mind you, I get a whole wing to myself apparently." His expression sobered. "And earlier I asked if I could have a talk with her dad. So he wants me to come see him at his office tomorrow morning."

"Why would you want to? Oh holy shit, man, are you doing it?"

Morty looked up, confused. "What?"

"Are you getting married, you asshole? And you didn't tell me first?"

"What? No!" Morty chuckled nervously. "Hell, no. I am in no way ready for that."

"Good. Because that is a whole other level of obligations right there."

Morty sighed. "Yeah, I mean, I don't know. Maybe someday." He cradled his phone in both hands, replying to Darcy, his brows scrunched in worry.

Kim studied his friend. Morty hadn't dated much, only once before in the years Kim had known him, and by his own account only a couple of girls had gone out with him in college. His average looks, average height, and unathletic body hadn't exactly drawn the honeys to him, and his introverted tendencies meant he never approached a girl, even if he was obviously attracted. As far as Kim knew, Darcy was his first really serious relationship. Though it was obvious Darcy liked this cynical, underachieving geek right now, they didn't seem to have much in common. Kim had seen how she had flirted with Morty, and put it down to a wealthy girl's rebellion against her conservative parents. He expected it would end within the year when Darcy graduated and moved on. Who knows, though, maybe Morty was secretly amazing in bed. Kim hoped his friend understood Darcy was destined to find some other rich boy and settle down to raise rich kids. She wasn't going to marry a nerdy bookstore clerk, though she was having fun right now. Plus, if he kept acting weird, she'd dump him. The fallout would be ugly; Kim knew Morty didn't think much of himself to begin with.

"So why a chat with Mr. Fracking?"

Morty licked his lips, then gave Kim a sheepish glance. "I need to try to talk him out of the fracking project at Bad River. It's going to hurt a whole lot of people."

"Since when did you become such an activist?"

Morty shrugged. "Come on, don't give me that. I've always cared. Just was never in a position to do anything meaningful about it before."

"Talking to Daddy Big Oil is going to accomplish nothing."

Morty sighed. "It can't hurt, I guess. I mean, I'm dating his daughter. Darcy has already been talking to him about it. Who knows. Maybe I can convince him the company's money will be wasted; that it's too much trouble to drill there."

Kim felt this was too much of a long shot. Also, though Morty was an expert-level critic of all things corporate, becoming involved in any sort of eco-warrior action wasn't his style. "Aren't they planning to sell it all overseas? They have to be making a profit to bother in the first place."

"Yeah, but I have to try." Morty shook his head. "Crap. She's talking about skipping class to drive me to Green Bay in the morning. She's already missed a few days of classes dealing with all of my nonsense."

"Tomorrow morning?"

"Yeah."

Kim shrugged. "I'll drive you."

"Kim, you don't have to."

"Goddamned right I don't. You should get on your knees and thank me for being such a good friend to you." Kim shrugged. "We both have closing shift tomorrow. Easy to pop up there, you have a polite little chat with the destroyer of the earth, we come back here in time for work. Cool?"

Morty smiled. It looked a bit strained. "Cool. Seriously though, you don't have to go out of your way for me."

"Knees, bitch!" Kim said, pointing at the floor in front of him.

Morty started lowering himself to the floor, shaking his head. "Well, okay, man, but I sure hope you have a magnifying glass. It was really hard finding it the last time."

Kim backed off, laughing, and Morty grinned at him. "As if you wouldn't gag trying to eat me," Kim scoffed, mirth fading when Morty paled. "Dude. You know I'm kidding. You're not my type."

"Yeah, I know. Not walrusey enough." Standing, Morty shook his legs a bit to straighten his jeans out. He'd definitely lost the excess padding around his waist and belly he'd carried ever since Kim had known him, up until these last couple of weeks. Kim nodded at him.

"Gettin' too skinny. You know I loves me some girls with curves." Morty managed only a weak smile, and Kim's unease returned. "What time should I pick you up at Darcy's tomorrow morning?"

Morty ran a hand through his hair, eyes on his phone. "Well, I need to go home first. Get my suit. I figure maybe I'll make a better impression if I dress more respectably. Let's meet at my place, eight a.m."

"You're really serious about this. A suit?"

"Yes, my one suit," Morty snapped. "Corporate bloodsuckers don't take anyone seriously if they're not dressed like they belong in a fucking boardroom."

Kim held up both hands. "All right, Jesus."

"Sorry. I'm sorry. Assmonkeys. All of this is insane and it's wiped me out."

Kim nodded. The sleepless circles around Morty's eyes made him seem older, and a little ghostly. "Try to get actual sleep in the cushy guest wing. You haven't acted like yourself in weeks."

"I know." Morty looked him in the eye at last. "You really don't have to drive me. I can take the bus."

"Screw that, you'll get your fancy suit all wrinkled. I need to keep an eye on you, keep your sarcasm from laying waste to a big corporation and starting a class war or something." Kim clasped Morty's arm briefly, and Morty nodded. Police radio chatter sounded at the swinging door, followed by a knock. "Guess the cops are here." Kim went to allow them into the back room, casting a worried eye back at Morty. Morty tucked his phone away, looking up expectantly, his wide eyes full of what Kim could only unhappily describe as fear.

Whatever is going through your head, you'd better let me in on it before you turn into a nervous wreck. Whether it's your future with Darcy, or crazy assholes stalking you, or dead old people next door, you'd better talk to me and soon.

Bracing himself for too many questions after too much weirdness, Kim opened the door.

38

By the time Morty left work, it was dark outside. He turned his coat collar up against a stiff wind which blew snow into his face, and turned north at the history museum, wanting to escape the traffic still puffing along the main drag of College Avenue. Spotlights cast the museum's crenellated towers into sharp relief against the dark gray sky. Morty glanced at it as he passed, thinking about the exhibit for the town's most famous son, Harry Houdini, on the top floor of the old Masonic hall-turned-public-building. Maybe old Harry had some tips for keeping a *wendigo* hidden from sight.

The rest of his workday had been uneventful. He and Kim had talked to the cops. The officers promised to do a few drive-by patrols at Morty's place. They wrote down Quell's description as well as his cell phone number. Morty had already erased Quell's voicemails, which he judged a fortunate thing, although the police were disappointed. The last thing he needed was them wondering why he was anywhere near the murder in Mellen.

Though that death had been written off as a rabid animal attack, he was relieved that no one, save Quell, was looking at him for it. And the cops thought they had the guy who killed Sturgensen and Mrs. Hietpas. Best to leave it at that. Guilt fluttered at the back of his mind. He tamped it down, trudging along the deserted sidewalk.

Though no new snow fell, the wind whipped drifts against houses and parked cars, and sent swirls of it into the air when he turned right onto Washington Street. Morty slowed beneath a streetlamp, unable to see his breath. His fingertips had pale scars, barely visible against his skin, all color washed out under the diffuse amber light. He shoved his hands in his pockets, though he wasn't chilled. If anything, he felt comfortable. Good thing Kim wasn't here. Morty had promised to bundle up warmly when he left the store, arguing it was only a few blocks north and east to Darcy's parents' home along the Fox River. He could certainly walk there in less time than it would take to wait for the next bus, which wouldn't get him far into the older neighborhood anyway.

He passed the modern steel-and-glass buildings of Larry U which sat incongruously next to their large, Federal-revival chapel. A darkened street led north from campus, toward City Park. Only blackness remained where two weeks ago a tall Christmas tree had still been brightly glimmering each night. It was too far across the park to make out the house with his apartment. He was uneasy about veering anywhere near there right now.

He passed the university's music center, glancing into the lit windows. He saw a student in the glass atrium, her nose buried in a book. Her hair was blond, and he thought of Darcy. Their first conversation had been about her music studies.

He might have seen her in the bookstore a time or two before they first spoke; he wasn't sure. He'd been shelving poetry, picking a few titles to display in what he felt was a sorely neglected section, when this pretty, blond, young woman in a hoodie and well-fitting leggings had approached him. Her tone sounded hesitant. "Um. Excuse me? You work here?"

Morty turned directly to her then, struck immediately by how deep and dark chocolate brown her eyes were, how warm and healthy her skin was, and how anxious she seemed about interrupting him. He gave her his most polite smile. "No, I just like rearranging the books. They get bored looking at the same view all the time." She stared at him, and he chuckled uncomfortably. "Yes. I work here. How can I help?"

"I was looking for the music section. I mean books about music, not CDs."

"Ah. You a student?"

She blushed. "Yes. Lawrence. Performing arts major. I play violin."

He noted her slender, delicate fingers, and well-trimmed nails. "Gotcha. Very cool. I'm no good with instruments; a surly tuba used to beat me up for my lunch money every day when I was at Larry U. Music is this way. Is there a particular book you need? Textbook?"

"A tuba player used to beat you up?"

"No, the tuba did. Brass instruments are assholes."

She giggled, and walked alongside him, hands shoved in her hoodie pockets. He tried not to stare at her, or to inhale too deeply of the warm, sweet scent she wore. *Don't be a creeper, dude. And lay off the stupid jokes.*

He had no idea how to interact with anybody, really. He much preferred spending his days in the stockroom, sorting through stacks and stacks of books at the wide table which was his undisputed territory. His new supervisory position meant far more time on the floor, overseeing other employees, which he hated, but the pay was better, and it came with another week of paid vacation, so he was learning to tolerate it.

"Actually, not a textbook. We're supposed to do a paper for Psychology of Music, on the personal life of a composer," she explained as they reached the correct shelves.

"Psychology of Music? That's a thing?"

"It is totally a thing. And I really need to pass it, and the professor is..." She shook her head.

"A complete poopyhead?"

She giggled. "That is accurate. Also, how old are you? If you don't mind me asking."

Morty drew himself up on his toes, lifting his chin and deepening his voice. "Young lady, I'll have you know I graduated that august university ten years past, under the very stern noses of the poopiest professors on campus, in the English Literature department." *What am I doing? This is not cute. This is not cool. I am not being cool. I look like an idiot.*

To his shock, she mimicked his posture, flicking one hand dismissively at the bookshelf for good measure. "Oh reallllly," she said, dropping her own tone as well; her voice took on a musical quality which immediately let him know she was far, far out of his league. "Well then, kind sir, do please show me the book here most likely to impress the poopyheads."

Morty took a step back, a nervous chuckle in his throat. "Well do you want something that'll impress your instructor, or would you really rather read something fun that still might impress him?"

She glanced at the row of music textbooks, and the shelves of biographies above those. "Well, fun, obviously." She picked up a biography of a boy-band-singer-turned-actor. "Unfortunately, I don't think 'fun' would impress this prof."

Morty took the trash bio away from her gently, and placed an old, cloth-bound book in her hands. "Try this."

She quirked an eyebrow at him, then opened it to read the title page. *"Evenings with the Orchestra.* How old is this?" She squinted at the date on the next page. Morty was gratified she at least knew where to check for publication info. Few things annoyed him as much as a customer asking for a classic title and responding "whatever" when he asked which edition they wanted.

"This is a first Barzun English edition from Nineteen fifty-six. Berlioz wrote in French," he explained when the girl glanced up at him. "It's an excellent translation, from what I've heard. I don't speak French."

"Berlioz, like 'Symphonie Fantastique'?"

"Same guy. He was not only a composer, but a conductor, a reviewer, and an absolutely scathing wit. If you're a musician, particularly if you play in an orchestra," he turned a querying look to her, and she nodded, "then you need this book."

She sampled a page, reading silently. *Please don't say it's too old. Please don't say it's too dry or you don't get it.*

And then she had laughed at something she'd read. She looked up at him in delight and wonder, as if he'd shown her the moon was not only indeed made of cheese, but that it was aged cheddar and free for the taking. He gave her a hesitant smile. "What do you think?"

"I love it! How have I never heard of this before?" She turned the pages, and Morty's heart warmed. "Is this about his life?"

"Kind of. He toured all over Europe, and ran into backwards orchestras who didn't know what to make of his weird modern music. There were local divas who demanded to be coddled even if they were terrible—especially if they were terrible—and all other sorts of adventures in the music world of his day. Those tours improved his reputation, since the Paris poopyheads didn't want him to play there for decades and he had to make a living somehow." She continued to page through the book. Morty tried not to sound as nervous as he felt. "So he toured a lot, and then he wrote about it. This is fiction, but it's all written by him from his own experiences. There's notes for each chapter. And this is a good biography, if you want to delve any deeper." He offered her a bio of the composer as well.

She smiled, accepting the second book. "This is great. Thank you so much!"

Morty hoped her enthusiasm wasn't feigned. Her smile radiated what felt to him like the genuine happiness of finding a treasure you never knew existed. "Cool. Hope it helps you write the best paper ever on sarcastic mid-nineteenth-century French composers."

"Definitely," she agreed, hugging the books to her breasts. Morty immediately yanked his gaze upwards, returning her smile. "Would you ring these up for me?"

"Sure," he said, a bit puzzled. As they came to the registers, he saw two employees working there. She could've just gone in line. He took over the unoccupied register at the end; fortunately there was only one person waiting, so he didn't have to endure a bunch of glares for giving this young woman special treatment. "Okay, so with tax..."

The first edition was priced higher than many of the hardbacks in the store. She didn't so much as blink. "Do you know a lot about music?" she asked as he bagged the books.

Morty shrugged. "I'm mostly into electronica, some alt-rock, some metal. I don't know a lot about classical beyond the few artists who really resonated with me. No modern pop at all. Country doesn't exist except for Johnny Cash."

She grinned at him. "'My name is Sue, how do you do?'"

He laughed. "Is it really?"

"It's Darcy. Darcy Mueller."

"Even better!" He nodded, then realized reciprocation was the expected social thing. He tapped the name tag on his lanyard. "Morty."

"Hi," she said, taking her books, hesitating. Morty wasn't sure what else to say.

"Hi back. So, anything else you needed?"

She brushed her hair away from her face. Her cheeks were pink. "This will probably sound really stupid." Behind her, a customer walked by with a ghostwritten financial success book by a reality TV star. The cover caught Morty's eye, and he spat out the first thing which came to mind.

"No, having a president who doesn't read sounds really stupid," he said, then checked himself. He cleared his throat. "Sorry, I mean what? Who said that out loud? Rude."

To his relief, she giggled. "I'd like to ask you something."

"Anything," Morty said, and in that instant meant it.

"Do you have a girlfriend?" He stared at her, surprised, and she quickly added, "Or a boyfriend? I mean, I don't judge."

"Me? No?"

"God, I am such an idiot. Never mind. Thank you for the books. And the jokes."

"Oh, you came for the jokes. Why is a bassoon better than an oboe?" She shrugged her shoulders. "A bassoon burns longer. What do you do with a flaming oboe? Set the bassoon on fire."

She laughed, and he proceeded to tell her every one of the jokes he recalled from his college roommate, who'd been a music ed major. "He's the only reason I'm able to be funny today," Morty explained. "How many lit majors does it take to change a light bulb?"

"How many?"

Morty pursed his lips in deep thought. "Apologies, m'lady, I was just thinking about how the darkness reminds me so vividly of Dylan Thomas' famous poem. I think I'll just sit here in the dark and write a thirty-page critique."

Darcy laughed again, a melodic, wonderful sound, and Morty grinned. *Wow. I think she's actually enjoying these stupid jokes. Okay, good call, Wending. You might not be a complete loser.*

He realized he should probably get back to work, as the cashiers were staring curiously at him. He was not in the least prepared for what Darcy said next. "Would you like to go out sometime?"

"Would I what now?"

She shrugged. "You know. Out for a drink or something. There's that arcade bar that just opened, down the street. Do you like old videogames?"

His jaw dropped. Fortunately he recovered before any drool could escape. "You mean like go out? With me?" The moment the words left his mouth he realized how incredibly immature they sounded, and blushed.

She was pink all over as well, he saw, right down her neck and possibly well below the collar of her shirt. He forced his gaze to stay at her eye level. Her chin lifted and she smiled at him. "Yes, Morty the BookStop Guy, do you want to go on a casual date with me to play some old arcade games and drink a few beers?"

"I would very much like that," he said quickly, before she could take it back.

"Tonight?"

"I work 'til nine."

"Tomorrow night."

"Okay," he agreed, his brain continuing to short-circuit.

"What time?"

"I could meet you there at six or seven?"

"Seven sounds great," she said, then leaned forward. Baffled, Morty did as well, and she confessed in a low voice, "I don't know much about gaming. Promise you won't make me look stupid?"

Morty stared into her eyes, and felt a dizzying rush of something he couldn't name. He swallowed hard, trying to regain his voice. It had gone all squeaky-scratchy. "I won't make you look stupid. Hell, if anything, I'm rusty on those old arcade consoles. I'll probably die a lot."

"It's okay. I'll get us lots of tokens." She nodded behind him. "Your friend said you enjoy gaming, so I thought maybe you'd be up for that."

Morty whirled to find Kim smirking at him from a few steps away. Morty glanced from Kim to Darcy, bewildered. "He said—?" *Back up a minute here, this makes absolutely no sense. This girl wants me to come to the arcade bar with her, although she's not a gamer, but she talked to Kim who told her what now?*

"See you at seven tomorrow," Darcy said, grabbing her purchases and heading swiftly for the front door. "Thanks again for the books. Bye!"

Morty half-raised a hand to wave back at her, then stood there dumbly until Kim shoved him. "Close your mouth, someone will stick something in it."

"What did you say to that girl?" Morty hissed, dragging Kim behind the wall of the sales counter, well away from anyone else.

"She asked me what kinda stuff you liked. Obviously I told her you preferred to stay at home, stretching your nose out more in a book and petting your hair before it all falls out, but she's cray, man. Wanted to know what would be likely to tease you out of your burrow."

Morty eyed him. "Don't screw with me."

Kim burst out laughing. "You want me to get tinfoil and make you a new hat? You look like the aliens just landed and offered to take you for years of anal probing." Kim shook his head. "Yes, that lovely honey asked me about you, which just proves she's insane because she didn't ask me out even when I was standing right in front of her in this shirt." He flexed his biceps, stretching the taut sleeves of his fitted tee.

Morty shook his head. "What is she, eighteen? I can't do this."

"She said she's a senior, and she can presumably get into a bar without a fake ID, so probably twenty-one, twenty-two. You can't do what? Go have some beers and play some classic games with a gorgeous college girl."

"Why would she?"

Kim nudged his shoulder. "Seriously, ease up on yourself. You're not that bad-looking."

"Dammit, Kim, I'm serious. Did you set this up?"

"Morty, I swear it. I did not. She asked me about you out of the blue. Okay, not totally out of the blue. I ran into her a couple days ago, we got to talking; you know, just casual, on the trade counter. You didn't notice her? You were up here too."

Morty shook his head, trying to think back. He was still trying to process the question, *'Would you like to go out sometime?'*

"You seriously need to look up from the books once in a while." Kim sighed. "At first I thought she was chatting me up, but she kept checking you out. I asked her what she studies, what kind of stuff she's into, and then she asked about you. So I told her you like reading, and you game with me weekly." He grinned. "I think she wanted an excuse to talk to you."

"Oh," Morty said, dismayed. "I thought she really liked the book."

Kim rolled his eyes. "Oh my God, you are hopeless."

"What?" Morty followed his friend around to the trade counter, aggrieved. "What?"

Morty smiled at the memory. Their first date had been every bit as awkward as he'd anticipated, but also amazing. She'd kissed him that night, and every desire he'd thought had been dormant and doomed within him had flared back to life. He would have never predicted Darcy would still be with him months later. It didn't make sense to him, but she'd nearly succeeded in making him feel he was worth something as a lover, was capable of being loved. And now all this.

Morty picked up his pace, moving from the campus area into the historic City Park neighborhood. He shook the snow from his hair; gentle flakes continued to drift down on him. He passed larger and nicer homes.

As he kept heading east, he'd reach the river, and their home was ostenta-
tiously perched right on the bluff above the water.

Christmas lights still gleamed on a few porches, and a large nativity
scene sprawled over an entire yard, the angels frozen in heavenly adoration,
painted eyes cast upward to the darkness. Darcy's parents would both be
there for dinner. No way to safely bring up the drilling then. Possibly
he could approach her dad afterwards. Morty frowned. No, Darcy would
probably sneak out of her room to join him in the guest wing. She did mention it was at the opposite end of the house from her parents' room. *Definitely all about the hanky-panky.* Unfortunately the thought didn't bring a
smile with it. What if he started to change again? It had happened today,
right there in the store. Hopefully that irritating shaman wouldn't be
around, and Morty would make damned sure no peeping squirrels were
outside. He touched his head, relieved to feel no bumps where antlers
might grow. *That squirrelly little spy said it wasn't them. And the shaman
said the ice in my hands was all me.*

His gaze turned to the sky; the starless mass of gray, and the wind
whistling past his ears offered no insights. *What the fuck is happening to me?*

Desperately he turned his thoughts to more practical matters which he
might be able to handle. There had to be some argument he could make to
Mueller. Something which would hit home.

You know what you can say. And how to say it. Morty shivered. *No. I can't
show him that. I can't be that.*

None of the Ojibwe were speaking up, except for that Wolf-Hunting
lady and she wasn't really accepted by the tribe, from what he'd gathered.
He wasn't positive she officially spoke for them, no matter that her impas-
sioned words had been on their behalf. If they weren't able to fight this in
court, Morty had no idea what other options existed.

He felt eyes upon him, and looked around until he spotted an owl in a
tree. They locked gazes. "Bite me. I'm on my way to see someone right now,
to get them to stop the drilling," Morty told it. The owl simply stared at
him. Morty resumed his trek, glancing back several times. The owl watched
him for a little while, but when he checked behind him again, it was gone.
He released a breath he didn't know he'd been holding. He couldn't even
tell which ones were just animals anymore.

He probably wouldn't have the chance to talk to Mueller tonight. He'd have to go to his office tomorrow, try to convince him to call off the drilling. But if that didn't work, what then?

Something in the back of his head whispered, *You know what then. You're going to have to scare him.*

He'd never be able to keep dating Darcy, when her father knew Morty was a monster. How would he keep working at the bookstore, with a crazy Bigfoot hunter after his ass, and creepy little forest men wanting him dead if he wouldn't help them? *I don't know. I don't know what to do.*

The wind hurried his steps. A cross-breeze between houses stung the corners of his eyes, and he wiped them furiously. *No. No, I can't do this. I'm not the winter* manitou. *I'm just a stupid asshole whom everyone thinks is some kind of environmental crusader, and all I want is to to be left alone.*

He reached the bluff where the street curved. White, steep lawns fell away to the icy river below. The surface was covered thick with snow, though in the center, the ice would be thinner, the water black beneath. Morty stopped, gazing down through the bare tree branches, imagining sinking into that darkness, the sluggishly-flowing water, pushing relentlessly north to Lake Michigan.

The wind blew against him, pushing him forward a step, startling him out of his reverie. Morty turned and trudged up the street of large, wealthy houses until he stood before a broad stone-and-timber Tudor manse. He'd only been here once before, and several of these ostentatious brick homes looked the same to him. He fumbled his phone out to double-check the house number. The screen wouldn't register his touch. A thin sheen of ice coated his fingers. Alarmed, he rubbed his hands briskly together until he felt moisture on his palms. He wiped them on his jeans and after another two tries succeeded in unlocking his phone and confirming he was at the right mansion among a street full of them. He walked to the front door and knocked.

The door opened, and Darcy smiled at him. "I thought that was you," she said, and opened her arms to him. "Come on. Get in here before you freeze, you goob."

Morty nodded. Darcy kissed him, pulled him inside the house, and reassured him in a whisper, "I'm glad you came. I've been wanting to see what the guest bed feels like forever." Morty was saved having to reply when Darcy's mother walked into the hallway. They exchanged hellos, and Darcy held onto Morty's arm, leading him into the bowels of the house, where a hot supper and her father waited. "Don't worry, it's okay," she whispered, squeezing his arm. "You can do this. Dad won't bite."

She smiled. He knew she believed in him, believed he was worth something. Morty still couldn't manage a smile back.

39

Quell didn't know when he'd nodded off; hours had been spent watching the old Victorian house, waiting for people to return home. All he'd observed was the landlord again – Quell had ducked below the window of his truck to avoid being seen – and a middle-aged woman with a child in tow entering the front door. No one else had come or gone. No lights had shown in the second-floor windows.

Once, later in the night, a police car cruised by, and Quell scrunched his body painfully below the dash and waited for the sound of the car to pass by. When they left, he drove to an all-night convenience store for a bathroom break and a cup of joe before returning to his stakeout. He fervently wished he had a partner, an apprentice, someone to share this tiring, tense duty. There wasn't anyone else. Just him, standing between the monsters and civilization.

The slamming of a car door startled him awake. Groggily, Quell looked around, dismayed to find he'd spilled his coffee at some point and stained his jeans. "God dang it," he muttered, picking up the cold, half-full cup.

Voices carried to him faintly through the closed, fogged windows of the truck. "Good luck, babe. Don't let him intimidate you," a feminine voice called out, full of hope and pride.

And then an answering voice which made Quell sit up straight in shock. "Yeah, make sure you have a body bag ready. RIP my ego." The voice was male, tenor, dry and scratchy around the edges, and unless Quell was seriously mistaken, a dead ringer for the one on that Wending fella's voicemail message. Quell frantically wiped the condensation off the window.

The man heading for the apartment house was not what Quell had expected; he seemed far too unimpressive to be a deadly monster, neither particularly tall nor muscular at all. A horn beeped, and the young man turned to wave, giving Quell a good look at his face. Quell fumbled with the door, cursing himself for having locked it at all last night. A little red sports car zoomed off, passing him. The instant it was out of his way, he threw the truck door open, turning toward the house in time to see the front door close.

Quell was not a man given to foul language, but he said a few choice words in his head right then. This had to be settled, one way or another. Either Wending knew something, or he was the murderous elk-thing. Taking a deep breath, nerves jittering, Quell lifted his rifle down from the rack behind him and thumbed the safety off. He'd only get one shot at this, if this was the beast that killed his own neighbors. Quell had no doubt the vicious creature he'd seen in Mellen would disembowel him as soon as say hello, if he forced it out into the open.

Quell stepped down from the cab, unkinking his back, all too aware of the arthritis in his joints. Nobody else was going to do this. The police would never understand, not until they saw the body, saw the monster for themselves. He needed to taunt it out into the open before killing it.

He looked around. Monday morning. Cars pulled out of driveways up and down the street, people going to work. Quell tucked the rifle under his coat when he saw a school bus stopping a block or so away, and children climbing into it. Maybe he should try to get inside the house. Confront the beast in its lair, sure, now that sounded like a fine idea. Anxious, he glanced up; a light was on in one of the second-floor windows now, though the blinds were down. He stood next to the truck, watching the bus pass by, worried someone would see the gun and get the wrong idea about all this.

Quell crossed the street toward the apartment house, skirting the obvious icy patches on the sidewalk. Last thing he needed was to slip and fall right as he was about to take a shot at this murderer. A car pulled up across the street, engine idling. Quell glanced back at it, but nobody got out. They must be visiting a different house. He continued toward the sagging porch of the old Victorian, peering up at the windows again. The second story was dark once more. The front door opened, and the same man from earlier trotted down the stairs in a navy blue suit which hung loose on his shoulders, his eyes on his cell phone. As he tucked the phone away in a pocket, Quell screwed his courage to the sticking-point and stepped into his path. "Excuse me," Quell said, and Wending's head jerked up.

They stared at each other a second. The younger guy blinked. "Excuse me," he responded, and made to go around Quell. Quell blocked his way.

"You know who I am?"

"Should I?" Despite the bluster in his scratchy voice, Quell saw what might be fear in the guy's eyes. He let his gun slide down from his armpit, getting his fingers into position. The man's eyes widened.

"You're Wending. You said you knew something about the murders here. How come you've been ignoring my calls?" Quell demanded.

Wending took a step back. Quell raised the rifle a bit, shaking his head. Wending swallowed visibly, slowly lifting his palms up. "Listen, I can't help you. Those things I said in my email, that was just a prank. I didn't think it would go this far."

"Son, don't lie to me," Quell said, taking a deep breath to steady his hands. "Now you and I are gonna go back inside there, and you are going to tell me everything you know."

*****

Morty stared at the gun. It was pointed roughly at his thighs. The hunter had left enough distance between them so he could raise it quickly, probably before Morty could grab it and point it away. Not that he felt such a strategy was the smartest plan.

Behind the hunter, across the street, movement caught Morty's attention. Kim slowly stepped out of his car, his phone at his ear. Kim held his fingers to his lips, silently telling Morty to stay quiet. Morty looked back down at the firearm. "I have no idea what you're talking about," Morty said, flinching as the gun jerked up a few inches.

"Don't you give me that," the Bigfoot hunter said, his voice low and dangerous. His eyes darted from Morty's hands to his face. "Your neighbors were torn apart, butchered by something that had them for dinner, something without any human compassion. Now I know you had some sorta disagreement with the old lady next door, rest her soul; and I know you were in the parking lot when two hideous beasts got into a nasty fight, and a woman died. I know you know damned well what I'm talking about, son."

Morty felt the hairs at the back of his neck prickling, felt rising anger at this stupid, pointless confrontation. "You need to leave," he said, holding himself motionless. "I have nothing to say to you. Get out of here."

"Was it you?" the hunter demanded, the rifle inching up a little more, pointing at Morty's chest. "Was it you that killed 'em? What are you?"

Kim crept closer, using the snowy box hedge as cover. Wrenching his gaze back to the hunter, who was frowning suspiciously, Morty repeated, "You need to leave. Now. I'm not telling you again."

"It was you," the hunter breathed, eyes widening and then narrowing. "You're the deer-thing. You tore that woman's throat and run off! Had everybody thinking you're some poor lost tourist, didn't ya? You murdered your neighbors, you bastard."

Morty shook his head, trying to keep himself calm. "No. That wasn't me. You don't understand anything you think you do. Just get out of here. There aren't going to be any more killings."

Kim continued to advance, closing in on the hunter from behind. Morty stared at the gun, at the hunter's hard eyes, and tried his best to signal Kim to fall back, shaking his head. Kim frowned, tiptoeing around the icy patches on the sidewalk, his hands out toward the hunter's back. *Dammit Kim, no! This isn't a game, this guy is dangerous!* Anguished, Morty's fingers curled into fists, his whole body tensed, straining to hold in the tremors rippling down his spine. All the hunter had to do was turn around, and Kim would be badly hurt.

Morty's breath hitched. His fingers twitched. He glanced down at them. His sharpened bones pierced his fingertips, bloody icicles immediately dripping from them, a searing chill shooting up his arms. An ache began in his skull. He looked up at the hunter, whose wide eyes said everything. *Oh shit.*

The hunter swiftly pointed the gun at Morty's face and pulled the trigger. Morty flinched. A loud *clack* sounded in the clear, cold air as the hammer came down on an empty chamber.

Kim leaped onto the man's back, grabbing for the rifle barrel. Panicking, Morty lunged, one hand closing around the rifle and yanking it away. The gun bounced off the sidewalk into the snowdrifts. The hunter yelled, fighting with Kim, as Morty backed off, panting, straining to pull the claws back in, to stop his skull from splitting.

"Morty, give me a hand!" Kim shouted, breaking Morty's shock. Morty rushed forward right as the hunter managed a punch to Kim's jaw. Kim staggered back. Quell swung at Morty but went ass-up as his foot found an icy spot. Morty fell onto him, grabbing one wrist, holding it behind Quell's back as the older man howled and twisted his wiry body. Pushing Morty out of the way, Kim slammed his knees down on the man's back, evoking a yelp. "Asshole!" Kim yelled, yanking the hunter's other wrist back.

"No, he's a monster! Kill it, kill it!" howled Quell. He stared up at Morty, who backed away, breathless. "Look at him! Look at his hands!"

Morty quickly wiped his bleeding fingers on his pants legs. Kim straddled the hunter's back, both of Quell's wrists held in a lock in Kim's strong hands. "You okay?" Kim gasped.

Morty nodded quickly. "Yeah. You?"

Kim nodded back. "Called the cops soon as I saw him. They're on the way, you crazy old coot." He kneed Quell in the spine again, eliciting another howl. "I can't believe this. He tried to shoot you!"

"Yeah," Morty said, trying to get his heart under control. He staggered back, taking stock of his appearance, brushing one hand through his hair. No antlers. Kim didn't see his fingers. Cops already knew this bastard was crazy. *Chill, breathe, this could work out all right. Kim's okay.*

"What were you thinking?" he demanded. Sirens wailed, the sound coming closer.

Kim blinked at him. "Fuck me, see if I ever save your life again."

Morty gestured where the gun had landed. "That thing could've been loaded. You could've been killed!"

Kim glowered, still holding Quell face down on the sidewalk. "He was pointing it at you and ranting about monsters. What else was I supposed to do, let him shoot you?"

"You could've been killed," Morty repeated, panic turning to an ache in his chest.

"You're still welcome."

Two uniformed officers ran up the walk. Kim continued to glare at Morty until the cops relieved his hold on Quell. Kim rose, massaging his jaw. "I took a punch for you, asshole."

"I'm sorry," Morty gulped. "That looked like it hurt like hell."

"Yeah it did. But I got beat up worse in junior high. 'Til I learned how to fight back."

The cops hauled Quell to his feet, slapping handcuffs on the man's bony wrists. The hunter jerked around, desperate. "No. You got it all wrong, officers! That man is the killer. He's a monster! He ripped a woman's throat out right in front of me!"

"Any idea what's he's talking about?" one of the cops asked.

Morty forced strength into his voice. "No, sorry."

"Dude's crazy," Kim told them. "This is the same guy who's been stalking my friend here. He came into our store last night raving about monsters."

A second patrol car pulled up to the curb. A third policeman walked up to them. "Hey there, got it under control?" His colleagues nodded; with a sigh he gestured at the truck parked across the street. "I ran the plates there, and turns out this guy's wanted for questioning upstate, too. Something about a body they found outside a trailer. He left a note with his phone number at the scene." He shook his head, watching Quell struggle. "Some criminals, ya know, they say they want to get caught."

"It wasn't me," Quell protested. "It was the other beast! That lynx-thing. Had to be the lynx-thing. I don't know what their beef is with each other, but you have to believe me! They are vicious killers and the death is not gonna stop until I put an end to both of 'em!"

"This asshole just tried to shoot my friend," Kim panted, gesturing at the yard where the gun had fallen. "We got the gun away from him, but he wasn't messing around."

"He'll kill again! You have to listen," Quell pleaded, struggling. His head jerked toward Morty. "I saw him. Saw his claws! In another second he'd have killed me; I had to shoot!"

"Well, sounds like a confession to me," one cop said. "Mister, you're under arrest for assault and I'm thinkin' also attempted murder here. Anything you say can and will be used against you—"

"Dadgummit, you morons!" Quell yelled over his Miranda-izing. His eyes were wild and furious, and his stare never left Morty. "That's the monster, right there! The one who killed those poor people right in this house and next door too. Ask him. Ask him why he did it! Look at his hands!"

The cops exchanged a frown. "Sir, do you mind if we—"

"Actually, I have a meeting to keep," Morty said, "And I really need to get going. I'll be back this afternoon. I work downtown at the BookStop. I'd be happy to talk to you then. I really can't be late to this."

The officer with the notebook sighed. "What's your name?"

"Wending. Morty Wending. I spoke to a couple of your colleagues just yesterday, after this man barged into the store, yelling about monsters."

Kim glared at Quell. "I see you ever again, gonna pay you back, dick-head."

One of the cops raised both hands. "Now, hey there, let's all just calm down."

"Can we just go, and you can come find us later if you need to take our statements or whatever?" Morty begged. "I'm interviewing with my girl-friend's father, at AmShale, up in Green Bay. I can't be late."

The police conferred a moment, then the officer who seemed to be in charge nodded. "Yeah, okay, Bobby says he saw that report from yesterday from the bookstore. All righty, go on, but we are gonna need to talk to you when you get back."

"Thank you, officer," Morty said. He looked at Kim. "We good?"

Kim sniffed. "Yeah. Let's go. Don't want you to be late for the big meet-ing." They thanked the police and headed for Kim's car.

Behind them, Quell shouted, "You don't fool me, monster! Whatever you are, I will find you again, and you won't kill anyone else on my watch!" Morty kept his head down, shoulders squared, moving quickly for the car and freedom. "And you, kid, you watch yourself. Nobody is safe around him. He ain't what he seems."

Morty shut the car door, buckling in, smoothing down his tie and suit-jacket. *I'm done. I'm so done with this insanity.* Kim slid into the driver's seat and started the engine, then sat there a moment, silent. Morty swallowed down his unease. "Hey, sorry you got hurt. Sorry I yelled at you."

Kim didn't look at him. A bruise was blooming on his jaw. "You're an asshole."

Morty sat quietly, accepting this. He wished none of this was real. Wished Kim hadn't been dragged into the middle of it. Wished he'd never gone to the dig site, never encountered that creepy dead thing. He glanced at his palm. The scar the antler had left remained, red against his pale skin, alone vivid among all the various wounds he'd received and recovered from in the last fortnight. "I'm sorry," he said again, softly.

Kim side-eyed him. "You are turning into a freak magnet."

Morty sank into the seat, staring dully at his hands. They appeared perfectly normal now, scar excepted. "Seems that way."

They sat in silence a few seconds, waiting for the police car blocking their exit to drive away. "You still want to have this stupid chat with an oil executive, after all this?"

Morty tried to straighten up. "Yeah. I do. Thanks for driving me." Hesitantly, he tapped his chest twice, and held his fist out to Kim.

Kim glanced at it. He sighed, and bumped Morty's fist with his own, then jerked his hand away. "Jeez, you are freezing! Are you sure you're not still sick?"

Morty touched a palm to his cheek; he felt fine to himself. He rubbed his hands together, blowing on them. "Pretty sure. That was kind of scary, though."

Kim nodded. "Yeah. The crazy bastard really meant to shoot you. The world is a very screwed-up place." With the cop car gone, Kim pulled out onto the street.

"Amen with a chorus of hooker nuns on crack," Morty agreed. Kim turned the heater up, flicking the passenger-side vents toward Morty, who immediately felt too hot. He swallowed, loosening his tie, but didn't dare object. "Thanks. I mean it."

They pulled into traffic, heading for the highway and Green Bay. Kim shook his head with a sharp laugh. "Let's sum up here. In one week, you stumbled around feverish and lost in the Northwoods and were rescued by rangers; a crazy homeless guy tried to give you a dead raccoon; a crazy Bigfoot hunter tried to shoot you in the face. Am I leaving anything out?"

Morty felt sweat breaking out on his brow and upper lip. He did his best to ignore it. "I slept with my girlfriend in her parents' guest bed."

Kim held up a finger, nodding. "Right. Can't forget that. How was it?"

"Very nice bed," Morty said. "Though I wasn't a fan of the seafoam green color scheme."

Kim snickered. "Think her parents noticed any hanky-panky?"

"Nah, I'm sure the maid already washed the sheets."

Kim offered him a fist-bump followed by finger-fireworks. "You stud, you."

Morty didn't feel it necessary to mention he'd been too afraid of what might happen to indulge in much with Darcy. He'd done his best to please her, though he was too keyed up for anything himself. Trying for casual, Morty shrugged. "I learned from the best."

"Damned right." Kim sighed. "Think we can make it?"

Morty checked the time on his phone. "Depends on if you have a grenade launcher in this thing. Might need it for traffic."

"Damn it. Shoulda grabbed the rifle from the old man."

Morty shivered. "Just drive. Drive like there's a laser-toting cyborg after us."

"Clearly you're taking the Sarah Connor part."

"Blow me," Morty offered. "I'll take that. Sarah was badass."

"She had more balls than you, for sure."

Morty held onto the passenger bar as Kim slid them in and out of heavy traffic on the interstate, relieved his friend hadn't seen anything. Now he just had to convince a man who lived for profit to stop drilling on a cursed site without letting the freaking *manitou* run amok. He'd rehearsed arguments in his head; nothing sounded passionate enough, powerful enough to penetrate Mueller's thick head. He suddenly pictured a bony muzzle full of teeth biting down on Mueller's skull, crunching through, blood and brains spraying. Morty cringed. *Shitgoblins. Just stay calm. Stay focused.*

He watched the snowy scenery zip by, afraid his best efforts wouldn't be enough to satisfy the *Bagwajinini's* demands. Afraid he would need to threaten his girlfriend's father. Afraid doing so would lose him the sweetest person in his life, at best. And at worst...

Morty swallowed, his throat thick with fear, and pretended he wasn't overheating as they sped toward a meeting he dreaded.

40

The lobby of AmShale's corporate offices was as soulless as Morty expected. The receptionist's desk was a model of professional coldness, with a small bronze statue of an oil rig, a phone bank, an appointment calendar, and little else. The art on the walls depicted all the places the company planned to ravage for a profit, landscapes of the Arctic and northern prairies. Nice touch.

Morty perched on the edge of a flat couch, waiting. Kim relaxed next to him, leafing through an upscale men's magazine. *Remember the routine. Act humble. Pretend you want this. Get him amiable before you try to change his mind.*

"This says purple is back in," Kim announced, holding up the style section. "What do you think, should I get a purple shirt?"

Morty shrugged. "You would know better than me."

"Right. Forgot I was talking to the guy who once wore a sweatshirt to a wedding."

"In my defense, it was a cousin I don't know well, and it was laundry day, and I forgot about it 'til the last minute."

"If you took a job here, you'd have to get a completely new wardrobe." Kim gave a nod at Morty's tie. "You actually clean up pretty well, dude."

"No, and oh hell no."

Kim lowered his voice, eyes on the magazine. "You really think you'll be able to talk Darcy's dad out of fracking?"

"I hope so. I came across some perturbing information which might dissuade him."

"Bringing your English major skills to the front. Good call."

Morty sighed. "Look, that woman who was in the store, the one I met up at the reservation? She told me a few things. Plans to disrupt the land-clearing AmShale is doing right now."

Kim was immediately more interested. "Like protests? People chaining themselves to the bulldozers?"

"More like imminent violence."

"Cooooool. You realize if you tell him that, you're putting people in danger."

"No, I'm trying to keep this from escalating."

"By ratting out protestors' plans?"

Morty shook his head. "No. I don't want anyone to get hurt, and people will be." Frustrated, he smoothed down his tie for the hundredth time. "I'll do whatever I have to, to prevent violence. You heard about the Native American protestors who were beat up by the cops over the Keystone XL pipeline, right? This could be worse. Much worse."

"More power to you, man."

The receptionist spoke quietly into her headset a moment, then stood and beckoned Morty. "Mr. Wending? Mr. Mueller will see you now. This way, please."

Kim gave a victory salute with a smile as Morty was ushered towards the elevator. Morty rode the box to the fifth floor, as the receptionist had directed. The office digs on the upper level were posh, if just as soulless as the downstairs lobby. Another receptionist welcomed Morty and walked him to Mueller's office. The big, chrome nameplate said it all.

Once Morty stepped inside, the receptionist closed the door, leaving the two men alone in the large, wood-paneled room. He took the hand the older man offered and shook it firmly. "Glad you could come in," Mueller said.

Morty nodded. Mueller gestured at the seat in front of the desk. Everything in here was midcentury modern, all sharp angles and browns and burnt oranges. Morty found the style too bland and clinical. It certainly fit Mueller. "Thank you for seeing me," he said.

Mueller folded his hands together on the empty surface of his desk. "Darcy tells me you two have been discussing the Bad River project. And that you attended a meeting in Ashland, hosted by the county resources officer." Morty nodded, and Mueller's eyes swept over Morty's face, assessing. "I hope it was instructive for you."

"It was interesting."

"We're providing quite an economic boost to the entire area. We'll be hiring dozens of new positions."

"I heard," Morty said. He took a deep breath. "Darcy mentioned AmShale is also involved in alternative energy, especially wind power."

"Oh yes. We own several wind farms across Wisconsin, Minnesota, Michigan, and up into Canada. And we're planning on expanding more into the lower plains states."

"I'd think, since it's a growing sector, that AmShale might be shifting more operations into renewables. As opposed to fracking, or traditional oil and gas drilling."

Mueller's mild smile didn't change. "We're investing more, that's true."

"I did some research," Morty continued, his mouth feeling dry, "and it seems as though fracking can be more costly. I mean, due to the cleanup and the lawsuits which follow every major fracking operation."

"As with any energy processes, there are costs involved which need to be taken into account. It's not more expensive in particular. If anything, it's a cost-effective way to get to gas reserves which conventional drilling can't easily reach." Mueller's tone was faintly patronizing.

"What if there's strong resistance? What if you get tied up in lawsuits that drag on and on? I imagine that would raise the expenses considerably."

Mueller gave a light shrug. "As I said, there are costs which must be considered. Are you saying Ashland is reconsidering our agreement with them?"

Morty shook his head. "Not the county, no." *Obstinate county official. I should've just eaten him anyway.* He tried not to outwardly flinch.

Mueller frowned. "Darcy didn't give me many details of the meeting. We've heard about other objections from people who really have no legal right to be involved at all. You were there. What can you tell me about the mood that night?"

"Uh, well, some people seemed happy at the mention of jobs, but others were pretty upset."

"Who was upset? The Indians?"

Morty stared at him, brain working overtime to frame his argument. "Well, I mean, the fracking will directly affect them."

"Not as badly as they're claiming. Did any of them say anything about religious objections?"

Morty furrowed his brow. "Religious?"

"There has been a bit of negativity from the tribal council, I hear. Disruption to our operations. Something about breaking a taboo." Mueller made a dismissive gesture. "I'm guessing it has to do with the artifacts we unearthed. Even though we're building them a museum for all of it." Mueller's eyes bored into Morty's. "Did you hear anyone talking about that?"

"Actually, yes," Morty said. "I've been told the burial mound should never have been disturbed; that it—"

Mueller interrupted Morty with a quick rap on the desk. "Would you be able to stay a little longer?" Mueller asked, checking his watch. "I have an officer's board meeting in just a minute to discuss what's been going on over there. I'd like you to come speak in a few minutes, tell everyone what exactly you heard."

"I—sure," Morty agreed. "Now?"

Mueller smiled. "I'll have my secretary fetch you. Just wait in the lobby, if you wouldn't mind." He stood and gestured at the door.

Morty rode the elevator back down to the lobby. Kim looked up, then glanced at the clock.

"Wow, that was fast. Your powers of persuasion must be better than I thought. Jedi mind trick for the win."

Morty shook his head, sitting down on the uncomfortable sofa. "No. He wants me to come talk at his board meeting. Tell 'em all about how unhappy the natives are."

Kim returned his attention to the fashion magazine. "My friend, the mole."

Morty kept his voice low. "I'm not giving them any names. I just need them to reconsider clearing and drilling, and maybe if they think there's enough public sentiment against them, they'll hold back, for now at least."

"What'll that fix?"

"It'll buy me some time," Morty hissed.

Kim frowned at him. "Buy you some time? Why are you the chosen one here?"

"Damned if I know. Maybe I can slow them down long enough for the Ojibwe to get a judge to stop the whole thing."

Kim shrugged. "Okay. Good luck with that. I mean it."

"Thanks."

Morty's knee jigged. He tried to stay calm, running through arguments in his head. If he told the board that people would get hurt if the logging continued, they'd just increase security. He could tell them the burial mound was a sacred site, and that they'd unleashed an angry ancient god. Right. Because corporate executives always listened to portents of doom.

"Mr. Wending?" Startled out of his increasingly gloomy thoughts, Morty stood up quickly. A man about his own age, wearing a neat gray suit and a clipboard under his arm, gave him a brief smile. "Would you come with me, please?"

Swallowing dryly, Morty followed the gray suit to the elevator. They rode up four floors, exiting to walk along a thick, carpeted hallway which muffled their footsteps and terminated at a pair of large wood-paneled doors. The gray suit knocked once, then ushered Morty inside. Mueller stood on one side of a long, polished table cut from a single giant tree trunk. Ostentatious and wasteful. Great.

Sixteen people in total, all grand old white people, were seated at the table. An elderly man with neatly combed gray hair presided at the far end. He smacked his palm on the dead tree, repeatedly, punctuating his angry words. "I don't care what Pocahontas wants, they had their chance and they took the money. As the acting CEO, I will tolerate this no longer."

"Everyone," Mueller announced, "This is Mr. Wending, a friend of my daughter's." The table slapping stopped. A couple of people nodded and conversation quieted. "He was at the Ashland meeting, and he overheard information pertinent to the Bad River issue. Mordecai, would you please elaborate on what you heard for us?" Mueller brushed down his suit coat as he sat.

Morty stood at the foot of the table, all eyes turning to him. The doors behind him closed; he felt the movement of the air on the back of his neck. He flicked his gaze from Mueller to the man at the head of the table. "Um. Yes. I overheard some people on the reservation saying digging into the burial mound was an extremely bad idea."

A woman with glasses and a tight bun of hair sniffed, curling her lips. Under her breath she muttered to the man next to her, "See? What did I say. Superstitious savages." Morty glared at her; she gazed calmly at him.

"Did they say why?" asked another man. His open, curious gaze appeared welcoming.

Morty nodded with relief at the mild question. "Yes. They believe the mound is cursed. That the grave is that of a *manitou,* a sort of powerful spirit. The *manitou* of the Starving Moon." A ripple of snickering traveled around the table. Morty's stomach twisted. He kept his expression neutral. "I know how it sounds. Some of the tribe take it very seriously."

"I thought most of them had converted to Christianity? This has to be a small minority."

"Well, your small minority barged onto the site in war paint and disrupted the loggers three days in a row," snapped the woman with glasses. "The foreman reported there were at least a dozen of them, all going on about bad spirits."

Mueller raised his hands placatingly. "I'm sure this can all be smoothed over with the right incentives. Mordecai, did the people you spoke with say what they wanted, to put everything right? If we've inadvertently given offense to their religion, what would constitute a proper apology?"

"First off, I don't believe this is a minority. Forcibly relocating the burial site is disrespectful, and even if you reburied it all at this point, I'm not sure that would fix it. Also, if you insist on continuing with fracking, people are going to get hurt."

The older man at the opposite end of the table frowned. "What people? So far, the sheriff has acted with considerable restraint in removing these trespassers from our site. However, if these reports I'm hearing about some young bucks charging in armed are correct, security will be fully within their rights to protect our workers."

Morty spread his hands out in front of him. "I wasn't aware of what happened after the meeting. But these tribespeople have every right to be concerned," he argued. "The fracking is going to spill toxins into the wild rice sloughs. And you've desecrated a sacred site. Of course they're upset, and they're going to protest."

Mueller crossed his arms and leaned back in his chair. "So, we issue a formal apology for any proper religious attention which we neglected. They signed the paperwork and we wired the funds, so we are mostly in the clear." Morty's splayed hands fell to his side as Mueller continued. "Regardless, we invite their shaman or whomever in to perform a ceremony, and we relocate the remains safely out of the way as planned. Minimal time disruption."

"That's not going to solve anything." Morty unclenched his fingers, which were curling into fists. "If they're already upset about you digging up the ancient burial mound, just imagine how much worse things will get once you start drilling." He looked at each of them in turn, seeing no sympathy in any face. They didn't care. They knew perfectly well what the result would be, and they really didn't care. He tried a different tack. "Just think of the expense. Think of the lawsuit which—"

"There's a lawsuit?" the CEO demanded, turning to another executive with thinning red hair. "John, do you know about this? I thought legal already covered this possibility."

"We did, sir. I haven't heard of any formal objection to the project." John from legal turned narrowed eyes to Morty. "Who specifically was talking about bringing suit? Did you get a name?"

"No, I didn't," Morty replied, "and that's not the point. I'm saying, think of all the trouble and the money you're going to waste, for what? Is it really worth it?"

"Mordecai," Mueller's clipped voice rose in the boardroom, "we need to know specifics. Can you provide us with names of the people you overheard planning on disrupting our project?"

"You keep calling it a project, like it's a goddamn science fair." Morty's twitch of anger at the condescending way his name had rolled off Mueller's tongue began turning into a brushfire. "No. I'm not giving you specifics. There is going to be violence at your drilling site if you don't shut it all down immediately."

That set off a murmur. "You heard one of them actually say that?" asked John from legal.

Morty flushed. "Yeah. I did. And they sounded serious. So reconsider. For the safety of your own employees, take a step back here. Shut down the logging, call off the drilling, and turn your operations elsewhere. I know you have other interests; you don't need this site that badly."

Several demands pelted him at once. "Give us a name!" "Is this some kind of eco-terrorist crap?" "Do you have an actual head count of these protestors?" Morty tried to focus on one person and failed. Outrage filled the air. "They had their chance to object, and the Indians accepted our offer to build them a museum. Took our money! Ungrateful red bastards, lied to our faces—"

"What did I say?" tutted the bespectacled lady, shaking her head. "They haven't changed. They're still an ignorant, superstitious, backstabbing people."

A dull throbbing spread across Morty's skull. He took a deep breath. "My mother was part Menominee. Those are my relatives you're talking about."

"Oh, so this is about your own native family concerns," said John, sneering. "Why don't you go back to the rez and tell your cousins if they set foot on our site again, we'll have them all dragged off to jail. And if they're armed, our workers have every right to defend themselves."

Glasses-woman scowled at the man next to her. "This is exactly why it's not worth the time to talk to these lazy pagans." She jabbed a finger in Morty's direction. "A hundred years of trying to civilize them, and they're still incapable of being honest. Trying to squeeze us for more money with these threats, beating their outdated war drums!"

Morty strode over to the woman and her colleague. A deepening chill seeped down his body. "What did you just say?"

"I didn't say anything," the woman snapped, "Not to you anyway."

An aide who'd been sitting next to the CEO dropped his notebook and headed for Morty. Reflexively, Morty shoved an angry fist, bones creaking, in the aide's direction. Sparkling ice blossomed on the rug where he gestured, a trail of frost eddying around Morty's feet. The aide slid on the iced carpet and he went down, his back hitting the floor with a crack. Morty gripped the armrest of the woman's chair, knuckles white.

"You just called them lazy. And earlier you called them savages."

The woman's eyes were wary. "You're mistaken. As head of HR, I wrote the cultural sensitivity rules for this company. AmShale treats all its employees and everyone it deals with equally and fairly."

"Now who's lying to whose face?" he snarled.

In a rush, Mueller was on his feet. He pointed at a young woman standing by the door. "You. Call security. Get him out of here."

"Oh, so now you don't want to hear what I have to say, Mr. Mueller?" Morty shouted, rage tinging every word. "When it's no longer something you can twist around to your advantage?" The door opened, and a tall, muscular guy with a military crew cut strode in. The woman by the door pointed at Morty, then ducked out. The security guard headed for Morty.

"Who is this man and why was he allowed in here?" the chief executive demanded. "This is exactly why we don't permit visitors in the boardroom!"

"You need to leave," Mueller barked at Morty.

"Every one of you would sell out your own families, as long as you made money," Morty yelled, weaving around the table as the guard advanced. "Don't any of you care? All this for what? A few more thousand in your bank accounts? A fat bonus at the end of the year?" He bumped into John from legal, who shoved him toward the guard. A strong hand clamped over Morty's wrist and twisted his arm behind his back. Morty cried out, cold fury exploding. Small trails of ice shot from beneath Morty's feet in all directions. With a grunt he rammed the guard with his shoulder, wresting himself free. Pain wracked his spine; his clothing felt too tight, too hot. He ripped the tie from his neck and tugged at the top buttons of his shirt.

"You have to stop! You woke up something you don't understand at all and if you keep drilling, people will die!" Stabbing agony ripped through his fingertips and his temples. He fought to remain coherent. He glared at the CEO. "You can't let it continue. Call off the drilling and leave the Bad River!"

"Those Indians had their chance to speak up. All they wanted was a payout, and they got it," the old man snapped, glowering at Morty. "And now they have the balls to renege on the deal? I have run this company too long to bow to a shakedown by a few greedy, lazy savages."

"How many years has your company been a blight on the land? How many years have you fattened your bank account on others' misery?" Morty advanced on the old man. With a snarl he kicked his feet free from the restrictive dress shoes, his toes shifting, bones lengthening.

The bespectacled woman stood up and screeched, "We've done nothing wrong. If the Indians don't want to live downstream from our operations, then tell them to move!"

"It's their land!" Morty snarled, shoving her away; she cried out as her back slammed into the wall.

The old man rose from his seat. "Get out of my boardroom, you half-breed bastard. And you tell those lying, dirty sons of bitches we have the right to drill right through their God-damned rice if we want to!"

Morty succumbed. Cold fire burned through his skull as the antlers burst upward in a spray of blood, his arms stretching, his vision turning red. "How dare you speak of rights, you locust? Taking everything and never giving a shit how many lives you ruin, how many people you poison." His throat was hoarse, teeth cutting his gums. There were too many people in his way; he leaped onto the table. "You have fucked up the earth long enough!"

Morty could hear the CEO's shallow, rapid breathing, could smell the perspiration breaking across the man's brow. He watched the old man's rheumy eyes follow his ascent. Morty crouched down, heading for the CEO, claws digging into the wood of the table. Wood these people had carved from the carcass of what was once a strong, mighty tree. The scent of it filled his nostrils, along with the acid reek of sweat and piss from the terrified people around him. Shouts and screams sang in his ears. *They don't care. None of them care. All they love is money. Parasites! Time for you to feed the earth. Time for you to reap what you sowed.*

With a roar, he shoved his antlers into the old man's chest. The executive twitched, eyes rolling up, his arms flapping loosely like a puppet coming free of its strings. *Fucking parasites. Meat sacks sucking the land dry, I will make you water the land with your blood.* Snarling, he thrust deeper, piercing between ribs, pushing down hard until he felt the fragile bones give way with a crunch. *Let's open that up and see if you do have a heart.*

Morty lifted his head, pulling the piked man up from his seat. With a shake of his head, he flung the old man from his antlers. The body hit with a delicious wet thud. Screams rose all around him. Morty grinned.

Something sharp stabbed his leg. He whirled, bony muzzle swinging around to meet a frightened stare. Morty yanked the fountain pen from his tendon; blood seeped out, matting his ragged fur. "Fuck," whispered the man who'd stabbed him.

Morty smiled. His teeth scissored into the man's throat, a crimson fountain spraying Mueller next to him. Mueller choked, stumbling backwards. Iron and light surged over Morty's tongue in a dizzying rush. He took a deep, heady breath. He bit deeper, claws tearing the soft outer layers away from his victim, taking what he was owed.

A chair thumped against his ribs, knocking him off balance. The *wendigo* roared, hooves regaining footing on the rug, rearing up to his full height to confront his attacker. John from legal strained to keep hold of the chair like a shield, one castor of it spinning crazily.

"You think you can hide? You think anything will protect you now? Your laws are not mine," Morty snarled, grabbing the chair. John whined, struggling to keep his protection a moment longer. Morty flung the chair at the doors. Where it crashed, ice exploded over the door handles and raced crackling up the jamb, solidifying quickly, a wall of frozen water glistening in the warm light of the lamps overhead.

"You are all takers," Morty hissed, his stomach drawing taut against his spine, hips shifting, claws lengthening, his head weighted by the bloody antlers spreading further into multiple thorny branches. The guard lurched forward, pulling a revolver from a holster under his jacket. Morty lashed out with one hand, razored claws just missing the guard's face, finding the chest instead and ripping sideways. The guard gurgled out a shriek.

The *wendigo's* jaws opened wide, the scent of the meat causing drool to drip from his long, hungry tongue. "How dare you willingly work for these vermin!"

"Oh my God," cried the bespectacled woman, yanking his attention away from the guard. With her back to the wall, she fumbled under her shirt and drew out a small cross on a chain around her neck, holding it up in shaking fingers.

"You hypocrite!" Morty vaulted across the table at her, and she screamed.

He thrust his muzzle up to her nose. "Your god commanded you to be kind," he growled, his voice roughening, reverberating between the bones of his throat. "You are not kind." She screamed again, and Morty crushed her face between his jaws.

Terror filled the room. Blood splashed his chest. Hunger overwhelmed him. He sliced into her stomach, ripping downward, hot and glistening organs spilling out. The *wendigo* caught her as she fell, bony muzzle thrust inside the fleshy shell, tugging out something delicious in his teeth. He gulped it down, then bit the next thing, and the next, soft, juicy morsels bursting between his teeth and over his tongue, swallowing everything quickly.

Deafening bangs clapped his ears; several hot, sharp things plunged into his back. Morty bellowed, dropping his nearly finished morsel. He whirled to see the wounded guard holding his revolver in bloody hands. The guard gaped. In two long strides the *wendigo* reached the foolish man, and ripped the weapon away along with the guard's hand. The guard screamed. Irritated by the noise, Morty snapped at the guard's head, and his claws found the guard's ribcage. He grabbed either side of the man's sternum, and with a powerful wrench of both hands cracked it open wide. Bits of brain dribbled from Morty's teeth as he feasted on the exposed lungs and heart.

Pounding at the door, shouting, chaos. The smells of blood and offal filled his nostrils. Morty threw another chair aside to reach another selfish taker. This one tried to run, and ended up on the floor, stump of a thigh spurting blood. As the *wendigo* started to eat, another parasite attempted to race past. Morty struck one long, bloody hand to the floor. Ice shot along the polished wood at the edge of the carpet. The escapee slipped and bashed their head against the table.

Blood soaked the *wendigo's* patchy fur, coating his ribs red, his muzzle painted thickly in it. Over and over he ripped soft, delectable organs still pulsing with life free of their confines, swallowing them down. There was always one more trying to scramble away from his reaching claws. Always one more spraying his face with crimson when he tore them open to find the best parts within.

Until there weren't. Morty panted. His long tongue licked his jaws. Nothing moved. Thick layers of ice coated the doors and the floor and the rug, gleaming red where bodies lay, missing arms, bellies hollowed out, many of their lying faces crushed and unrecognizable. A soft sound reached his hearing. The *wendigo* crouched, listening, sniffing. He oriented on the sound of stifled breathing, and his eyes met Mueller's wide, terrified ones. Mueller's bulk was curled into an impossible ball under a serving table against the far wall. Bodies surrounded him, and his face and clothing were spattered with blood.

This was all his fault. He was the one who thought he could pay for desecration with a few paltry gestures. Morty effortlessly shoved the bulky grand table out of his way.

Mueller held up a trembling hand. "Please," he whispered, "Please—no—stay away from Darcy!"

Darcy? Her smile brightened in his memory. Morty halted, confused, the *manitou* warring with the man. The muffled shouts and pounding on the boardroom door from the outside penetrated. The carnage swam into his vision. He saw his elongated claws, sticky with blood. Felt it dripping off the end of his bony muzzle. He saw it in the terror in Mueller's eyes.

Morty fell back onto his haunches, reeling, gasping, claws shrinking. He groaned as his spine twisted.

"Stay away from my daughter," Mueller pleaded, tears streaking through the blood on his face. Morty could hear Mueller's thudding heart. He looked around again, taking in the stench, the blood, the doors shaking as someone outside tried to break the grip of the ice holding them shut.

Oh fuck me.

Morty backed away, wheezing. His hands shook. He touched his head, feeling the antlers, and looked at his shredded clothing. His frightened eyes met Mueller's once more. He scrambled to his feet and ran for the door, yanking it open, ice shattering. With a wordless cry of terror, Morty sprinted past the startled guards and other people crowding the hallway. A woman shrieked as he lunged forward and careened around the corner; he narrowly avoided spearing her with his antlers.

At the end of the hall, the elevator dinged. Before it opened, he slammed into the door next to it. As he'd hoped, the emergency stairs were there. He descended, cloven feet clopping, echoes bouncing off the stairway walls. He was drenched in blood. His mouth was full of it.

Two floors down he staggered into a wall, retching. Bits of shining meat came up. What felt like gallons of blood fountained out of him and splashed down the concrete stairs. Eyes blurring, Morty sank to the floor, bracing one hand against the wall to keep from toppling over into his own wretched puke. The gray floor was cool. He couldn't stop crying, as he vomited again and again. When he reached dry heaves, he collapsed with his back pressed to the wall. He strained to pull in the claws and antlers, willed his bones to snap back into their shorter lengths, felt air brushing his skin again. He heard heavy breathing, and slowly raised his head.

A few steps down, Kim stood with one hand clasped over his mouth, face pale. Morty stared back, panting, too weak to get up. Nausea rumbled, and he leaned over, coughing. He spat out a chunk of bone. His belly felt distended, as though he'd gone back for inadvisable thirds at Thanksgiving. Closing his eyes, Morty waited for the inevitable. *Just haul me away. Fuck my entire nightmare of a life at this point.*

Silence. Slow footsteps came towards him. The sound stopped as it climbed and passed the last step next to him. Morty dared to open his eyes. Kim sat on the other side of the stairs, regarding him with a serious face. Morty swallowed, and wiped his mouth with what was left of his sleeve. "Hey," he managed, his voice weak.

Kim gave him a cautious nod. "Hey." They sat there in the chilly stairwell, hearing doors slamming somewhere above. No one was investigating this area yet. Kim eyed him. "You, uh. You hurt?"

"This...This isn't mine." He looked down at the blood coating his chest beneath the shreds of his dress shirt.

"Ah." Kim fell silent, studying him. Morty forced himself to meet his friend's gaze, miserable. *No excuses this time. This is real. He saw me. Saw the thing I let myself become.*

"So," Kim began slowly, "We're eating people now?"

Morty choked back a badly timed, strangled laugh. "Guess so."

Kim nodded, eyes traveling from Morty's bare and bloody feet, up the tatters of his one actual suit, and to his face again. Morty didn't move, his heart thumping, keeping his hands open and limp. He could feel the blood drying on his nose and cheeks, over his chin and throat. "You...all of them?"

Morty winced. "No. Not all of them." He slumped further. "Not Mueller."

"Because Darcy?"

Morty nodded, eyes shut, pain in his chest. "Because Darcy."

More silence, for what felt to Morty like an hour. Then Kim said, "So that Bigfoot guy wasn't a complete asshole."

Morty felt like laughing. If he didn't he was going to lose it. He choked out a terrible laugh, but it sounded so hideous he made himself stop. His voice was rough and strained. "Not completely."

"So." Kim's brown eyes were wary when Morty met his gaze. "Now that I know, you gonna eat me?"

Morty dry heaved. "Gods no."

Kim nodded. "Just checking." He stood, and offered his clean, dry hand to Morty's bloody one. "Come on, get up. We need to get you out of here. Cops are already here. They'll probably search the stairs next."

Morty blinked at him. Impatient, Kim waggled his fingers. "Get your sorry ass up. We need to move."

Numbly, Morty grasped Kim's hand and was hauled to his feet. Feeling faint, he grabbed the stair rail. "Can you walk?" Kim asked. Morty wobbled, steadied, and nodded."Okay. So I'm guessing everyone saw that. With the antlers."

"Yeah."

"Any of 'em see your face?"

"Did you?"

"Only after you, uh, reverted."

Morty bit his lip. "Only Mueller." He felt a tremble of nausea again. "The rest of them are lying in pieces in the boardroom."

"I have no idea what security cameras caught. I don't see any right here, though," Kim said. "So here's the story: some terrible creature suddenly appeared in the meeting. You have no idea what it was or where it came from. You escaped, ran and hid in the stairwell." He glanced back at the bloody hoofprints Morty had left on the landing. "It blew past you a minute ago. You didn't see where it went. We'll get the paramedics to check you out." Morty shook his head, panic rising again. Kim tugged his arm, forcing him to continue down the stairs. "Listen to me, you asshole! You have to do this. Be vague. Act terrified and traumatized."

Morty gulped. "Not an act."

"Yeah. I get that."

"Kim, I killed those people. My neighbors. The woman at the road-house. Those dickheads upstairs just now. I ate them!"

"Yeah. I got that too." They shuffled silently down a down a few more stairs. "This started with the burial mound, right?"

"Yeah. That thing, it's inside me." Morty strained to breathe. His chest had a vise clamped around it. "I went to a shaman to cure it but he just made it worse. So much worse."

"Maybe we can figure out a way to stop it. To change you back."

Morty shook his head vehemently. "No. The shaman—the shaman bound the *manitou* to me—it's in me—I can't stop it..." Morty felt tears sliding down his cheeks. His breath stuttered. "I can't fucking stop it."

"Now that's just crazy talk," Kim said, his imitation of a Midwestern biddy so out-of-place Morty stared at him, blinking through his blurred vision. "You're gonna have to fill me in on some shit, obviously, but tell me this: did you go in there intending to eat people?"

Morty sobbed harder, shaking his head. "Fuck no!"

"So what set you off?" Kim gently tugged his arm. Morty staggered down the stairs, leaning on Kim.

"They wouldn't listen. They wouldn't care about anything. It's just all about the money to them." He stopped a moment; his heart beating itself into panic again. "They called the Ojibwe savages, lazy—"

"Well all of that is horrible. Is that thing Ojibwe?"

"It's a *wendigo*. A cannibal monster. Worse. A *manitou,* a spirit, bound to my body. A very old spirit. A winter god." Morty gulped, wiping his nose on his ripped sleeve. "I was so furious."

"Understandable."

Morty halted, refusing to allow himself to be walked down any farther. "Jesus, Kim. When some asshole insults me, I don't eat them!"

Kim sighed. "I know, man. And I know you'd never do any of this awful shit. Obviously this thing has a temper. So let's get you out of here. Away from here. Someplace you won't be tempted to hurt anyone. And I guess we'll figure this out." Morty hiccuped, his eyes still leaking, and took a small step towards Kim. Kim raised a warning finger. "You hug me with blood all over you, I will slap you into next week."

A garbled laugh escaped before he could help it. "Nah, I know, cannibals aren't your type."

"True dat. I don't waste my time on straight guys." He grabbed Morty's arm and tugged. "Close your mouth before I change my mind. Let's go."

"Wait. You—you're—?"

"Bi, asshole, yes. Jesus, you really are oblivious. We all learned something today. Now move your ass. There is gonna be a shitstorm all over this place, and you need to be sitting with the medics, being treated and sedated, when it hits us."

Morty followed his friend down the rest of the stairs and out the emergency exit. Fierce wind buffeted them. Kim swore. "What the actual fuck. I said shitstorm, not snowstorm. Forecast was for a few clouds today, not a blizzard!"

Snow slapped their faces. Morty hung onto Kim's arm as they made their way toward an ambulance. His stomach hurt. Someone spotted them and shouted, waving one of the paramedics away from the front door. Before help reached them, Morty held his face up to the sky. "Um. I think maybe this is my fault too."

"Winter god, you said?" Morty nodded. "You are just a special kind of asshole, you know that?"

"Thanks," Morty mumbled. Within moments he was bundled into the back of an ambulance, wrapped in blankets, having lights shone in his eyes. He shook his head at all the questions the medic fired at him. No, he wasn't hurt. No, he had no idea what happened. No, he didn't know what that thing was or where it came from or where it went. It had clawed at him and he ran. Kim spun a story about his buddy fleeing from horrible violence up in the boardroom, a costumed psychopath. They answered all the same questions again from a police officer. Once the paramedics cleaned the blood off him enough to determine Morty was not in fact desperately wounded, they were allowed to leave. Police scurried in and out of the building. Gurneys came out bearing black, zippered bags.

Snow came down thick and fast as Kim warmed up the engine of his car. Morty hunched over in the passenger seat, feeling woozy, stomach unpleasantly overfull.

Kim peered out. "Not sure we can make it home in this. I bet they haven't even plowed the highway yet." The wind howled around the car windows, the sky completely white with snow.

"I can't go home," Morty said, trying to sit up straighter. He'd objected to a sedative but the paramedic had insisted he needed it since he was babbling about monsters and blood.

"You want me to call Darcy?"

"No, no—I can't." Morty didn't realize he was crying again until he felt the tears turning to ice on the end of his nose. "God damn it."

"What are you going to tell her?"

Morty shuddered. "I can't. I can't ever." He felt ill, and grabbed the armrest for support. Tendrils of ice spread out from his touch. He stared at them, trembling.

"Dude. Could you not freeze my car?"

"Sorry." Morty curled his hands against his chest. "She'll hate me. I'm a monster. Take me into the woods, kick me out like a vicious dog. That's where I belong, Kim," Morty whimpered and wrapped his arms around his body, doing his best not to touch anything. "Just dump me in the woods, okay?"

Kim sighed. "Maybe the sedative wasn't such a great idea."

Morty snuffled and swallowed down the persistent taste of iron. "I don't feel so good."

"Hang in there, pasty white boy. I have an idea."

"What?"

Kim glanced at him. "Just buckle up. And any chance you can do something about all this snow?"

Morty gazed out the window. He felt unmoored, surreal; his pain felt as though it was happening to someone else. Some other guilty bastard who just ate a whole boardroom full of greedy executives. He stared at the snow, seeing its patterns, watching the wind, realizing he could feel its rage. It wanted to bury everything. All this awfulness. All these horrible people who only cared about themselves. He raised both hands, making a petting gesture at it. *Calm down. Shhhh. You're too noisy, snow. Calm down.*

He stared at the last few flakes drifting down, entranced. Although the clouds remained, the wind dropped. "Shhh," he whispered.

Kim stared at the sky, then at Morty, then laughed. "Scratch what I said earlier. I think I see the solution to your problem." Morty blinked at him. "We need to keep you high. You are so chill right now."

Morty started giggling. "I'm so chill. Get it? I'm a *wendigo*. Get it? Chill?"

"You, my friend, are seriously fucked up." Kim's tone was mild, but weariness and heartsickness washed over Morty, sobering him.

"Understatement of the year. Please just get me away from everyone. I don't want to kill anyone else."

Kim turned the wheel, and drove slowly away from the AmShale building. Morty glanced in the side mirror, and saw the paramedics bringing out more closed bags on stretchers. He shut his eyes. He wasn't so stoned he didn't remember all of it. And that taste. So rich. He wanted to keep eating and eating. Feeling sick, he leaned his forehead against the cool glass of the passenger window, and tried not to think of anything at all.

41

The lock-up was cold, and full of smelly drunks. Quell shifted away from the mumbling one on the bench. At least the police had taken off the cuffs when they shoved him in here. He'd been told nothing yet about a hearing. "How about my right to a speedy trial, there?" he shouted at a passing cop. The cop ignored him and kept walking.

Quell rubbed his elbows and knees. This cold wasn't too good for his arthritis. He'd paced for a while, but his bones hurt too much, especially his back where that fool kid had kneeled on him. He shuddered to think what would happen to the kid if he kept hanging around with that monster. Quell rubbed his aching hands together. "They just don't listen," he muttered. "I tried, I tried to tell 'em."

"Hey, did ya hear about Green Bay?" The cop who'd ignored Quell planted his rump on the corner of the cell guard's desk.

"Hey, Jake. Yeah. Packers thinking about trading."

"No, not the Packers. The murders in Green Bay, like an hour ago."

Quell heaved his aching body off the bench to the front of the holding cell. Murders? Didn't that monster say he had a meeting he was going to up there?

"Came in over the radio; they were asking for back-up, some kinda manhunt going on. Some crazy person went into an oil company office up there and killed everyone! Like ten or twelve dead, they said, and a couple other folks wounded."

"What happened?" Quell asked, raising his voice. "How were they killed, these people?"

"Just the craziest thing I ever heard. The paramedics found only two guys left alive, both of 'em goin' on about crazy stuff, a monster that ate people, if ya can believe it." Quell's heart hitched, and he clutched at the bars. "The guy that did it got away, and cops up there are still looking for him. Some kinda costumed psycho, with knives maybe. Reports of a skeleton wearing a deer head. Uff da. I tell ya, I'm sure glad we don't live up there. It's all that lake-effect snow, ya know. Drives people nuts after a whole winter of it."

"God dang it, I warned you," Quell shouted, "I warned you and you wouldn't believe me! Think I'm crazy now?"

"You just calm down there, old-timer," the guard said, frowning. "Don't go gettin' all worked up."

"You know anything about this killer?" Jake asked. Quell nodded, breathless.

"You bet I do! Seen it myself, up at Mellen a week ago. And I know what he looks like when he's not a monster."

"Jake, don't waste your time." The guard tapped the side of his head. "This guy tried to shoot a fella in the face this morning. Would've killed him, if it'd been loaded. Went on a rant about monsters and it took three officers to bring him in. Wiry old fella."

"Huh," Jake raised his eyebrows in Quell's direction. "Really? Three officers for this old coot?"

The guard shrugged. "I guess it's some kinda adrenaline imbalance or something. Dementia. My sister, she works over there at the retirement home in Kimberly, ya know; and she says some of these old folks, they can surprise ya there, how strong they get when they get all worked up over somethin.'"

"I am not that old," Quell yelled, "And I'm not crazy! This proves it, don't you see? Did anyone get a good look at it? Was that Wending fella there? You have to listen to me. I know who he is! Don't know quite what he is yet, but I'm working on it."

"Tried to shoot someone in the face?" Officer Jake asked quietly.

The guard nodded. "In broad daylight. There were kids going to school right around the corner. And him waving a rifle around and yelling about how some guy was a monster and he had to kill him." He sighed. "The shrink can't get here fast enough for my liking, I tell ya."

Quell slapped the bars, though it hurt his hands, trying to hold their attention. "I need to get up there. Need to track this bastard before more innocent people die. You have ta to let me out of here!"

"You'll get your turn," Officer Jake said, holding a hand up. "Now you just settle down and stop giving Terry here so much trouble. Do you have family, anyone who takes care of you, maybe, you want us to call?"

"I take care of myself!" Quell snapped. "Why won't you just listen? I'm telling the truth. I can help."

"You can help by quieting down. You're gonna stir up these other guys, and not all of 'em are as kindly as you, old man," the guard warned.

"Gotta go. See you at break," Jake paused at the doorway, "good luck with this one here," and left.

The guard returned his attention to his cell phone screen. Quell waved at him until the guard looked up."I'm not trying to make your life harder, here; but you have to listen. I know what killed those people, the ones here and up in Green Bay. I can even tell you where he lives. You need to let me out of here; I have to bring him down. You fellas just ain't prepared for this."

"If you want to cooperate, that's great," the guard said. "I'll let the detectives know you want to talk to them, and someone'll be down in an hour or so." He reached for the desk phone.

"Oh, I'll talk, all right," Quell agreed. "You don't know what you're hunting for. This wasn't a man that killed those people; it was a flat-out murderous beast."

"Uh huh." Into the phone the guard said, "Yeah, the old fella that came in this morning, the attempted murder? He wants to talk to somebody." He tapped his fingers on the desk, listening to whatever was on the other end. "Yeah, tell 'em to bring the shrink along. This guy has issues."

Quell's brain hurt. He returned wearily to the bench, sitting well away from the unkempt, hung-over man now glaring at him. *Oh, I have issues, son, but not the way you think. I just need to get out of here, and fast.*

He squinted across the basement lock-up. Through the narrow window, he could see a blanket of white outside. The sudden blizzard earlier had swiftly piled snow against the building. All he could hope was that it had stopped in time to leave tracks unburied, and that he'd get out of here soon enough to go find them, wherever this office was in Green Bay. He'd find the monster, and end his trail of butchery.

The tapping of the guard's fingers on his phone screen, and coughing from one of the other cell occupants, were the only sounds in the small jail. Quell huddled into himself for warmth, and waited.

*****

Darcy burst through the front door. "Dad? Dad, are you okay?" Her mother met her in the foyer, and hugged her. "Where is he? Is he hurt?"

"In the kitchen. The hospital released him a half-hour ago. He was too shaken up to drive home, so one of the employees dropped him off." Mrs. Mueller put trembling fingers to her lips. Darcy pushed past her, hurrying to the large, open kitchen. She found her father on the sofa next to the kitchen hearth, the gas fire blazing, with a drink in his hand. "Dad?"

He looked smaller, feeble. He folded her into a hug, rocking her and stroking the back of her hair. When he released her, his lips were trembling. Darcy was shocked to see a tear streaking down his cheek. "Dad? Are you all right?"

"My sweet girl. Thank God you're alive."

Darcy shook her head. "Yes, I'm fine. I came home as soon as I got Mom's message." She looked into his eyes, worried at the fear she saw there. "What happened? Are you okay?" He nodded, and fear crept up her spine. "What about Morty? Is he okay? He's not answering his phone."

"Don't you call him ever again," her father sat upright with a snap. "Don't you ever see him again, do you understand me?"

"What happened?" she asked, confused. All her mother's voicemail had said was something awful had happened at work, and her father was in the hospital in Green Bay, and to come home right away. Darcy had been in classes all morning and she'd rushed home as soon as she'd called her mom.

Her father set down his drink and gripped her arms, his eyes wide. "You are never to see him, never again!"

"Ow. Dad, what the hell?" She pulled away, rubbing her arms. "What happened?" He hesitated. "Why were you in the hospital? Was there an accident?"

"No."

Darcy turned to her mother. "Mom? Will one of you please tell me what's going on?"

"There was a— Someone went into your father's office and—" Her mother sniffled, hands going up to her mouth. "A-and they hurt people."

"Are you hurt?" She grasped her father's arm tightly. "Tell me everything, please!"

"I'm not hurt." He picked up his glass and gulped down the last of his drink. "The doctors said my blood pressure was too high, wanted me to stay in the hospital overnight, but I had to come home. Had to make sure he hadn't hurt you. My sweet girl..."

"Who hadn't hurt me?"

"That monster you call your boyfriend!" her father roared. He shot to his feet, shaking a finger at her. "You are never, ever to go near him again, wherever he is!"

"Why?" Darcy cried, "What did he do? Why are you mad at him?"

Abruptly her father shut up, eyes wide. A tremor ran all through him and he sank to the couch, clutching his empty glass.

Darcy threw both hands in the air, frustrated. "Why are you acting like this? What did he do? Did he say something you didn't want to hear? Did he tell you to stop the fracking?" To her surprise, her father flinched.

"There won't be any fracking," he said, his voice uncharacteristically soft. "Not anymore."

"What about the rest of the board? They're going to call off the Bad River project, just like that?"

His head jerked up, red-rimmed eyes glaring at her. "The board is dead, Darcy."

Her mother let out a sickening sob. Darcy watched her mother retreat from the room. Her father was pouring himself another tumbler of his best Scotch; the golden liquid splashed over the edge of the glass and onto the genuine Navajo carpet by the hearth. Her father never spilled drinks on the family antiques. "What do you mean, dead?"

"I mean every last one of them was murdered today." He tossed back half the drink in one go. "Everyone except me."

"Oh my God." Her legs wobbled. She dropped to the sofa next to him. Her reaching hand found his, and clasped it tight. "I'm so glad you're okay. What happened?" He shook his head, eyes shut. "Who was it? Did the police stop him?" she asked. He shook his head again. "Everyone? How many people?"

Her father took a deep, shuddering breath. "I don't know. Fourteen? Fifteen? Everyone at the officers' meeting. No, I think maybe Sara got out before it started."

"So someone just walked into the meeting and started shooting people?"

His eyes opened, and he squeezed her hand. "Not exactly. Darcy, I need you to promise me you will stay home. Right here. I've called up extra security; they should be here any minute."

"You think this maniac is going to come after you here?"

"I don't know. I don't know." His frightened eyes bored into her, scaring her. "You need to stay here. Right here, where I can keep you safe."

"For how long?"

"As long as it takes for them to catch the monster and kill it!" Darcy watched as the veins on her father's neck started throbbing.

Darcy pulled back. "The semester just started two weeks ago. I have a tour coming up, the whole orchestra is going. I am not giving that up."

"You can go back next semester," he slammed his glass on the table, "once it's safe again. Until then, you stay right here, young lady."

"This doesn't make any sense. Why would some crazy psycho—"

"You are staying in this house until I say so and that's an order!"

Standing up, Darcy took a step away from her father. "Dad, I love you. You're really upset right now, you've just been through a horrible experience, and I'm really, really glad you're all right." She gathered up her courage. "But you can't just forbid me from attending school or keep me from going on tour. This is important. I'll be graduating in just a few months. And you can't tell me whom I can and can't see."

He reached for her hands; reluctantly, she let him hold them. He felt cold to her. "Was Morty there when this happened?" she asked.

Her father swallowed hard. "Darcy. Forget about him. He's not good for you."

She pulled away. "Yes he is, Dad. He makes me happy. He doesn't need me to be perfect. I can just be me, and he loves me anyway." Her father met her glare only a moment before his gaze fell. Darcy's resolve firmed. "Whatever he said to upset you, I'm sorry; but he's a sweetheart and I'm not going to stop dating him just because you don't like him."

"Darcy," her father groaned, wavering as he stood up. "Please, you don't understand—"

"I know he went to your office today to try to impress you," she interrupted, worried Morty had been hurt. He still hadn't replied to her texts this morning. "Was he there when this happened? Did you see if he was hurt?"

"Yes, he was there. And I hope he is hurt. And you may never see him again as long as I'm alive!"

She took another step back from him. "I cannot believe you. Jesus! You've been through horrible trauma today, but Dad, you are drunk, and you're being absolutely hateful!"

"Darcy—"

"No, Dad!" She stormed from the room, running up the back stairs and along the upper hall. She passed her own room, heading for the guest wing. Alma wouldn't be in to clean until tomorrow; the sheets were mussed, the covers thrown back.

Darcy dove into the bed, burying her face in the pillow. It still smelled of Morty's aftershave, the sandalwood one she'd given him for Christmas.

She heard tires crunching through the snow in the driveway, and checked out the window. An SUV with the logo of a private security firm had pulled up to the house, and three large men in heavy black coats climbed out. She wound a strand of hair around her fingers uncertainly, watching until the men went in the front door. *Great. So he's going to try and keep me prisoner in here? Keep me from going to class? This is ridiculous.* She pulled her cell phone out of her pocket and texted Morty again: *"Hey, please call me as soon as you get this. What happened at Dad's office? Are you ok?"*

She sent it and waited; no reply came. She launched the browser and looked up *Green Bay AmShale shooting.*

The first result was a breaking news story on a local website. She watched a video of a reporter standing outside a police cordon in a snowy street; the AmShale corporate office stood gray in the background. An ambulance rolled out of the front drive, lights off and siren quiet. The reporter's voice was grim.

"Tragedy and confusion here today in Green Bay, as reports of an active shooter came earlier from the offices of oil company AmShale. Police aren't releasing names of the victims at this time, but sources confirm at least fourteen

people are dead, with others being treated for minor injuries. Police were called to the scene at nine-forty-six this morning, when security reported sounds of a struggle, screams, and gunshots from the boardroom on the fourth floor.

"Police have released no information on the attacker at this time. However, we've obtained an inside source who confirms the killer wore a Halloween costume, and unconfirmed reports of the killer eating the victims have shocked—" Repulsed, Darcy shut off the video.

She checked other sites; nobody seemed to have any further details yet.

Remembering Kim had driven Morty this morning, she tried calling him. He didn't answer. She found the number for the hospital in Green Bay, but neither Morty nor Kim had been admitted. Darcy fished a ponytail holder from a pocket and pulled her hair back. Head bowed over her phone, she kept texting, kept searching for news, until her mother found her some time later. She assented to the plea to stay in for the night, and returned to her search as the day slid into evening. Morty didn't respond to any of her calls.

Darcy set her phone down, staring numbly out the window. Twinkling garden lights shone on the thick snow in the yard. The sky was dark and calm overhead. She thought of Morty lost in the snow, cold and hungry and feverish, and hugged herself. *Please text back. Please let me know you're all right. And as soon as I can sneak past these stupid rent-a-cops, I'll come find you, Mordecai. Dad doesn't know the real you. Whatever happened between you two, you can tell me. Just please, please be all right.*

She gazed out at the darkness, and pulled the knit throw off the edge of the bed to wrap around her shoulders. Even inside, it was a bitterly cold night.

*****

Marie lounged in the heated pool at the Bad River Resort, sipping a delicate champagne, watching the steam rise into the night sky. Stars shone far away. She ignored the balding man eyeing her from the other side of the pool; she wasn't in the mood for company. She needed to think.

The logging trucks had been called away two days ago, the cleared land left inexplicably empty. She had watched as men had come by night, carrying away items wrapped in furs and skins from the shanty, a *Midewiwin* priest leading them in song. Curious, she had followed them deep into the woods, and watched the Anishinaabeg rebury the bones of the dead god with song and ceremony. The dance was still going on when she left this morning. The people would be fasting for days, to cleanse the tribe of any dread illness which the unearthing of the burial mound had brought into their midst. Marie wondered if the winter *manitou* knew of any of this. And if he would approve or even care.

The other resort guest eventually trudged out of the pool, leaving her in blissful solitude. Marie sipped her champagne, savoring the crisp bubbles tickling the roof of her mouth. If they had abandoned the site, it must mean Morty had succeeded. She wondered if he really did talk them out of drilling. She pouted. *So much meat I could have eaten! He ruins all the fun.*

She caught a gleam of black out of the corner of her eye. She lazily floated her body around to see a large rabbit at the edge of the pool. It had made no noise, had no scent, and it now sat next to her wine, its solid black eyes betraying its origin.

"Have a glass, if you wish. Or should I order you a salad?"

The rabbit's nose twitched, and Marie felt foolish. *Silly. I cannot tell when it's just an animal any more.*

The rabbit sat up on its haunches, staring at her. Its mental speech jolted into her mind. "You did what was asked. We thank you."

"Good. It was not at all pleasant, setting foot in their filthy city." She toyed with her glass, running her nails around the rim. "So the *windigo* was able to charm the whites into stopping the drilling? How did he manage it? Does he really have medicine?"

"He ate fourteen of them," said the *Bagwajinini.*

Marie stood up, setting the glass aside. "Really? He ate them? How do you know?"

"We watched from outside. We listened. They brought out the dead in black bags." The rabbit took a few steps around the rim of the pool. "We saw the *windigo* covered in their blood, his stomach full."

"*Sacre bleu.*" A chuckle rose in her throat. She raised her glass. "Well good for him! It is about time he had some fun."

The rabbit shook its head. "Sister *Mishibizhu*, he must be watched. The winter spirit's power awakes. He called down a storm, snow and wind and death. He is becoming more dangerous, as we feared."

Marie scoffed. "You wanted him to stop the men destroying the land, and clearly he has done so. What more will you ask?"

"Do not dismiss this so lightly, sister."

"*Oui, oui,* he is the *manitou* of the Starving Moon in the flesh, I understand," she growled, lifting her glass to her lips. She never saw it move; one moment the rabbit had her glass in its paws, the next it had dumped the champagne onto the ground. Marie protested, *"Hii!* What do you think you're doing?"

"He must be watched," it repeated. "He has devoured the flesh of his kind and no food or drink will satisfy him again."

"Of course he has, he is a *windigo*. What did you expect?" Marie crossed her arms. "He did what you wanted. You should be pleased. He stopped the intruders in my river. I am pleased with him." She glared defiantly at the fat gray rabbit.

The little guardian of the forest gazed steadily at her, unblinking. "If he continues to use his winter medicine, he will grow so hungry it will be impossible for his mortal spirit to contain it. If he lashes out we will have to destroy him. We fear he may be already too strong. Go and speak with your father. We wish to smoke the pipe with him."

"My father?" Marie sputtered. "Have you lost your mind? Why would he speak with you?"

"Tell him of the *manitou's* power. We may need his help to strike down the *wendigo*, if he is unable to control his urges. If the old spirit becomes too strong." Its black eyes stared into hers, and Marie fought the desire to look away. "He once covered the land in ice, sister. All the lakes froze solid, and no fish swam, and the First People nearly perished. This may not be allowed to happen again. If it does, even your kind will suffer. Tell your father that, and then we will smoke with him and discuss what needs to be done."

"I am not your servant," Marie began hotly, but the *Bagwajinini* was gone. She rose from the pool, shivering, casting sharp eyes in all directions. There was no trace of it, not even a scent beyond the faint odor of pine needles in the air.

Marie wrapped a thick towel around herself, and retreated to her warm, comfortable suite. She ordered a hot toddy from room service and waited to unpack her dinner until after the drink was delivered. She sat before the fireplace, the remains of a cross-country skier laid out in a suitcase, and picked at her food. She had both long, delicious legs to enjoy, as well as the intact head with its delicate brains, but she found herself unable to fully relish the meal.

Winter medicine? Called down a storm? Impossible. She thought of the *windigo's* long, foolish face, his reluctance to even let his claws out, and shook her head. *I am shocked he was able to eat one silly white man. Fourteen! Good for you, Morty.* She frowned, thinking of the command she'd been given. *Go and tell my father, indeed. What am I, their errand girl? Nasty little hairy things.*

She sniffed, thoughtfully chewing on a forearm. Perhaps she would, at that. She could tell Papa how the *windigo* killed a group of greedy *waabishkiiwewaad* who wanted to poison her river. Papa complained all last summer of the ones dumping barrels of chemicals into the lake. He was getting too old and fat to do things himself. If Morty had learned finally to love the taste of his prey, perhaps he could be talked into eating a few of those bastards with their little boats.

She laid back on a pile of pillows, licking her fingertips. She refused to do anything until summer. Papa would not wake until then anyway. She stretched languorously from the top of her spine all the way to the tips of her toes, and put the unease the *Bagwajinini* had brought out of her mind. Finished with her feast, she packed up the bones, slurping the remaining marrow from a femur, and closed the bits inside heavy plastic in her suitcase.

She called the front desk. "Henri?" she purred, "Would you come see me? I am tired, and I wish to go to bed." She set the phone down with a smile, and stretched out on the pillows before the fire again, wiping a smear of blood from her breast while she waited for her favorite room service.

42

Morty closed the cabin door behind them while Kim set the grocery bags down on the counter. Kim nodded at the bags. "Okay, I figure this should last a couple weeks."

Morty swept his eyes over the bags full of coffee and snacks, frozen pizzas, and lots and lots of raw beef. "Yeah, thanks." Seeing the bounty his friend had brought wracked Morty with guilt.

The rural cabin, isolated even from other vacation homes in the state forest, offered privacy which Kim had declared would help Morty get his shit back together. Morty was dubious that simply holing up in the Northwoods boonies would change anything, but at least it meant he wasn't near enough to civilization to hurt anyone. It wasn't close by good ice-fishing lakes or snowmobile trails, and should remain undisturbed, at least until spring. Renting the place in the off-season hadn't been the hard part; assuring the owner Morty absolutely didn't need anyone checking in on him at all was more difficult.

"Just be sure to leave the typewriter out on the table, okay? In case anyone does swing by to see if you're all right after a blizzard or anything. Remember, you're the eccentric writer on sabbatical," Kim cautioned.

"All work and no play makes Morty a dull boy," Morty agreed. "Been meaning to finish my novel anyway, right?" He thumbed through a stack of books. "And thank you again. For these." Kim had brought every book he could locate, from both the BookStop and the library, having to do with Anishinaabe legends, *wendigo* stories, or medicine ceremonies.

"This thing is legendary, right? So there has to be something in one of those books that'll help." Kim paused, then clapped Morty on the shoulder. "We'll fix you." Morty wished he were able to share his friend's optimism. *Yeah. Sure. Fix me.* Like a car which just needed the right part to work again. Or maybe more like "fixing" a cat so it stopped peeing on the walls and beating up the other cats.

"Is this going to be enough to eat?" Kim asked.

Morty glanced at the meat, shame washing through him. "I have no idea. Guess we'll find out."

Kim picked up Morty's cell phone, plugged in to charge on the counter. He swiped it on. "She still texting you?"

Morty swallowed, throat dry. "Off and on."

"I saw her again yesterday. She's going on her orchestra tour next week." He put the phone down. "Told her again all I know is you're off visiting sick family in New Mexico." Kim frowned. "She's not going to buy that forever. You need to at least text her back."

"Kim, I can't." Morty rubbed a hand over his jaw, feeling unkempt, despite shaving and showering every day as though he were still going to work.

"How long you think you're gonna stay here?"

"'Til my leave runs out, at least. You can take whatever you need out of my savings. Should be a couple thou left."

"No, dude, it's not the money. I mean how long are you going to hide out here in the ass end of nowhere? Nobody is searching for you. The cops think it was some weirdo in a costume. You can come back to work any time. In fact I really wish you would soon." Kim scowled. "Leila has me covering your shifts, you know. Acting supervisor, but without the actual upgraded benefits."

"No, I can't. Not until I'm sure this thing is dead. Or controllable. Not until I am positive I'm not going to kill anyone else." They locked eyes, and Kim lowered his first.

"Okay. Yeah. That's probably best. You seem fine now, though. I mean it's been a week, and you haven't gone all death-elk again."

Despite this being true, he suffered horrible dreams every night. Snow, anger, and so much goddamned hunger. His stomach growled just thinking about it. Morty hesitated, glancing at the grocery bags. *I might as well show him. This is nowhere near normal.*

He grabbed a package of cold, raw kidney, tore it open, and shoved a hunk of it into his mouth. He chewed, wiping the rivulet of blood from the corner of his lips. Kim paled and averted his eyes. Morty kept chewing. "This is why I can't come back. Not until I figure out how to stop it from ever happening again."

"Point taken."

"Good," Morty said around another mouthful of raw organ. He swallowed, and fetched a glass of cool water from the tap. He washed the meat down, wiped his lips, and nodded at Kim. "I am grateful, man. Really. And I'm sorry Leila is busting your balls."

"I get it. Just don't give up. We'll beat this thing. Every curse has a cure, right? If this thing is an evil god, there must be a benevolent one out there, somewhere, dedicated to kicking its ass. We just have to find it." He grinned at Morty. "Besides, what god would want to be in your body for more than a week?"

"Sure. Yeah. Has to be something." There was zero conviction in his voice.

They stood in the kitchen for another silent moment. Kim jangled his car keys. "You need anything else before I head back?"

"No, should be all good."

"Think you could do that sexy snow magic again? It was coming down pretty good on the drive out here."

"Which route you taking?"

"Straight south. Whatever that state road is."

Morty closed his eyes, calming himself, reaching for the sky. After a few seconds he could feel the snow clouds bumping up against his awareness like potent, sullen, fat geese. *Clear out. Let him pass.* He envisioned them over the forest, the narrow road, and when he was sure he could feel the snow exactly in Kim's path, he coaxed the falling flakes to stop. When he felt the wind and clouds obey him, he opened his eyes. "You're good to go. All clear."

Kim whistled. "That shit is useful."

"Rent me out for winter parties."

"Don't say it unless you mean it. I will one hundred per cent pimp you out." Kim pulled his coat on. "Text me if you need anything. Remember it's a long damned walk to the nearest town, and nobody's up here this time of year. You know how to start the generator if the power goes out?"

"Google is my friend." Morty followed Kim to the door. Snow was piled high against the log walls; the woodpile was nearly buried. "Drive safe. See you in a couple weeks."

"Don't eat the library books. I have to take those back. If you find anything online you want, order it and send it to my place, and I'll bring it next time." He reached out and pulled Morty in for a hug. "Kick this thing's ass."

"Thanks." Morty watched Kim drive off, snow tires crunching over the nearly inaccessible road. He'd have to drive in the dark for hours to get back to Appleton. Morty glanced up at the sky. Dusk was falling, along with the temperature. He stood gazing out as the breeze picked up, rolling over the fir trees surrounding the cabin. He only had on a tee shirt and shorts, and socks to cushion his feet. He still wasn't cold. He might never be cold again.

He closed the door, went to the kitchen counter, and pulled another chunk of raw meat from the open package. He chewed on it as he put the rest of the groceries away. Raw meat wasn't good cold. But if he heated it, it tasted overcooked. He hadn't mastered the art of finding the perfect warm point for the meat. What his tongue really wanted, what his stomach growled for, was hot and rich and raw.

Morty tried not to think about that. His phone buzzed with an incoming text. He licked his fingertips clean, and after several swipes with his stupid cold fingers managed to unlock the screen.

Another message from Darcy joined the dozens of others she'd sent. *"Hope you're doing okay. Look, if you don't want to see me, could you at least just say so? Not a fan of this silent treatment. I'm going on tour next week. Madison first, then Milwaukee, then Manitowoc. Wish you could come hear us."*

His chest hurt. As he was about to set the phone down, another text came in. *"I miss you, Mordecai."*

Morty dropped onto the overstuffed sofa in front of the fireplace, staring dully at the crackling log there. The fire had almost died down. It made him think of a brighter, warmer time, sitting with Darcy in front of the hearth at the Bad River Resort. Was that only a month ago? It felt like years. He looked at his hands. His skin was pale, with only one scar in the palm of his left hand. No claws. No ache in his skull. All his pain right now centered in his chest, where his heart kept beating and beating.

He picked up a book from the table in front of him. *You're just a sorry loser, Wending. Just a dumb geek who never learned discipline, or self-denial. You're not strong. And you really think you can beat down a god?* He sighed. *Maybe. Fuck it. I'm a book nerd.*

And the one thing he knew how to do well was read. So he'd research the hell out of this. He'd find an answer. And maybe then... His gaze returned to the phone, with its cache full of unanswered texts.

Mordecai opened the book and began to read.

The Reluctant Wendigo will return.

Author's Note

Months of research of Anishinaabe legend, history, and customs have gone into this work; however, as a non-Native American, I may have still committed some error in my portrayal of the characters or in language usage. I apologize in advance, and welcome correction. The fictional Mashkiki Reservation overlaps the range of the actual Bad River Reservation; however, I very much doubt the actual tribal council there would agree to fracking anywhere near them, for any amount of compensation. They have been fighting oil pipelines crossing their land for years, and are instrumental in conserving local land, water, and wildlife.

There are many descriptions of the *windigo,* also known as the *wendigo,* and *witiiko.* In numerous sources of distinct Algonquian tribes, their description varies from giants with hearts of ice to animate, corpselike beings. Despite the popular image of a *wendigo* having antlers or deerlike features, I have found no original texts supporting this. However, as there's little agreement on what a *wendigo* or *windigo* looks like (some stories say they can look like anything in the forest), I feel free to advance my own interpretation. After all, Morty's not just a *wendigo,* he's harboring a cruel winter spirit who, bent on punishing the greedy who consume too much, is older than historical record.

The geography of Appleton and of Wisconsin in general is more or less accurate in this story. The legend of the black lodge was reported in the local folklore book *Gone Missing!* by Dennis Boyer; I have relocated it about 70 miles east along the Lake Superior shore. I have taken liberties as well with the timing of blizzards in the winter of 2019, and of the Book Across the Bay festival.

Hopefully, the feel of the land and the winter comes through in this tale. I moved here in the late autumn of 2014 and I love the snow, the people, and the local legends, all of which continue to inspire my writing.

Glossary

Anishinaabe (pl. Anishinaabeg): Ojibwe self-identifying name.

Bagwajinini (aka mimigwesi, mimakwesi, pukwudgies): mischievous forest creatures, said to care for animals, and who sometimes aid children lost in the woods. They can appear as animals or as hairy little gnomes, but are seldom seen by any but the very young. If offerings are made to them, they might give one luck in hunting, or protection from the dangers of the wilderness, but if insulted, they could play mean tricks, such as loosing tied canoes or destroying food caches.

Gitchigami (aka Gitchigumi): Lake Superior.

Gitchi-manitou: Great Spirit. A creator, but not usually one who interacts directly with humanity in Ojibwe legend. The role of guides, teachers, and benefactors falls to the Seven Sacred Manidoog, who guided the Anishinaabe from the east coast to the Great Lakes hundreds of years ago.

Gitchi-mishibizhu: Great water panther; Marie's father. Largest and oldest monster in Lake Superior.

Gitchi-mookomaan (pl. gitchi-mookomaanag): literally "knife spirit." White people, particularly hunters.

Ho-chunk: Wisconsin native tribe; probable descendants of the mound-builders in central and southwest Wisconsin. Their residence in the area dates back centuries, predating the Anishinaabe migration west.

Hodag: a hoax monster, invented by a Northwoods entrepreneur in the spirit of P.T. Barnum to drum up tourist business. Still celebrated by at least one Wisconsin town today.

Kabibona'kan, the Winter-maker: Ojibwe manitou of winter, associated with the north.

Manitou (aka manido, pl. manidoog): spirit, anima, mystery. Often mistranslated as "god."

Menominee, Odawa, Ojibwe: Algonquin tribes living in Wisconsin, Minnesota, and Canada in the Great Lakes region, from whom these legends and most of these words are drawn.

Midewiwin: a secret, sacred society, whose purpose it is to teach spiritual lessons in traditional Anishinaabe culture.

Mishibizhu (pl. mishibizhug; aka mishipeshu, mishibishiw): underwater panther. Fierce monsters living at the bottom of lakes and rivers, described as feline but with scales, horns, and extremely long tails. They eat anyone foolish enough to venture near their waters.

Naabesim: literally "male dog," a spirit animal serving the shaman of the black lodge.

Noondezhi: simpleton, fool.

Rougarou: Bigfoot, Sasquatch. From French trappers.

Voyageur: French hunters and trappers who roamed Canada and the Upper Midwest in past centuries, often trading with and intermarrying among the tribes they encountered.

Waabishkiiwed (pl. waabishkiiwewaad): "pale like a stick." White man; white people.

Wendigo (aka windigo, wentiko; pl. wendigook or windigook): Cannibal monsters who stalk the subarctic forests in winter. They may be spirits who possess the unlucky and slowly turn them cannibalistic, or physical monsters of varying description. Most legends agree they have hearts of ice and are extremely hard to kill.

Wiisini Namegos: Literally "fish eater." Marie's youngest brother.

Resources

Dangerous Spirits: The Windigo in Myth and Legend, Shawn Smallman, Heritage House, 2014.

The Ojibwe People's Dictionary: *https://ojibwe.lib.umn.edu/* - great language aid, with audio clips of word pronunciations as well.

Native languages and legends: *http://www.native-languages.org/chippewa.htm* (also has entries for Menominee and Odawa legends and monsters referenced in this story).

Legend Stories: recorded Ojibwe myths and tales: *https://www.dibaajimowin.com/myths*

Mazina'igan, periodical published by Great Lakes Indian Fish & Wildlife Commission, various issues 2018-2019.

Chippewa Customs, Frances Densmore, annotated edition, Minnesota Society Historical Press, 1979.

Northern Frights: A Supernatural Ecology of the Wisconsin Headwaters, Dennis Boyer, Prairie Oak Press, 1998.

Gone Missing! A Supernatural Tour of the Great Lakes, Dennis Boyer, Badger Books Inc, 2002.

Mysterious Islands: Forgotten Tales of the Great Lakes, Andrea Gutsche & Cindy Bisaillon, Lynx Images Inc, 1999.

Haunted Lakes: Great Lakes Ghost Stories, Superstitions, and Sea Serpents, Frederick Stonehouse, Lake Superior Port Cities, 1997.

Fearsome Creatures of the Lumberwoods, Hal Johnson, Workman Publishing, 2015.

Shingebiss: an Ojibwe Legend, Nancy Van Laan, Houghton Mifflin, 1997.

Many, many thanks to:

My partner, soul mate, and Biggest Goob Scott, for endless support and encouragement and my antler engagement ring. Also, for being an amazing cook. And for cooking all those nights I was too busy writing.

Publisher and bestie Sue London, for taking on this labor of love with me and guiding it through all necessary hoops. You rock so hard, chica.

Editor Jen Sylvia, for time, trouble, and remarkable patience as I struggled through the unfamiliar side of the writer/editor dynamic. And for convincing me to reduce the number of fucks. Behold, I am nearly fuckless.

All of my family from Florida to Wisconsin and from Nor'Dakota to Georgia, for being my cheering squad on so many occasions, for making me feel like the Cool Weird Aunt, and for the Gnome Games. To Ash, Juan, Shane, Autumn, and Dom: Bocce next time is *on,* and I will destroy you all. Much love to Mom & John, Ken & Colleen, Marlys & Gary, Darron & Danielle, and of course my nieces Salema & Sasha, way too young to read this book. Also it has scary things.

Extended Aunts and Uncles and family friends, for your continued love and support. Special shout-outs to Aunt Bobby and to Uncle John as beta readers.

All my Bookmans peeps wherever they are now, as the BookStop is a fictional clone of the Speedway store. Thanks to Lex and Julia who first welcomed me in; Peter, John O, Boyd, Ben, and Kat who taught me the intricacies of book buying; Marty, who kept me relatively sane with constant MST3K quips; and all the folks who felt like a family to me in Tucson: Jack, Heather, Ryan W, Mario, Jeff, Chino, Wilson, Ryan V, Audrey, Nature, Mazzy, Scott C, Lindy, Ian, Rhys, Kerrie, Kerry, Big Jim, Sarah, and all those who made my time there more like hanging out with friends than work.

All my friends who've offered encouragement, jokes, songs, and moral support in truly bizarre times during the writing of this book. The Dumbpocalypse is survivable with excellent folks like you.

Cover artist Sally Jackson, who displayed immense patience to match her amazing talent in getting the art just right, through all my "just one more thing" emails.

Anyone who preordered. I find your faith gratifying.

And lastly, Bob Odenkirk, whom I don't know personally, but who inspired Morty and unwittingly helped my wendigo ideas finally gel into this work. This story wouldn't have gone anywhere had I not come across the perfect model for Mordecai.

All of you rock. Thank you!

Made in the USA
Monee, IL
09 June 2020

32988563R00225